THE STORIES OF MARY LAVIN

By the same author
Tales from Bective Bridge
The Long Ago
The House in Clewe Street (novel)
The Becker Wives
At Sally Gap
Mary O'Grady (novel)
A Single Lady
The Patriot Son
A Likely Story
Selected Stories
The Great Wave
The Stories of Mary Lavin (Volume 1)
In the Middle of the Fields
Happiness
The Second Best Children in the World
A Memory
The Stories of Mary Lavin (Volume 2)
The Shrine and other stories

THE STORIES OF

Mary Lavin

VOLUME THREE

CONSTABLE

LONDON

This selection first published 1985 by
Constable and Company Limited
10 Orange Street, London WC2H 7EG
Copyright © 1985 Mary Lavin
Set in Monophoto Garamond 10pt by
Servis Filmsetting Limited, Manchester
Printed in Great Britain by
St Edmundsbury Press
Bury St Edmunds, Suffolk

British Library CIP data
Lavin, Mary
The stories of Mary Lavin
Vol. 3
I. Title
823'.912 [F]   PS3523.A914

ISBN 0 09 464570 1

Contents

To my grandchildren
Kathleen, Kevin and Margaret MacMahon,
Mathew Ryan,
Eoghain, Adam and Tadgh
and to the memory of Eliza Peavoy

Lilacs

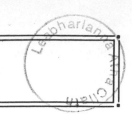

"That dunghill isn't doing anyone any harm, and it's not going out of where it is as long as I'm in this house," Phelim Mulloy said to his wife Ros, but he threw an angry look at his elder daughter Kate who was standing by the kitchen window with her back turned to them both.

"Oh Phelim," Ros said softly, "if only it could be put somewhere else besides under the window of the room where we eat our bit of food."

"Didn't you just say a minute ago people can smell it from the other end of the town? If that's the case I don't see what would be the good in shifting it from one side of the yard to the other."

Kate could stand no more. "What I don't see is the need for us dealing in dung at all."

"There you are, what did I tell you?" Phelim said. "I knew all along what was in the back of your minds, both of you. And the one inside there too," he added, nodding his head at the closed door of one of the rooms off the kitchen. "All you want, the three of you, is to get rid of the dung altogether. Why on earth can't women speak out, and say what they mean. That's a thing always puzzled me."

"Leave Stacy out of this, Phelim," said Ros, but she spoke quietly. "Stacy has one of her headaches."

"I know she has," said Phelim, "and I know something else. I know I'm supposed to think it's the smell of the dung gave it to her. Isn't that so?"

"Ah Phelim, that's not what I meant at all. I only thought you might wake her with your shouting. She could be asleep."

"Asleep is it? It's a real miracle any of you can get a wink of sleep, day or night, with the smell of that harmless heap of dung out there, that's bringing good money to this house week after week." He had lowered his voice, but when he turned and looked at Kate it rose again without his noticing. "It paid for your education at a fancy boarding school, and for your sister's too. It paid for your notions of learning to play the piano, *and* the violin, both of which instruments is rotting away inside in the parlour and not a squeak of a tune ever I heard out of the one or the other of them since the day they came into the house."

"We may as well spare our breath, Mother," Kate said. "He won't give in, now or ever. That's my belief."

"That's the truest word that's ever come out of your mouth," Phelim said to her, and stomping across the kitchen he opened the door that led into the yard and went out, leaving the door open. Immediately the faint odour of stale manure that hung in the air was enriched by the smell of a

I

fresh load, hot and steaming that had just been tipped into the huge dunghill from a farm cart that was the first of a line of carts waiting their turn to unload. Ros sighed and went to close the door, but Kate got ahead of her and banged it shut, before going back to the window and taking up her stand there. After a nervous glance at the door of the bedroom that her daughters shared, Ros, too, went over to the window and both women stared out.

An empty cart was clattering out of the yard and Phelim was leading in another from which, as it went over the spud-stone of the gate, a clod or two of dung fell out on the cobbles. The dunghill was nearly filled, and liquid from it was running down the sides of the trough to form pools through which Phelim waded unconcernedly as he forked back the stuff on top to make room for more.

"That's the last load," Ros said.

"For this week," Kate said. "Your trouble is you're too soft with him, Mother. You'll have to be harder on him. You'll have to keep at him night and day. That is to say if you care anything at all about me and Stacy."

"Ah Kate. Can't you see there's no use? Can't you see he's set in his ways?"

"All I can see is the way we're being disgraced." Kate said angrily. "Last night, at the concert in the Parish Hall, just before the curtain went up I heard the wife of that man who bought the bakehouse telling the person beside her that they couldn't open a window since they came here with a queer smell that was coming from somewhere, and asking the other person if she knew what it could be. I nearly died of shame, Mother, I really did. I couldn't catch what answer she got, but after the first item was over, and I glanced back, I saw it was Mamie Murtagh she was sitting beside, and you can guess what that one would be likely to have said. My whole pleasure in the evening was spoiled."

"You take things too much to heart, Kate," Ros said sadly. "There's Stacy inside there, and it's my belief she wouldn't mind us dealing in dung at all if it wasn't for the smell of it. Only the other day she was remarking that if he'd even clear a small space under the windows we might plant something there that would smell nice. 'Just think, Mother,' she said, 'just think if it was a smell of lilac that was coming in to us every time we opened a door or a window.'"

"Oh Stacy has lilac on the brain if you ask me," Kate said crossly. "She never stops talking about it. What did she ever do to try and improve our situation?"

"Ah now Kate, you know Stacy is very timid."

"All the more reason Father would listen to her, if she'd speak to him. He may not let on to it, but he'd do anything for her."

Ros nodded. She'd never speak to him, all the same, Stacy would never have the heart to cross anyone."

"She wouldn't need to say much. Didn't you hear him, today, saying he supposed it was the smell of the dung was giving her her headaches? You let that pass, but I wouldn't not that he'd have taken much more from me, although it's me has to listen to her moaning and groaning the minute the first cart rattles into the yard. How is it that it's always on a Wednesday she has a headache? And it's been the same since the first Wednesday we came home from the convent." With that last thrust Kate ran into the bedroom and came out with a raincoat. "I'm going out for a walk," she said, "and I won't come back until the smell of that stuff has died down a bit. You can tell my father that, too, if he's looking for me."

"Wait a minute, Kate. Was Stacy asleep?" Ros asked.

"I don't know and I don't care. She was lying with her face to the wall, like always."

When Kate went out, Ros took down the tea-caddy from the dresser and put a few pinches of tea from it into an earthenware pot on the hob of the big open fire. Then, tilting the kettle that hung from a crane over the flames, she wet the tea, and pouring out a cup she carried it over to the window and set it to cool on the sill while she went on watching Phelim.

He was a hard man when you went against him. A man who'd never let himself be thwarted. He was always the same. That being so, there wasn't much sense in nagging him but Kate would never be made see that. Kate was stubborn too.

The last of the carts had gone, and after shutting the gate Phelim had taken a yard-brush and was sweeping up the dung that had been spilled. When he'd made a heap of it, he got a shovel and gathered it up and flung it up on the dunghill. But whether he did it to tidy the yard or in order not to waste the dung, Ros didn't know. The loose bits of dung he'd flung up on the top of the trough had dried out, and the bits of straw that were stuck to it had dried out too. They gleamed bright and yellow in a ray of watery sunlight that had suddenly shone forth.

Now that Kate was gone, Ros began to feel less bitter against Phelim. Like herself, he was getting old. She was sorry they had upset him. And while she was looking at him, he laid the yard-brush against the wall of one of the sheds and put his hand to his back. He'd been doing that a lot lately. She didn't like to see him doing it. She went across to the door and opened it.

"There's hot tea in the pot on the hob, Phelim," she called out. "Come in and have a cup." Then seeing he was coming, she went over and gently opened the bedroom door. "Stacy, would you be able for a cup of tea?" she asked bending over the big feather-bed.

Stacy sat up at once.

"What did he say? Is it going to be moved?" she asked eagerly.

"Ssh, Stacy," Ros whispered, and then as Stacy heard her father's steps in the kitchen she looked startled.

"Did he hear me?" she asked anxiously.

"No," said Ros, and she went over and drew the curtains to let in the daylight. "How is your poor head, Stacy?"

Stacy leaned toward Ros so she could be heard when she whispered. "Did you have a word with him, Mother?"

"Yes," said Ros.

"Did he agree?" Stacy whispered.

"No."

Stacy closed her eyes.

"I hope he wasn't upset," she said.

Ros stroked her daughter's limp hair. "Don't you worry anyway, Stacy," she said. "He'll get over it. He's been outside sweeping the yard and I think maybe he has forgotten we raised the matter at all. Anyway, Kate has gone for a walk and I called him in for a cup of tea. Are you sure you won't let me bring you in a nice hot cup to sip here in the bed?"

"I think I'd prefer to get up and have it outside, as long as you're sure father is not upset."

Ros drew a strand of Stacy's hair back from her damp forehead. "You're a good girl, Stacy, a good, kind creature," she said. "You may feel better when you're on your feet. I can promise you there will be no arguing for the time being anyway. I'm sorry I crossed him at all."

*   *   *

It was to Stacy Ros turned a week later, when Phelim was taken bad in the middle of the night with a sharp pain in his chest that the women weren't able to ease, and after the doctor came and stayed with him until the early hours of the morning, the doctor didn't seem able to do much either. Before Phelim could be got to hospital he died.

"Oh Stacy, Stacy," Ros cried, throwing herself into her younger daughter's arms. "Why did I cross him over that old dunghill?"

"Don't fret, Mother," Stacy begged. "I never heard you cross him over anything else as long as I can remember. You were always good and kind to him, calling him in out of the yard every other minute for a cup of tea. Morning, noon and night I'd hear your voice, and the mornings the carts came with the dung you'd call him in oftener than ever. I used to hear you when I'd be lying inside with one of my headaches."

Ros was not to be easily consoled.

"What thanks is due to a woman for giving her man a cup of hot tea on a bitter cold day? He was the best man ever lived. Oh why did I cross him?"

"Ah Mother, it wasn't only on cold days you were good to him but on summer days too. Isn't that so, Kate?" Stacy appealed to Kate.

"You did everything you could to please him, Mother," Kate said, but seeing this made no impression on her mother she turned to Stacy. "That's more than could be said about him," she muttered.

But Ros heard her.

"Say no more, you," she cried. "You were the one was always at me to torment him. Oh why did I listen to you? Why did I cross him?"

"Because you were in the right. That's why," Kate said.

"Was I?" Ros said.

Phelim was laid out in the parlour, and all through the night Ros and her daughters sat up in the room with the corpse. The neighbours that came to the house stayed up all night too, but they sat in the kitchen, and kept the fire going and made tea from time to time. Kate and Stacy stared sadly at their dead father stretched out in his shroud, and they mourned him as the man they had known all their lives, a heavy man with a red face whom they had seldom seen out of his big rubber boots caked with muck.

Ros mourned that Phelim too. But she mourned many another Phelim besides. She mourned the Phelim who, up to a little while before, never put a coat on him going out in the raw, cold air, nor covered his head even in the rain. Of course his hair was as thick as a thatch. But most of all, she mourned the Phelim whose hair had not yet grown coarse but was soft and smooth as silk, like it was the time he led her in off the road and up a little lane near the chapel one Sunday when he was walking her home from Mass. That was the time when he used to call her by the old name. When, she wondered, when did he stop calling her Rose? Or was it she, herself, gave herself the new name? Or perhaps it was someone else altogether, someone outside the family. A neighbour maybe? No matter, Ros was a good name anyway, wherever it came from. It was a good name and a suitable name for an old woman. It would have been only foolishness to go on calling her Rose after she faded and dried up like an old twig. Ros looked down at her bony hands, and her tears on them. But they were tears for Phelim. "Rose," he'd said that day in the lane, "Rose, I've been thinking about ways to make money. And do you know what I found out? There's a pile of money to be made out of dung." Rose thought he was joking. "It's true," he said. "The people in the town, especially women, would give any amount of money for a bagful of it for their gardens. And only a few miles out from the town there are farmers going mad to get rid of it, with it piling up day after day and cluttering up their farmyards until they can hardly get in or out their sheds. Now, I was thinking, if I got hold of a horse and cart and went out and brought back a few loads of that dung, and if my father would let me store it for a while in our yard, I could maybe sell it to the people in the town. I could sell it by the sack to women for their gardens."

"Women like the doctor's wife," Rose said, knowing the doctor's wife was mad about roses. The doctor's wife had been seen going out into the street with a shovel to bring back a shovelful of horse manure.

"That's right; women like that. After a while the farmers might deliver the loads to me. I might offer to pay for it myself. Then if I made as much money as I think I might, maybe soon I'd be able to get a place of my own where I'd have room to store enough to make it a worthwhile business." To Rose it seemed an odd sort of way to make money, but Phelim was only eighteen then, and probably he wanted to have a few pounds in his pocket while he was waiting for something better. "I'm going to ask my father about the storage today," he said, "and in the afternoon I'm going to get hold of a cart and go out the country and see how I get on."

"Is that so?" Rose said, for want of knowing what else to say.

"It is," said Phelim, "and do you know the place I have in mind to buy if I make enough money? I'd buy that place we often looked at, you and me when we were out walking, that place on the outskirts of the town, with a big yard and two big sheds that only need a bit of fixing, to be ideal for my purposes."

"I think so," Rose said. "Isn't there an old cottage there all smothered with ivy?"

"That's the very place. Do you remember we peeped in the windows one day last Summer. There's no one living there."

"No wonder," Rose said.

"Listen to me, Rose. After I'd done up the sheds," Phelim said. "I could fix up the cottage too, and make a nice job of it. That's another thing I wanted to ask you, Rose. How would you like to live in that cottage, after I'd done it up of course, live in it with me? " he added when he saw he'd startled her. "Well Rose, what have you to say to that?"

She'd bent her head to hide her blushes, and looked down at her small thin-soled shoes that she only wore on a Sunday. She didn't know what to say.

"Well?" said Phelim.

"There's a very dirty smell of dung," she said at last in a whisper.

"It only smells strong when it's fresh," Phelim said, "and maybe you could plant flowers to take away the smell."

She kept looking down at her shoes.

"They'd have to be flowers with a strong scent," she said, but already she was thinking of how strongly sweet rocket and mignonette perfumed the air of an evening after rain.

"You could plant all the flowers you liked, you'd have nothing else to do the day long," he said. How innocent he was, for all that he was thinking of making big money and taking a wife. She looked up at him. His skin was as fair and smooth as her own. He was the best looking fellow for miles around. Girls far prettier than her would have been glad to be led up a lane by him, just for a bit of a lark, let alone a proposal of marriage. "Well, Rose?" he said, and now there were blushes coming and going in his cheeks too, blotching his face. She could see that he was bent on carrying out his plan. "You ought to know, Rose Magarry, that there's a lot in the way people look at a thing. When I was a young lad, driving along the country roads in my father's trap, I used to love looking down at the gold rings of dung dried out by the sun, as they flashed past underneath the horses' hooves."

Rose felt like laughing, but she knew he was deadly serious. He wasn't like anybody else in the world she'd ever known. Who else would say a thing like that? It was like poetry. The sun was spilling down on them and in the hedges little pink dog roses were swaying in a soft breeze.

"Alright, so," she said. "I will."

"You will? Oh, Rose. Kiss me so," he said.

"Not here Phelim," she whispered. People were still coming out of the chapel yard and some of them were looking up the lane.

"Rose Magarry, if you're going to marry me, you must face up to people and never be ashamed of anything I do," he said, and when she still hung back he put out his hand and tilted up her chin. "If you don't kiss me right here and now, Rose, I'll have no more to do with you."

She kissed him then.

And now, at his wake, the candle flames were wavering around his coffin the way the dog roses wavered that day in the Summer breeze.

Ros shed tears for those little dog roses. She shed tears for the roses that were in her own cheeks in those days. And she shed tears for the soft kissing lips of young Phelim. Her tears fell quietly, but it seemed to Kate and Stacy that, like rain in windless weather, they would never cease.

When the white light of morning came at last, the neighbours got up and went home to do a few chores of their own and be ready for the funeral. Kate and Stacy got ready too, and made Ros ready. Ros didn't look much different in black from what she always looked. Neither did Stacy. But Kate looked well in black. It toned down her high colour.

After the funeral Kate led her mother home. Stacy had already been taken home by neighbours, because she fainted when the coffin was being lowered into the ground. She was lying down when they came home. The women who brought Stacy home and one or two other women who had stayed behind after the coffin was carried out, to put the furniture back in place, gave a meal to the family, but these women made sure to leave as soon as possible to let the Mulloys get used to their loss. When the women had gone Stacy got up and came out to join Ros and Kate. A strong smell of guttered-out candles hung in the air and also a faint scent of the lilies that had been on the coffin.

"Oh Kate! Smell!" Stacy cried, drawing in as deep a breath as her thin chest allowed.

"For Heaven's sake, don't talk about smells or you'll have our mother wailing again and going on about having crossed him over the dunghill," Kate said in a sharp whisper.

But Ros didn't need any reminders to make her wail.

"Oh Phelim, Phelim, why did I cross you? Wasn't I the bad old woman to go against you over a heap of dung that, if I looked at things rightly, wasn't bad at all after it dried out a bit. It was mostly yellow straw."

"Take no heed of her," Kate counselled Stacy. "Go inside you with our new hats and coats, and hang them up in our room with a sheet draped over them. Black nap is a caution for collecting dust." To Ros she spoke kindly, but firmly. "You've got to give over this moaning, Mother," she said. "You're only tormenting yourself. What harm was it for you to let him see how we felt about the dung?"

Ros stopped moaning long enough to look sadly out the window.

"It was out of the dung he made his first few shillings," she said.

"That may be. But how long ago was that? He made plenty of money other ways as time went on. There was no need in keeping on the dung and humiliating us. He only did it out of obstinacy." As Stacy came back after hanging up their black clothes, Kate appealed to her, "Isn't that so, Stacy?"

Stacy drew another thin breath.

"It doesn't smell too bad today, does it?" she said. "I suppose the scent of the flowers drove it out."

"Well, the house won't always be filled with lilies," Kate said irritably. "In any case, Stacy, it's not the smell concerns me. What concerns me is the way people look at us when they hear how our money is made."

Ros stopped moaning again for another minute. "It's no cause for shame. It's honest dealing, and that's more than can be said for the dealings of others in this town. You shouldn't heed people's talk, Kate."

"Well, I like that!" Kate cried. "May I ask what do you know, Mother, about how people talk? Certain kinds of people I mean; good class people. It's easily seen you were never away at boarding school like Stacy and me, or else you'd know what it feels like to have to admit our money was made out of horse manure and cow dung."

"I don't see what great call there was on you to tell them," Ros said.

"Stacy, Stacy, did you hear that?" Kate cried.

Stacy put her hand to her head. She was getting confused. There was some truth in what Kate had said, and she felt obliged to side with her, but first she ran over and threw herself down at her mother's knees.

"We didn't tell them at first, Mother," she said, hoping to make Ros feel better. "We told them our father dealt in fertiliser, but one of the girls looked up the word in the dictionary and found out it was only a fancy name for manure."

It was astonishing to Kate and Stacy how Ros took that. She not only stopped wailing but she began to laugh. "Your father would have been amused to hear that," she said.

"Well, it wasn't funny for us," Kate said.

Ros stopped laughing, but the trace of a small bleak smile remained on her face.

"It wasn't everyone had your father's sense of humour," she said.

"It wasn't everyone had his obstinacy either," Kate said.

"You're right there, Kate," Ros said simply. "Isn't that why I feel so bad? When we knew how stubborn he was, weren't we the stupid women to be always trying to best him? We only succeeded in making him miserable."

Kate and Stacy looked at each other.

"How about another cup of tea, Mother? I'll bring it over here to you beside the fire," Stacy said, and although her mother made no reply Stacy made the tea and brought over a cup. Ros took the cup but handed back the saucer.

"Leave that back on the table," she said, and holding the cup in her two hands she went over to the window, although the light was fading fast.

"It only smells bad on hot muggy days," she said.

Kate gave a loud sniff. "Don't forget Summer is coming."

For a moment it seemed Ros had not heard, then she gave a sigh.

"It is and it isn't," she said. "I often think that in January it's as true to say we have put the Summer behind us as it is to say it's ahead." Then she glanced at a calendar on the wall. "Is tomorrow Wednesday?" she said, and an anxious expression overcame the sorrowful look on her face. Wednesday was the day the farmers delivered the dung.

"Mother! You don't think the farmers will be unmannerly enough to come banging on the gate tomorrow, and us after having a death in the family?" Kate said in a shocked voice.

"Death never interfered with business yet, as far as I know," Ros said coldly. "And the farmers are kind folk. I saw a lot of them at the funeral. They might think it all the more reason to come, knowing my man was taken from me."

"Mother!" This time Kate was more than shocked, she was outraged. "You're not thinking, by any chance, of keeping on dealing with them; dealing in dung?"

Ros looked her daughter straight in the face.

"I'm thinking of your father and him young one day, and the next day, you might say, him stretched on the bed inside with the neighbours washing him for his burial." She began to moan again.

"If you keep this up you'll be laid alongside him one of these days," Kate said.

"Leave me be," Ros said. "I'm not doing any harm to myself by thinking about him. I like thinking about him."

"He lived to a good age, Mother. Don't forget that," Kate said.

"I suppose that's what you'll be saying about me one of these days," Ros said, but she didn't seem as upset as she had been. She turned to Stacy. "It seems only like yesterday, Stacy, that I was sitting up beside him on the cart, right behind the horse's tail, with my white blouse on me and the gold chain he gave me bouncing about on my front, and us both watching the road flashing past under the horse's hooves, bright with gold rings of dung."

Kate raised her eyebrows. But Stacy gave a sob. And that night, when she and Kate were in bed, she gave another sob. "Kate, it's not a good sign when people begin to go back over the past, is it?"

"Are you speaking about Mother?"

"I am. Did you see how bad she looked when you brought her home from the grave?"

"I did," said Kate. "It may be true what I said to her. If she isn't careful we may be laying her alongside poor father before long."

"Oh Kate. How could you say such a thing?" Stacy burst into tears. "Oh Kate. Oh Kate, why did we make her go against father over the dunghill? I know how she feels. I keep reproaching myself for all the hard things I used to think about him when I'd be lying here in bed with one of my headaches."

"Well, you certainly never came out with them," Kate said. "You left it to me to say them for you. Not that I'm going to reproach myself about anything. There was no need in him keeping that dunghill. He only did it out of pig-headedness. And now, if you'll only let me, I'm going to sleep."

Kate was just dropping off when Stacy leant up on her elbow.

"You don't really think they will come in the morning, do you, Kate, the carts I mean, like our mother said?"

"Of course not," Kate said.

"But if they do?"

"Oh go to sleep Stacy, for Heaven's sake. There's no need facing things until they happen. And stop fidgeting. You're twitching the blankets off me. Move over."

Stacy faced back to the wall and lay still. She didn't think she'd be able to sleep, but when she did, it seemed as if she'd only been asleep one minute when she woke to find the night had ended. The hard, white light of day was pressing on her eyelids. It's a new day for us, she thought, but not for their poor father laid in the cold clay. Stacy shivered and drew up her feet that were touching the icy iron rail at the foot of the bed. It must have been the cold wakened her. Opening her eyes she saw, through a chink between the curtains, that the crinkled edges of the big corrugated sheds glittered with frost. If only, she thought, if only it was Summer. She longed for the time when warm winds go daffing through the trees, and when in the gardens to which they delivered fertiliser, the tight hard beads of lilac buds would soon loop out into soft pear-shaped bosoms of blossom. And then, gentle as those thoughts, another thought came into Stacy's mind, and she wondered whether their father, sleeping under the close, green sods, might mind now if they got rid of the dunghill. Indeed it seemed the dunghill was as good as gone, now that father himself was gone. Curling up in the warm blankets, Stacy was preparing to sleep again, when there was a loud knocking on the yard-gates and the sound of a horse shaking its harness. She raised her head off the pillow, and as she did, she heard the gate in the yard slap back against the wall and there was a rattle of iron-shod wheels travelling in across the cobbles.

"Kate! Kate!" she screamed, shaking her. "I thought I heard Father leading in a load of manure."

"Oh shut up, Stacy. You're dreaming, or else raving," Kate muttered from the depths of the blankets that she had pulled closer around her. But suddenly she sat up. And then, to Stacy's astonishment, she threw back the bedclothes altogether, right across the footrail of the bed, and ran across the floor and pressed her face to the windowpane. "I might have known this would happen," she cried. "For all her lamenting and wailing, our mother knows what she's doing. Come and look."

Out in the yard Ros was leading in the first of the carts, and calling out to the drivers of the other carts waiting their turn to come in. She was not wearing her black clothes, but her ordinary everyday coat, the colour of the earth and the earth's decaying refuse. In the raw cold air, the manure in the cart she was leading was still giving off, unevenly, the fog of its hot breath.

"Get dressed, Stacy. We'll go down together." Kate ordered and grabbed her clothes and dressed.

When they were both dressed, with Kate leading, the sisters went into the kitchen. The yard door was open and a powerful stench was making its way inside. The last cart was by then unloaded, and Ros had come back into the kitchen and began to warm her hands by the big fire already roaring up the chimney. She had left the door open but Kate went over and banged it shut.

"Well?" said Ros.

"Well?" Kate said only louder.

Stacy sat down at once and began to cry. The other two women took no notice of her as they faced each other across the kitchen.

"Say whatever it is you have to say, Kate," Ros said.

"You know what I have to say," said Kate.

"Don't say it so. Save your breath." Ros said, and she went as if to go out into the yard again, but Stacy got up and ran and put her arms around her.

"Mother, you always agreed with us. You always said it would be nice if . . ."

Ros put up a hand and silenced her.

"Listen to me, both of you," she said. "I had no right agreeing with anyone but your father. It was to him I pledged my word. It was him I had a right to stand behind. He always said there was no shame in making money anyway it could be made, as long as it was made honestly. And another thing he said was that money was money, whether it was in gold coins or in dung. And that was true for him. Did you, either of you, hear what the priest said yesterday in the cemetery? 'God help all poor widows'." That's what he said. And he set me thinking. Did it never occur to you that it might not be easy for us, three women with no man about the place, to keep going, to put food on the table and keep a fire on the hearth, to say nothing at all about finery and fal-lals."

"That last remark is meant for me I suppose," Kate said, but the frown that came on her face seemed to come more from worry than anger. "By the way, Mother," she said, "You never told us whether you had a word with the solicitor when he came with his condolences? Did you by any chance find out how father's affairs stood?"

"I did," Ros said. But that was all she said as she went out into the yard again and took up the yard-brush. She had left the door open but Stacy went over and closed it gently.

"She's twice as stubborn as ever father was," Kate said. "There's going to be no change around here as long as she's alive."

Stacy's face clouded. "All the same, Kate, she's sure to let us clear a small corner and put in a few shrubs and things," she said timidly.

"Lilacs, I suppose," Kate said, with an unmistakable sneer, which however Stacy did not see.

"Think of the scent of them coming in the window, Kate."

"You are a fool, Stacy," Kate replied. "At least I can see that our mother has more important things on her mind than lilac bushes. I wonder what information she got from Jasper Kane? I thought her very secretive. I would have thought he'd have had a word with me, as the eldest daughter."

"Oh Kate." Stacy's eyes filled with tears again. "I never thought about it before, but when poor mother . . ." she hesitated, then after a gulp she went on "when poor mother goes to join father, you and I will be all alone in the world with no one to look after us."

"Stop whimpering, Stacy," Kate said sharply. "We've got to start living our own lives, sooner or later." Going over to a small ornamental mirror on the wall over the fireplace, she looked into it and patted her hair. Stacy stared at her in surprise, because unless you stood well back from it you could only see the tip of your nose in that little mirror. But Kate was not looking at herself. She was looking out into the yard, which was reflected in the mirror, in which she could see their mother going around sweeping up stray bits of straw and dirt to bring them over and throw them on top of the dunghill. Then Kate turned around. "We don't need to worry too much about that woman. She'll hardly follow father for many a long day. That woman is as strong as a tree."

But Ros was not cut out to be a widow. If Phelim had been taken from her before the dog roses had faded in the hedges that first Summer of their lives together, she could hardly have mourned him more bitterly than she did when an old woman, tossing and turning sleeplessly in their big brass bed.

Kate and Stacy did their best to ease her work in the house. But there was one thing Kate was determined they would not do, and that was give any help on the Wednesday mornings when the farm carts arrived with their load. Nor would they help her to bag it for the townspeople although as Phelim had long ago foreseen, the townspeople were often glad to bag it for themselves, or wheel it away in barrowfuls. On Wednesday morning when the rapping came at the gates at dawn, Kate and Stacy stayed in bed and did not get up, but Stacy was wide awake and lay listening to the noises outside. And sometimes she scrambled out of bed across Kate and went to the window.

"Kate?" Stacy would say almost every day.

"What?"

"Perhaps I ought to step out to the kitchen and see the fire is kept up. She'll be very cold when she comes in."

"You'll do nothing of the kind I hope. We must stick to our agreement. Get back into bed."

"She has only her old coat on her and it's very thin, Kate."

Before answering her, Kate might raise herself up on one elbow and hump the blankets up with her so that when she sank back they were well pegged down around her. "By all the noise she's making out there I'd say her circulation would be kept up no matter if she was in nothing but her shift."

"That work is too heavy for her, Kate. She shouldn't be doing it at all."

"And who is to blame for that? Get back to bed, like I told you, and don't let her see you're looking out. She'd like nothing better than that."

"But she's not looking this way, Kate. She couldn't see me."

"That's what you think. Let me tell you, that woman has eyes in the back of her head."

Stacy giggled nervously at that. It was what their mother herself used to tell them when they were small. Then suddenly she stopped giggling and ran back and threw herself across the foot of the bed and began to sob.

After moving her feet to one side, Kate listened for a few seconds to the sobbing. Then she humped up her other shoulder and pegged the blankets under her on the other side.

"What ails you now?" she asked then.

"Oh Kate, you made me think of when we were children, and she used to stand up so tall and straight and with her gold chain and locket bobbing about on her chest." Stacy gave another sob. "Now she's so thin and bent the chain is dangling down to her waist."

Kate sat up with a start. "She's not wearing that chain and locket now, out in the yard, is she? Gold is worth a lot more now than it was when father bought her that."

Stacy went over to the window and looked out again. "No, she's not wearing it."

"I should hope not," Kate said. "I saw it on her at the funeral but I forgot about it afterwards in the commotion."

"She took it off when we came back," Stacy said. "She put it away in father's black box and locked the box."

"Well, that's one good thing she did anyway," Kate said. "She oughtn't to wear it at all."

"Oh Kate!" Stacy looked startled.

"What?" Kate asked, staring back at her.

Stacy didn't know what she wanted to say. She couldn't put it into

words. She had always thought Kate and herself were alike, that they had
the same way of looking at things, but lately she was not so sure of this.
They were both getting older of course, and some people were not as
even-tempered as others. Not that she thought herself a paragon, but
being so prone to headaches she had to let a lot of things pass that she
didn't agree with, like something Kate said recently about the time when
they were away at school. Their mother had asked how many years ago it
was, and while Stacy was trying to count up the years Kate, answered at
once.

"Only a few years ago," she said. That wasn't true but perhaps it only
seemed like that to Kate.

Gradually, as time passed, Stacy too, like Kate, used to put the blankets
over her head so as not to hear the knocking at the gate, and the rattle of
the cart wheels, or at least to deaden the noise of it. She just lay thinking.
Kate had once asked her what went through her head when she'd be lying
saying nothing.

"This and that," she'd said. She really didn't think about anything in
particular. Sometimes she'd imagine what it would be like if they did clear
a small space in the yard and planted things. She knew of course that if they
put in a lilac bush it would be small for a long time and would not bear
flowers for ages. It would be mostly leaves, and leaves only for years, or so
she'd read somewhere. Yet she always imagined it would be a fully grown
lilac they'd have outside the window. Once she imagined something
absolutely ridiculous. She was lying half awake and half asleep, and she
thought they had transplanted a large full grown lilac, a lilac that had more
flowers than leaves, something you never see. And then, as she was half-
dozing, the tree got so big and strong its roots pushed under the wall and
pushed up through the floorboards, bending the nails and sending
splinters of wood flying in all directions. And its branches were so laden
with blossom, so weighted down with them, that one big pointed bosom
of bloom almost touched her face. But suddenly the branch broke with a
crack and Stacy was wide awake again. Then the sound that woke her
came again, only now she knew what it was, a knocking on the gate
outside, only louder than usual, and after it came a voice calling out. She
gave Kate a shake.

"Do you hear that, Kate? Mother must have slept it out."

"Let's hope she did," Kate said. "It might teach her a lesson, it might
make her see she's not as fit and able as she thinks."

"But what about the farmers?"

"Who cares about them," Kate said. "I don't. Do you?"

When the knocking came again a third time, and a fourth time, Stacy
shook Kate again.

"Kate. I wouldn't mind going down and opening the gate," she said.

"You? In your nightdress?" Kate needed to say no more. Stacy
cowered down under the blankets in her shame, then suddenly she sat up

again.

"There wouldn't be anything wrong with mother, would there?" she cried. This time, without heeding Kate, Stacy climbed out over her to get to the floor. "I won't go out to the yard, I promise, I'll just go and wake mother," she said and ran out of the room.

"Come back and shut this door," Kate called after her. Stacy mustn't have heard. "Stacy. Did you hear me?" Kate shouted.

Stacy didn't come back.

"Stacy." Kate yelled. "Stacy?" At last she sat up.

"Is there something wrong?" she asked. Getting no answer now either, she got up herself.

Stacy was in their mother's room, lying in a heap on the floor. As Kate said afterwards, she hardly needed to look to know their mother was dead, because Stacy always flopped down in a faint the moment she came up against something unpleasant. And the next day, in the cemetery when the prayers were over and the gravediggers took up their shovels, Stacy passed out again and had to be brought home by two of the neighbours, leaving Kate to stand and listen to the stones and the clay rumbling down on the coffin.

"You're a nice one, Stacy. Leaving me to stand listening to that awful sound."

"But I heard it, Kate," Stacy protested. "I did. Then my head began to reel, and I got confused. The next thing I knew I was on the ground looking up at the blue sky and thinking the noise was the sound of the horses going clip-clap along the road."

Kate stared at her.

"Are you mad? What horses?"

"Oh Kate, don't you remember? The horses mother was always talking about. She was always telling us how when she and father were young, she used to sit beside him on a plank across the cart and watch the road flashing by under the horse's hooves, glittering with bright gold rings of dung?"

Kate, however, wasn't listening.

"That reminds me. Isn't tomorrow Wednesday?" she said. "Which of us is going to get up and let in the farm carts?" When Stacy stared vacantly, Kate stamped her foot. "Don't look so stupid, Stacy. They came the day after father was buried, why wouldn't they come tomorrow? Mother herself said it was their way of showing that as far as they were concerned the death wouldn't make any difference."

"Oh Kate. How do you think they'll take it when you tell them . . ."

"Tell them what? Really Stacy, you *are* a fool. Tomorrow is no day to tell them anything. We'll have to take it easy, wait and see how we stand, before we talk about making changes."

Kate was so capable. Stacy was filled with admiration for her. She would not have minded in the least getting up to open the gate, but she never would be able to face a discussion of the future. Kate was able for everything, and realising this, Stacy permitted herself a small feeling of excitement at the thought of them making their own plans and standing on their own two feet.

"I'll get up and light the fire and bring you a cup of tea in bed before you have to get up, Kate," she said.

Kate shrugged her shoulders. "If I know you, Stacy, you'll have one of your headaches," she said.

Stacy said nothing. She was resolved to get up, headache or no headache. On the quiet she set an old alarm clock she found in the kitchen. But the alarm bell was broken, and the first thing Stacy heard next morning was the rapping on the gate. When she went to scramble out, to her surprise Kate was already gone from the room. And when Stacy threw her clothes on and ran out to the kitchen, the fire was roaring up the chimney, and a cup with a trace of sugar and tea leaves in the bottom of it was on the windowsill. The teapot was on the hob but it had been made a long time and it was cold. She made herself another pot and took it over to sip it by the window, looking out.

Kate was in the yard, directing the carts and laughing and talking with the men. Kate certainly had a way with her and no mistake. When it would come to telling the farmers that they needn't deliver any more dung, she'd do it tactfully and they wouldn't be offended.

One big tall farmer, with red hair and whiskers, was the last to leave, and he and Kate stood talking at the gate so long Stacy wondered if, after all, Kate mightn't be discussing their future dealings with him. She hoped she wouldn't catch cold. She had put a few more sods of turf on the fire.

"Do you want to set the chimney on fire?" Kate asked when she came in. Stacy didn't let herself get upset though. Kate was carrying all the responsibility now, and it was bound to make her edgy.

"I saw you talking to one of the men," said she. "I was wondering if perhaps you were giving him a hint of our plans and sounding him out?"

"I was sounding him out alright," Kate said, and she smiled. "You see, Stacy. I've been thinking that we might come up with a new plan. You mightn't like it at first, but you may come round when I make you see it in the right light. Sit down and I'll tell you." Stacy sat down. Kate stayed standing. "I've been looking into the ledgers, and I would never have believed there was so much money coming in from the dung. So, I've been thinking that, instead of getting rid of it, we ought to try and take in more, twice or three times more, and make twice or three times as much money. No. No. Sit down again, Stacy. Hear me out. My plan would be that we'd move into a more suitable house, larger and with a garden maybe."

When Stacy said nothing Kate looked sharply at her. It wouldn't have surprised her if Stacy had flopped off in another faint, but she was only sitting dumbly looking into the fire. "It's only a suggestion," Kate said, feeling her way more carefully. "You never heed anything, Stacy, but when I go out for my walks I take note of things I see, and there's a plot of ground for sale out a bit the road, but not too far from here all the same, and it's for sale. I've made enquiries about the cost of that too."

But Stacy had found her tongue. "I don't want to move out of here, Kate," she cried. "This is where we were born, where we were so happy together, where my mother and father . . ." She began to cry. "Oh Kate. I never want to leave here. Never. Never."

Kate could hardly speak with fury.

"Stay here so," she said. "But don't expect me to stay with you. I'm getting out of here at the first opportunity that comes my way. And let me tell you something else. That dunghill isn't stirring out of where it is until I've a decent dowry out of it. Cry away now to your heart's content for all I care." Going over to their bedroom Kate went in and banged the door behind her.

Stacy stopped crying and stared at the closed door. Her head had begun to throb and she would have liked to lie down, but after the early hour Kate had risen she had probably gone back to bed. No. Kate was up and moving about the room. There was great activity going on. Stacy felt better. She knew Kate. Kate had never been one to say she was sorry for anything she said or did, but that did not always mean she didn't feel sorry. She must be giving their room a good turn-out. Perhaps this was her way of working off her annoyance and at the same time show she was sorry for losing her temper. Stacy sat back, thinking her thoughts, and waited for Kate to come out. She didn't have long to wait. In about five minutes the knob of the bedroom door rattled. "Open this door for me, Stacy. My arms are full. I can't turn the handle," Kate called and Stacy was glad to see she sounded in excellent form, and as if all was forgotten. For the second time in twenty-four hours Stacy felt a small surge of excitement, as Kate came out, her arms piled skyhigh with dresses and hats and a couple of cardboard boxes, covered with wallpaper, in which they kept their gloves and handkerchiefs. She'd done a real spring cleaning. They hadn't done one in years. She hadn't noticed it before but the wallpaper on the boxes was yellowed with age and the flowery pattern faded. They might paste on new wallpaper? And seeing that Kate, naturally, was carrying only her own things she ran to get hers, but first she ran back to clear a space on the table so Kate could put her things down.

But Kate was heading across the kitchen to their mother's room.

"There's no sense in having a room idle, is there?" she said, disappearing into it. "I'm moving in here."

There was no further mention of the dunghill that day, nor indeed that week. Stacy felt a bit lonely at first in the room they had shared since childhood. But it had its advantages. It had been a bit stuffy sleeping next to the wall. And she didn't have so many headaches, but that could possibly be attributed to Kate's recent suggestion that she ought to ignore them, and not give in to them.

Every Wednesday Kate was up at the crack of dawn to let in the carts and supervise the unloading. As their father had also foreseen, they were now paying the farmers for the manure, but only a small sum, because the farmers were still glad to get rid of it. The townspeople on the other hand were paying five times more than before for it. Kate had made no bones about raising her prices. The only time there was a reference to the future was when Kate announced that she didn't like keeping cash in the house, and that she was going to start banking some of their takings. The rest could be put as usual in the black box, which was almost the only thing that had never been taken out of their mother's room. A lot of other things had been thrown out.

Kate and Stacy got on as well as ever, it seemed to Stacy but there were often long stretches of silence in the house because Kate was never as talkative as their mother. After nightfall they often sat by a dying fire, only waiting for it to go out, before getting up and going to bed. All things considered, Kate was right to have moved into the other room, and Stacy began to enjoy having a room of her own. She had salvaged a few of her mother's things that Kate had thrown out and she liked looking at them. If Kate knew, she never said anything. Kate never came into the old room anymore.

Then when Con O'Toole, the whiskery farmer with whom Kate had been talking the first day she took over the running of things, started dropping in to see how they were getting on, Stacy was particularly glad to have a room of her own. She liked Con. She really did. But the smell of his pipe brought on her headaches again. The smell of his tobacco never quite left the house, and it pursued her through the keyhole after she had left him and Kate together, because of course it was Kate that Con came to see.

"How can you stand the smell of his pipe?" she asked Kate one morning. "It's worse than the smell of the dung." She only said it by way of a joke, but Kate, who had taken out the black box and was going through the papers in it, a thing she did regularly now, shut the lid of the box and frowned.

"I thought we agreed on saying fertiliser instead of that word you used."

"Oh but that was long ago, when we were in boarding school," Stacy stammered.

"I beg your pardon. It was agreed we'd be more particular about how we referred to our business when we were in the company of other people, or at least that was my understanding. Take Con O'Toole for instance. He may deliver dung here but he never gives it that name, at least not in front of me. The house he lives in may be thatched and have a mud wall, but that's because his old mother is alive and he can't get her to agree to knocking it down and building a new house, which of course they can well afford. I was astonished at the amount of land he owns. Of course, you understand, Stacy, that I am not urging him to make any changes. So please don't mention this conversation to him. I'll tell him myself when I judge the time to be right. I'll make him see the need for building a new house. He needn't knock down the old one either. He can leave the old woman in it for what time is left her. But as I say, I'll bide my time. I might even wait until after we are married."

That was the first Stacy heard of Kate's intended marriage, but after that first reference there was talk of nothing else, right up to the fine blowy morning when Kate was hoisted up into Con O'Toole's new motor-car, in a peacock blue outfit, with their mother's gold chain bumping up and down on her bosom.

Stacy was almost squeezed to death in the doorway as the guests all stood there to wave goodbye to the happy couple. There had been far more guests than either she or Kate had bargained on because the O'Tooles had so many relations, and they all brought their children, and, to boot, Kate's old mother-in-law brought along a few of her own cronies as well. But there was enough food, and plenty of port wine.

It was a fine wedding. And Stacy didn't mind the mess that was made of the house. Such a mess: Crumbs scattered over the carpet in the parlour and driven into it by people's feet. Bottle tops all over the kitchen floor. Port wine and lemonade stains soaked into the tablecloth. It was going to take time to get the place to rights again. Stacy was almost looking forward to getting it to rights again because she had decided to make a few changes in the arrangement of the furniture small changes, only involving chairs and ornaments and she intended attacking the job that evening after the guests left. However, when the bridal couple drove off with a hiss of steam rising out of the radiator of the car, the guests flocked back into the house and didn't go until there wasn't a morsel left to eat, or single drop left to refill the decanters. One thing did upset Stacy and that was when she saw the way the beautiful wedding cake on which the icing had been as hard and white as plaster had been laid waste by someone who didn't know how to cut a cake. And the children that hadn't already fallen asleep on the sofas were stuffing themselves with the last crumbs. Stacy herself hadn't as much as a taste of that cake, and she'd intended keeping at least one tier aside for some future time. Ah well. It was nice to think everyone had had a good time, she thought, as she closed the door on the last of the O'Tooles, who had greatly outnumbered their own friends. Jasper Kane, their father's solicitor, had been the principal guest. He had not in fact left yet, but he was getting ready to leave.

"It will be very lonely for you now, Miss Stacy," he said. "You ought to get some person in to keep you company, at least for the nights."

It was very kind of him to be so concerned. Stacy expressed her gratitude freely, and reassured him that she was quite looking forward to being, as it were, her own mistress. She felt obliged to add, hastily, that she'd miss Kate, although to be strictly truthful, she didn't think she'd miss her as much as she would have thought before Con O'Toole had put in his appearance.

"Well, well. I'm glad to hear you say that, Miss Stacy." Jasper Kane said, as he prepared to leave. "I expect you'll drop in to my office at your convenience. I understand your sister took care of the business, but I'm sure you'll be just as competent when you get the hang of things." Then for a staid man like him, he got almost playful. "I'll be very curious to see what changes you'll make," he said, and she saw his eye fall on a red plush sofa that Kate had bought after Con started calling, and which Stacy thought was hideous. She gave him a conspiratorial smile. But she didn't want him to think she wasn't serious.

"I intend to make changes outside as well, Mr Kane," she said, gravely. And the very first thing I'm going to do is plant a few lilac trees.

Jasper Kane looked surprised.

"Oh? Where?" he asked and although it was dark outside, he went to the window and tried to see out.

"Where else but where the dunghill has always been. You see I am going to get rid of it," Stacy said, and just to hear herself speaking with such authority made her almost light-headed.

Jasper Kane remained staring out into the darkness. Then he turned around and asked a simple question.

"But what will you live on, Miss Stacy?"

Happiness

Mother had a lot to say. This does not mean she was always talking but that we children felt the wells she drew upon were deep, deep, deep. Her theme was happiness: what it was, what it was not; where we might find it, where not; and how, if found, it must be guarded. Never must we confound it with pleasure. Nor think sorrow its exact opposite.

"Take Father Hugh," Mother's eyes flashed as she looked at him. "According to him, sorrow is an ingredient of happiness, a necessary ingredient, if you please." And when he tried to protest she put up her hand. "There may be a freakish truth in the theory for some people. But not for me. And not, I hope, for my children." She looked severely at us three girls. We laughed. None of us had had much experience of sorrow. Bea and I were children and Linda only a year old when our father died suddenly after a short illness that had not at first seemed serious. "I've known people to make sorrow a substitute for happiness," Mother said.

Father Hugh protested again. "You're not putting me in that class, I hope?"

Father Hugh, ever since our father died, had been the closest of anyone to us as a family, without being close to any one of us in particular, even to Mother. He lived in a monastery near our farm in County Meath, and he had been one of the celebrants at the Requiem High Mass our father's political importance had demanded. He met us that day for the first time, but he took to dropping in to see us, with the idea of filling the crater of loneliness left at our centre. He did not know that there was a cavity in his own life, much less that we would fill it. He and Mother were both young in those days, and perhaps it gave scandal to some that he was so often in our house, staying till late into the night and, indeed, thinking nothing of stopping all night if there was any special reason, such as one of us being sick. He had even on occasion slept there if the night was too wet for tramping home across the fields.

When we girls were young, we were so used to having Father Hugh around that we never stood on ceremony with him but in his presence dried our hair and pared our nails and never minded what garments were strewn about. As for Mother, she thought nothing of running out of the bathroom in her slip, brushing her teeth or combing her hair, if she wanted to tell him something she might otherwise forget. And she brooked no criticism of her behaviour. "Celibacy was never meant to take all the warmth and homeliness out of their lives," she said.

On this point, too, Bea was adamant. Bea, the middle sister, was our oracle. "I'm so glad he has Mother," she said, "as well as her having him, because it must be awful the way most women treat them, priests, I mean, as if they were pariahs. Mother treats him like a human being, that's all."

When it came to Mother's ears that there had been gossip about her making free with Father Hugh, she opened her eyes wide in astonishment. "But he's only a priest," she said.

Bea giggled. "It's a good job he didn't hear that," she said to me afterwards. It would undo the good she's done him. You'd think he was a eunuch."

"Bea, do you think he's in love with her?" I said.

"If so, he doesn't know it," Bea said firmly. "It's her soul he's after. Maybe he wants to make sure of her in the next world."

But thoughts of the world to come never troubled Mother. "If anything ever happens to me, children," she said, "suddenly, I mean, or when you are not near me, or I cannot speak to you, I want you to promise you won't feel bad. There's no need. Just remember that I had a happy life and if I had to choose my kind of heaven I'd take it on this earth with you again, no matter how much you might at times annoy me."

You see, according to Mother, annoyance and fatigue, and even illness and pain, could coexist with happiness. She had a habit of asking people if they were happy at times and in places that, to say the least of it, seemed to us inappropriate. "But are you happy?" she'd probe as one lay sick and bathed in sweat, or in the throes of a jumping toothache. And once in our presence she made the inquiry of an old friend as he lay upon his deathbed. "Why not?" she asked when we took her to task for it later. "Isn't it more important than ever to be happy when you're dying? Take my own father, do you know what he said in his last moments? On his deathbed, he defied me to name a man who had enjoyed a better life. In spite of dreadful pain, his face radiated happiness." Mother nodded her head comfortably. "Happiness drives out pain, as fire burns out fire."

Having no knowledge of our own to pit against hers, we thirstily drank in her rhetoric. Only Bea was sceptical. "Perhaps you got it from him, like spots, or fever," she said. "Or something that could at least be slipped from hand to hand."

"Do you think I'd have taken it if that were the case" Mother cried. "Then, when he needed it most?"

"Not there and then," Bea said stubbornly. "I meant as a sort of legacy."

"Don't you think in that case, Mother said, exasperated, "he would have felt obliged to leave it to your grandmother?"

Certainly we knew that in spite of his lavish heart our grandfather had failed to provide our grandmother with enduring happiness. He had passed that job on to Mother. And Mother had not made too good a fist of it, even when Father was living and she had him, and later us children to help.

As for Father Hugh, he had given our grandmother up early in the game. "God Almighty couldn't make that woman happy," he said one day, seeing Mother's face, drawn and pale with fatigue, preparing for the nightly run over to her own mother's house that would exhaust her utterly. There were evenings after she came home from the County library where she worked, when we saw her stand with the car keys in her hand, trying to think which would be worse, to slog over there on foot, or take out the car again. And yet the distance was short. It was Mother's day that had been too long. "Weren't you over to see her this morning?" Father Hugh demanded.

"No matter," said Mother She was no doubt thinking of the forlorn face our grandmother always put on when she was leaving.

"Don't say good night, Vera," Grandmother would plead. "It makes me feel too lonely. And you never can tell, you might slip over again before you go to bed."

"Do you know the time?" Bea would ask impatiently if she happened to be with Mother. Not indeed that the lateness of the hour counted for anything, because in all likelihood Mother would go back, if only to pass by under the window and see that the lights were out, or stand and listen and make sure that as far as she could tell all was well.

"I wouldn't mind if she was happy," Mother once said to us.

"And how do you know she's not?" we asked.

"When people are happy, I can feel it. Can't you?"

We were not sure. Most people thought our grandmother was a gay creature, a small birdy being who even at a great age laughed like a girl, and more remarkably sang like one, as she went about her day. But beak and claw were of steel. She'd think nothing of sending Mother back to a shop three times if her errands were not exactly right. "Not sugar like that, that's too fine; it's not castor sugar I want. But not as coarse as that, either. I want an in-between kind."

Provoked one day, my youngest sister, Linda, turned and gave battle. "You're mean!" she cried. "You love ordering people about."

Grandmother preened, as if Linda had paid her a compliment. "I was always hard to please," she said. "As a girl, I used to be called Miss Imperious."

And Miss Imperious she remained as long as she lived, even when she was a great age. Her orders were then given a wry twist by the fact that as she advanced in age she took to calling her daughter Mother, as we did.

There was one great phrase with which our grandmother opened every sentence: "*if only*". "If only," she'd say, when we came to visit her, "if only you'd come earlier, before I was worn out expecting you." Or if we were early, then she'd say, if only it was later, after she'd had a rest and could enjoy us, be able for us. And if we brought her flowers, she'd sigh to think that if only we'd brought them the previous day when she'd had a visitor to appreciate them or if only the stems were longer, or that we had picked a few green leaves, and included a few buds. Because she'd say disparagingly, the poor flowers we'd brought were already wilting. We used to feel we might just as well not have brought them. As the years went on grandmother had a new bead to add to her rosary: if only her friends were not all dead. By their absence, they reduced to nil all real enjoyment in anything. Our own father, her son-in-law, was the one person who had ever gone close to pleasing her. But even here there had been a snag. "If only he was my real son," she used to say, with a sigh.

Mother's mother lived on through our childhood and into our early maturity, although she outlived the money our grandfather left her, and in our minds she was a complicated mixture of valiance and defeat. Courageous and generous within the limits of her own life, her simplest demand was yet enormous in the larger frame of Mother's life, and so we never could see her with the same clarity of vision with which we saw our grandfather, or our own father. Them we saw only through Mother's eyes.

"Take your grandfather," she'd cry, and instantly we'd see him, his eyes turning upon us, yes, upon us, although in his day only one of us had been born: me. At another time, Mother would cry, "Take your own father," and instantly we'd see him, tall, handsome, young, and much more suited to marry one of us than poor bedraggled Mother. Most fascinating of all were the times Mother would say "Take me." By magic then, staring down the years, we'd see blazingly clear a small girl with black hair and buttoned boots, who, though plain and pouting, burned bright, like a star. "I was happy, you see," Mother said. And we'd strain hard to try and understand the mystery of the light that still radiated from her. "I used to lean along a tree that grew out over the river," she said, "and look down through the grey leaves at the water flowing past below, and I used to think it was not the stream that flowed but me, spreadeagled over it, who flew through the air like a bird. That I'd found the secret." She made it seem there might be such a secret, just waiting to be found. Another time she used to dream that she'd be a great singer.

"We didn't know you sang, Mother?"

She had to laugh. "Like a crow," she said.

Sometimes she used to think she'd swim the Channel.

"Did you swim that well, Mother?"

"Oh, not really, just the breast stroke," she said. "And only then by the aid of two pig bladders blown up by my father and tied around my middle. But I used to throb, yes, throb with happiness."

Behind Mother's back, Bea raised her eyebrows.

What was it, we used to ask ourselves, that quality that she, we felt sure, misnamed? Was it courage? Was it strength, health, or high spirits? Something you could not give or take? A conundrum, or a game of catch-as-catch-can?

"I know what it was," cried Bea one day. "A sham."

Whatever it was, we knew that Mother would let no wind of violence from within or without tear it from her. Although, one evening when Father Hugh was with us, our astonished ears heard her proclaim that there might be a time when one had to slacken hold on it, let it go for a moment, to catch at it again with a surer hand. In the way, we supposed, that the high-wire walker up among the painted stars of his canvas sky must wait to fling himself through the air until the bar he catches at has started to sway perversely from him. Oh no, no! That downward drag at our innards we could not bear, the belly swelling to the shape of a pear. Let happiness go by the board. "After all, lots of people seem to make out without it," Bea said. It was too tricky a business. And might it not be that one had to be born with a flair for it?

"A flair would not be enough," Mother said when we once asked her. "Take Father Hugh. He, if anyone, had a flair for it, a natural capacity. You've only to look at him when he's off guard with you children, or helping me in the garden. But he rejects happiness. He casts it from him."

"That is simply not true, Vera," said Father Hugh, overhearing her. "It's just that I don't place an inordinate value on it like you. I don't think it's enough to carry one all the way. To the end, I mean—and after."

"Oh, don't talk about the end when we're only in the middle," said Mother. And, indeed, at that moment her own face shone with such happiness it was hard to believe that her earth was not her heaven. Certainly it was her constant contention that of happiness she had had a lion's share. This, however, we, in private, doubted. Perhaps there were times when she had had a surplus of it, when she was young, say, with her redoubtable father, whose love blazed circles around her, making winter into summer and ice into fire. Perhaps she did have a brimming measure in her early married years. By straining hard, we could find traces left in our minds from those days of milk and honey. Our father, while he lived, had cast a magic over everything, for us as well as for her. He held his love up over us like an umbrella and kept off the troubles that afterwards came down on us, pouring cats and dogs.

But if she did have more than the common lot of happiness in those early days, what use was that when we could remember so clearly how our father's death had ravaged her? And how could we forget the distress it brought on us when, afraid to let her out of our sight, Bea and I stumbled after her everywhere, through the woods and along the bank of the river, where, in the weeks that followed, she tried vainly to find peace.

The summer after Father died, we were invited to France to stay with friends, and when she went walking on the cliffs at Fécamp our fears for her grew frenzied, so that we hung on to her arm and dragged at her skirt, hoping that like leaded weights we'd pin her down if she went too near to the edge. But at night we had to abandon our watch, being forced to follow the conventions of a family still whole, a home still intact, and go to bed at the same time as the children of the house. It was at that hour, when the coast guard was gone from his rowing boat offshore, and the sand was as cold and grey as the sea, that Mother liked to swim. And when she had washed, kissed, and left us, our hearts almost died inside us and we'd creep out of bed again to stand in our bare feet at the mansard and watch as she ran down the shingle, striking out when she reached the water where, far out, wave and sky and mist were one, and the greyness closed over her. If we took our eyes off her for an instant, it was impossible to find her again.

"Oh, make her turn back, God please!" I prayed out loud one night.

Startled, Bea turned away from the window. "She'll have to turn back sometime, won't she? Unless—?"

Locking our cold hands together, we'd stare out again. "She wouldn't," I whispered. "It would be a sin."

Secure in the deterring power of sin, we let out our breath. Then Bea's breath caught again. "What if she went out so far she used up all her strength and couldn't swim back? It wouldn't be a sin then."

"It's the intention that counts," I said.

A second later, we could see the arm lift heavily up and wearily cleave down, and at last Mother was in the shallows, wading back to shore.

"Don't let her see us!" cried Bea. As if our chattering teeth would not give us away when she looked in at us before she went to her own room on the other side of the corridor, where later in the night the sound of her weeping would reach us.

What was it worth, a happiness bought that dearly?

But Mother had never questioned its worth. She told us once that on a wintry day she brought her own mother a snowdrop. "It was the first one of the year," she said, "a bleak bud that had come up stunted before its time, and I meant it as a sign of Spring to come. But do you know what your grandmother said? 'What good are snowdrops to me now?' Such a thing to say! What good are snowdrops at all if they don't hold their value for us all our lives? Isn't that the whole point of a snowdrop? And that is the whole point of happiness, too. What good would it be if it could be erased without trace? Take me and those daffodils." Stooping, she buried her face in a bunch that lay on the table waiting to be put in vases. "If they didn't hold their beauty absolute and inviolable, do you think I could bear the sight of them after what happened when your father was in hospital?"

It was a fair question. When Father went to hospital, Mother went with him and stayed in a small hotel across the street so she could be with him all day from early to late. "Because it was so awful for him, being in Dublin," she said. "You have no idea how he hated it."

That he was dying neither of them realised. How could they know, as it rushed through the sky, that their star was a falling star? But one evening when she'd left him asleep Mother came back home for a few hours to see how we were faring, and it broke her heart to see the daffodils were out all over the place, in the woods, under the trees, and along the sides of the avenue. There had never been so many, and she thought how awful it was that Father was missing them. "I know you send up little bunches to him, you poor dears," she said. "Sweet little bunches, too, squeezed tight as posies by your little fists. But stuffed into vases they can't really make up to him for not being able to see masses of them growing." So on the way back to the hospital she stopped her car and pulled a great bunch of them, the full of her arms. "They took up the whole back seat," she said, "and I was so excited at the thought of walking into his room and dumping them on his bed, you know just plomping them down so he could smell them, and feel them. I didn't mean them to be put in vases in his room, not all of them. It would have taken a rainwater barrel to hold them. Why, I could hardly see over them as I came up the steps; I kept tripping. But when I came into the hall, that nun—I told you about her—that nun came up to me, sprang out of nowhere it seemed, although I know now that she was waiting for me, knowing that somebody had to bring me to my senses. But the cruel way she did it. Reaching out she grabbed the flowers, letting lots of them fall. I remember some of them getting stood on. 'Where are you going with those foolish flowers, you foolish woman?' she said. 'Don't you know your husband is dying? Your prayers are all you can give him now.' She was right. I was foolish. But I wasn't cured. And that Summer it was nothing but foolishness the way I dragged you children after me all over Europe. As if any one place was going to be different from another, any better, any less desolate. But there was great satisfaction in bringing you places your father and I had planned to bring you, although in fairness to him I must say that he would not perhaps have brought you so young. And he would not have had an ulterior motive. But above all, he would not have attempted those trips in such a dilapidated car."

Oh, that car! It was a battered old red sports car, so depleted of accessories that when, eventually, we got a new car Mother still stuck out her hand on bends, and in wet weather jumped out to wipe the windscreen with her sleeve. And if fussed, she'd let down the window and shout at people, forgetting she now had a horn. How we ever fitted into it with all our luggage was a miracle.

"Oh. There was plenty of room, you were never lumpish, any of you," Mother said proudly. "But you were very healthy and very strong." She turned to me. "Think of how you got that car up the hill in Switzerland."

"The Alps are not hills, Mother," I pointed out coldly, as I had done at the time, when the car failed to make it on one of the inclines. Mother let it run back until it wedged against the rock face, and I had to get out and push till she got it going again in first gear. But when it got started it couldn't be stopped to pick me up until it reached the top, where they had to wait for me. And for a very long time.

"Ah, well," Mother said, sighing wistfully at the thought of those trips. "You got something out of them, I hope. All that travelling must have helped you with your geography and your history."

We looked at each other and smiled, and then Mother herself laughed. "Remember the time when we were in Italy, and it was Easter, and all the shops were chock-full of food? The butchers' shops had poultry and game hanging up outside the doors, fully feathered, and with their poor heads dripping blood, and in the windows they had poor little lambs and suckling pigs and young goats, all skinned and hanging by their hindfeet." She shuddered. "Continentals are so obsessed about food. I found it revolting. I had to hurry past. But Linda, who must have been only four then, dragged at me and stared and stared. You know how children at that age have a morbid fascination for what is cruel and bloody. Her face was flushed and her eyes were wide. I hurried her back to the hotel. But next morning she crept into my room, and pressed up close to me. 'Can't we go back, just once, and look again at that shop?' she whispered. 'The shop where they have the little children hanging up for Easter.' She meant the young goats, of course, but I'd said *kids*, I suppose. How we laughed." But here her face was grave. "You were really very good children in general. Otherwise I would never have put so much effort into rearing you, because I wasn't a bit maternal. You brought out the best in me. I put an unnatural effort into you, of course, because I was taking my standards from your father, forgetting that his might not have remained so inflexible if he had lived to middle age and was beset by life, like other parents."

"Well, the job is nearly over now, Vera," said Father Hugh. "And you didn't do so badly."

"That's right, Hugh," said Mother, and she straightened up, and put her hand to her back the way she sometimes did in the garden when she got up from her knees after weeding. "I didn't go over to the enemy anyway. We survived." Then a flash of defiance came into her eyes. "And we were happy. That was the main thing."

Father Hugh frowned. "There you go again!" he said.

Mother turned on him. "I don't think you realise the onslaughts that were made upon our happiness. The minute Robert died, they came down on me, cohorts of relatives, friends, even strangers, all draped in black, opening their arms like bats to let me pass into their company. 'Life is a vale of tears,' they said. 'You are privileged to find it out so young.' Ugh! After I staggered on to my feet and began to take hold of life once more, they fell back defeated. And the first day I gave a laugh, pouff, they were blown out like candles. They weren't living in a real world at all; they belonged to a ghostly world where life was easy: all one had to do was sit and weep. It takes effort to push back the stone from the mouth of the tomb and walk out."

Effort. Effort. Ah, but that strange-sounding word could invoke little sympathy from those who had not learned yet what it meant. Life must have been hardest for Mother in those years when we older ones were at college, no longer children, yet still dependent on her. Indeed, we made more demands on her than ever then, having moved into new areas of activity and emotion. And came and went as freely as we did ourselves, so that the house was often like a hotel, and one where pets were not prohibited but took their places on chairs and beds, as regardlessly as the people. Anyway it was hard to have sympathy for someone who got things into such a state as Mother. All over the house there was clutter. Her study was like the returned-letter department of a post-office, with stacks of paper everywhere, bills paid and unpaid, letters answered and unanswered, tax returns, pamphlets, leaflets. If by mistake we left the door open on a windy day, we came back to find papers flapping through the air like frightened birds. Efficient only in that she managed eventually to conclude every task she began, it never seemed possible to outsiders that by Mother's methods anything whatever could be accomplished. In an attempt to keep order elsewhere she made her own room the clearing house into which the rest of us put everything: things to be given away, things to be mended, things to be stored, things to be treasured, things to be returned; even things to be thrown out. By the end of the year, the room resembled an obsolescence dump. And no one could help her; the chaos of her life was as personal as an act of creation. One might as well try to finish another person's poem.

As the years passed, Mother rushed around more hectically. And although Bea and I had married and were not at home any more, except at holiday time and for occasional weekends, Linda was noisier than the two of us put together had been, and for every follower we had brought home she brought twenty. The house was never still. Now that we were reduced to being visitors, we watched Mother's tension mount to vertigo, knowing that, like a spinning top, she could not rest till she fell. But now at the smallest pretext Father Hugh would call in the doctor and Mother would be put on the mail boat and dispatched to London. For it was essential that she get far enough away to make phoning home every night prohibitively costly.

Unfortunately, the thought of departure often drove a spur into her and she redoubled her effort to achieve order in her affairs. She would stay up until the early hours ransacking her desk. To her, as always the shortest parting entailed a preparation as for death. And as if her end was at hand, we would all be summoned, to be given last minute instructions, although she never got time to speak a word to us, because five minutes before departure she would still be attempting to reply to letters that were the acquisition of weeks and would have taken whole days to answer.

"Don't you know the taxi is at the door, Vera?" Father Hugh would say, running his hand through his grey hair and looking very dishevelled himself. She had him at times as distracted as herself. "You can't do any more. You'll have to leave the rest till you come back."

"I can't, I can't!" Mother would cry. "I'll have to cancel my plans."

One day, Father Hugh opened the lid of her case, which was strapped up in the hall, and with a swipe of his arm he cleared all the papers on the top of the desk pell-mell into the suitcase. "You can sort them on the boat." he said, "or the train to London."

Thereafter, Mother's luggage always included an empty case to hold the unfinished papers on her desk. And years afterwards a steward on the Irish Mail told us she was a familiar figure, working away at letters and bills nearly all the way from Holyhead to Euston. "She usually gave it up about Rugby or Crewe," he said. "She'd get talking to someone in the compartment." He smiled. "There was one day coming down the corridor of the train I was just in time to see her close up the window with a guilty look. I didn't say anything, but I think she'd emptied those papers of hers out the window."

Quite likely. When we were children, even a few hours away from us gave her composure. And in two weeks or less, when she'd come home, the well of her spirit would be freshened. We'd hardly know her, her step so light, her eye so bright, and her love and patience once more freely flowing. But in no time at all the house would fill up once more with the noise and confusion of too many people and too many animals, and again we'd be fighting our corner with cats and dogs, bats, mice, bees and even wasps. "Don't kill it!" Mother would cry if we raised a hand to an angry wasp. "Just catch it, dear, and put it outside. Open the window and let it fly away!" But even this treatment could at times be deemed too harsh. "Wait a minute. Close the window!" she'd cry. "It's too cold outside. It will die. That's why it came in, I suppose. Oh dear, what will we do?" Life would be going full blast again.

There was only one place Mother found rest. When she was at breaking point and fit to fall, she'd go out into the garden, not to sit or stroll around but to dig, to drag up weeds, to move great clumps of corms or rhizomes, or indeed quite frequently to haul huge rocks from one place to another. She was always laying down a path, building a dry wall, or making compost heaps as high as hills. However jaded she might be going out, when dark forced her in at last her step had a spring of a daisy. So if she did not succeed in defining happiness to our satisfaction, we could see that whatever it was, she possessed it to the full when she was in her garden.

I said as much one Sunday when Bea and I had dropped round for the afternoon. Father Hugh was with us again. "It's an unthinking happiness, though," he cavilled. We were standing at the drawing-room window, looking out to where in the fading light we could see Mother on her knees weeding in the long border that stretched from the house right down to the woods. "I wonder how she'd take it if she were stricken down and had to give up that heavy work," he said. Was he perhaps a little jealous of how she could stoop and bend? He himself had begun to use a stick. I was often a little jealous of her myself, because although I was married and had children of my own, I had married young and felt the weight of living as heavy as a weight of years. "She doesn't take enough care of herself," Father Hugh said sadly. "Look at her out there with nothing under her knees to protect her from the damp ground." It was almost too dim for us to see her, but even in the drawing room it was chilly. "She should not be let stay out there after the sun goes down."

"Just you try to get her in then," said Linda, who had come into the room in time to hear him. "Don't you know by now that what would kill another person only seems to make Mother thrive?"

Father Hugh shook his head again. "You seem to forget it's not younger she's getting." He fidgeted and fussed, and several times went to the window to stare out apprehensively. He was really getting quite elderly.

"Come and sit down, Father Hugh," Bea said, and to take his mind off Mother she turned on the light and blotted out the garden. Instead of seeing through the window, we saw into it as into a mirror, and there between the flower-laden tables and the lamps it was ourselves we saw moving vaguely. Like Father Hugh, we, too, were waiting for her to come in before we called an end to the day.

"Oh, this is ridiculous!" Father Hugh cried at last. "She'll have to listen to reason." And going over to the window he threw it open. "Vera! Vera!" he called, sternly, so sternly that, more intimate than an endearment, his tone shocked us. "She didn't hear me," he said, turning back blinking at us in the lighted room. "I'm going out to get her." And in a minute he was gone from the room. As he ran down the garden path, we stared at each other, astonished; his step, like his voice , was the step of a lover. "I'm coming, Vera!" he cried.

Although she never failed to answer him when he called, whatever about us, Mother had not moved. In the whole-hearted way she did everything, she was bent down close to the ground. It wasn't the light only that was dimming; her eyesight also was failing too, I thought, as instinctively I followed Father Hugh.

But halfway down the path I stopped. I had seen something he had not seen. Mother's hand that appeared to support itself in a forked branch of an old tree-peony she had planted as a bride, was not in fact gripping it but impaled upon it. And the hand that appeared to be grubbing in the clay in fact was sunk into the soft mould. "Mother!" I screamed, and I ran forward, but when I reached her I covered my face with my hands. "Oh Father Hugh," I cried. "Is she dead?"

It was Bea who answered, hysterically. "She is! She is!" she cried, and she began to pound Father Hugh on the back with her fists, as if his pessimistic words had made this happen.

But Mother was not dead. And at first the doctor even offered hope of her pulling through. But from the moment Father Hugh lifted her up to carry her into the house we ourselves had no hope, seeing how effortlessly he, who was not strong, could carry her. When he put her down on her bed, her head hardly creased the pillow.

Mother lived for four hours. Like the days of her life, those four hours were packed tight with concern and anxiety. Partly conscious, partly delirious, she seemed to think the counterpane was her desk, and she scrabbled her fingers upon it as if trying to sort out a muddle of bills and correspondence. No longer indifferent now, we listened, anguished, to the distracted cries that had all our lifetime been so familiar to us. "Oh, where is it? Where is it? I had it a minute ago. Where on earth did I put it?"

"Vera, Vera stop worrying," Father Hugh pleaded, but she waved him away and went on sifting through the sheets as if they were sheets of paper. "Oh, Vera," he begged. "Listen to me! Do you not know—"

Before he could say what he was going to say Bea pushed between them. "You're not to tell her!" she commanded. "Why frighten her?"

"But it ought not to frighten her," said Father Hugh. "This is what I was always afraid would happen, that she'd be frightened when it came to the end."

At that moment, as if to vindicate him, Mother's hands fell idle on the coverlet, palm upward and empty. And turning her head she stared at each of us in turn, beseechingly. "I cannot face it," she whispered. "I can't. I can't. I can't."

"Oh, my God!" Bea said, and she started to cry.

"Vera. For God's sake listen to me!" Father Hugh cried, and pressing his face to hers, as close as a kiss, he kept whispering to her, trying to cast into the dark tunnel before her the powerful light of his own faith.

But it seemed to us that Mother must already be looking into God's exigent eyes. "I can't!" she cried again. "I can't face it."

Then her mind came back from the stark world of the spirit to the world where her body was still detained, but even that world was now a whirling kaleidoscope of things which only she could see. Suddenly her eyes focused, and, catching at Father Hugh, she pulled herself up a little and pointed to something we could not see. "What will be done with them?" Her voice was anxious. "They ought to be put in water anyway," she said, and, leaning over the edge of the bed, she pointed to the floor. "Don't step on them," she said sharply. Then, more sharply still, she addressed us all. "Have them sent to the public ward," she said peremptorily. "Don't let that nun take them, she'll only put them on the altar. And God doesn't want them. He made them for us, not for Himself."

It was the familiar rhetoric that all her life had characterised her utterances. For a moment we were mystified. Then Bea gasped. "The daffodils!" she cried. "Don't you remember? The day Father died." And over Bea's face came the light that had so often blazed over Mother's. Leaning across the bed, she pushed Father Hugh aside. And, putting out her hands, she held Mother's face between her palms as tenderly as if it were the face of a child. "It's all right, Mother. You don't have to face it. It's over." Then she who had so fiercely forbade Father Hugh to do so blurted out the truth. "You've finished with this world, Mother," she said, and, confident that her tidings were joyous, her voice was strong.

Mother made the last effort of her life and grasped at Bea's meaning. She let out a sigh, and, closing her eyes, she sank back, and this time her head sank so deep into the pillow it seemed that it would have been dented had it been a pillow of stone.

The New Gardener

Clem was the man for us. "No matter. I'll get it to rights," he said blithely, when he saw the state of our garden. Five weeks of early spring with no man in it, and a wet season at that, it was a fright. "And now where's the cottage?" he asked.

He had crossed over from Holyhead on the night boat, come down to Bective on the bus and walked up from the crossroads. "I left the family in Dublin," he said. "I want to get the cottage fixed up before they see it. It was a rough crossing, and Pearl got a little sick."

Which was Pearl? The snapshots he'd sent in lieu of an interview had shown him surrounded by a nice-sized family for so young a man. Holding on to one arm was a woman, presumably his wife, but she must have stirred as the snap was being taken, because it was blurred. Her dark hair was cloudy anyway and partly hid her face. In spite of the blurring, her features looked sharp though, but this was of small moment as long as she could take care of the young children that clung about Clem, especially the baby girl, who snuggled in his arms.

"They're coming down on the evening bus," he explained. "Where can I get a horse and cart? I want to pick up a few sticks of furniture for the place. I suppose I'll get one in the farmyard?" In a few minutes he was rattling off in the farm cart, standing with his legs apart, his yellow hair lifting in the breeze of his departure, and the white tennis shoes, which he had worn also in the snap, looking, to the last glimpse, magnificently unsuitable. In less than an hour he was back with a load of fat mattresses, bulging pillows and bedding, the lot barricaded into the cart by a palisade of table legs and up-ended chairs. "Another run and the job is done," he cried, as he toppled everything out on the grass patch in front of the cottage, and galloped off to town once more.

The second time he could be heard coming a mile away with a load of ewers and basins, pots and pans, a wash-hand stand, an oil cooker and tin cans, all clattering together in the cart behind him. "These things must be got into the house at once," he said to a young lad sent up from the yard to help him. "There's damp in the air, and I don't want them rusted. Don't stand there gawking, boy," he added, as Jimmy stared at the bedding already beaded with mist. "Bedding is easy aired," said Clem. "But rust is a serious matter. Learn to distinguish!"

Then there began such a fury of lifting and carrying, pushing and pulling, such banging of nails and bringing down of plaster, but above all, such running in and out of the cottage that Clem's tennis shoes came at last into their own. They were so apt for the job on foot.

By evening every picture was hung, every plate in place, the tables and chairs were right side up and the oil cooker lit and giving off its perfume. The bedding was still outdoors. "No matter. Food comes first. Learn to distinguish!" cried Clem again, as he held a plate under a brown-paper bag and let plop out a mess of cream buns. "The family will be starving," he said. "Pearl isn't much of a feeder," he added sadly, "but the others have powerful appetites."

He still hadn't said which one was Pearl, but it wasn't the wife anyway, because when Jimmy saw them trudging up the drive a while later, there was no wife, there was only Clem with two small boys, a bigger girl, and a little one in his arms snuggled close to him, as she was in the snap, with only her curls to be seen. Yet when Clem let down the child, Jimmy wondered no more, for she was the dead spit of a pearl.

"Did you ever see the like of her!" Clem exclaimed delightedly, as he saw Jimmy looking at her. "She puts me in mind of apple blossom. That's what I should have called her: Blossom. But no matter. I don't like fancy names anyway. Come now, Moll," he said, turning to the bigger girl, "let's get her to bed. She's dog-tired." Planting Pearl in Moll's arms, he ran out and pulled in one of the mattresses. "It's a bit damp all right," he said, in surprise. But, undismayed, he dashed into the garden and came back with three large rhubarb leaves. "We'll put these under the sheet," he said. "Leaves are waterproof. Trust nature every time." Then as Moll was about to stagger away with Pearl in her arms, he ran after them and gave Moll a hug. "She's the best little mother in the world," he said. "I don't know what I'd do without her."

It was the first and last reference, oblique as it was, to the absence of a Mrs. Clem.

As the days went on, however, the absence of Mrs. Clem was seldom felt, for if Clem was a good father, he was a still better mother. True, he sometimes had to knock off work in the garden to cook a hot meal for them all, to fetch them from school, or oftenest of all, to wash Pearl's hair, but he still did more work in one day than another man would in six. And it wasn't just hard work; Clem had a green hand if ever a man had.

On his first morning with us, he made his only complaint. "There isn't enough shelter in this garden," he said. "Living things are very tender." And disregarding the fact that he'd just whitened his tennis shoes, he leaped into the soft black clay of the border and broke off branches recklessly from syringa, philadelphus and daphne. Then he rushed around sticking the twigs into the ground, here, there and everywhere.

He must be marking the places where he's going to plant shrubs, thought Jimmy. But before a week was out, the twigs, that at first had wilted and lost their leaves, stiffened into life again and put forth new shoots. A green hand? When Clem stuck a spade into the ground at the end of a day, Jimmy half-expected to see it sprouting leaves by morning. There was nothing Clem couldn't do with a plant. In any weather he'd put down a seed. In any weather he'd take up a seedling. "It'll be all right if it's properly handled," he'd say, planting seeds gaily, with rain falling so heavily on the wet clay that it splashed back into his face and spattered it all over. And when the sun did shine, as often as not he'd be down on his knees with his box of seedlings, pricking them out.

"Won't they die in the sun?" asked Jimmy.

"Why would they die?" Clem asked. "Like all living things, they only ask to be treated gently." To see Clem handle a young plant, you'd think it was some small animal that he held between his palms. Even seeds got their full share of his love and care, every single one, no matter how many to a packet. Once he made Jimmy sweep up a whole cement floor in the potting shed where he'd let one seed fall. "We can't leave it there with no food and no drink and no light and no covering," he said, as he lit match after match to help in the search.

Jimmy felt a bit put upon. "What about all the packets of seeds that are up there on the shelf?" he protested. "The last gardener forgot to sow them until it was too late."

"But it's never too late," said Clem. "Where are they?" And the next minute he had rummaged out the packets of old seeds with their faded and discoloured flower prints. "Everything should get its chance," he said, and he gathered up every flower pot in sight and, filling them with the finest of sieved clay, he poked a seed into each one. "If there's life in those seeds, they'll take flight before the end of the week," he told Jimmy. And in less than a week, over each pot there hovered two frail green wings. Yet, for all the energy he spent on plants and chores, Clem still had energy to spare. "How is the fishing around here?" he asked Jimmy one Saturday afternoon, a few weeks after his arrival. "I'd like to take the children fishing." He turned to Pearl. "Wouldn't you like to go fishing, Pearl?" She was a good little thing, and she never gave any trouble. All the minding she got was following Clem around the garden. Now and again he'd tell her to get up off damp grass, or to mind would a wasp sting her. There was one thing he was very particular about though, and that was that she should not take off the little woolly coat she always wore.

"Pearly hot!" Pearl would cry. No matter. He made her keep the coat on. It was, however, very hot indeed on an afternoon in May, and when Clem bent down to dibble in a few colchicums for the autumn, Pearl stamped her foot.

"Pearly hot!" she cried, defiantly, and pulled off the yellow woolly coat and she threw it down on the ground.

Jimmy bent down to pick it up, but when he looked up, he was astonished to see Clem's eyes filled with tears.

"I hate anyone to see it," said Clem. "I can't bear to look at it myself. But I knew it couldn't be kept covered forever."

On the inner, softer side of Pearl's arm was a long, sickle-shaped scar. It was healed. It wasn't really very noticeable. Many a child had a scab twice as big on its knee, or on its elbow, or even its nose. But all the same, Pearl's scar made Jimmy shudder. Perhaps because it was on the soft underflesh, perhaps because of the look it had brought to Clem's eyes, this scar of Pearl's seemed to have a terrible importance.

"Was it an accident, Clem?"

"No," said Clem so shortly Jimmy was startled.

Could Clem——? Oh no, no! She was his seedling, his fledgling, his little plant that, if he could, he would cup between his hands, breathe upon, press close and hold against himself forever. As it was, he put his arms around her. "Wouldn't you like to catch a little fish, Pearl?" he was asking her. "I'll get a sally wand for you, and I'll peel it white. Maybe you'll catch a great big salmon."

His own ambition was more humble. He turned abruptly to Jimmy. "I suppose there's plenty of pike? Can we get a frog, do you think? Frogs are the only bait for pike. Get hold of a good frog, Jimmy, and we'll meet you down at Clady Bridge in ten minutes."

Where was he to get a frog on a fine May evening in Meath? On a wet day yes, the roads were plastered with them, sprawled out where cars had gone over them. But this afternoon Clem and the children must have been a full hour down by Clady pool before Jimmy came running back to them, his hand over his pocket.

The children were all calling to each other and laughing, and Clem was shouting excitedly, but it was Pearl's small voice that caught the ear, babbling as joyously to Clem as the pebbles to the stream. There was joy and excitement in the air, and joy welled up in Jimmy's heart, too, as he scrambled over the wall and tumbled happily down the bank, filling the air with the bittersweet smell of elder leaves as he caught at a branch to save himself from falling.

"Good man! You've got the bait," cried Clem, his expert eye picking out the bulge in Jimmy's pocket. He was helping Pearl to cast her line. It was a peeled willow wand and dangling from it was a big black hairpin bent into a hook. As Jimmy took the frog out of his pocket, however, Clem reached for his own rod which, to have out of harm's way, he had placed crosswise in the cleft of an elder bush that hung over the stream. As he took it down, the taut gut slashed through tender young leaves and, once again, their bitter scent was let out upon the air.

"Here, Jimmy. Here's the hook," he said. "Put on the frog!" Taking a tobacco tin out of his pocket, Clem selected a hook and, fingering it gently free of other hooks and flies, he laid it in Jimmy's palm. Then he begun to unwind his reel. For a few minutes the sound of the winding reel asserted itself over all the other sounds in the glade, until gradually it was absorbed into the general pattern of sound.

Suddenly there was another sound; a screech. It split the air. It turned every other sound into silence. It was the frog. There was nothing human in that screech, but every human ear in that green place knew what the screech held: it held pain, and pain as humans know it.

"What did you do to him?" yelled Clem, and his face went black with rage. Throwing down the line, he caught hold of the screeching frog. Quick as thought, he pulled out the hook that had only gone a small way into the bulging belly, but had brought out a bubble of its bile-like blood. Then, throwing down the hook and stamping on it, he held the little slimy creature between his two hands. "You are all right now," he told it, looking into its bulbous eyes, as if he'd force it to cast out its fear. Then he turned to Jimmy again. "You didn't know any better," he said sadly. "You're only a child yourself. But let this be a lesson to you. Never in your life hurt or harm a defenceless thing! Or if you do, then don't let me see you do it, because I could not stand it. I could not stand it," he repeated, less gently. "I never did a cruel thing in my life. I couldn't do one if I tried and I could not stand by and see one done either. I only saw a cruel deed done in my presence once." Then he lowered his voice so only Jimmy could hear, "and once was enough! I couldn't stand it. Then he closed his eyes and pressed his hands over them as if he saw it all again. When he took down his hands after a minute, and opened his eyes again, he had a dazed look. It was as if he was astonished to find himself there, where he was, on the sunlit bank. More than that, he looked amazed that the sun could shine, amazed that the birds could sing.

"Are you feeling all right?" Jimmy asked.

Clem looked at him dazed. Then it was as if he took a plunge back into the happiness around him.

"Here, give me a hook!" he cried, rooting around in the box. "This is the way it's done." Deftly tucking up the legs of the frog so it fitted snugly into one hand, he nicked its back with the point of the barb, and then swiftly he passed the hook under the skin and brought it out again as if it were a needle and thread and he had just taken a long, leisurely stitch. "There! You see. It didn't feel a thing," he said, and hastily fixing the hook to the end of the line he reeled out a few yards of it and let the frog hang down.

Delightedly he gazed at it for a minute, as it moved its legs rhythmically outward and inward in a swimming motion. "Wait till we let him into the water!" he cried then, and he ran to the edge of the pool, scattering the children to either side and throwing the line out over the pool. Suspended in the air the frog hung down, as still as the lead on the end of a plumb line, its image given back by the clear water that gave back also the blue sky and the white clouds as if they were under, not over, the pebbles and stones. Then Clem began to unwind the reel, and the frog in the air and the frog in the pool began to draw close to each other, till the real frog hit the water with a smack. Once there, its legs began to work again. "Swim away, son," said Clem indulgently, and he unwound more of the line. "You'd think he was taking swimming lessons, wouldn't you?" he said, watching it amiably.

"But won't the pike eat him?" said Jimmy. "Isn't that worse than getting the hook stuck in him?"

Clem turned around. "Nonsense!" he cried. "Death and pain are two different things. Learn to distinguish, boy!" And he called to Pearl. "Would you like to hold the line for a while, Pearl?"

But Pearl was not looking at the frog. Something behind them had caught her attention.

"Who are those men, Daddy?" she asked, as two big men in dustcoats, who had been watching the scene for some time from the small bridge over the stream, began to get over the wall and slide down the bank towards them.

Clem looked back. "Here, Jimmy," he said. That was all, and he handed him the line.

"You know why we're here?" asked one of the detectives. Clem simply answered their question with a question of his own. "What about the children?" he asked.

Never would Jimmy have thought that detectives could be so gentle and kind. "The children will be well treated, Clem," said one. The other addressed Jimmy. "Stay here with them, you Jimmy, and keep them amused. We've got a police-woman in the car up on the drive, and she'll come down to you in a minute and see what's to be done." They turned to Clem. "We'll have to ask you to come with us, I'm afraid."

Clem nodded briefly. Then he turned to Jimmy. "Here, give me the line again for a minute," he said, and as Pearl had snuggled close to him, her two arms around one leg as if it was a pillar, he freed her grasp and put the rod into her hand.

"You can have the first turn, Pearly," he said. "Then Moll. Then the others. After that it will be turn and turn about for you all." His voice was as kind as ever but it was also authoritative. Then he nodded to the men, and finding it slippery to walk in the dirty tennis shoes, he caught at some of the elder branches, and by their help scrambled up the bank alongside the men.

Lemonade

"Wake up, Maudie! Wake up for your first glimpse of Ireland."

It was nine days since they'd left Pappa on the wharf at Boston and it was only four o'clock in the morning. Mama picked Maudie up to look out of the porthole. If it had been daylight, the coast of Ireland could have been seen like a thin string of seaweed drifting on the horizon, but in the dark all that could be seen of the land was the flash from the lighthouse. "That's Fastnet Rock," Mama said in a rapture Maudie found hard to understand. Through the porthole misted with their warm breath, when Maudie's eyes got used to the dimness the only other thing she could see by the light from the engine room was the same grey waste of water that had washed against the sides of the ship all week, lit occasionally by a cold white flash of spray as waves clashed together. Then there was another flash from the lighthouse, and another and another. Maudie squealed with delight: it was just as if a great fist had opened and thrown out a big ball of light that closed again, only to keep on opening and closing until she saw that the lighthouse was set on the top of an enormous black rock.

"That isn't really Ireland?" Maudie asked timidly. She was afraid to show her disappointment.

Mama didn't even hear her she was so busy dressing and getting Maudie into her clothes. "We must go up on deck. We mustn't miss a minute of it," she said. Yet later in the day, even when the sun came out, the shore of Ireland seemed very far away and if it was fields they saw they were as thin a line of seaweed, but so brilliantly green the sight took Maudie's breath away. Soon however, a little steamer arrived alongside the ship. This was the tender that was to take them to Cobh but Maudie was so sleepy the town looked to her like any old town and when they got into a train she sank back weakly against the red repp upholstery of the seats that smelled strongly of dust and fumes of smoke. She was asleep in an instant. And it felt as if it was only another instant before Mama was shaking her to wake her again.

"I must tidy you up. This is the second next station to home," she said.

Then suddenly before the train had properly stopped at the platform two of the handsomest men Maudie had ever seen wrenched open the carriage door, and jumping in they began to hug and kiss Mama. It was the uncles.

"But we are only at Ennis Junction!" Mama cried.

"That's right, but we were so impatient to see you, we hired a sidecar and came to meet you here."

Maudie was overwhelmed. No wonder Mama missed them and was always telling her about the larks they played on people. Even the Uncle Paud ran up and down the platform shouting in the other carriages at the startled strangers, pretending he was the guard of the train.

"Is there anybody there for here?" he called out.

When they finally got home Uncle Paud got a trolley and brought Mama's trunk and all their other belongings into the house. The trolley was for bringing porter barrels out to the bottling shed he explained when Maudie asked, "but it comes in useful for lots of things." Then he laughed. "Perhaps you never heard of porter out in America," he said.

"Is it like lemonade?" Maudie ventured.

Mama laughed. "So you remember that old joke after all those years," she said.

"Ah yes. Poor Dinny," said Uncle Matt. "How is he anyway?"

"Oh, he's fine, just fine," Mama said. "He'll be coming over to bring us back in March. That was what we planned anyway."

"Nonsense," said the uncles, both together. "Sure you only went out there for a little holiday."

"I was there ten years!" A long sort of holiday," Mama said. "According to Dinny *this* is a holiday."

Uncle Matt had taken Maudie up in his arms. "Don't mind your Mama," he said. "We have plans too. We intended to persuade your Pappa to buy a little place and settle down over here for good."

"I'm afraid that depends on just one factor," Mama said gloomily.

"Oh, cheer up," said Uncle Paud. "He'll be a new man when he finds himself a bachelor again."

"He certainly made good resolutions, if he can keep them," Mama did cheer up.

The next morning when Maudie got up Mama had already gone out into the shop and was waiting on customers just like the uncles.

"How about some lemonade," Uncle Paud asked. At that hour of the morning! Before breakfast? "Go on!" he cried recklessly. "Let's see if you remember how to use the bottle opener."

Not to hurt his feelings Maudie had a glass but she only drank some of it.

"I'm sure she'd prefer a biscuit," Uncle Matt said, and she saw there was a big glass case in the middle of the shop showing all sorts of biscuits. Each biscuit tin had a little window that you could open and take out the kind you wanted. Uncle Matt showed her how to open the biscuit case too.

"Make yourself at home. Take one anytime you like."

"Please take a plain one dear," Mama cautioned, but Uncle Matt had already given four, two with pink and two with white icing on.

Mama sighed. "She won't appreciate them if she eats too many at the one time," she said. "And I don't like to see her indulging in excess!"

Then happening to look out of the shop window, she gave an exclamation. "Look!" she cried. "There is a poor child that I'm sure would give her two eyes this minute for one bite of a biscuit."

Maudie swung around. In the street, with her face pressed to the shop window, she saw for an instant a girl her own size, before the girl, with a glowering look at Maudie, slunk away. But oh, she had looked so thin, her dress was so dirty and her long hair hung about her shoulders raggy and seemed all tats and snags as if it was never combed. Her dress was black like as if was cut down from the dress of a grown up.

"Why didn't *you* give her a biscuit Mama?" Maudie demanded. Then she had an inspiration. She'd been told to take as many as she liked. Ramming her own biscuits in her pockets, she ran over to the case again and opening the lid, she plunged in her hand and took out a whole fistful of the first biscuits that came to her hand. "I'll give her some," she said and she ran out into the street.

"Come back here, you bold girl," Mama cried, and even Uncle Matt was taken off his feet.

"That is going a bit too far," he muttered. They both ran to the door but Maudie was half way up the street after the girl, who had disappeared around the corner at the top.

At first Maudie thought she had vanished into thin air, until she suddenly caught sight of her crouching down between a load of cardboard boxes outside a hardware shop, her bony shoulders hunched together the way the wings of angels are sometimes depicted in holy pictures, wrapped around them so tightly the knobs of their wing bones almost meet on their chest.

"Hello!" Maudie said brightly. She was so glad she found the girl. "Would you like a biscuit?" she asked.

"No," said the girl. "I have no money."

"Oh, but they are a present," Maudie said. "I'm giving them to you." "Why?"

Maudie's confidence was inclined to totter at getting this monosyllable for a reply, but she was not put off by it.

"Well, I got them for nothing myself and I thought you might like to share them. I have more in my pocket."

The girl only looked more scared than ever. "Did you steal them?" she whispered, and she shuddered violently. "If you did you'll go to Hell or else you'll have to tell the priest in confession and he'll shout at you. I heard him shout at a woman one day." Here, after another violent shudder, she began to run again and this time she went so fast Maudie didn't try to follow her. When she went back to the shop she knew at once Mama and Uncle Paud were talking about her and Uncle Matt had joined them. Mama was furious.

"Do you mean to say you two don't see any difference between her taking them for herself and taking them to distribute with largesse all over the town."

"Oh, come now, don't exaggerate," said Paud, "and if you ask me I think the child should be commended for showing a charitable instinct."

As they had not noticed Maudie had come back she stood inside the door as quiet as possible, till they'd stop talking about her.

"Who was that child, anyway?" Mama asked. "I never saw such a neglected creature."

"Of course you couldn't have know her. She probably wasn't born until after you went away. She's Mad Mary's daughter. People say she's as mad as the mother, but that's only malice, and because she's hardly ever seen about the town. I don't know where she spends her time."

But Maudie's ears pricked up like a rabbit's, and such curiosity took possession of her, she threw discretion to the winds.

"Oh, the poor girl!" she sobbed, running out into the middle of the shop. "Why is her mother called Mad Mary? Is she really mad?"

Mama and the uncles had got such a fright when Maudie spoke, they forgot for a moment what they were saying, but when they remembered they seemed to be lost for words and stared at each other dumbly. Instead of answering Maudie they spoke to each other. "I never thought of it before but I suppose it is a cruel way to speak of the unfortunate woman. And I suppose she knows what she's called?" said Uncle Paud.

"You may be sure the girl knows," Uncle Matt said. "Children can be very cruel."

Maudie was all agog but unfortunately Mama remembered her misdeed. "Well, sorry and all as we may be for the girl, you must admit she's no fit companion for Maudie." She wagged her finger at her. "Don't let me catch you having anything to do with that girl again," she said, and she actually shook her fist at Maudie.

"You needn't worry," Maudie said. "She doesn't want to have anything to do with me."

"Well, thank God for small mercies," Mama said. "That's an end to that."

It was not the end though.

About a month after they had arrived in Ireland Maudie got into some little scrape or other of very little significance, but as time went on she got into another and another. When the novelty of her Mother's old home began to wear off she began to feel lonely, not only for Pappa but for her school friends on the other side of the world. She had met all her cousins when their mothers and fathers came to see Mama but they were all younger than her and when the uncles brought other children from the town to visit her the visits were not a great success. For one thing they had to go home early to do their homework, or so they said.

Then one day when she was playing shop and spilled a whole bin of tea that Matt said cost a fortune, Uncle Paud was twice as cross as him, although it was him who usually took her part.

"What can we expect?" he cried. "The devil makes work for idle hands. The child ought to be at school."

"But Paud," Mama protested. "Our plans are so indefinite. As well as that there is only the National School."

"It was good enough for us, wasn't it?" Matt and Paud asked both together.

Mama bit her lip, but she was not to be defeated "In any case I can't take a decision like this on my own initiative. I'll have to write to Dinny," Mama said, but seeing by the look on the faces of the uncles this excuse was considered feeble Mama became more animated. "Tell me!" she said, "where does that poor child we were talking about recently, where does she go to school—Mad Mary's daughter? I know she is to be pitied but I can't believe she's the right kind of company for Maudie."

"You needn't worry," said Paud. "I hear she's as ostracised at school as she is by the rest of this charitable town. May I ask what you think should be done with a child like that? Where else could she get an education except in the local school?"

Oh, it's not my business," Mama said testily, "but I'm sure there would be a special provision for someone like her in America."

"America! America!" said Matt angrily. "If it was so wonderful, why did you take her away from there? Not that we don't love having her, but I thought it was the company Dinny kept that was one of your main objections to America."

"Who told you that?" Mama was furious now.

"You did write to us occasionally," said Matt, "or do you forget that too?"

Mama threw a look at Paud and Matt like the looks she sometimes threw at Pappa.

"There's one thing I don't forget," she said, "and that's the way people in this family store up every word a person says, although only half meaning it most of the time, so they can throw it back in their face when the person least expects it."

"But you *did* say it!"

"Oh, what if I did! You put a different complexion on my words. Indeed it might be no harm to have the child away from the atmosphere in this house at times." Catching Maudie by the hand she marched her towards the lobby between the shop and the swelling quarters, where street coats were kept. "I'll get my hat and coat and go down to the convent this minute and make the necessary arrangements."

"Easy! Easy!" cried Paud, "You'd better send word you're coming. You can send a note and I'll drop it in when I'm passing that way this morning."

"Alright, but say I'm coming right away." Maudie said nothing but she knew it wasn't only the lemonade that was coming to an end. She was going into captivity.

The school house was at the far end of the town. There were two ways of going to it, one that was a short cut, but Mama took the road that ran under the old ruined archway, that was part of a high old wall that Mama said once ran all around the town. She said she wanted me to see it because it was mentioned in history books and that inside there were the other ancient ruins, an old church, but nobody ever went in there. "You won't come this way dear, when you come alone, you'll come through the town, but today I want to get my talk with the nuns over and done with as quick as possible."

As we went along the street, ahead of us, running along in bare feet, with their boots sticking out of bulky satchels strapped to their backs, were a number of little boys.

"Are they going to my school," Maudie asked.

Mama frowned. "Yes, but they are the country children from outside the town. You won't have to mix with them." Then surprisingly, she laughed. "In my day the country scholars had to bring a sod of turf every day for the teacher's fire. We town children only had to bring a penny. I wonder is that old custom dead?"

"You'd better give me a penny just in case," Maudie said, but she said it absently because they were passing a row of cottages, a whole row of them, all so small and neat, so dazzlingly whitewashed and all of them thatched with shiny golden straw that she hung back to look at them in amazement. They were just like doll's houses. "Are they real?" she said. "Do real people live in them?"

"Of course," Mama said impatiently. "They're working class people but highly respectable, but please come on. We're nearly at the pathway up to the convent. I can already see the school through the archway."

The archway must have been very old because even passing quickly under it you could feel a chill in the air, and Maudie was astonished to think the public road ran through it just like a river under a bridge. "Ouch!" she cried, as while she was staring up at the glistening wet slabs that roofed it, a big drop of icy cold water fell straight into her eye. This was probably why she didn't notice that there was another row of cottages on the other side of the archway until they had nearly passed them. They must once have been just the same as the ones on the other side, they were the same size, that is to say, those of them that were still standing, but except for one, their roofs had all fallen in and the windows and doors were boarded up, except for one at the end of the row. It had a roof but it was a tin roof and even then that was rusty. It had glass in the windows and a proper door, but whereas Maudie thought the windows and doors of the other cottages looked like a cute little face, because the windows each side of the door were like two eyes and a mouth, this cottage had a hungry little face! There couldn't be anyone living in it, she thought. There was grass sprouting out of the gutter and in front of the door there was a pool of water. Since it had not rained all week it looked as if someone threw out slop from inside.

"Maudie!" Mama almost dragged her arm out of its socket with the force of the way she pulled her on. "Stop staring," she hissed. "That woman would think nothing of coming out and flinging stones at us. We shouldn't have come this way at all, but I forgot she lived here."

Instinctively Maudie knew who lived in the hovel. "Is it Mad Mary's?" she whispered and the tears rushed into her eyes. This then must be where the sad girl lived who wouldn't take the biscuits from her. She held tighter to Mama's hand and didn't need to be told again to hurry, but she couldn't help glancing back over her shoulder. The tumbled down cottages, including Mad Mary's, were built right up against the wet and slimy wall that surrounded the ruins of which she could just see the tops, smothered in ivy. "What else is inside there," she asked, because although there were gaps in the wall, but they were almost altogether blocked with ivy too. "What is behind the wall?" she whispered.

"Only an old cemetery. Nobody is buried there anymore. Stop looking back Maudie." They had come to a low iron gate that led up a cement path to where, beside the convent there was the school, as neat as a shoebox. When they got to it and Mama pushed open the door there were rows and rows of children and all of them stared at Maudie with open mouths.

"Ah," said a tall young nun coming to meet them. "Is this our new pupil?" she asked. "A little Yank!" She took Maudie's hand, but it was to Mama she spoke. "I don't suppose she knows any of the other children?" she said.

"I'm afraid not," said Mama.

"Ah, well, she'll soon make friends. Now, who will I put her beside I wonder?" she mused as she scanned the faces all eagerly smiling.

But just then Maudie saw a familiar face.

"I know *her*," she said excitedly and pointed to where all by herself on the last bench she saw the girl in the raggy black dress. "Can I sit beside her?"

Instinctively she knew there was something wrong. Some of the class tittered and the nun clutched her hand very tightly while she and Mama exchanged looks of dismay.

"Oh, but wouldn't you like to sit up in the front row?" the nun asked quickly. "You'll be near the blackboard."

"And near the fire," Mama said.

Maudie knew Mama would be angry but she didn't care.

"I want to sit beside that girl," she repeated.

At once the sugary look that the nun had been bestowing on her faded from her face and she gave a very sour look at the girl in the back row before she started to lead Maudie up to the top of the class.

"*You* may want to sit beside her Maudie," she said, "but I don't think Sadie would want you to sit beside *her*. I'm sorry to say Sadie is not a very friendly girl. That's why she sits down there alone. You see Maudie Sadie hasn't learned yet that people have to behave in a certain way if they want people to like them." Confidently she was proceeding forward when Maudie broke away from her.

"In America we can sit where we like in class," she said," and anyway I don't care if Sadie doesn't like me, I like her." Then, just like the drop of water that fell into her eyes as she went under the archway, Maudie smiled straight into Sadie's eyes. There was a moment of suspense for everyone and then Sadie smiled back right into Maudie's eyes.

"Well, you may sit there for today," the nun said crisply, and she whispered something to Mama.

"Say goodbye to your mother now," she said, with some resemblance of her earlier manner, but when Mama was kissing Maudie she took the opportunity of giving her a piece of her mind.

"How can you be so like your father!" she cried. "Why did you have to pick out this child out of all the children in the class?"

"I'm sorry Mama," Maudie said but she knew it was for the future she was apologising. Then she ran down to the back of the classroom and slipped into the bench beside Sadie.

But the impulse that had made Sadie smile had died and her face had a sullen and withdrawn look, which she undeviatingly maintained all the rest of the morning until the bell rang for play time, and all the children jumped up and rushed out to the school yard. Then she looked fiercely at Maudie. "Which way did you come to school?" she asked.

"Past your house," Maudie said recklessly.

First Sadie stared dejectedly down at the desk, then in spite of herself she giggled.

"It's awful isn't it?" she said.

Emboldened by the giggle, Maudie shrugged her shoulders. "Who cares!" she said and then she asked a question. "Why don't we go out like the others?"

Now it was Sadie who shrugged her shoulders.

"What happens at play time?" Maudie asked.

"They eat their lunch and they play," Sadie said.

Maudie noticed the pronoun. "Don't you play?"

"No," said Sadie. "They don't want me. You heard what the nun said."

"I don't believe a word of it," said Maudie. "But anyway, I can be your friend, can't I?"

"Then nobody will be friends with you," Sadie said darkly.

"But what do you do. You don't sit in here all the time?"

"No. I go out but I sit up on the wall."

Maudie looked out the open door. "Let's go out now and we'll both sit on the wall," she said. "We'll pay no heed to the others. I think it's them that don't know how to behave. We'll eat our lunch and talk."

When Sadie and Maudie appeared in the yard all the others stared but no one spoke to them. The pair sat up on the wall and took out their lunches.

Maudie hadn't got a satchel yet but she had an apple and an orange, and a slice of cheese wrapped in a napkin paper in her pocket. Sadie had taken her lunch from her schoolbag, but it was wrapped in a bit of greasy paper and consisted of two thick and unappetising slices of bread with a slab of lard between them, but it was Sadie who was critical of Maudie's meal. "Is that all you've got to eat?" she asked anxiously and for a moment Maudie was afraid she was going to offer to share her bread with her, but instead she was staring at Maudie's orange. "The first day I came to school," she said, "I had no lunch so the nun went into the convent and came back with an orange. But when she gave it to me I bit into it like an apple, skin and all, because I never had an orange before. It was awful. The whole class laughed at me, even the nun," she said, and as if it was yesterday, tears of shame came into her eyes.

Once more Maudie threw discretion to the winds.

"Oh Sadie, can't you see now how funny it was. If I was there I'm sure I'd have laughed too. And if it was another girl that did it I'm sure you'd have laughed as well, you'd have died laughing."

Solemnly Sadie shook her head. "I'd never laugh at anybody, ever, ever, no matter what they did," she said.

Maudie dangled her legs and thought over this before she answered. "I bet you'll be different when you grow up Sadie."

"No, I'll never be different from what I am now," Sadie said passionately.

"Well, I suppose I won't change a lot," Maudie said, but without much conviction. "Maybe nobody does. Who knows!" She was considering this new idea in the light of her limited experience when she became aware that Sadie was no longer listening. She was staring back to where, due to a fall in the level of the land, the ancient archway could be seen and in its shadow her own cottage. Then Maudie saw that at the door of the cottage a woman was standing. "Is that your mother?" she asked fearfully.

"Yes," Sadie said tensely, but when the woman went inside again she slumped with relief. "I always sit where I can see her," she said, "because if I saw her coming up here I'd run away." For a moment it seemed she could find no words for a circumstance she dreaded. "You see," she said then slowly. "She did come once to complain about me having to bring a sod of turf instead of a penny. I didn't mind bringing the turf because the archway is the boundary of the town, and we are outside the arch so we're not really townspeople, although that doesn't apply to the doctor and lots of other people who built new houses beyond us, but my mother thought they were making other distinctions, that they were belittling me."

"What did you think?"

"Oh, I didn't care about that," Sadie sounded tired of the matter. "It was the way she came into the class in a rage that I minded. At the thought of it, she put her hands over her face.

"Was she very angry?" Maudie asked, thanking her stars that she had not asked if the woman was very mad, which was what she nearly said.

"No. She wasn't angry. She was very quiet, and she spoke softly and politely. What was dreadful was the way everyone gave in to her right away and said I could bring whatever suited her, a sod of turf, or a penny."

Maudie was mystified. "Wasn't that great Sadie?"

"No, no, no," Sadie said emphatically! "It was terrible because it showed they were *afraid* of her."

Maudie sat dumbly listening until it occurred to her that it was a good thing Sadie knew how people felt about her mother and there would be no need for Maudie herself to have to watch her words all the time. She never felt that was as important as Mama did.

"Sadie, when did your mother get like that, or was she always a bit queer?" she asked.

She was very happy when Sadie turned around eagerly and her face lighted up. "I don't think she was like that always. I can't remember very well but I once saw a picture of our cottage and it was just like the ones on the other side of the arch, only nicer. It had a pot of geraniums on the window sills and the thatch wasn't covered with tin, it was shining like gold. I think she only got like that after my little brother died," she said, her face assuming its sad lifeless expression.

"Oh, I didn't know you had a brother. What happened to him?"

Sadie seemed all at once less anxious to talk about the matter. Her voice got dull and she spoke very slowly, as if at any minute she'd stop and tell nothing more.

"Nobody talks about it," she said. "You see it was because of something my mother herself did that my brother died."

Maudie's throat began to throb with fright at what she might be about to hear, but Sadie's next words reassured her.

"Poor, poor Ma," Sadie said. "She did what she did out of love and ignorance as well, of course, but not as ignorant as the people who told her to do it. I think they were bad, bad people. I think they were the ones who were astray in the head."

"But what was it? What did they tell her to do?" Maudie wasn't quite so frightened, but a vein was throbbing violently in her throat.

"I hate to think of it," Sadie said, "but my little brother got a rash, a terrible rash, all over his face and his body and the doctor couldn't cure him, no matter how hard he tried, and then, oh Maudie, I hate to say it, then someone told my poor Ma that she ought to wash him all over with—" She stopped. "I can't say it. I can't! I can't! Perhaps you can guess?" she asked, her cheeks flaming. Just then however, the bell rang and she jumped down off the wall. "Anyway we have to go back to class now," she said.

All during the afternoon Maudie was cudgelling her brain but she couldn't imagine what on earth it was that Sadie's mother used to wash the poor little boy in, and even if she dared to ask, she and Sadie didn't get a chance to talk till the end of the day, and when they went outside Mama was waiting for Maudie. She wanted to show her the other way home, through the town.

"Goodbye Sadie," Maudie called out. "Keep my place for me tomorrow."

"I don't think there is any danger of anyone wanting your place beside that child," Mama said coldly. "And let me tell you Maudie I'll take it as a favour if you don't talk about your new companion at the tea table tonight."

Yet it was Mama herself who brought up Sadie's name. Twice, at least twice. When Maudie had gone out of the room for a minute she returned to hear her talking about her friend, although she stopped immediately when Maudie came back. "No more for the moment!" she cautioned the aunts. "We can talk about it later." From Mama's face it was clear that the topic was irresistible, and so, although she knew it was a bit mean Maudie left the room again deliberately and when she came back she crept in quietly. After all she felt justified in finding out the truth if it meant she might be able to help Sadie. She only heard a few words before she was discovered, but she heard all she needed to know.

"Wasn't there another child?" Mama was asking when Maudie got within earshot as she tiptoed back. "What happened to it?"

Unfortunately Paud answered in such a low voice Maudie missed what he said, but not Mama's screech of disbelief.

"How revolting," she said. "It's like something you hear done by a primitive tribe. You can't mean it. His own urine? She washed him in *that*?"

Maudie barely knew the word but some instinct told her it meant pee-pee. She didn't have time to think about it because Mama was still railing against Mad Mary and saying she never heard anything so disgusting and that she ought to have been put away, whatever that meant.

Uncle Paud was much kinder.

"Don't forget the poor woman paid for it," he said. "The sores became infected and she had to watch her little son die in terrible agony, poor child."

"Is it since then she's been queer?" Mama asked.

"I think so," said Uncle Paud. "When I was young, before the boy was born, and she had only the girl, I never noticed anything abnormal about her. There was no sign of a husband, but that wasn't altogether unusual among people of that class. I know she kept the place fairly clean. She'd slap a bit of lime on the walls and the girl was well kept looking, but after the death of the child things changed. Would anyone wonder at that?"

At that moment they spied Maudie.

"I thought you were out in the kitchen," Mama said, as if she'd committed some crime. They were all silent after that, till Mama ordered her to clean the table and swept out of the room.

"Were you very sad when your brother died?" she asked Sadie next day, when they got up on the wall to eat their lunch, trying to appear as if his death was just like any other death—from scarlet fever or hooping-cough.

"You've no idea how I loved him," Sadie said. "He was too small to talk about anything like you and me. He was only seven, and his funeral was so sad. Only a few people came to it, like the doctor and the priest, and a few odd people that went to all funerals, and maybe a few who came to see how Ma would behave. We didn't even have a proper coffin, not because we were poor, but because he was so small. He was put in a little wooden box that the undertaker gave Ma for nothing and she painted it white." Suddenly she began to cry. "When they put the box into the ground and threw the clay over it, I thought Ma would go really mad. She was nearly mad about not being able to cure the rash, but I could see the priest staring at her anxiously. I felt awful. Do you know what I wished.? I wished it was me that was in that box. It being white, and Tony being in it didn't seem to make it so bad being dead. It didn't seem half as bad as having to stand there beside Ma thinking she'd do something wild and make a show of us for good and all."

"But she didn't?" Maudie said.

"No. She didn't," Sadie said, and she said it wonderingly as if it was the first time she'd realised it.

"I bet you were sorry then about wishing you were dead too. Wouldn't it be awful for her if she didn't have you, if she didn't have anybody left at all?"

"I never thought of that either," Sadie said. "I'm always only thinking about what it would be like for me, if I didn't have her disgracing me all the time." A sudden new thought hit her. "Maudie? would you like to see Tony's grave? She keeps it gorgeous. I always had to say that for her. And it's not easy to keep it nice. Poor little Tony is not up in the new cemetery where a single weed is never let put up its head before it's scotched by Jim Clegg, the caretaker. He's buried behind our cottage in the old cemetery that's been closed to burials for years. It's all weeds and briers. If anyone cared, but nobody does, they'd no sooner have cut them back from their own plot, than they'd have rambled in again from the other plots, but Ma is in there almost all day and she makes sure that Tony's grave is kept marvellous, it's kept better than any of Jim Clegg's graves."

Maudie swallowed hard to keep her next words, but without success. "Isn't it creepy having him buried just back of your cottage.?"

"I don't see what differ that makes." Sadie was seemingly surprised at such an idea. "And it makes it better for Ma, not just having him near us, but people can't be prying on her and all the time she spends by the grave because they can't see her going in or out. She goes in through a gap in the wall that's almost hidden by big clumps of ivy, but she can get through it as easy as a rabbit. It's right beside our house and as well as that Tony's grave is not far away from the gap. The whole place is all nettles and thistles but Ma has flattened down a pathway to it and the sting is gone out of them. It's the nicest grave I ever saw. She's always finding new things to put on it. There's the head of a big marble angel at the top, with its two wings sprouting out of its neck like the ones in the new cemetery, only the tips of the wings are gone, but you'd never notice that because she planted it down in the clay and trained a bit of young ivy around the bottom. The ivy is some use, you see, although mind you she had a hard job keeping it from spreading. She chooses the tender young little shoots. And she has lots of plaster roses and sprays of plaster lilies, and what I love best is a little silver dove with a silver leaf in its mouth." Sadie was breathless trying to describe it all. "Of course they all came off other old graves people never visited, graves of people that probably nobody remembers, not even the oldest people in the town. She found them by rooting and she didn't mind that her hands got all stung except once or twice when the nettle rash reminded her of Tony, but that's all over now because there's no room for any more decorations, except a few jampots that she fills with wild flowers in the summer. I think it's sad that nobody ever sees it but even the tourists that come to see the friary get the key from Jasper Kane, the solicitor, and go in by the main gates at the Market Square. There's a path kept cleared from those gates to the ruins, but I don't believe those people know there is a cemetery here at all because the old tombstones have fallen, and some of them were only small stones to begin with. And oh yes, some of the stones have sunk down into the ground. You see if a coffin is cheap it caves in and the whole grave caves in then too. You have to be very careful I can tell you! You could easily twist your ankle or maybe even break your leg in that place. And it's not lucky to fall in a graveyard. Did you know that? If you do it means you'll be buried yourself within the year."

"I don't believe that," Maudie protested feebly because she was almost overcome by the unexpected torrent of words that had broken from her friend, usually so silent. "Who told you that anyway?" she asked.

"I forget," said Sadie carelessly. "I suppose it was Ma, but you learn a lot of things in an old graveyard just by walking around and reading the words on the tombs. You can do that by rubbing the lettering hard with fistfuls of grass. Do you know there is a man buried in there with three wives buried along with him? What do you think of that? They all died a few years after he married them, and although you're supposed to be buried with your first wife only, I suppose he was very rich and was able to get his way. He lived to be ninety and he never married again so I suppose he loved them all the same way and wanted them near him when he did die. But the tombstone over that grave has a big split down the middle. I bet you don't know why?"

"Maybe because the grave had to be opened so often." Maudie hazarded a guess, just to show interest, but the stories were getting very gruesome.

"Not at all," Sadie scoffed. "The grave was robbed one night, not long after the man himself was buried! I don't suppose you know, but there was a time when people called body-snatchers dug up dead people and sold them to doctors to cut them up to learn all about their bones and their insides. But that was not the kind of robbers I'm talking about. There were robbers that just dug up graves of women to steal their gold wedding rings. If they couldn't get the ring off they cut off the finger, and they thought they'd get a great haul in the grave where this man's three rich wives were buried but they got a proper let-down, because he'd used the one ring to marry the three of them, and when the last one died he took it off and had it put on the little finger of his own hand, but they never thought of opening his coffin, and so that was that!"

"I never knew a graveyard could be so interesting," Maudie said.

"Oh, they're not all."

At this point the bell rang and they had to jump off the wall.

"I could tell you hundreds of stories about graveyards," she said. "Of course, they're not all interesting. The new cemetery is the dullest place I ever set foot. I would not be caught dead in it. All the same I'm not like my poor Ma. I know that when you're dead, you're dead."

"Doesn't she know that?" Maudie asked amazed, as they got into their bench and had to be quiet.

"If you saw Tony's grave you'd know what I mean," Sadie said.

"Why don't you come and have a look at it today on your way home?"

"I'm supposed to go home through the town," Maudie said, but she flinched under Sadie's look of contempt.

"Do you want to see it or do you not?" Sadie asked.

For the rest of the day, whenever Maudie thought of going into the old cemetery with Sadie her heart fluttered with a queer pleasurable fear, but at four o'clock when she was guided in through the ivy, that did indeed almost conceal the gap in the wall of the graveyard, her fear was not so pleasurable. There was a sort of path alright and the trodden nettles didn't sting her, but in places where there were no weeds the grass was tough and matted and once or twice it netted over her feet as if to snare her. Was it true she wondered what Sadie had said about what would happen if you fell in a cemetery?

"Oh, wait for me Sadie," she cried, because Sadie was taking high springing steps and was already way ahead of her.

"Ssh, ssh," Sadie whispered back urgently. "We don't want people outside to hear us."

There didn't seem to be much chance of their being heard, Maudie thought.

When they were still outside the wall the place seemed so still and silent, but now it seemed to her that it was the town that had gone silent, like a clock that had stopped, where in here all around were strange ghostly sounds. When a light breeze blew through the ivy that clambered against each other they made a strange tapping sound as if sending out some mysterious message. And then somewhere in the grass, not far from them, a weird sound surged into her ears, a sound that was half-singing, half-sighing.

"Oh, what is that?" Maudie didn't need to be told to whisper. Her mouth was too dry to speak any louder.

Sadie laughed.

"That's an old broken immortelle," Sadie said, "and the wind whispers through its rusty wire. That's all that's left of it." But try as best she could she could not make Maudie understand what an immortelle was like, even a new one before it was violated by time, its glass dome shattered and its false flowers lost in the weeds. "Don't bother about it," she said. "Some day I'll show you one that's not broken. I hate them. I think the flowers Ma puts on Tony's grave are so much nicer. Those immortelles are only put on graves because people want them to last forever and not have the bother of taking care of real flowers. Hurry up, though, I'm dying to show you our grave. I can see it from here," she added encouragingly, pointing with her finger. "It's just over there," she said.

Maudie however had only ventured to take one more step when, unaccountably Sadie seemed to change her mind.

"Perhaps you don't really want to see it?" she cried. "Perhaps your mother will notice at home that you haven't come home from school yet. Perhaps we'll come another day? Perhaps a Saturday would be better?" She had already jumped down off the stump and was trying to turn Maudie around to go back.

Maudie dug her feet into the ground. Sadie had given too many reasons for changing her mind. "There's something you don't want me to see," she said, and knowing now from the way Sadie had pointed she ran forward full tilt, not even caring now whether she stumbled or not.

"Oh," she gasped with delight when she came upon the grave. It was like a little glade in the surrounding wilderness. It was the same shape and size as any of the graves she had seen in the new cemetery, although she'd only seen them from the road when she went for a walk with the uncles, but the wall up there was low and you could easily see over it. But Tony's grave was, oh, so beautifully decorated, she had never seen anything like it. At the head of it, as Sadie said, was the marble angel and all the little ornamental roses and sprays of plaster lillies, the little silvery dove with the silvery leaf in its mouth, and most breathtaking of all were the jam pots, not one like Sadie said, but three or four at least filled with all kinds of wild flowers, and even some garden kinds like wallflowers.

"Oh, it's lovely Sadie," she murmured. "I'm so glad you brought me to see it," she cried until, right in the middle of the grave she saw something very odd and she knew at once why Sadie didn't want her to see the grave that day. What she saw was a lemonade bottle, a full one, unopened.

Sadie who had hung back, came slowly up to her.

"I didn't want you to see the lemonade," she said slowly, and she looked very miserable. "She doesn't put it there very often. It's a long time now since she did it at all. I thought she'd given up doing it, that she couldn't spare the money, or better still, that perhaps she got some of her senses back and knew it was a crazy thing to do. I wouldn't have brought you if I knew she'd done it again, but well, you've seen it now," she said, and to Maudie's distress she began to cry.

A vague oppressive feeling had come over Maudie and she looked around. The whole place was like a big untidy garden except for Tony's little grave, and suddenly she too began to cry.

Sadie stared at her incredulously. "I thought you'd laugh," she said. "I thought you'd stop being my friend and think I was as queer as Ma. I thought you'd think it was no wonder she's called what she's called! She thinks Tony will come back and drink it!"

"Oh, don't cry Sadie. Please don't cry," Maudie said, but she had to wipe her own eyes dry. "I suppose you could laugh if you looked at it another way," she said on a sudden inspiration. "It *is* very funny looking there when you come to think of it." Indeed she felt that she might start to laugh herself any minute and she might have done so if the sight of the bottle of lemonade hadn't had a peculiar effect upon her: It had made her thirsty.

How was it that she'd got sick of lemonade when the uncles were always lavishing her with it, and now, at this moment she'd give anything for even one little sip of it. Why, the sight of the bottle on Tony's grave had already made her throat as dry as blotting paper. She closed her eyes and. ran her tongue over her lips to moisten them. She could just imagine prising up the cap, although of course it would have to be done with a sharp stone or a piece of tin, if they could find one. She could imagine how slowly the cap would start to lift at first and then it would jerk into the air with millions of little beady bubbles welling up out of it and pouring down the sides of the bottle unless she held it up quick and put the bottle to her mouth and let the foamy part roll down her throat. After that of course, Sadie could have some, if she wanted. But oh gracious goodness, what a longing for a drop came over her. She'd have to go home at once and ask for some. She opened her eyes and dared to look again at the source of her temptation. The label on the bottle was bright and glossy. Surely that was queer. It wouldn't be the same bottle she put every time. She was going to ask Sadie when a gleam of sun made its way through the gloom of the ivy and a gleam of broken glass caught her eye under the wall, and when she looked closer she saw there were other bits of broken glass, and one bit was the neck of a bottle with its gilt top still tightly clawed down on its unopened top. "Oh Sadie, would you think it's to you she'd give it? What does she do when she finds he hasn't come?" She pointed towards where she'd seen the gleam of broken glass. "Does she throw it away to break it?"

"No," Sadie said, and she hung her head. "I find it. I throw it away and break it, in case anyone would see it." She paused. "And I suppose I think it must make her happy to think Tony took it."

"It's you who throws it away? Unopened?" Maudie couldn't believe her ears. "What a waste. Oh Sadie," she cried, "would your mother be delighted if she came back and found it was empty? She might think Tony came back and drank it."

"I never thought of that," Sadie said. "Do you think we ought to open it and spill out the lemonade?"

Maudie had had such a different solution she was taken aback. "We could do that of course," she said, "but that would still be a waste. And waste is a sin," said Maudie, drawing from new-found information she'd learned in Ireland. "Of course it's alright for your Ma because she doesn't know it's wasted and anyway she is not 'responsible' as people say, but we are and I don't think we ought to spill it out." She paused, "specially as I'm very thirsty. It's very stuffy in this old place. How about you?"

There was a pause before Sadie answered. "I'm gasping," she said then.

"That settles it, so," Maudie grabbed the lemonade bottle. "How will we open it?" she asked, exhilaration almost sweeping her off her feet.

"Ma always left a bottle opener," Sadie said. "It's under one of the jam pots so it won't get rusty, but she left the end of the wooden handle sticking out for Tony to see it."

Maudie looked her straight in the eye. "I guess your mother was not as mad as people think," she said, and she was glad to see that Sadie's cheeks were flaming red with excitement, and she even cracked a joke. "If Ma could only see us now," she said, but the mere thought of Mad Mary made the sweat break out all over her. Then she located the bottle opener and put it to work. The cap flew off like a bird and the foam of the drink bubbled upwards. "Quick! Lick it," Maudie cried, and then because by now neither of them wanted to waste a drop, they both together began to lick at the stream of golden liquid that poured forth in an ineffable stream.

It was while they were still holding the bottle over their heads that Maudie looked across the grave and saw Mad Mary.

At sight of that figure, silent and still in her black rags, appearing without warning, that all the fears that had been dampened down, burst into flames of terror and panic. Not a limb could she move, not even her tongue that was paralysed in the middle of a lick.

Then Sadie saw her mother. "Oh Jesus, Mary and Joseph, she'll crucify us," she cried, as if the tall silent woman in black was deaf, or dead.

Were they far from the gap in the wall was Maudie's first thought, but she didn't dare to turn around to see, because to do so she'd have to take her eyes off Mad Mary, and she felt her eyes were all she had to defend her. She stared into Mad Mary's eyes and then to the astonishment of Sadie, instead of running back, Maudie ran forward. "We didn't mean any harm," she cried. "It was only that we didn't want to see it going to waste. It was an awful waste, you know."

To Sadie's even greater amazement her mother put out her arms and Maudie threw herself into them.

"I know that child, but I only know it now," Sadie's mother said, and she was looking not at Maudie but at the sadly decked out little grave. "Tony is gone beyond where I can give him anything, and I'm glad to have realised it. He was only a child, but sure that's all Sadie is too. It would be fitter if I gave her more love. And I myself must seem only a sort of a child, with the way I have been behaving? Who but a child would put food on a grave? If I'd been found out doing that I'd have been put away into an institution." She looked at Sadie. "And what would become her then?"

"Oh, that's no kind of way to talk," Maudie said authoritatively.

Mad Mary looked more closely at her. "Whose child are you?" she asked, but she didn't wait for a reply. "What did you do with the lemonade?" she asked. "Did you let it spill?" For the bottle had fallen from Sadie's limp fingers. "No harm done," said Mad Mary. "I'll get you some more. Take this girl home to the cottage Sadie and I'll get some for both of you."

Maudie however, knew that enough was enough for one day. "Let Sadie come back to my house," she said. "We'll get lemonade from my uncles and no one will have to pay for it. I get it free." She turned persuasively. "Think of all the money you've wasted," she said, as just then a bit of a bleached label that had once been glossy and new fluttered past them as a dead leaf.

Mad Mary considered the suggestion. "Your family wouldn't want the likes of her being friends with you?"

"Why not?" Maudie countered.

Mad Mary looked at Sadie as if she was seeing her for the first time, or at least for the first time in years.

"That's right," she agreed. "Why wouldn't they?" Then her voice became more like the voice of Maudie's own mother. "Do you never put a comb through your hair?" she said crossly.

"She can comb her hair in my house, because I think we ought to start getting home. My mother will be wondering where I am," Maudie said.

"Can I go Ma?" Sadie asked.

"You can," said her mother. "It will give me a chance to put the cottage to rights while you're away." She looked at Tony's grave. "I'd have been better employed long ago doing a bit of readying up at home than always readying this place. Poor little Tony. Sure he's gone to a Better Place."

"Good bye Ma," Sadie said gently.

"Wait," said her mother. "I'll be with you as far as the gap in the wall."

As they began to move away Maudie looked back. "You kept the grave lovely," she said to Sadie's mother. "The lemonade bottle spoiled it, really, don't you think?"

"I do," said Tony's mother. They all looked back then and they all nodded in agreement at Maudie's statement. They went out through the gap together and Sadie and Maudie ran under the archway and back into the town.

Oh, but what was that Maudie saw? "Oh! Oh! Oh! She broke into a run and left Sadie stranded in the middle of the street. In front of the shop was a side-car, or as they used to call it in America, a jaunting car, and on the seat to one side of it, there were two big trunks, which the jarvey was just about to drag down on to the sidewalk with the help of Uncle Paud and Uncle Matt. On the other side was a man in a smart striped suit and a bowler hat. "It's Pappa!" Maudie screamed. It was only two months since they'd left him and they weren't expecting him till March, yet here he was! Mama was there too, but she seemed as surprised as Maudie, but there was a great look of triumph on her face, and indeed Pappa looked very pleased with himself too. As he got down on to the footpath Maudie raced over to him and he held out his arms for her to jump into them.

"I suppose I'd better go home," Sadie said sadly, catching at Maudie's sleeve to get her attention, as everyone had begun to go into the house. It was Pappa who noticed her.

"Is this your little friend?" he said. "Aren't you going to bring her in? I'm sure Uncle Paud will have enough lemonade and biscuits for us all."

Maudie saw Mama give a sharp look at Pappa, but Pappa laughed at her.

"You thought you knew me inside out, didn't you?" he asked her. Then he turned to Maudie. "Your old Pappa didn't spend all his money in the way your Mama thought. I had a nice little nest egg tucked away that she knew nothing about. We're not going back to America; none of us. We're going to buy a place over here like I always promised myself!" He looked back at Mama. "How about Dublin?" he asked. "We'll go up there and start looking around as soon as you like." Then he saw the sad look had come back on Sadie's face. "You'll still be friends. And I'm going to buy a motor car so Maudie will be coming down here in the holidays." Then he had another idea. "And we'll bring you back with us for visits."

Sadie said nothing. Tears had come into her eyes, but they were sort of happy tears, because she was smiling.

"I wouldn't want to leave Ma alone," she said, but then Uncle Paud said something surprising. "We'll look after your Ma whenever you go to see Maudie," he said. "In fact we'll see if she'd mind letting us give her a hand right away. We could get the walls white washed and get a bit of gravel spread in front of the door. No woman can be expected to do jobs like that. Do you think she'd let us help.?"

"I don't know," Sadie said simply.

"Well, there's plenty of time to see about it," said Uncle Paud. "We are not going to let those Yanks go off to Dublin until they've found a suitable house, a sound investment. So you'll see Maudie at school tomorrow anyway and maybe a lot of tomorrows."

As Sadie had finished her lemonade, Maudie went with her to the door. "You mustn't worry when I go," she said. "Now that you've made one friend, you'll find you'll make lots and lots more. And we can always write to each other."

"I don't write very well," Sadie said, as she stepped into the street. Behind in the parlour Maudie heard Pappa telling his adventures on the ship and she was impatient to go back to him to join in it. So before she closed the door she wagged her finger at Sadie. "Well, you'd better hurry up then and learn how to write," she said. Sadie laughed. It was the first time she'd ever seen her laugh, and she waved at her until Sadie was out of sight.

In the Middle of the Fields

Like a rock in the sea, she was islanded by fields, the heavy grass washing about the house, and the cattle wading in it as in water. Even their gentle stirrings were a loss when they moved away at evening to the shelter of the woods. A rainy day might strike a wet flash from a hay barn on the far side of the river. Not even a habitation! And yet she was less lonely for him here in Meath than elsewhere. Anxieties by day, and cares, and at night vague, nameless fears, these were the stones across the mouth of the tomb. But who understood that? They thought she hugged tight every memory she had of him. What did they know about memory? What was it but another name for dry love and barren longing? They even tried to unload upon her their own small purposeless memories. "I imagine I see him every time I look out there," they would say as they glanced nervously over the darkening fields when they were leaving. "I think I ought to see him coming through the trees." Oh, for God's sake! she'd think. She'd forgotten him for a minute.

It wasn't him she saw when she looked out at the fields. It was the ugly tufts of tow and scutch that whitened the tops of the grass and gave it the look of a sea in storm, spattered with broken foam. That grass would have to be topped. And how much would it cost?

At least Ned, the old herd, knew the man to do it for her. "Bartley Crossen is your man, Ma'am. Your husband knew him well."

Vera couldn't place him at first. Then she remembered. "Oh, yes, that's his hay barn we see, isn't it? Why, of course. I know him well, by sight." And so she did, splashing past on the road in his big muddy car, the wheels always caked with clay, and the wife in the front seat beside him.

"I'll get him to call around and have a word with you, Ma'am," said the herd.

"Before dark," she cautioned.

But there was no need to tell Ned. The old man knew how she always tried to be upstairs before it got dark, locking herself into her bedroom, which opened off the room where the children slept, praying devoutly that she wouldn't have to come down again for anything, above all, not to answer the door. That was what in particular she dreaded: a knock after dark.

"Ah, sure, who'd come near you, Ma'am, knowing you're a woman alone with small children that might be wakened and set crying? And, for that matter, where could you be safer than in the middle of the fields, with the innocent beasts asleep around you?" If he himself had come to the house late at night for any reason, to get hot water to stoup the foot of a beast, or to call the vet, he took care to shout out long before he got to the gable. "It's me, Ma'am!" he'd shout.

"Coming! Coming!" she'd cry, gratefully, as quick on his words as their echo. Unlocking her door, she'd run down and throw open the hall door. No matter what the hour! No matter how black the night!

"Go back to your bed now, you Ma'am," he'd say from the darkness, where she could see the swinging yard lamp coming nearer and nearer like the light of a little boat drawing near to a jetty. "I'll put out the lights and let myself out." Relaxed by the thought that there was someone in the house, she would indeed scuttle back into bed, and, what was more, she'd be nearly asleep when she'd hear the door slam. It used to sound like the slam of a door a million miles away. There was no need to worry. He'd see that Crossen came early.

It was well before dark when Crossen did drive up to the door. The wife was with him, as usual, sitting up in the front seat the way people sat up in the well of little tub traps long ago, their knees pressed together, allowing no slump. Ned had come with them, but only he and Crossen got out.

"Won't your wife come inside and wait, Mr. Crossen?" she asked.

"Oh, not at all, Ma'am. She lies sitting in the car. Now, where's the grass that's to be cut? Are there any stones lying about that would blunt the blade? Going around the gable of the house, he looked out over the land.

"There's not a stone or a stump in it," Ned said. "You'd run your blade over the whole of it while you'd be whetting it twenty times in another place."

"I can see that," said Bartley Crossen, but absently, Vera thought. He had walked across the lawn to the rickety wooden gate that led into the pasture, and leaned on it. He didn't seem to be looking at the fields at all though, but at the small string of stunted thorns that grew along the riverbank, their branches leaning so heavily out over the water that their roots were almost dragged clear of the clay. When he turned around he gave a sigh. "Ah, sure, I didn't need to look. I know it well," he said. As she showed surprise, he gave a little laugh, like a young man. "I courted a girl down there when I was a lad," he said. "That's a queer length of time ago now, I can tell you." He turned to the old man. "You might remember." Then he looked back at her. "I don't suppose you were born then Ma'am," he said, and there was something kindly in his look and in his words. "You'd like the mowing done soon, I suppose? How about first thing in the morning?"

Her face lit up. But there was the price to settle. "It won't be as dear as cutting meadow, will it?"

"Ah, I won't be too hard on you, Ma'am," he said. "I can promise you that."

"That's very kind of you," she said, but a little doubtfully.

Behind Crossen's back, Ned nodded his head in approval. "Let it go at that, Ma'am," he whispered as they walked back towards the car. "He's a man you can trust."

When Crossen and the wife had driven away, Ned reassured her again. "A decent man," he said. Then he gave a laugh, and it was a young kind of laugh for a man of his age. "Did you hear what he said about the girl he courted down there? Do you know who that was? It was his first wife. You know he was twice married? Ah, well, it's so long ago I wouldn't wonder if you never heard it. Look at the way he spoke about her himself, as if she was some girl he'd all but forgotten. The thorn trees brought her to his mind. That's where they used to meet, being only youngsters, when they first took up with each other."

"Poor Bridie Logan! She was as wild as a hare. And she was mad with love, young as she was. They were company-keeping while they were still going to school. Only nobody took it seriously, him least of all, maybe, till the winter he went away to the agricultural college in Clonakilty. They started writing to each other then. I used to see her running up to the postbox at the crossroads every other evening, and sure, the whole village knew where the letter was going. His people were fit to be tied when he came home in the summer and said he wasn't going back, but was going to marry Bridie. All the same, his father set them up in a cottage on his own land. It's the cottage he uses now for stall-feds, it's back of his new house. Oh, but you can't judge it now for what it was then. Giddy and all as she was, as lightheaded as a thistle, you should have seen the way Bridie kept that cottage. She'd have had it scrubbed away if she didn't start having a baby. He wouldn't let her take the scrubbing brush into her hands after that."

"But she wasn't delicate, was she?"

"Bridie? She was as strong as a kid goat, that one. But I told you she was mad about him, didn't I? Well, after she was married to him she was no better. Worse, I'd say: She couldn't do enough for him. It was like as if she was driven on by some kind of a fever. You'd only to look in her eyes to see it. Do you know! From that day to this, I don't believe I ever saw a woman so full of going as that one. Did you ever happen to see little birds flying about in the air like they were flying for the divilment of it and nothing else? And did you ever see the way they give a sort of a little leap in the air, like they were forcing themselves to go a bit higher still, higher than they ought? Well, it struck me that was the way Bridie was acting, as she rushed about that cottage doing this and doing that to make him prouder and prouder of her. As if he could be any prouder than he was already with her condition getting noticeable."

"She didn't die in childbed?"

"No. Not in a manner of speaking, anyway. She had the child, nice and easy, and in their own cottage too, only costing him a few shillings for one of those women that went in for that kind of job long ago. And all went well. It was no time till she was let up on her feet again. I was there the first morning she had the place to herself. She was up and dressed when I got there, just as he was going out to milk.

"'Oh, it's great to be able to go out again,' she said, taking a great breath of the morning air as she stood at the door looking after him. 'Wait, why don't I come with you to milk?' she called out after him. Then she threw a glance back at the baby to make sure it was asleep in its crib by the window.

"'It's too far for you, Bridie,' he said. The cows were down in a little field alongside the road, at the foot of the hill below the village. And knowing she'd start coaxing him, Bartley made off as quick as he could out of the gate with the cans. 'Good man!' I said to myself. But the next thing I knew, Bridie had darted across the yard.

"'I can go on the bike if it's too far to walk,' she said. And up she got on her old bike, and out she pedalled through the gate.

"'Bridie, are you out of your mind?' Bartley shouted as she whizzed past him.

"'Arrah, what harm can it do me?' she shouted back.

"I went stiff with fright looking after her. And I thought it was the same with him, when he threw down the cans and started down the hill after her. But looking back on it, I think it was the same fever as always was raging in her that was raging in him, too. Mad with love, that's what they were, both of them, she only wanting to draw him on, and he only too willing.

"'Wait for me!' he shouted, but before she'd even got to the bottom she started to brake the bike, putting down her foot like you'd see a youngster do, and raising up such a cloud of dust we could hardly see her."

"She braked too hard?"

"Not her! In the twinkle of an eye she'd stopped the bike, jumped off, turned it round, and was pedalling madly up the hill again to meet him, with her head down on the handle-bars like a racing cyclist. But that was the finish of her."

"Oh, no! What *happened*?"

"She stopped pedalling all of a sudden, and the bike half stopped, and then it started to slide back down the hill, as if it had skidded on the loose gravel at the side of the road. That's what we both thought happened, because we both began to run down the hill too. She didn't get time to fall before we got to her. But what use was that? It was some kind of internal bleeding that took her. We got her into the bed, and the neighbours came running, but she was gone before night."

"Oh, what a dreadful thing to happen! And the baby?"

"Well, it was a strong child. And it grew into a fine lad. That's the fellow that drives the tractor for him now, the oldest son, Barty they called him not to confuse him with Bartley."

"Well, I suppose his second marriage had more to it, when all was said and done."

"That's it. And she's a good woman, the second one. Look at the way she brought up that child of Bridie's, and filled the cradle, year after year, with sons of her own. Ah sure, things always work out for the best in the end, no matter what!" the old man said, and he started to walk away.

"Wait a minute, Ned," Vera called after him urgently. "Do you really think he forgot about her, until today?"

"I'd swear it," said the old man. Then he looked hard at her. "It will be the same with you, too," he added kindly. "Take my word for it. Everything passes in time and is forgotten."

As she shook her head doubtfully, he shook his emphatically. "When the tree falls, how can the shadow stand?" he said. And he walked away.

I wonder! she thought as she walked back to the house, and she envied the practical country people who made good the defaults of nature as readily as the broken sod knits back into the sward.

Again that night, when she went up to her room, Vera looked down towards the river and she thought of Crossen. Had he really forgotten? It was hard for her to believe, and with a sigh she picked up her hairbrush and pulled it through her hair. Like everything else about her lately, her hair was sluggish and hung heavily down, but after a few minutes under the quickening strokes of the brush, it lightened and lifted, and soon it flew about her face like the spray over a weir. It had always been the same, even when she was a child. She had only to suffer the first painful drag of the bristles when her mother would cry out, "Look! Look! That's electricity!" And a blue spark would shine for an instant like a star in the grey depths of the mirror. That was all they knew of electricity in those dim-lit days when valleys of shadow lay deep between one piece of furniture and another. Was it because rooms were so badly lit then that they saw it so often, that little blue star? Suddenly she was overcome by longing to see it again, and, standing up impetuously, she switched off the light. It was just then that, down below, the iron fist of the knocker was lifted and, with a strong, confident hand, brought down on the door. It was not a furtive knock. She recognised that even as she sat stark with fright in the darkness. And then a voice that was vaguely familiar called out from below.

"It's me, Ma'am. I hope I'm not disturbing you?"

"Oh, Mr. Crossen!" she cried out with relief, and unlocking her door, she ran across the landing and threw up a window on that side of the house. "I'll be right down!" she called.

"There's no need to come down, Ma'am," he shouted. "I only want one word with you."

"Of course I'll come down." She went back and got her dressing-gown and was about to pin up her hair, but as she did she heard him stomping his feet on the gravel. It had been a mild day, but with night a chill had come in the air, and for all that it was late spring, there was a cutting east wind coming across the river. "I'll run down and let you in from the cold," she called, and, twisting up her hair, she held it against her head with her hand without waiting to pin it, and she ran down the stairs in her bare feet and opened the hall door.

"Oh? You were going to bed, Ma'am?" he said apologetically when she opened the door. And where he had been so impatient a minute beforehand, he stood stock-still in the open doorway. "I saw the lights were out downstairs when I was coming up the drive," he said contritely. "But I didn't think you'd gone up for the night."

"Not at all," she lied, to put him at his ease. "I was just upstairs brushing my hair. You must excuse me," she added, because a breeze from the door was blowing her dressing-gown from her knees, and to pull it across she had to take her hand from her hair, so the hair fell down about her shoulders. "Would you mind closing the door for me?" she said, with some embarrassment, and she began to back up the stairs. "Please go inside to the sitting-room off the hall. "Put on the light. I'll be down in a minute."

Although he had obediently stepped inside the door, and closed it, he stood stoutly in the middle of the hall. "I shouldn't have come in," he said. "You were going to bed," he cried, this time in an accusing voice as if he dared her to deny it. He was looking at her hair. "Excuse my saying so, Ma'am, but I never saw such a fine head of hair. God bless it!" he added quickly, as if afraid he had been too familiar. "Doesn't a small thing make a big differ," he said impulsively. "You look like a young girl."

In spite of herself, she smiled with pleasure. She wanted no more of this kind of talk, all the same. "Well, I don't feel like one," she said sharply.

What was meant for a quite opposite effect however, seemed to delight him and put him wonderfully at ease. "Ah sure, you're a sensible woman, I can see that," he said, and, coming to the foot of the stairs, he leaned comfortably across the newel post. "Let you stay the way you are, Ma'am," he said. "I've only one word to say to you. Let me say here and now and be off about my business. The wife will be waiting up for me, and I don't want that."

She hesitated. Was the reference to his wife meant to put *her* at ease? "I think I ought to get my slippers," she said cautiously. Her feet were cold.

"Oh, yes, you should put on your slippers," he said, only then seeing that she was in her bare feet. "But as to the rest, I'm long gone beyond taking any account of what a woman has on her. I'm gone beyond taking notice of women at all."

But she had seen something to put on her feet. Under the table in the hall there was a pair of old boots belonging to Richard, with fleece lining in them. She hadn't been able to make up her mind to give them away with the rest of his clothes, and although they were big and clumsy on her, she often stuck her feet into them when she came in from the fields with mud on her shoes. "Well, come in where it's warm, so," she said. She came back down the few steps and stuck her feet into the boots, and then she opened the door of the sittingroom. She was glad she'd come down. He'd never have been able to put on the light. "There's something wrong with the centre light," she said as she groped along the skirting board to find the plug of the reading lamp. It was in an awkward place, behind the desk. She had to go down on her knees.

"What's wrong with it?" he asked, as, with a countryman's interest in practicalities, he clicked the switch up and down to no effect.

"Oh, nothing much, I'm sure," she said absently. "There!" She had found the plug, and the room was lit up with a bright white glow.

"Why don't you leave the plug in the socket?" he asked critically.

"I don't know," she said. "I think someone told me it's safer, with reading lamps, to pull the plugs out at night. There might be a short circuit, or mice might nibble at the cord, or something. I forget what I was told. I got into the habit of doing it, and now I keep on." She felt a bit silly.

But he was concerned about it. "I don't think any harm could be done," he said gravely. Then he turned away from the problem. "About tomorrow, Ma'am," he said, somewhat offhandedly, she thought. "I was determined I'd see you tonight, because I'm not a man to break my word, above all, to a woman."

What was he getting at?

"Let me put it this way," he said quickly. "You'll understand, Ma'am, that as far as I am concerned, topping land is the same as cutting hay. The same time. The same labour. The same cost. And the same wear and tear on the blade. You understand that?"

On her guard, she nodded.

"Well now, Ma'am, I'd be the first to admit that it's not quite the same for you. For you, topping doesn't give the immediate return you'd get from hay."

"There's *no* return from topping," she exclaimed crossly.

"Oh, come now, Ma'am! Good grassland pays as well as anything. You know you won't get nice sweet pickings for your beasts from neglected land, but only old tow grass knotting under their feet. It's just that it's not a quick return, and so, as you know, I told you I'd be making a special price for you."

"I do know," she said impatiently. "But I thought that part of it was settled and done."

"Oh, I'm not going back on it, if that's what you think," he said affably. "I'm glad to do what I can for you, Ma'am, the more so seeing you have no man to attend to these things for you, but only yourself alone."

"Oh, I'm well able to look after myself," she said, raising her voice.

Once again her words had an opposite effect to what she intended. He laughed good-humouredly. "That's what all women like to think," he said. "Well, now," he went on in a different tone of voice, and it annoyed her to see he seemed to think something had been settled between them, "it would suit me, and I'm sure it's all the same to you, if we could leave your little job till later in the week, say till nearer to the time of the haymaking generally. Because by then I'd have the cutting bar in good order, sharpened and ready for use. Whereas now, while there's still a bit of ploughing to be done here and there, I'll have to be chopping and changing, between the plough and the mower, putting one on one minute and the other the next."

"As if anyone is still ploughing this time of the year! Who are you putting before me?" she demanded.

"Now, take it easy, Ma'am. I'm not putting anyone before you, leastways, not without getting leave first from you."

"Without telling me you're not coming, you mean."

"Oh, now, Ma'am, don't get cross. I'm only trying to make matters easy for everyone."

She was very angry now. "It's always the same story. I thought you'd treat me differently. I'm to wait till after this one, and after that one, and in the end my fields will go wild."

He looked a bit shamefaced. "Ah now, Ma'am, that's not going to be the case at all. Although, mind you, some people don't hold with topping, you know."

"I hold with it."

"Oh, I suppose there's something in it," he said reluctantly. "But the way I look at it, cutting the weeds in July is a kind of a topping."

"Grass cut before it goes to seed gets so thick at the roots no weeds can come up," she cried, so angry she didn't realise how authoritative she sounded.

"Faith, I never knew you were so well up, Ma'am," he said, looking at her admiringly, but she saw he wasn't going to be put down by her. "All the same now, Ma'am, you can't say a few days here or there could make any difference?"

"A few days could make all the difference. This farm has a gravelly bottom to it, for all it's to lush. A few days of drought could burn it to the butt. And how could I mow it then? And what cover would there be for the 'nice sweet pickings' you were talking about a minute ago?" Angrily, she mimicked his own accent without thinking.

He threw up his hands. "Ah well, I suppose a man may as well admit when he's bested," he said. "Even by a woman. And you can't say I broke my promise."

"I can't say but you tried hard enough," she said grudgingly, although she was mollified that she was getting her way. "Can I offer you anything?" she said then, anxious to convey an air of finality to their discussion.

"Not at all, Ma'am. Nothing, thank you. I'll have to be getting home."

"I hope you won't think I was trying to take advantage of you," he said as they went towards the door. "It's just that we must all make out as best we can for ourselves, isn't that so? Not but you are well able to look after yourself, I must say. No one ever thought you'd stay on here after your husband died. I suppose it's for the children you did it?" He looked up the well of the stairs. "Are they asleep?"

"Oh, long ago," she said indifferently. She opened the hall door. The night air swept in. But this time, from far away, it brought with it the fragrance of new-mown hay. "There's hay cut somewhere already," she exclaimed in surprise. And she lifted her face to the sweetness of it.

For a minute, Crossen looked past her out into the darkness, then he looked back at her. "Aren't you never lonely here at night?" he asked suddenly.

"You mean frightened?" she corrected quickly and coldly.

"Yes,! Yes, that's what I meant," he said, taken aback. "Ah, but why would you be frightened? What safer place could you be under the sky than right here with your own fields all about you."

What he said was so true, and he himself as he stood there, with his hat in his hand, so normal and natural it was indeed absurd to think that he would no sooner have gone out the door than she would be scurrying up the stairs like a child. "You may not believe it," she said, "but I am scared to death sometimes. I nearly died when I heard your knock on the door tonight. It's because I was scared that I was upstairs," she said, in a further burst of confidence. "I always go up the minute it gets dark. I don't feel so frightened upstairs."

"Isn't that strange now?" he said, and she could see he found it an incomprehensibly womanly thing to do. He was sympathetic all the same. "You shouldn't be alone. That's the truth of the matter," he said, It's a shame."

"Oh, it can't be helped," she said. There was something she wanted to shrug off in his sympathy, while at the same time she appreciated the kindliness. "Would you like to do something for me?" she asked impulsively. "Would you wait and put out the lights down here and let me get back upstairs before you go? Ned often does that for me if he's working here late: After she had spoken she felt foolish, but she saw at once that, if anything, he thought it only too little to do for her. He was genuinely troubled about her. And it wasn't only the present moment that concerned him; he seemed to be considering the whole problem of her isolation and loneliness.

"Is there nobody could stay here with you, at night even? It would have to be another woman, of course," he added quickly, and her heart was warmed by the way, without a word from her, he rejected that solution out of hand. "You don't want another woman about the place," he said flatly.

"Oh, I'm all right, really. I'll get used to it," she said.

"It's a shame, all the same," he said. He said it helplessly, though, and he motioned her towards the stairs. "You'll be all right for tonight, anyway. Go on up the stairs now, and I'll put out the lights." He had already turned around to go back into the sitting-room.

Yet it wasn't quite as she intended for some reason, and it was somewhat reluctantly that she started up the stairs.

"Wait a minute! How do I put out this one?" he called out from the room before she was halfway up.

"Oh, I'd better put out that one myself," she said, thinking of the awkward position of the plug. She ran down again, and, going past him into the little room, she knelt and pulled at the cord. Instantly the room was deluged in darkness. And instantly she felt that she had done something stupid. It was not like turning out a light by a switch at the door and being able to step back into the lighted hall. She got to her feet as quickly as she could, but as she did, she saw that Crossen was standing in the doorway. His bulk was blocked out against the hall light behind him. "I'll leave the rest to you," she said to break the peculiar silence that had come down on the house. But he didn't move. He stood there, the full of the doorway, and she was reluctant to brush past him.

Why didn't he move? Instead he caught her by the arm, and, putting out his other hand, he pressed his palm against the door-jamb, barring her way.

"Tell me," he whispered, his words falling over each other, "are you never lonely at all?"

"What did you say?" she said in a clear voice, because the thickness of his voice sickened her. She had barely heard what he said. Her one thought was to get past him.

He leaned forward. "What about a little kiss?" he whispered, and to get a better hold on her he let go the hand he had pressed against the wall, but before he caught at her with both hands she had wrenched her all free of him, and, ignominiously ducking under his armpit, she was out next minute in the lighted hall.

Out there, because light was all the protection she needed from him, the old fool, she began to laugh. She had only to wait for him to come sheepishly out. But there was something she hadn't counted on; she hadn't counted on there being anything pathetic in his sheepishness, something really pitiful in the way he shambled into the light, not raising his eyes. And she was so surprisingly touched that before he had time to utter a word she put out her hand. "Don't feel too bad," she said. "I didn't take offence."

Still he didn't look at her. He just took her hand and pressed it gratefully, his face turned away. And to her dismay she saw that his nose was running water. Like a small boy, he wiped it with the back of his fist, streaking his face. "I don't know what came over me," he said slowly. "I'm getting on to be an old man. I thought I was beyond all that." He wiped his face again. "Beyond letting myself go, anyway," he amended miserably.

"Oh, it was nothing," she said.

He shook his head. "It wasn't as if I had cause for what I did."

"But you did nothing," she protested.

"It wasn't nothing to me," he said dejectedly.

For a minute, they stood there silent. The hall door was still ajar, but she didn't dare to close it. What am I going to do with him now, she thought, I'll have him here all night if I'm not careful. What time was it, anyway? All scale and proportion seemed to have gone from the night. "Well, I'll see you in the morning, Mr. Crossen," she said, as matter-of-factly as possible.

He nodded, but made no move to go. You know I meant no disrespect to you, Ma'am, don't you?" he said, looking imploringly at her. "I always had a great regard for you. And for your husband, too. I was thinking of him this very night when I was coming up to the house. And I thought of him again when you came to the door looking like a young girl. I thought what a pity it was him to be taken from you, and you both so young. Oh, what came over me at all? And what would Mona say if she knew?"

"But surely you wouldn't tell her? I should certainly hope not," Vera cried, appalled. What sort of a figure would she cut if he told the wife about her coming down in her bare feet with her hair down her back. "Take care would you tell her!" she warned.

"I don't suppose I ought," he said, but he said it uncertainly and morosely, and he leaned back against the wall. "She's been a good woman, Mona. I wouldn't want anyone to think different. My sons could tell you. She's been a good mother to them all these years. She never made a bit of difference between them. Some say she was better to Barty than to any of them. She reared him from a week old. She was living next door to us, you see, at the time I was left with him," he said. "She came in that first night and took him home to her own bed, and, mind you, that wasn't a small thing for a woman who knew nothing about children, not being what you'd call a young girl, in spite of the big family she gave me afterwards. She took him home and looked after him, although it isn't every woman would care to be responsible for a newborn baby. That's a thing a man doesn't forget easy. There's many I know would say that if she hadn't taken him someone else would, but no one only her would have done it the way she did. She used to keep him all day in her own cottage, feeding him and the rest of it. But at night, when I'd be back from the fields, she'd bring him home and leave him down in his little crib by the fire alongside of me. She used to let on she had things to do in her own place, and she'd slip away and leave us alone, but that wasn't her real reason for leaving him. She knew the way I'd be sitting looking into the fire, wondering how I'd face the long years ahead, and she left the child there with me to distract me from my sorrow. And she was right. I never got long to brood. The child would give a cry, or a whinge, and I'd have to run out and fetch her to him. Or else she'd hear him herself maybe, and run in without me having to call her at all. I used often think she must have kept every window and door in her place open, for fear she'd lose a sound from either of us. And so, bit by bit, I was knit back into a living man. I often wondered what would have become of me if it wasn't for her. There are men and when the bright way closes to them there's no knowing but they'll take a dark way. And I was that class of man. I told you she used to take the little fellow away in the day and bring him back at night? Well, of course, she used to take him away again coming on to the real dark of night. She used to keep him in her own bed. But as the months went on and he got bigger, I could see she hated taking him away from me at all. He was beginning to smile and play with his fists and be real company. 'I wonder ought I leave him with you tonight,' she'd say then, night after night. And sometimes she'd run in and dump him down in the middle of the big double bed in the room off the kitchen, but the next minute she'd snatch him up again. 'I'd be afraid you'd overlie him. You might only smother him, God between us and all harm!'

" 'You'd better take him,' I'd say, I used to hate to see him go myself by this time. All the same, I was afraid he'd start crying in the night, and what would I do then? If I had to go out for her in the middle of the night, it could cause a lot of talk. there was talk enough as things were, I can tell you, although there was no grounds for it. I had no more notion of her than if she wasn't a woman at all. Would you believe that? But one night when she took him up and put him down, and put him down and took him up, and went on and went on about leaving him or taking him, I had to laugh. 'It's a pity you can't stay along with him, and that would settle all,' I said. I was only joking her, but she got as red as fire, and next thing she burst out crying. But not before she'd caught up the child and wrapped her coat around him. Then, after giving me a terrible look, she ran out the door with him. Well, that was the beginning of it. I'd no idea she had any feelings for me. I thought it was only for the child. But men are fools, as women well know, and she knew before me what was right and proper for us both. And for the child too. Some women have great insight into these things. That night God opened my own eyes to the woman I had in her, and I saw it was better I took her than wasted away after the one that was gone. And wasn't I right?"

"Of course you were right," she said quickly.

But he had slumped back against the wall, and the abject look came back into his eyes. "And to think I shamed her as well as myself."

I'll never get rid of him, Vera thought desperately. "Ah, what ails you?" she cried impatiently. "Forget it, can't you?"

"I can't," he said simply.

"Ah, for heaven's sake. It's got nothing to do with her at all."

Surprised, he looked up at her. "You're not blaming yourself, surely?"

he asked.

She'd have laughed at that if she hadn't seen she was making headway. Another stroke and she'd be rid of him. "Why are you blaming any of us?" she cried. "It's got nothing to do with any of us, with you, or me, or the woman at home waiting for you. It was the other one you should blame, that girl, your first wife, Bridie! Blame her!" The words had broken uncontrollably from her. For a moment, she thought she was hysterical and that she could not stop. "You thought you could forget her," she cried, "but see what she did to you when she got the chance."

He stood for a moment at the open door. "God rest her soul," he said, without looking back, and he stepped into the night.

The Lucky Pair

Vera picked him out in the sea of dancers. He had kept his head above water, jostled but never submerged, as he jerked his partners up and down. He was not sucked under even when in the final flourishes of a number the ends of dresses lashed together into a wild and briary foam. Not even when the spotlights showed the motes of dust to be a rising flood in which the violinists raised their violins—shoulder-high as if in the last minutes before catastrophe. She knew him by sight, of course. She knew his name, too. He was Andrew Gill, incoming Auditor of the Students Law Society, an office that made him automatically chairman of the dance. And because he was tall, of course the red ribbon with the auditorial insignia was very conspicuous across his shoulders. Did he have to wear those other medals, though, she wondered? Perhaps he was conceited, as his fellow students in the Law Faculty declared. She herself felt sure he just wore them tonight to give dignity to the dance.

He was certainly taking his duties as chairman seriously, talking affably to everyone, like the host at a private dance. He seemed bent on making the night a success. Yet she could see that he himself was hardly enjoying it. He did not appear to have brought along a girl, or to belong to a proper party, and he danced only duty dances. She kept watching him. Wasn't there something patronising in being so determined that others enjoy what he himself so obviously disdained? Well, she wasn't enjoying it, either. She'd far rather be writing up her notes in the reading-room of the National Library. And when the night came to an end and she caught sight of him again, in the vestibule, turning up the collar of his overcoat, it occurred to her that he was doing so less as a precaution against the weather than against further contamination by his fellows. She put up her own collar. That was the very way she felt about most of her then fellow students. It was all she could do not to smile at him, which would have been absurd. Neither tonight nor at any other time had he ever noticed her.

But the very next evening, at the library, when he came in and took the only vacant seat, which happened to be the one next to her, she saw a faint look of recognition on his face as he put down his notebooks. Faintly she let recognition show on her own face. And, incredibly, he smiled. "Did you enjoy the dance last night?" he asked.

"Oh, yes," she said eagerly, thinking of his efforts to make it a success. Immediately, she repented her hypocrisy. "That kind of thing isn't much in my line, though," she added.

73

He looked surprised. "I thought all girls were mad about dancing," he said. The attendant brought him his books just then, but before he started to read, he looked at her again. "Haven't I seen you somewhere?"

"Last night, I suppose."

"No, somewhere else," he said severely, before he settled down to study. After that, he neither spoke nor looked at her till the bell rang at ten o'clock. Then he turned to her. "I know where I've seen you," he said, and he seemed very pleased at placing her. "In Leeson Street."

"That's right," she said. "You live there, too, don't you?"

She was quite unprepared for the cross look that came over his face. "I do not," he said coldly. "I live in Kildare." Gathering up his books, he stalked out of the library.

Well, that's that, she thought.

But it was not. Outside on the landing, he was standing, obviously waiting for her because the minute she came out he took up their conversation as if it were an immensely important discussion. "I have to stay in Dublin from Mondays to Fridays," he explained. "But that's not the same as saying I live here. I couldn't bear it. I hate Dublin!" His forcefulness took her breath away.

"But it's such a beautiful city," she protested. They had reached the door and stepped out into the evening air, where, between the columns of the stone colonnade, sky, cloud, and tree were so wayward and free that the heart was troubled by their vernal beauty. "I love Dublin," she said intensely, though she felt that the slender connection between them would surely now snap like a twig. "Well, I'll say good night!" she said more timidly. A little sadly, she went out of the gates and up the street.

Yet the next afternoon they met again. This time in Leeson Street. He had taken off his hat, and there was something about the way he was sauntering along that made it hard to believe he was not enjoying the air and the sunlight.

"Oh, good afternoon," he said stiffly.

"Isn't it a lovely afternoon?" she said.

"The air is fresh," he allowed, but he frowned as he looked up the street.

Vera looked up the street too. How could he not appreciate the beauty of the architecture? The light that had left one side of the street was following further on the other side, striking the white plastered recesses of the windows and the white painted window sills which gave back the light in diminishing scale, as a hand passing over the keys of a piano gives back notes divinely graded.

His face was severe. "I suppose you'd say these old houses were beautiful. To me they're ugly and ought to be pulled down."

He was very aggressive, but she felt there was some tribute in his remembering their brief conversation of the previous evening. "I don't see how anyone could call them ugly," she said.

"Wait a minute," he said. "Are we talking about the outsides or the insides, because I'm afraid I'm only thinking of the insides? Do you know, I often stand at the door of the digs with my latchkey in my hand, dreading to open the door on the dinginess, the dark, and the smell!"

"The smell? That must be damp, I suppose. "Doesn't your landlady have fires?"

He looked as if he had not thought it might be damp. "Oh, you know the sort of fires they have in a lodging-house," he said then. "Once, I threw an orange peel on to the fire in the morning and it was still there when I came back that night."

"But that's not the fault of the house," she protested.

He wasn't listening. "I was in another digs, in Fitzwilliam Street, when I was a first-year student, and there were initials carved into the banister rail all the way up the stairs, the way you'd see them carved into the bark of a tree, but one day the curtains on the landing window were taken down, and when the light fell across the stairs I saw it wasn't into the wood they were carved at all but into a coating of grease and dirt on the top of the rail."

She had to laugh at that, but she still made a protest. "That wasn't the fault of the house, either. You're not being fair! And anyway, houses aren't like people; they don't get ugly just because they get old. There's an old house out in the country in Summerhill—" She broke off, because straight in front of them, set in a circle cut out of the cement, was a young sycamore tree, its sooty branches showered with young green leaves, fine as rain. "Oh, just look at that tree!" she cried. "What have you got in Kildare to equal that? And have you heard the Dublin birds?"

"I hear a few starving sparrows now and then, in the backyard of the digs," he said.

"Oh, they're probably country birds that ought never to have left home. I'm talking about the city birds that live in the creeper on the houses. Did you hear that?" she cried excitedly, as just then, just above them, a small bird gave a vesper call.

"Where is it?" he asked, staring at the grey and withered creeper, thin as a cobweb, on the brick. They could not see even a stir. It was as if the bricks were singing.

"It probably has a nest somewhere in the creeper. I must try if I can see it from my window because this is where I live," she said, putting her hand on the iron rail that led up a flight of steps.

"Oh, the house with the bird," he said gallantly, but she saw that the look he threw over the house was sharp and critical. "I'll see you in the library some time, I suppose," he said vaguely.

"I suppose so," she said, vaguely, too, and she was glad that her answer was drowned by another note, single but clear as water, that came just then from the creeper.

After that it was well over a week before they met again. She was already at her desk in the library when he appeared, but the minute he saw her he came straight over. "Was I rude the other day, talking like that about the street where you live?" He seemed concerned.

"Oh, I didn't mind. The houses on this side are in good condition."

"I hope you're not just saying that to make me feel better," he said earnestly. "I think it's something in my nature that makes me hate the city. I feel a different person the minute I step off the bus on the country road."

"Isn't it good you can get away like that," she said, feeling more sympathy with him than the last time.

"It is. I don't know what I'd do if I couldn't," he said, and she realised there was a note of desperation in his voice.

"There's no reason why you shouldn't always be able to go home, is there?"

"No immediate reason," he said slowly, and then his words came with a rush. "My mother died two years ago and I never feel the same about going down there since she died." But at this point an old gentleman at the desk in front of them turned around and frowned. "We're disturbing people. I'll tell you another time," he said. "Perhaps we might walk up the street together at ten o'clock?"

"If you like," she said, trying to sound different.

"I'll tell you about it as we're walking along," he said.

All the same when the bell rang, she thought he'd forgotten her. He walked out of the library without giving her a glance. Like the last time, however, he was waiting for her outside, and he took up what he had been saying as if he'd left off the previous minute. "Things had never been the same since my brother married, anyway," he said, and sighed. "My sister-in-law is very kind. She tries hard to please me. And my brother sends one of the workmen to meet the bus at Clane every Friday night with my bicycle. But it's not the same as when my mother was alive. I can't feel I'm wanted in the same way. To tell you the truth, I spend most of the time out with my gun, wandering about the woods."

"Oh, I'm sure they like having you," she said. And why wouldn't they? she thought, looking at him. He was really very nice. But he wasn't listening to her.

"I know one thing," he said determinedly. "I wouldn't go down there very often if there was a family on the way."

"What difference would that make?" She was obviously surprised. "It hardly seems fair to hope they won't have any," she said, finding it hard not to laugh.

"Oh, I wasn't thinking about them. I was thinking about myself. I'd hate to be there if there was anything like that going on. Something happened last summer, you see," he said, lowering his voice. "They didn't tell me what was the matter, but my sister-in-law was in bed for several days. It was during the holidays, and I was at home for two months. It was very awkward for me. I stayed out most of the day, but I had to go in sometimes. I felt very uncomfortable."

"Did she have a miscarriage?"

"I suppose so," he said, and he gave her a glance that she found hard to interpret, except that he looked less uncomfortable. He must have been embarrassed. "The house was full of women, anyway," he went on, and more easily, more naturally, she thought. Was it possible that he had appreciated her explicitness? "Her sisters came, two of them, and extra local women to help with the housework. There were women going up and down the stairs all the time, whispering. "I'd never want to get married if there was much of that going on."

This time she did laugh outright. "But why would there be? It doesn't often happen."

"Oh, I don't know," he said cautiously. "Women feel differently about these things. They revel in it, if you ask me."

"Not all of them!" she protested. "Not me."

"Not you, maybe," he agreed absently. "But then, you're not like other girls. I never met a girl like you before. By the way," he said, "you said something about Summerhill the other day. That's very near where I live. How do you know it so well?"

"I live there," she said. "Near there, anyway, about a mile outside the village."

"But I thought you said you lived in that house in Leeson Street." He looked so confused she felt like laughing.

"No. I've got a flat there, but I only stay there on week days. Like you I go home every Friday too."

He stared at her. "I might have known!" he said then.

She laughed outright. "Thank you. I take it that's a compliment?" They had reached where she lived. "Oh, look at our tree!" she exclaimed. Only a week had passed since they'd looked up at it for the first time together, but the green buds that had looked as if they'd rained upon the branches were now as big as birds.

"They're as big as birds!" he exclaimed, exactly as if he had read her mind. "You'd think if you clapped your hands they'd rise up and fly away."

Oh, but if those buds were birds, not for anything would she clap her hands. Ordinary as the moment was, she wanted to prolong it as long as possible, and with it the new delicate delight it held for her. But even while she held her breath, the magic went, and without looking down she knew that his attention had been taken by something else. "I must ask you to excuse me," he said abruptly. "I forgot I had promised to meet someone tonight."

She didn't need to look to know it was another girl, but she didn't expect the girl who was waiting impatiently for him on the other side of the street to be so striking, tall like him, and with a strong but perfect face.

But as the girl impatiently stepped off the pavement and came across the street to meet him, it was her eyes that held attention. What word would describe them? The only word that came to mind hardly made sense, but it fitted exactly, they were ranging eyes. She felt she was never going to see him again.

On the following Monday evening however, when she went to the library, he was there, although he didn't seem to see her. She sat down and tried to concentrate. It was a fine evening, and on the dome overhead, still daylit and blue, a few pigeons paraded. They could be very distracting, because although through the frosted glass their bodies were blurred, their pink feet formed patterns exact and clear cut. After a few minutes, one of them caught up a lump of dislodged masonry with his pink toes and clinked it against the glass. Lifting it, he let it drop again, and then repeated the performance and it was soon apparent that this noise would be kept up as long as there was light in the sky. One or two people tittered. One or two frowned.

Almost immediately, Andrew Gill stood up and came over to her. "I can't settle down with that wretched bird," he said. "How about you? Will we go?"

He wants to talk about that girl, she thought, and I don't want to hear about her. All the same she got up and went with him. Hoping perhaps to forestall his confidences, she was the first to speak when they were out of the Reading Room. "Did you enjoy the weekend?" she asked.

"Oh, I didn't go home," he said.

That girl, of course! She was sure this had something to do with her. "Why?" she asked, in a small voice, but evidently she was wrong.

"Family reasons," he said, almost as if she should have known. "I'll tell you when we get outside," he added.

"I thought it had something to do with that girl you met the other night," she said, before she realised she was giving something away.

"Olive?" He looked surprised. "Why would I stay in Dublin for her?" His words were so impersonal, as was his voice, and even the expression on his face, that her heart lifted, and she didn't mind his next words in the least, although they were all in praise of the girl. "You saw her? Isn't she very striking? And she's brilliantly clever. She's been qualified a year, and she's younger than me. What did you think of her?" Before she could answer, he lowered his voice and went on. "She's very strange, though," he said. "I know her fairly well. I met her last summer in London. I was over there with the Debating Society, expenses paid, of course, and I stayed on a few days with a chap I know who has a room in Chelsea. I ran into her in the King's Road one afternoon. I recognized her at once from law lectures. Who wouldn't recognise a face like that. I didn't expect her to know me. Our eyes met, though, and she stopped. We talked for a few minutes, and I thought I ought to ask her to have a cup of tea. I didn't expect she'd accept, but she did, and would you believe it, we weren't halfway through the tea when she asked me for a loan. Can you imagine that?"

"Did you give it to her?"

"You don't know how much she wanted, or you wouldn't ask that," he said. "Thirty pounds! I don't suppose I had thirty shillings in my pocket at the time."

"Did she tell you what she wanted it for?"

"No. And I didn't ask. I felt safer not knowing. You feel kind of responsible for people from home when you meet them in a strange city, don't you think? But I knew that I wasn't the only one to whom she could turn because she mentioned a medical student we both knew, and mentioned that she was meeting him that night. Convery was his name. I always thought him a nice fellow, although I didn't know him well. He'd failed his finals, she said, and she seemed upset about it, so I felt they must know each other fairly well. Oddly enough I ran into the two of them again that evening, I mean I saw them. They didn't see me. It was in a restaurant in Soho, one of those places where there's a small space for dancing. They were so taken up with each other they didn't see anyone. He was leaning across the table and whispering in her ear, but when I looked closer I saw there were tears in her eyes. I felt very sorry that I couldn't help her. And I think she knew I was sincere in that, because when we were both back in Dublin she looked me up. And she's been looking me up ever since, off and on, and asking me to meet her, like the other evening when you saw her. It's hard to know what she wants from me, though. She never stays long with me. She's very restless. But yet there are times when she rings me up and says she simply must see me or she'll go mad."

"What about the other fellow?"

"Oh, he's back in Dublin, too. He did his finals again but he barely scraped a pass. I think he's not practising either. I don't know why."

"Are they seeing each other still?" She hesitated. "What I mean is that she must have some interest in you, in spite of what you said about the other fellow."

Andrew gave a laugh. "Not at all." But he must have seen she wasn't satisfied. "Look here," he said: "there's something I didn't tell you. I was only told it myself in confidence."

"Oh, why tell me? It has nothing to do with me," she said coldly.

"But I'd like to tell you. I wish I could." He frowned. "But it's a bit of a responsibility having someone's confidence in a matter that's very intimate. I probably will tell you some time. Not now, though," he said, dismissing the topic. "There's something else I want to talk about tonight, if you don't mind?" They had reached the bottom of Leeson Street and were walking slowly. "It's about my weekends. I'd like your advice," he said gravely. "My brother was up in town this afternoon. My sister-in-law has been in bed again, and this time they had another doctor, not the local doctor, but one down from Dublin, a woman's doctor."

"A gynaecologist, you mean," she said.

"Yes," he said humbly, as if he knew that she found his approach to this topic irritatingly naive. "She has to stay in bed for several weeks. It's too bad, really. That's what I wanted to ask you about. Do you think it would be all right for me to continue to go down there?"

Her first impulse was to urge him to go, but she hesitated, thinking that his embarrassment might come from something in his experience she didn't understand. Then, overcome by a sudden impulse, she heard herself utter the most astonishing words. "Why don't you come down to us for this weekend?"

He stared at her in amazement.

"Well, why not?" she said. "You'd get away from Dublin, and it would give them a bit of privacy."

"Wouldn't your people mind?" he asked after a pause.

"Oh, there's only my father," she said offhandedly, "and he likes having people about."

Clearly, he himself didn't come from gregarious stock. "Does your father shoot?" he asked after another pause.

She saw that the answer to this would be of great importance to him.

"Only rabbits I'm afraid," she said smiling.

But even rabbits seemed to put things on a better basis. "How would I get down?" he said cautiously.

"Oh, there are several buses," she said, trying to give an impression of carelessness, though it was of vital importance to her now that he come, if only to prove he had not thought the invitation outrageous. She felt like holding her breath, in case one breath might scare him away. But she couldn't hold it forever. "I think there are plover in the fields," she said timidly.

"Golden plover?" he asked eagerly.

"Are there different kinds?"

"You don't mean to say you don't know the difference?"

"Are they a bit like magpies?" she asked cautiously.

"Oh no, that's green plover, the common sort! They're easy enough to find in most places. They make quite good shooting, though," he added hastily, but she saw he was disappointed.

"Last Sunday, I saw a pheasant," she said.

"On your own land?" he asked eagerly. "A hen?"

"I think so. Yes, it was a hen, of course, the duller of the two, isn't it?"

"I should think so," he said. "You can't mistake the male at this time of year. They get so daring coming up to the close season. You can see every feather, not just the mottle on the body but the ring of white feathers around the neck, and even the fiery rim of feathers about the eyes."

But she interrupted him. "They're not feathers, that red rim about the eyes. Surely that's skin or inflamed flesh?"

He was so taken by surprise, he stared vacantly for a moment. "You're right," he said then. "You're absolutely right. But how did you know that?"

"I've seen them in the poulterer's," she said, so apologetically that he threw back his head and gave a loud laugh.

"Well, will you come?" she cried, quick on the laugh, taking him a bit off guard. "The bus gets to the gate about eight, but if I'm not there to meet you, it will still be light enough for you to make your way up to the house."

"It's very kind of you, I must," he said after a minute, and she knew he had capitulated.

"Well, I'll see you then," she said, to show it was settled, although she hoped to see him again before then.

When several evenings passed and she did not see him, she got uneasy. On Thursday evening, she felt certain he'd be in the library, but as she went up the library steps she saw, not him, but that girl Olive! Immediately she was unhappy, although she went into the library and tried to forget her. When a short time afterwards, however, Andrew came in, she knew at once that something was wrong. He looked around the room and came straight to her desk.

"Must you study tonight?" he asked abruptly. "I'd like to talk to you about the weekend."

"You're not coming?"

"How did you know?" he asked in surprise.

She got up, and they went out together.

"I was coming," he said as they went down the stairs.

"I know! Till you met that girl!" she cried. "I saw her on the steps when I was coming in."

He looked unhappy. "She didn't say anything, she was just surprised," he said. "She hadn't realised we knew each other so well."

"And what did you say?"

"I told her the truth," he said simply. "I said we didn't know each other well at all, but that you lived in the country and knew I'd be glad of a chance to get out of Dublin."

"What did she say to that?"

"She only shrugged her shoulders and walked away. She's like that. She wanted to talk to me about something and I suppose she was disappointed. She'd begun to count on being able to confide in me."

Vera pondered this for a minute. "Are you sure she isn't interested in you?" she said then, very slowly and carefully.

"Not in the least," he said stoutly. "Do you remember I said there was something about her I hadn't told you? Well, I'm going to tell you now. I feel differently about it since she interfered in my affairs. She's married. She's married to that fellow I saw her with in London. They were married even then, but I didn't know it!"

"I don't understand."

"They don't live with each other, by the way. There's some reason, his mother doesn't know about the marriage, or something like that, but that's not the real reason. They have some awful effect on each other, she says. The minute they're together, they quarrel. It's happening all the time, and yet when they're apart they're miserable too. She says it's like a curse on them, whatever she means by that." An unhappy look came over his own face at the thought of it. "What do you make of it?" he asked. "I wanted to tell you ever since I met you. I wanted to talk it over with you, and see what you'd say. What do you make of it?"

"I told you I just don't understand."

"Nor me!" he said.

"Well, then!" she cried suddenly. "If *we* can't understand them, how could *she* possibly understand us? I don't think she should have said anything to you, about me, I mean."

"Neither do I!" he said firmly, but he was still troubled about something. "Apart from that, though, perhaps I ought not to go home with you tomorrow anyway, for other reasons. I've been seeing a lot of you. For a person of my disposition, I mean," he added when she raised her eyebrows. "You see. I've never enjoyed talking to anyone as much as I've enjoyed talking to you, or not for years. Not since I used to go out with my brother all day long on the bog."

"Is that the brother who's married now?"

"No—a younger brother. He died."

"Oh, I'm sorry," she murmured.

"It's all right. I don't mind now. I've got over it. I was only explaining that being with you was the nearest thing I've ever known to being with him. But I suppose I've been foolish, and there is a difference. This friendship might easily turn into something else."

"And what harm if it did?" she said boldly.

"Oh, but we wouldn't want that to happen, would we?" he said with great concern. "It would spoil everything." He looked genuinely distressed. "You wouldn't want it, would you?"

"I don't know," she said prudently. "But if it did turn into something else, I don't see how it could matter, as long as we both felt the same way about it, as we do about the way we feel now."

He was listening very carefully. "I suppose so," he said. "I'm certain we'd never feel differently about anything. I can't imagine us ever disagreeing," he said confidently.

"Even about Dublin?" she said pertly.

He laughed at that.

"Well, then, why worry?" she said.

"You mean I ought to go down to your place as we arranged?" he said.

"I do," she said decisively.

"And I will," he said, equally strongly, and so loudly that a lady in the street stared in disapproval. "After all, tomorrow may never come."

"That's true," she said, but a small guilty feeling stole into her heart, as if somehow she had taken advantage of him. Because she had felt that not only would tomorrow come but other tomorrows, and that one day they'd get married. And the responsibility would be hers. It rested with her at that very moment.

He, however, was concerned only with the weekend. "Well, is it settled?" he asked. And when she nodded, he smiled. "Aren't we lucky? That we can talk over things, even an awkward matter like that, and not—"

"I know," She nodded, without letting him finish.

"How is it Olive and Convery are so different from us," he said.

"It's the kind of people they are, I suppose," she said cautiously "We've kept ourselves free of each other, and that will give us a right of choice in the future."

"I know, I know," he said, and he looked very sagacious. "They let themselves be caught up blindly in some sort of . . ."

"Almost its prey," she suggested.

"Yes, yes!" he said. "They put themselves at the mercy of some force outside themselves, I'd say." They walked on silently for a little way. "That's it!" he said with satisfaction, and then he looked at his watch. "Look here, it's early yet, couldn't we have a cup of coffee before I see you home?"

"That would be nice," she said. They turned back towards the city. But she was still thinking of the others. "It must be awful for them," she said.

"Simply awful," he said, measuring his step carefully to hers. "I often think about them, about him in particular. It must be terrible to have made a mess of things like that at the begining of your life. How can he hope to make a success of his profession with all that strain and tension in his private life."

"It must be anguish for them," she said, out loud. But as she said the word, its meaning, which she would have thought immutable, began to change and take on strange inflections that were not all of pain. There seemed even to be implications in it of something like exultation. And again she felt a strange sense of guilt towards him. She glanced at him. I'll never make him suffer, she vowed to herself.

But it was absurd. Had he not said himself that they were a lucky pair?

Heart of Gold

"That," said Lucy, "that is something I cannot remember." She knew they would not believe her, but she didn't care.

"Was it the first night he came back to see you?"

Lucy only smiled enigmatically. What they all wanted to know, specially her nieces and nephews, was when exactly Sam had proposed to her. That it was scandalously soon after Sam's first wife died—poor Mona—they already knew. The whole town knew for that matter. Tongues had begun to wag within minutes of his stepping out of the Dublin train and everyone had guessed he had come back to her after all the years. A lot of people maintained he would, but nobody dreamt he'd come so soon, and Lucy sensed disapproval in some quarters.

Dear Sam. Lucy couldn't understand why people didn't give him credit for so faithful a heart. Only the young had seen his love in its true light and responded to the romance of it. And that was why she would not have minded them knowing, the young people, knowing that Sam had indeed declared his intentions on that first night of all, that he had hardly stepped inside the door when he had broached marriage. But she couldn't tell them, dearly as she would like to have done because of course she had Sam's character to consider. And, as well as that a certain respect had to be shown towards the dead. Although, mind you, Lucy told herself, her own sisters had not shown much respect. The very day Mona died, Louise and Bay, the only two of the family who lived in the town had come running down the street screeching like oracles.

She was in the yard at the back of the house, which Louise and Bay still called the garden, although the real garden had long gone to glory. A large portion of it at the end, most of it indeed, had been compulsorily acquired by the town council when they were widening the main street which was behind their house. All Lucy had for a garden were some plants in tubs, but they in no time at all flourished and spread like wildfire until in no time at all they had covered up every unsightly thing in the place, the tin roof of the fuel shed, the walls to either side and above all the cast off rubbish of two generations.

"I'm out here in the back-yard," she said when she heard them calling her name. They ran out to her, yes, ran. She hadn't seen either of them run in years.

"Lucy! Did you hear!" they cried. "Sam's wife is dead."

"Oh, no!" she said, and she sank back against a bushy mass of jasmine. Like a living creature, it gave way at the shock of her weight, then braced to take it. "Not Mona Hendron?" A minute too late, she realised she had used Mona's maiden name.

Louise didn't miss the significance of that. "Take care!" she said. "You may find him at the door one of these days to see if you'll have him back."

"Oh, don't be silly, Louise," Lucy said, taking this for a compliment and feeling it should be disclaimed.

But Louise had not meant it for a compliment. "He'd be just the kind of old fool to do something like that," she said. "Why didn't you marry him, anyway when he was young. You never really told us."

Lucy bridled. "Why didn't I marry any of them if it goes to that?" she said coldly. "He wasn't the only pebble on the beach." It was a well enough established fact, and Louise and Bay had no business to forget it, that her beaux had been legion. Even those who had not known her in the old days had only to look at her now to believe in her legend. Louise and Bay seemed to forget how sought after she had been. Even now they were implying that Sam had been the only real string to her bow, she who went everywhere with a crowd of admirers circling around her.

Not that she ever took joy in her nimbus. She was forever shooing men away like wasps. But it only made them pester her all the more. At dances she was continually being waylaid behind some potted palm or Chinese screen. It got very tiresome, a fact that Louise and Bay never believed. They rarely gave her any sympathy, even after they were married themselves and when she—now she could face it—when she had been left behind by the tide. The fact was that Sam was the only one she might have married, because only with him did she feel friendly and at ease. Indeed, they were very modern in the way they took things for granted about each other. The trouble was that they sometimes took the wrong things for granted. Or Sam did. He assumed that she'd never marry him. He never asked her reason.

It was Sam she told about her first and premature proposal at sixteen. They were coming home from school with their satchels on their backs when she told him. He nearly doubled up with laughing. They had to put down their satchels till they got their breath back, they laughed so much. In the years that followed, Sam was a party to many a laugh of the same sort. He was almost as quick as herself to spot when some poor fellow was about to fall for her, some newcomer to the town, a bank clerk, or a solicitor's apprentice, or maybe just a visitor in the hotel. "Poor fellow!" he'd say. "Poor fellow. Another case of Lucyitis!" He was never mistaken about these prospective suitors, only about the outcome of their suit. "Take care, Lucy," he'd say each time. "This one will sweep you off your feet." He never learned to take her treatment of one as an indication of how she'd treat the next. And when at last it became clear that she gave them all short shrift, Sam being timid and humble, took it as a guarantee, that he had no chance at all.

Then when he was the last man on the scene and she had reached her thirtieth year, he surprised her one evening. "What are you waiting for anyway, Lucy?" he asked out of the blue.

"For you, Sam," she said promptly.

"Don't joke with me," he said soberly. "I know I have no hope."

"You have as good a chance as anyone," she said. And then, cautiously, she decided to give him a hint of certain misgivings. "Matrimony doesn't appeal to me," she said, "much less maternity." For a minute she thought she had uncovered her fears of childbirth, but she hadn't really disclosed anything, and so he didn't believe her.

He'd bent his head. "I envy fellows that are married," he said.

It was the first time she'd realised that, living alone in a room in the Central Hotel, he might well long for a home of his own, but she was impatient with him for not seeing what it was that held her back.

"Why are you single so?" she'd cried.

"Because of you, Lucy," he said. "I'd stay single forever if I could be sure you would. But you might walk off one day and leave me in the lurch."

"I'd never do that," she'd said. "We might be an old Darby and Joan yet. I wouldn't mind that at all." Then, thinking she'd been very meaningful, she ran off, laughing and happy. Next time, she thought, she'd give him a broader hint.

But there was no next time. Lucy was hardly awake next morning when her sisters came into the room. "Did you hear what's being said, Lucy?" they cried. "It's all over the town that Sam Lowndes is engaged. To Mona Hendron! It can't be true, can it?"

Never! she thought. Never! But she wasn't going to let herself down before them, "Why shouldn't it be?" she'd said coldly. Yet she sprang out of bed, and in a few minutes she had left the house and gone uptown in the direction of the Central Hotel.

Before she got halfway, however, coming towards her, hurrying, with his head down, was Sam. "Oh, Lucy, I was coming down to see you," he'd said.

"Is it true?" she'd cried.

That he didn't ask what she meant was the first sign she got that there was truth in what she'd heard. He looked frightened, too, or was he only unusually excited? "Is there talk, Lucy?" he asked anxiously.

"Talk! It's all over the town that you're engaged to Mona Hendron," she said, blurting it out.

What did she expect? Certainly not what he'd said.

"She was right so. I thought she was only having me on. I was going to come back and tell you last night, only it was very late. You see, Lucy, it was after I left you it happened." He looked away. "Isn't it strange how things do happen," he'd said dazedly. "It was because I thought I saw you looking at my collar, and I knew it was frayed, so I went in to Simmons' drapery to buy a new one before the shop closed. And to think I never bought it!" He'd put up his hand to the collar, which indeed was very frayed, and soiled as well. "She was there inside the counter." He gulped. "Mona," he said. "She was showing something to a young one that was buying ribbon. They were laughing. Then, when the young one went out, Mona came over to serve me. "Did you ever see one of these, Sam?" she said, and she had a card in her hand. It was a card cut in the shape of a hand, and it had nine or ten round holes in it. Each hole had a number. A ring card, she called it. Did you ever see one, Lucy?"

"Of course I did," she snapped. "For taking the measure of a girl's ring finger!"

"That's right," he'd seemed surprised that she knew. "I never saw one till then. That's why I took it up in my hand." He shook his head. "That's where I made my mistake. I see now it was stupid of me, but I held it out and asked her to show me how it worked. She started to put her finger into the little holes, one after the other, till she came to the one that was right for her. "That's my fit now," she said, and she laughed and held up her finger with the card dangling from it."

When he came to this point of his story, Sam had been overcome. "Oh, Lucy, wasn't I unfortunate!" he'd cried. "At that minute, the door opened and two young women came into the shop. I only knew them by sight, but Mona knew them well. One was the manageress of the Railway Hotel. It appears that two worse gossips you couldn't have found. 'They'll have it all over the town we're engaged, Sam,' said Mona when they went out."

"You didn't believe her?"

"Well, I did and I didn't," he'd said miserably. "She was very upset. She began to cry."

A tremendous relief had come over Lucy. She began to laugh.

But Sam didn't laugh. "Oh, it's not funny, Lucy," he said. "She could be compromised. She said those wouldn't rest till they'd spread the story all over the town."

"Ah, for heaven's sake!" she'd cried impatiently. "Who'd believe a story like that?"

"Didn't you believe it, Lucy?" he'd said dolefully. "And if you did, what can we expect from other people? I'm afraid I've put myself in a very tight corner," he said, taking out his handkerchief and wiping his forehead.

She'd stared at him. "You don't mean to say you'd contemplate—?" But she couldn't trust herself to utter the word "marriage". "That you'd contemplate going ahead with this nonsense?"

For a minute he said nothing. "I wouldn't want to do anything dishonourable, Lucy," he said.

"Nonsense Sam. Everybody knows you are a man of honour." It had been on the point of her tongue to add that everyone knew it was with her he was in love. But she swallowed the words. "If you ask me," she said, "it looks as if she was out from the start to catch you."

"Oh, hush, hush, Lucy," he said. "She didn't think anyone would come into the shop. It was nearly closing time. I didn't bother to buy the shirt. Instead I said I'd give her a hand with putting up the shutters. She has too much to do in that shop, I often thought that. And she's not very strong, either, I'd say."

"Well, she doesn't look delicate to me!" Lucy'd cried. Was he in the habit of helping with those shutters, she wondered.

But Sam was scrupulously considering her remark. "Oh, I don't mean she's delicate," he said. "Just not strong."

There was a long pause. "Ah, well, what does that matter, one way or another, to you, I mean?" she said at last, in a low voice.

"Oh, it could matter a lot," he said meditatively, "later on."

To her utter amazement, she realised that he was thinking of marriage. "Well, it seems she has no fears for herself in that respect if she's so determined to get a man," she said vindictively.

"Oh, don't be hard, Lucy," he said. "After all, it's a natural instinct in a woman. And there's another thing. I think maybe she's had a soft spot for me for a long time past."

"And that would excuse her, I suppose?"

This time, he didn't notice the bitterness. "She's a very decent girl," he added quickly. "A man could do worse."

In the face of that, how could she have said anything other than she did. "Good luck to her so!" she said. "And you, too! I wish you joy of each other." And she'd turned on her heel and gone into the house.

"Well!" said Louise and Bay, who had seen them through the gable window and come rushing to meet her.

"It's true," she'd said. "He's just told me."

And so, in a way, it was she who had put the seal on their engagement. What was more, for all her high spirits and her shining looks, from that moment she took a back seat in life. The strange thing was, though, that on the day Mona died it seemed that she'd been given back, in an instant, her lost role. She was once more what she had been, a romantic figure, tantalising, unpredictable. And now, with her nieces and nephews growing up around, she had a larger audience than ever. Clearly, this renewal of her affair with Sam had them all on tenterhooks.

"You wouldn't think of marrying him, Lucy?" her sisters cried in consternation.

They didn't seem to give a thought to her age. Not even the nieces and nephews. It was of Sam they were doubtful. "He must be an old fellow by now, Aunt Lucy," they said.

"He's the same age as me," she said dryly.

"But when did you see him last?" they persisted.

"Not for years," she admitted, and she laughed. "He may be bald for all I know." She was determined to take everything in good part. "Would you like to see a picture of him?" she asked, remembering an old faded photo that had been taken on an outing of the Temperance Society. They were all in it, herself, and Louise, and Bay, and several others, or course, too, and, in the middle of them, Sam. She hadn't looked at it for years. "How young we all were!" she exclaimed, glancing at it before showing it to them.

But the young people were looking at the clothes, not at the faces. The clothes look a million years old. "Which is Sam?" they asked.

"In the middle." She pointed to him.

They looked closer. "Oh, Aunt Lucy, I thought you were joking. He is bald."

That annoyed her a bit. "How could he be bald then? He was very young at the time."

"His hair must have been awfully fine, if so," one of them said, peering.

"It was very, very fine," she said, trying to be patient. "It was as soft as a child's."

"Oh, Aunt Lucy, you're blushing," they squealed. "Aunt Lucy's blushing."

It would have been just like the old days, the teasing and the innuendoes, if Louise hadn't damped them down. "I must say this conversation is in very bad taste," she said. "His wife is only a week dead."

Involuntarily, Lucy corrected her. "Two weeks," she said.

The young people giggled.

Louise glared. "Don't tell me you are counting the days!" she said.

It was only then Lucy realised that it wasn't at all the same as in the old days. Of course, her family didn't know the full story. They didn't know how Sam had been tricked into that first marriage. She'd never told a living soul. She was just about to tell them then when it occurred to her that it would be a betrayal of him. Already, her loyalties had begun to engage her less to them than to him.

If anything were to crop up again between Sam and herself, it would hardly suit Louise and Bay. Better for them to have her there, where she always was, in the old home. The house was hers, of course, by her mother's will, as the sole surviving single one of the family, so it would go to them when she died. But what was it worth? Nothing. Riddled with woodworm and flaking with dry rot, it wouldn't fetch a penny if it were to be sold. On the other hand, the site might well become very valuable in time to come. At some future date, they or their children might benefit from what she now had to preserve at such cost. Only for her, it would have fallen down long ago. It wasn't just the upkeep and maintenance but she'd paid the rates and taxes as well. And meanwhile they came and went as they pleased. Bay and Louise ran in and out as if they'd never left home. To observe the fomalities never occurred to them. It was the same with the rest. Even the ones that had left the town came back occasionally for their holidays, or spend a weekend. And as for their children! It has been a regular holiday home for those children: so safe, and free of charge. And when they grew up, the children, too, made their own of the house. Such an excellent place to study, quiet, dull. Such an excellent place to recuperate after an illness or an operation. A regular nursing-home, that's what it was on occasion, somewhere to put up their feet, with someone to dance attendance upon them. Selfish to the core, every one of them. But she'd never really seen this clearly until the matter of Sam arose. What she found contemptible was that they should begin their campaign against him so far in advance of events. For although she, too, thought it likely that Sam might come back to her, it did not cross her mind that he would make a move until Mona was a year dead, or until the year was nearly out.

But one night two weeks later, when there was a knock on her door, she knew it was him. She had the house to herself for once. Not that that made much difference, it might as well have had walls of glass from the way Louise and Bay knew all that went on in it. Indeed, within five minutes of his stepping off the train they knew about it. And, he had no sooner stepped out again to catch the train back, than the lot of them were down on top of her. Had they no shame?

That, however, was what they were saying about her. "No shame, no shame at all," they intoned as they came in the door.

"What are you talking about?" she cried. "What more natural than that he would turn to us in his bereavement?"

"To us? To you! He had to pass my house to come here," said Louise.

"And mine!" cried Bay.

"What did he have to say, anyway?" they demanded.

For a minute, she didn't answer. Instead, she walked over to the mirror and stared into it. Aware of them huddled behind her, she stared into the glass. Well, she had more looks left than either of them could lay claim to ever have had at all. With this knowledge, she felt her old power over them returning. And she remembered something. In the old days, they never knew what to make of her, that was what used to drive them mad, and she could still do it. "Wouldn't you like to know!" she said.

"You might have spared a thought for us," they said, "and not set the town by the ears."

"You'd think it was me went up to Dublin to see him," she said.

"That wouldn't have been as bad," Louise and Bay were beside themselves. "He could have written and arranged to meet you somewhere, and not make a laughing-stock of us all."

One of the children had to intervene. "Anyone would think he'd popped the question. He was only feeling his way, isn't that right, Aunt Lucy?"

If they only knew! For when she'd opened the door to him, his first words were an apology, not for his haste but his tardiness. "This was the earliest I could come down, Lucy," he'd said as he stepped inside, and her timid expression of sympathy was immediately absorbed into his own exclamations, as he took off his coat and hat and laid them on top of the piano. "A terrible thing, death! A terrible thing, Lucy," he said. "It leaves the living half dead, too. I was sick, actually sick, would you believe that, on the day she was taken to the chapel, let alone on the day of the funeral. The confusion! You've no idea what it was like. We had a good maid, fortunately, a very decent girl, too; she couldn't have felt it more if she was one of the family, but that only made matters worse, because whenever she came across something belonging to Mona she started to scream and cry. She hasn't got over it yet, indeed. She misses her a great deal, because although she's a great worker, she's lost without someone to tell her what to do. Too slow! no method! Do you know what time I got my lunch today? Three o'clock. It's a wonder I caught the train this evening. I've been trying to get down all week." The ease and familiarity with which he ran on was amazing. There was no constraint between them. "You're looking well, Lucy," he said practically, as he sat down. And then, without putting a tooth in it, he gave his reason for coming. "I'm not going to let you slip a second time, you know."

It seemed only proper to pretend she didn't understand, but he caught her eye, and she felt her face redden.

He looked at her fondly. "We can't afford to misunderstand one another again, Lucy. We haven't the whole of life before us, now, that we can be prodigal of it."

It was so true she was disarmed. "All the same," she murmured, "It's very soon to talk about it."

He stood up and moved nearer to her. "What's the difference between talking about it and thinking about it?" he said softly. "You never ceased to have your niche in my heart, Lucy. You must know that. I never pretended otherwise to anyone. And what more natural than that my thoughts would turn to you, run to you, when I was free again. To whom else would I turn? Aren't you nearer to me now than any living soul?"

It was what she felt herself, and yet she was troubled by feelings of sadness and regret. "Oh, Sam, if we could be young again."

But he shook his head. "This was the way it was ordained," he said, and somehow instantly the words, though trite, put everything into perspective. The years between past and present were reduced to scale at last, and his marriage to Mona put in its proper place, a mere incident in his romance with herself. "Oh, Lucy. Oh, Lucy," he said. "We need happiness more now than we needed it when we were young."

That was true, too. So true.

"Be kind to me Lucy," he said, almost in a whisper. "I need kindness badly."

"Oh, Sam," she said tenderly, as if it was her heart and not her voice that spoke.

"It's yes?" he cried, and he took her hand in a clasp that was gentle but experienced, and she felt that any effort to withdraw it would be hopelessly inadequate. He sensed her reluctance, though. "Still afraid to take the plunge, dear?" he said softly. "There's nothing to be timid about. I'm an old hand at the game now, and even if I do say it myself, if I made one woman happy, I don't see why I shouldn't do the same again. Well?" he said.

Lucy's head reeled. She had to gain time. "I never offered you any refreshment after your journey, Sam," she said, making a move towards the door. "You'll have a cup of tea, or something?"

With one hand he still detained her, but with the other he managed to pull out his watch. It was the same old-fashioned turnip type he'd always had. "I won't have time," he said. "I'll have to be leaving for the station in a few minutes. Next time, I'll try and get down earlier. I had only one purpose on this occasion. Quickly! Tell me, Lucy! Are you going to make me a happy man?"

"But you say you'll come down again, Sam. Can't we talk about it the next time?"

His big silver timepiece might be the same, but Sam himself had changed. His watch and his mouth clicked shut with the same finality. "I'm not asking you to name the day," he said. "Only to give me your promise."

Since she still presumed there wouldn't be any question of marrying until the year was out, she might have agreed there and then were it not for a silly scruple. If she gave her promise, might he not think fit to kiss her? And would that be seemly?

But he'd whipped out his watch again. "Let me decide for us both," he said. "There's no time to be lost." And then, as she thought he would, he leaned forward and kissed her. It was, however, the quickest of kisses. It wouldn't disturb a mouse. "It's settled," he said, and he snatched up his hat. "I must make tracks."

Well! After he'd gone, she leaned back against the hall stand, and her impulse was to giggle like a girl, not knowing that her sisters were already on their way down the street, about to break in on her with their strictures.

Not that she heeded them. On the contrary, their concern for themselves was so great it had made any concern for them on her part utterly superfluous. She need consider only herself and, of course, Sam, as on his next visit she told him. "I don't mind what the family say, Sam. It's not of them I'm thinking. After all, they cannot say much if we wait till the year is out." As Sam seemed about to interrupt her, she put up her hand. She had other scruples. "Wait a minute, Sam," she said. "Let me explain. I'm not upset by what anyone might say." She hesitated when it came to the point, she just couldn't tell him.

But he knew. "It's of Mona you're thinking, isn't it?" he asked gently.

Gratefully, she nodded her head.

"Listen, Lucy," he said kindly but carefully. "Listen to me. Mona would be the first to understand. She would be the first to want me to be happy, happy and well cared for. Do you know what I was thinking today while I was waiting for my meal to be served up to me?" As he saw the sympathetic inquiry in her eye, he broke off to answer it. "Oh, indeed yes, the same story. It was after three when I got it. And if you saw it when it was put in front of me." He shuddered. "Uneatable! The poor girl does her best, but she lacks direction. She can't be blamed. But what's this I was saying? Oh, yes. I was saying that while I was sitting there waiting for my meal to be dished up, and knowing well how unappetising it would be, ice cold, the chop stuck to the plate, I thought to myself that it would break Mona's heart if she could see me. And do you know what else I thought, Lucy? I thought that Heaven couldn't be Heaven for her if she were able to look down at me in that moment." He closed his eyes. Then, opening them wide, he looked bravely on a new day of thought. "God surely spares them such sights," he said.

It was certainly comforting to think so. All the same, she felt guilty, and she said so. "I can't help it, Sam," she whispered.

He took her hand. "Guilty for what, Lucy? Is it for the past?"

She felt like laughing. "Oh, no, no," she cried. "For the present. I feel I'm taking you away from her."

"It was God who took her away from me Lucy," he said. He was so wise. "Aren't you only taking me back?"

Gentle, and yet discriminating. How could she but trust him? But he was looking at his watch. It couldn't be time for his train already? "Oh no, no," he said reassuringly. "It's just that time flies, and we have a lot to arrange. First, let me put your mind finally at rest about poor Mona. Let me tell you, Lucy, that she urged me to marry again." He nodded his head and lowered his voice. "She spoke of it just before the end. I won't repeat her exact words. Such things are sacred, but you can rest assured we'd have her blessing on what we are about to do." He closed his eyes again, this time as if in prayer, and when he opened them it was briskly, as one rises from prayer strengthened to take a new command of things. "We have nothing to fear from our consciences," he said. "Tell me about your family. Did I understand you to say when you opened the door that they have been causing you anxiety?"

Although it was really the other way round, Lucy nodded.

She frowned. "They could give a lot of annoyance," he said, "unless, that is to say unless we go about things a clever way."

Thinking there could be no ambiguity in a truism, Lucy agreed happily.

"What we must do," said Sam, "is spring it on them." Then, before she had time to say anything, he snapped his fingers. "Why tell them at all, for that matter. I could have a word with the priest and get things arranged quietly. Then I could slip down the night before on the late train and we could be married as early as possible."

Lucy was speechless. She couldn't say anything, yet distinctly he appeared to be listening.

"Ah, you're right," he said, exactly as if she had spoken. "You're right, Lucy. It wouldn't do. The town is too full of gossips. Our little secret would be common property in five minutes. No, we'll have to think of something else." He pondered for a minute. "You could come up to Dublin and we could be married up there." But almost at once he shook his head. "No, no. That wouldn't do either. You'd want to be married here, in your own parish. It's quite natural. For sentiment's sake if for no other reason. It's different, perhaps, for me, but I'm able to put myself in your place. There will be enough that will be strange to you." He pondered again. "I'll tell you what we'll do," he said, and she had only time to notice in passing that the conditional mood had given way to the future positive. "I will come down on the evening train, but I won't come all the way," and he was so pleased with his little ruse, he winked at her. "I'll get off at a small station somewhere up the line, and in the morning I'll hire a car and come across country just in time for the ceremony. You will only have to walk up the street as if there was nothing at all afoot. And then, before anyone gets wind of it, the deed will be done."

Lucy was stunned. "Do you mean elope?"

"Elope?" It was a word Sam himself hadn't heard for years, but, seeing how it brought a light into Lucy's eyes, he repeated it. "Elope, that's it!" he said.

"And who'd tell my family?" she asked, doubtful in spite of a rising excitement.

"We can tell them ourselves when all is over," Sam said. "There's only Louise and Bay in the town, isn't that all? We can walk around and confront them, beard them in their dens."

Lucy laughed guiltily. "Arm in arm!" she said.

"That's the idea," said Sam. "Let them lump it or like it. And as for the ones in America, well, we needn't think about them. It can't matter to them one way or another, nor the ones in Dublin, either, although they can be told in the same way as the ones down here. We can walk around and call on them that night if it isn't too late when we get there."

"To Dublin? Is that where we'll go?" She'd given no thought at all to the honeymoon. In the old days, honeymoons were mostly spent in Kilkee or Tramore. "Is it to Dublin we'd go?" she repeated.

Sam had given no thought to the matter, either. He was sobered by his omission. "I've taken a lot of time off lately, I'm afraid," he said, "with one thing and another, when Mona was ill, and later for the funeral. I'd find it a bit awkward to ask for more time in so short a space. But wait a minute!" he cried. He really was resourceful. "We're forgetting that it will be all new to you, the house, I mean. The house will be a big change for you after this place. It's a nice little house, snug and dry."

He made it sound so like a nest Lucy had to smile.

"That's my girl!" he said approvingly. "I knew you'd take the right attitude. And let me tell you something. Honeymoons are overrated.

Believe you me! I can give you my solemn assurance on that. What is more, I have yet to meet the married couple that hasn't the same to say. That's one part of the business with which they'd dispense if they had to do it over again. Yes, take it from me, honeymoons are grossly overrated. I have no hesitation at all in asking for your trust on this point, Lucy. None whatever."

"Will I not see it so till, till afterwards, the house, I mean?" she asked timidly, trying hard not to sound doubtful.

"Isn't that best, don't you think?" He was very cheerful. "It's in good order. You've nothing to worry about on that score. You'll have nothing to do but walk in the door. Not only is it fully fitted, fully equipped, but as I'll only be one night gone from it, it will be well aired into the bargain." Remembering that in this respect Lucy did not know what she was being spared, he threw up his eyes in token of some past experience of his own. then he lowered them to rest gently on her. "I can only say that it's no more than we deserve, Lucy, after our long wait, our long, long wait," he repeated sighing. "Lucy, you're not going to make it much longer, are you?"

"Oh, Sam!" He made her feel so dilatory that she looked anxiously at the calendar on the wall behind his back. "Lent begins next month," she said. "We'll have to wait till after that, anyway."

But Sam had whisked the calendar off its nail and was examining it. "Unless we hustle, and get it over before Lent," he said. "I don't see what there is to stop us, do you?"

And so one day in early February, with a bunch of snowdrops pinned to her lapel, Lucy became a bride.

"Let me do that, Lucy. You might strain yourself," admonished Sam, as he took her dressing-case and put it up with the other suitcases on the luggage rack of the train. Doing so, he looked tenderly at her. "It wasn't such an ordeal after all, was it?" he asked, and he leaned across and patted her on the knee. "You look bewildered," he said, and he laughed. "Well, cheer up, love; it's all over now."

Bewildered she was. More than the ceremony seemed to have ended. What, for instance, was she to make of her family's new attitude towards her? Had they got wind of things in advance, that they had taken her news so coolly? What had happened to their fears of a scandal? Above all, what had become of their concern for themselves? Now it was only of her they thought.

"Well, it's your own business, Lucy," said Louise, almost as soon as she'd opened the door to them, when, as planned, she and Sam went round, arm in arm, after the wedding. She hadn't given them time to open their mouths. One look and Louise guessed. Their being together at that hour of the day may have made the telling superfluous, of course. And then there was her bunch of snowdrops. And oh yes, Sam had a snowdrop in his buttonhole.

Bay wasn't surprised, either. "It was more or less what I expected," she said when Louise's youngest had been sent up the street to inform her and bring her down. "Well, I hope you'll be happy," she added.

"Oh, naturally, we all hope that," said Louise.

And later, when Lucy and Sam were in the train and the family was standing on the platform, Bay's parting words were not the most encouraging. "You must make the best of it now," she called out as the train began to slide away from the platform.

"We're off!" cried Sam, and although he urged her to lean out and wave to them, she had barely time to raise her hand before the railway bridge snuffed them out. There was nothing to do after that but settle into her seat. Sam remained standing. Closing the window, he turned his attention to the luggage. "I'll fold our coats and put them on top of the cases, out of the way," he said.

His back was to her. But anyway she hardly heard him. Her mind still echoed with her sister's words. "I hope you know what you're doing." Did she know what she was doing? What had she done? Had she, in her endeavour to hide her intention from others, hidden it in part from herself as well? She stared out the carriage window. The flat fields through which they were travelling were familiar to her still, but field by field they were being flung back to either side as if flung out of existence. "Oh, Sam, did we do right?" she whispered.

Sam's mind, however, was on the overcoats. It was a mistake to have turned them inside out. With their slippy silk linings, they kept sliding off the rack. He had to stand up again and take them down and turn them right side out before he put them back. "That's better," he said contentedly, surveying them once more before he sat down. But he'd heard her. "It's funny you should say that," he said then. "Mona asked me that same question. In the same circumstances, too. But she had cause to ask. Poor Mona! There was a little cloud on her happiness." He sighed.

"A cloud? What was it!" she asked in dismay.

"She was very tenderhearted," said Sam. He made a discreet sign of the cross. On the opposite seat, Lucy felt obliged to do the same. "She was never able to enjoy her own happiness if it cast a shadow over that of someone else."

In the past few weeks, Lucy had heard many references to Mona, but somehow she'd never really thought much about her. For that matter, she hadn't thought about her for years. Sam and Mona were married almost immediately after the bogus episode of the engagement ring, and Lucy had taken care to be away at the time of the wedding; she went to Lisdoonvarna for several weeks, although it wasn't the best time of year for the spa. And when she came back, people had the grace not to speak about them to her. Then perhaps the fact that they had no children made it seem after a time as if they had passed out of existence. But in the train, when Sam spoke of her, Lucy suddenly pictured Mona again, as she must have been on the morning of her wedding trip. It might have been on this same train that they took their departure. It could have been in this very carriage they travelled. Perhaps on this very seat Mona, too, had sat. Suddenly she leaned forward. "Sam, would you like to change places?" she cried.

"But why?" Sam asked.

"Well, some people say it's bad to sit with your back to the engine," she said. "It could make you sick."

Sam was just about to cross his feet contentedly. "Not me," he said. "But I'll change with you all the same if you like."

"Please, Sam," she said faintly.

When they'd changed seats, he looked at her with a worried expression. "Do you feel better now?" he asked. "Mind you, Mona liked to face the engine, too, although I always think it's better to feel sick than to get a cinder in your eye."

"You mean she sat on this side?"

"Yes, always on that side," said Sam amiably, "unless the carriage was crowded. In which case—"

But the train roared through a tunnel just then, and Lucy couldn't hear. What did it matter anyway, she asked herself, and she was prepared to think about something else when they flashed out into the open again. From either side, the green fields rushed towards her, but it was the green fields of life that had rushed towards Mona. It was all very well to say that in the old days Mona couldn't hold a candle to her, but what figure would she cut now if placed by the side of that green, young girl? Fresh apprehensions chilled her, and she forgot that for Sam those early memories of Mona had long been overlaid by others, less exciting. By a strange transference, she began to think of Sam as young and green, too. I must look awful, she thought, putting up her hand nervously to her hair, to her forehead, to her cheek. She hadn't slept well the night before, and she wasn't used to early rising. She must be a sight. She didn't dare look in a mirror.

As if he were a mirror, however, Sam at that moment gave her back her reflection. "You look a bit tired," he said, and he sighed. "Mona failed a lot in late years," he said. "She looked very badly towards the end."

Lucy looked at him fixedly. To talk about Mona was hardly the best cure for her at that moment, but it might be better than thinking about her. "I never saw her again." she said. "Not after—"

She didn't need to finish the sentence. He nodded understandingly. "She was strong enough, you know," he said, easily conversationally. "I used to think she wasn't, but I was wrong. She was able for plenty of hard work. There was no doubt of that. We hadn't much money in the early days, and she worked hard to save every penny. I often went to bed at night and left her downstairs, and do you know what she'd be at? Glazing my collars, or waxing my shoes. I had no control over her when it came to work. But in the end she got pulled down by those pregnancies."

Lucy started.

"Didn't you know?" said Sam, seeing her surprise. "She had four or five miscarriages. She did indeed. And it nearly broke her heart. It was a real cross. She'd have been a good mother, just as she was a good wife, but it was not to be, it seems." He shook his head. "Many a time, I came home from work and found her sitting in the dark, brooding over it. I used to do my best to console her, but it was no use. I used to tell her that she was a mother. Time and time again, I'd tell her that. 'You are a mother, Mona.' That her children never came to full term did not deprive her of that title. But she was inconsolable. You see, Lucy, it wasn't of herself she was thinking but of me." His voice dropped. "The most unselfish of women. Do you know what she said to me one day? She said that if she'd known that she'd never give me a family, she wouldn't have married me at all. Can you imagine anything more unselfish? To think that she could bring herself to wish another woman in her place."

"Oh, she couldn't have meant it, Sam," Lucy protested.

Sam shook his head. "Indeed she did. You've no notion of her depth. And what is more, Lucy, it was you she was thinking about at the time."

That was too much. "Oh, no!" she cried, putting her two hands up to her face. It was one thing to know that she had held her place in his heart. It was another thing altogether for Mona to have known it. "She didn't mention me by name, Sam, did she?"

"Well, maybe not on that occasion," said Sam piously. "She had great delicacy," he added. "But I may as well tell you your name was not unmentioned in our home. She often spoke of you, especially in our early days, because you see, she knew she had only come second with me." He leaned forward. "Ah, yes, Lucy, your name was a household word with us in the early days of our marriage. Indeed, it became a kind of joke in the end. Ah, don't be offended. It was a playful little joke; there was no harm in it. Ah, there was a rare quality in Mona, that she could turn the tragic into the comic. In her place, another woman would surely have nourished bitterness against you, especially when she remembered what you were in those days, because, that's another thing, she was fully aware of how much better-looking you were than her. I often heard her say that beauties like you were no longer to be seen." He shook his head and sighed deeply this time. For a moment, Lucy thought it was for the passing of that beauty he sighed, but it was not. "Ungrudging!" he said. "Generous-hearted! That was Mona!" And to her dismay he took out his handkerchief. But when he unfolded it, it appeared it was only to blow his nose. "Her unselfishness was never more in evidence than at the end," he said then. "When she felt the end was near, it was not of herself but of me she was thinking. She couldn't bear the thought of me being neglected. Do you know, Lucy, one day when I went into the hospital I had a button missing off my waistcoat, and when she saw it the tears ran down her face. 'You can't say but I always had you well turned out, Sam,' she said. 'I can't bear to think you'd ever be otherwise.' It was on that day she made me promise I wouldn't let any thought of her stand in my way if I saw fit to marry again. But I told you that, didn't I?" he asked, suddenly anxious.

Something of the sort he had undoubtedly said, but she certainly had not understood she had been specifically designated by Mona to take her place. It was one thing to think of Mona's benisons vaguely showering down from Heaven; it was quite another to think of her dispensing them from her deathbed. Acquiescence from above seemed right and proper and in keeping with the supernatural state but from a hospital bed it seemed like a subtle accusation. "She didn't really mean me?" she cried.

She looked at him. Was this the constancy to which she had clung? Like the moon, it had two faces: on one side hers, and on the other Mona's. But which to which was shown? If Mona had to live with anecdotes about her, what would it be like for her, Lucy, in a few hours' time, when she'd be boxed up in Mona's house? Suddenly she felt faint. She'd have to get out in the corridor for some air. But she didn't want him to come with her. She got to her feet. "Will you hand me down my small case, Sam," she said. "I think I'll have a wash." That ought to keep him from following her.

But he hadn't thought of doing so, and after he'd put up a hand to assist her he settled back in his seat. "Remind me to tell you something when you come back," he said patiently. "A nice little thought that came into my head."

Impatiently, she stood in the doorway. "Tell me now!"

But he'd taken out his watch and was looking at it, and then he glanced out of the window. "My little plan would depend on what time we arrive in Dublin," he said, "and whether or not there is any daylight left."

Suddenly she knew what was in his mind. "Where is she buried?" she asked, and her voice in her own ears sounded like lead.

But his face lit up, and she saw that he marvelled at her intuition and what he took to be another affinity between them. "You had the same thought? That would mean twice as much to her." But there was a draught from the open door. "We'll talk about it when you return," he said affably, "and I'll tell you a little incident that happened six or seven years ago. You'll find it very touching, I know."

Oh, no, you won't, she thought, as emphatically as if she'd spoken. She got out into the corridor, and almost ran in her anxiety to get far away from him. The train was travelling fast. The noise of the wheels was deafening, and several times she would have been thrown from one side to the other if she hadn't steadied herself against the rattling woodwork, now of a window and now of a door. The train seemed to be crowded, although in their first-class carriage she and Sam had sat in state. But finally she came on a carriage with only one young couple occupying a corner. Not noticing that the floor was strewn with confetti, she was about to take refuge there when, outraged, the man sprang up and slapped the blind down in her face.

Tears rushed into her eyes. But what did it matter where she went? Sam would eventually miss her and come to look for her. If only the train would stop, she could get off? She glanced out of the window. It was getting dark outside, but the fields between the darkening hedges were pale with a thin mist that seeped up from the ground. If the train stopped for even a minute, she could jump down and stumble across the line and lose herself in that bright but concealing mist. She could imagine herself coming to a stand, out of breath, in time to watch the lighted train move forward again without her. She would see the carriages slide past one by one, till in one of them, sitting foolishly waiting, would be Sam. But the train wouldn't stop till it got to its destination. If she wanted to get off, she'd have to throw herself out. Involuntarily, she glanced at the door handle. It was green with verdigris around the stem, but the lever itself shone bright from handling. She'd only have to press it down and the door would fly open. Quickly, she clapped her hands into her pockets as if to save them from some act for which they alone would be responsible. She wasn't as unbalanced as all that. But she had begun to tremble, and the thought of continuing on to the end of the journey was unbearable. And that house! It was unbearable to think of facing into it cluttered with all the paraphernalia of another woman's life.

"I've left everything as it was, Lucy," he'd said. "You'll know better how to dispose of her little possessions than me."

Her little possessions! What did that mean? Presses full of clothes? Chests of drawers stuffed with every kind of rubbish? Boxes, portmanteaux, little cubby-holes here and there filled with God knows what junk. She'd known enough of Mona to guess she'd been a great one for finery and gewgaws of all kinds.

Gewgaws? A frantic thought came to her. Her own wedding ring! Where had Sam got it? During the ceremony, he had clapped it on her finger so fast it was as if he had handcuffed her to him, but it was very thick, thicker than wedding rings were at the present day, and now, looking closer, she saw it had at the same time a worn look. Was it possible that it was not new? She shuddered. And her engagement ring? She'd known it was not new, but she liked antique jewellery, but she remembered being surprised at the alacrity with which he'd produced it the moment he'd broken down her scruples. He'd pulled it out of his pocket, where, loose as a pebble, it had rattled around among his keys and his coins. That, she'd supposed, was why there was dust in the crevices of the setting. She hadn't washed it, because the setting looked so insecure. But now, examining it, too, very closely, she saw that it was grime, not dust, that clogged the claw. Feeling sick, she went to drag the rings off her finger. But they were a tight fit and her fingers swelled when she tugged at them, but she went on trying to drag them off until the skin broke and began to bleed. The sight of the blood steadied her for a minute. Anyway if she were to bare the bone, what difference would it make? For that matter, what difference would it make if she did get the rings off? If she threw them out the window, it would not alter her situation. It would have been to more purpose to have thrown herself out.

Insidiously, when it came again, this thought was less alien. A strange excitement made a vein in her throat throb, and at the same time it seemed that the train was gathering speed crazily, like a train derailed. The rattling carriages careered after each other, but every now and then they veered slightly, as if they would unlock their couplings and fly asunder. If at that moment she were to press the door handle, she knew exactly what would happen. In an instant the door would be dragged out of her hand and clatter back on its hinges, or else be wrenched off them altogether. Caught in a great current of air travelling as fast as the train itself, it might be a long time before the door would land on the tracks, perhaps not until the train had passed and the line was empty and silent again. And what about her? Snatched from her feet, freed from all volition, she, too, would be violently caught up and sucked out into that rushing current. Like a bit of paper, she'd be blown away. She went nearer to the door. Heaven had never been easily imaginable, but it would be heaven to feel those rushing winds sprout like wings from her shoulder-blades to uphold her and bear her through the air. To think that by a single act she might undo her folly and prove herself finally and forever to be what she had always been, a romantic figure.

But in her heart she knew it was too late. She was committed to being real at last. Sam had committed her. It was a long way back to the carriage where he sat, but she'd have to go back. She'd have to stumble along the train till she came to where she'd left him. She'd have to open the door and go in and sit down by his side.

Slowly she began to go back along the corridors. When she came to the compartment occupied by the lovers, she saw that the blind was up. It must have snapped up unnoticed by them. Tired of kissing and indifferent now to gapers, they sat hand in hand, staring in front of them. And although they didn't care this time, she averted her face and hurried on, looking outward to where on the other side of her the fields should have been. But now against the glass only darkness pressed. Like a backing of mercury, it had made the windows into mirrors. And in one of those windows, sitting patiently waiting for her, she saw Sam. He was asleep. He was having a little nap, which wasn't to be wondered at, because Sam was tired and Sam was old.

Poor Sam, she thought, and her heart softened. What if he did meander on about Mona! He'd earned the right to it. He had learned a larger love than she or Mona knew anything about. "Sam," she said, stepping into the carriage.

With a start, he jerked his head up. He had been in a sound sleep, but he spoke immediately, as if out of his thoughts. She didn't at once catch what he said. Does he know which of us it is at all, she wondered, Mona or me? And she tried not to mind. But Sam at that very moment repeated what he had said.

"Poor fellows!" That was what he'd said. "Poor fellows." And she realised with a start that not only was it of her he was thinking, and of the past, but that, in particular, he was thinking of the swains that had swarmed around her in the old days, and whom in the end he had bested. Little did he ever think he'd do it, he who had nothing to recommend him but his heart of gold.

The Cuckoo-spit

Drenched with light under the midsummer moon, the fields were as large as the fields of the sky. Hedges and ditches dissolved in mist, and down by the river the thorn-bushes floated loose like several branches. Tall trees in the middle of the fields streamed on the air, rooted by long, dragging shadows.

Vera stood at the French door, and then the night was so bright she ventured a little way down the garden path. It was a strange night. All that was real and erect had become unreal. The unreal alone had shape. And when close beside her in the long grass a beast stirred, it was only by its shadow she could see where it lay. Unnerved, she turned back to the house. The house, too, had an insubstantial air, its white gable merging in the white of the sky. But on the bright ground its shadow fell black as iron.

It was when she reached the edge of this shadow that the young man stepped out and startled her.

"I thought you saw me," he said defensively. "The night is so bright. I saw you. I was watching you as I was coming across the fields." Then his voice changed. "Are you all right?" he asked anxiously.

"Oh, yes," she said. His concern had already made nonsense of her fright. And in the strong light pouring down she could see him as plain as day, a young man with a kind face, his thin cheekbones splattered with large, flaky freckles. Their eyes met, and they smiled at each other, surprised and happy. "I ought to know you, I am sure," she said, since it was late and he wore no coat.

"I don't think so," he said. "I'm only down here sometimes in summer. I come to stay with an uncle of mine who lives across the river."

"Oh, I know him. Tim Hynes? At least, I know him by name. I never actually met him. My husband used to talk a lot about him."

"I know," The young man nodded. "Tim was very upset by his death. So, of course, was everyone," he added hastily.

"Your uncle more than most, though. I was told he took it very badly. There was something, wasn't there, about his losing interest in the election—not voting at all?"

"That's right. He more or less gave up politics after that."

"I remember I got a wonderful letter from him at the time."

"Tim?" He raised his eyebrows.

Remembering the old man's spelling, Vera herself laughed.

"I never forgot it. Something he said in it. He said it might have been difficult, even for a man like Richard, to save his soul in Dail Eireann."

"That's like a thing he'd say, all right, but I think it could have been to comfort you. Tim had no doubt whatever about the stature of the man we'd lost in your husband."

The plural pronoun caught her attention. "Are you interested in politics, too?" she asked, but she was hardly heeding his reply, she was so surprised at the sudden lessening of her interest in him. All the same, I ought to ask him into the house, she thought, if only for his uncle's sake. Or was it too late?

"Oh, it's far too late," he said. "I didn't intend to call. I was out for a walk, and I'd crossed over the bridge in the village and was going along the bank of the river below here when I saw that the windows were all lighted. To tell you the truth, I came up closer just out of curiosity. I was always fascinated by this house. Then I saw the French door open. Somehow or other, I got a strange feeling that the house was empty. So I came up and I was about to knock when I realised the odd situation I had got myself into, and I didn't know what to do. I was just standing there when I saw you coming back. Do you do that often, go out and leave the door open?"

She turned and looked over her shoulder to where the open door let out a stream of golden light that cut its own shape on the shape of the shadow. "I wasn't far away," she said vaguely.

"That's true," he said. "And it was a lovely night for a walk."

It annoyed her that, having been worried at the start, he was so easily satisfied about her safety. "I shouldn't have left the door open all the same," she said, "but I only meant to walk a little way, just up and down the garden path."

"I know!" he said. "The usual thing! You were tempted to go further."

Again she was irritated by his readiness to put his own interpretation on the situation. "As a matter of fact, there was nothing usual about it," she said. "This is the first time since my husband died that I've set foot outside the house after dark alone, except in the car, of course."

"I don't understand," he said quietly. "What could there possibly be to fear in the heart of the country?"

"That was what Richard used to say. But I wasn't brought up in the country, and that makes a difference. Even when he was alive, I was nervous out-of-doors after dark." She laughed. "I'll tell you something that happened one night. We kept a few hens. They were supposed to be my affair. The henhouse was over there." She pointed to a small triangular field near the house, a small field bounded on three sides by a wood. "I was always forgetting to shut them up at night, and we often had to go out late and do it, but once it was the middle of the night when I woke up and thought of them, and I had to wake Richard, and we had to put on our coats and go out to them."

"Couldn't he have gone alone?"

"Of course not. They were my hens. It wouldn't have been fair to let him go alone."

He shook his head. "He must have been a very patient man."

"But it was a night just like this," she cried.

Immediately, with her words the night seemed to press closer, lapping them round, not just with its mist and moonlight but with its summer smells of new-mown hay and sweet white clover. "We didn't go back to the house at all," she said, remembering that other night with quick and vivid pain. "We stayed out for ages." But suddenly she had an uneasy feeling that she was giving something away about that night, or about herself, or Richard.

There was a little silence.

"Is he long dead?"

"Four years this summer," she said, and turned her face away, although she felt his sympathy would not be so easily stemmed.

"You must miss him very much," he said. "I was thinking that as I was walking in the fields, and looking at the house. I was wondering how you were able to go on living here without him." But he must have felt tactless, or impertinent, because he looked away from her, out over the fields. "It's very beautiful here, of course," he added quickly.

"Tonight, yes," she granted. "This is a night in a thousand,"but she gave a cold glance over the moonlit stretches of which he spoke with such unconcern. Did he not know that there were other nights, when those fields could wear a different aspect?

But he missed the glance she'd given over the lonely fields and turned back to her. "I suppose the more beautiful it is, the more lonely it must be for you."

She looked into his face. "I got over the worst of it long ago," she said harshly. "Do you know what *I* was thinking? *I* was thinking that there is, after all, a kind of peace at last when you face up to life's defeats. It's not a question of getting stronger, as people think, or being better able to bear things; it's that you get weaker and stop trying. I think I couldn't bear anything now, even happiness." She paused. That was true, she thought, and yet she felt she had expressed herself inadequately. "It's just that I've got old, I suppose," she said more simply.

"Don't be silly," he said, but lightly, carelessly.

She sighed. "All the same," she said, "there is a strange peace about knowing that the best in life is gone forever."

"You mean love?"

She nodded. "And youth," she said, but she thought she saw doubt in his eyes. "Aren't they the one thing?"

She was startled by the haggard look that came over his face. "I don't know," he said. "I hope not. God knows I've never had much of either."

"What do you mean? What age are you, anyway?" But before he could answer she realised that she didn't even know his name. "You didn't tell me your name," she said.

"Fergus," he said, giving no surname.

He must be Tim's brother's child, she thought, and again at the thought of her old neighbour across the river she felt she ought to insist on his coming inside, no matter the hour.

"Oh, no, no," he said, actually beginning to move away. "I'm afraid to think how late it must be now."

"Well, perhaps you'll come again," she said formally, but she knew that in this invitation, generosity was not on her side. It was nice to see that he thought otherwise.

"That's very kind of you, Mrs. Traske," he said warmly. "I'd like very much to come." His pleasure was so genuine it added to hers, yet a ridiculous ache had gone through her when he used her surname, although anything else would have been unthinkable from a strange young man, a man years younger than her. Even if they got to know each other well, and he were to call again, and again, she could not imagine that he would call her Vera, ever. It was a name she had never liked. And lately she'd liked it less. At this moment, it seemed utterly unsuitable to her: a name for a young girl. It even seemed to have a strangely venal quality. But he was saying something, and she had to listen.

"I was only saying that I don't suppose you approve of calling people by their first names on a first meeting," he said.

Taken aback by the way their thoughts had run so close together, she hesitated. "Well, it doesn't give much chance for measuring one's progress with people, does it?"

"I never thought of that," he said, and he looked at her, delightedly. "I must remember that." Again he seemed about to go, but again he stopped. "I correct examination papers at this time of year. I may get word any day from my landlady in Dublin to say that they have arrived. I'll have to go back at once then. Would it matter, would you mind, if I came fairly soon? Very soon perhaps?"

"Whenever you like. I'm always here," she said, and then they said good night, and he walked away.

As she went into the house, she wondered if he would come again. She hoped he would; it was a pleasant encounter. And she kept on thinking about it as she went around the house, fastening the windows and locking the door. Even when she went upstairs, she stood for a while at the open window, looking out and going over scraps of their conversation. Some of the things she had said now seemed affected. Had she lost the knack of small talk? In particular, she thought of what she had said about happiness, and not being able now to bear it. That was so absurd, but surely he understood that she meant a certain kind of happiness, possible only to the young. Indeed, it might well be that it was when one let go all hope of ever knowing it again that the heart was emptied and ready for simpler relationships, those without tie, without pain. But when she put out the light and turned back the white counterpane, breaking the skin of light on it, she felt vaguely depressed. Would there not always be something purposeless in such attachments?

Did she expect him to come again? Certainly not the very next evening. And so early. Only a short time before, she was in the garden, weeding and staking plants, working away, without noticing the day had ended. It was by the light of a big yellow moon that she was trying to see what she was doing. It was so low a moon, so close to the ground, and it shed so gold a light that, like the sun, it gilded everything. Unlike the moon of late night, it did not take all colour from the earth but left a flush of purple in the big roses and peonies, and a glow of yellow in their glossy stamens. Yet it was night. The birds were silent; a stillness had settled over the farm. Nervously, she gathered together the rake, the hoe and the spade, but she didn't wait to put them in the tool shed. She hurried towards the house. In the doorway she delayed for a moment. There was a peculiar quality abroad. Was it expectancy? It's in the night, though, and not in me, she thought, but just then, like a high wind falling, the expectancy died down as a step sounded on the gravel.

"You didn't think I'd come so soon, did you?" Fergus said, smiling. "It's even more marvellous than last night, though, and I thought of you not liking to go out at night alone. But you *were* going out?"

"No. Going in," she said.

"Good. I'm glad I came. Get something to put over your shoulders. Hurry!"

In spite of her surprise, she didn't hesitate. "I'll only be a minute," she said, "Won't you come in while you're waiting?"

He shook his head. "Houses weren't built for nights like this."

When she came out, he was standing clear of the shadows of the house, in the full light. "I was telling my uncle about you," he said when she joined him. "He wasn't in bed when I got back last night. He sends you his regards. In fact, he sent you several messages, so many I'm sure I've forgotten the half of them." He smiled at her. "No matter, you can take them as given; they were all compliments and good wishes. And now," he said, surveying the view and taking her arm casually, "which way will we go? Down by the river? Or is the grass too high?"

"We can follow the cowpaths."

"Oh, but the cattle go in single file, and we want to talk," he said, and he linked her more closely. It made her uncomfortable, but she knew that when they crossed over the wooden fence around the house and went into the field in front of it, they would have to unlink. He realised it, too, after a few steps. "It's like wading through water, isn't it?" he said, amazed as the high grass weighted down their feet. "Does it never get eaten down? The place seemed heavily stocked to me as I came along here."

"It would take all the cattle in Ireland to graze it down at this time of year," she said carelessly.

He turned to her with an earnestness that was touching.

"You had courage to keep it when you are so nervous here," he said. "Any other woman would have sold it and gone back to the city."

"That never once entered my mind," she said, remembering how from the first she was aware of the security she drew from this piece of ground. But she saw by his face that he thought she had kept it for the sake of the past.

"I must tell you something," he said. "I nearly wrote you a letter last night after I went away from here. Would you have thought it very odd? The only reason I did not was because I'd have had to come back with it, and I thought that a footstep during the night might frighten you."

"It would have frightened the wits out of me," she said quickly. She did not ask what he would have said in the letter.

"I knew it would," he said. "I'm glad I did not do it. Anyway, I think that you know without my saying it how much meeting you meant to me."

"It was nice for me to meet you, too," she said politely.

"There is nothing rarer in the world than happiness," he said then.

"Happiness? Whose happiness are you talking about" she asked sharply.

"Yours," he said deliberately. "I know what you're thinking, but there is a kind of happiness that is indestructible; it lives on no matter what comes after. At least, that was how it seemed to me listening to you talking last evening."

"But we were only talking for such a little while," she protested.

"No matter," he said. "Anyway, last night was not the first time I'd seen you. I used to study down by the river long ago, on our side, and I used to see you and your husband walking together in the fields. You used to go with him to count the cattle, didn't you?"

"Yes. I always went with him," she said absently, because her mind was going back over the previous evening.

"How I used to envy your companionship," he said. They had reached the river bank and they had to walk slowly, because the ground was dented and uneven from where the cattle in wet weather had cut up the sod, which now was hard as rock. "Not that I have much experience," he went on, "but of the marriages I've seen at close quarters, not many were like yours. They weren't failures, either; I suppose they were happy enough in a way." He hesitated. "Only it wouldn't be my way," he said flatly.

"And what would be your way?" she asked laughingly.

"Well, that's just it," he said. "That's what I wanted to try to tell you in the letter. You see, I didn't have any clear idea of what I would want from marriage. I only knew what I wouldn't want, until last night, listening to you."

"I don't understand?" she cried nervously, but she did remember that at one moment the night before she had felt uneasy. Had he formed some impression of his own at that moment? If so, she would probably be powerless now to alter it. Distantly, she turned away and looked down into the river. "Supposing the impression I gave you was wrong," she said. "Supposing I falsified it." When he said nothing, she turned and looked at him and she saw he was bewildered. Filled with remorse, she put out her hand to him. "It wasn't false," she said quickly, "but that was one of the things I used to dread after his death, that the past would become altered in my mind, and that he would be made into something that he wasn't."

"Not by you, though?"

"No. By others, but it might have come to the same thing in the end. You cannot imagine how awful it was in those first months, having to listen to people talking about him, going on and on about him, mostly his family, of course, but my own people were nearly as bad, and friends and neighbours. Everybody. And all the time they were getting him more and more out of focus for me. He was—but you've heard your uncle talk about him, so you'll know what I'm going to say—he was nearly perfect, guileless. He knew only candour, the kind of person who'd make you doubt the doctrine of original sin. But to listen to his family you'd think he was a man of marble. They diminished him. Instead of adding to him, they diminished him. Can you understand that? I used to think, immediately, that that was the way they would speak of him whatever he'd been; the dead are always whitewashed. And he didn't need it. In the end, instead of listening to them, I used to sit trying to think of something about him that I didn't like."

"Did you?"

"Well, we used to quarrel when we were first married, but in all fairness to him it was usually my fault, although it always ended with his taking the blame. Not to be noble or anything like that, but just to stop us from arguing, which he hated; to get us back to being happy again. He used to say it didn't matter what happened, I'd always blame him anyway, so it might as well be first as last. Well, one evening a few weeks after his death, I was visiting his people and listening to the same old rigmarole about him, and I got into a kind of a panic. Soon I wouldn't be properly able to remember him at all; I thought I'd lose hold of what he was really like. I was so unhappy. And when I went out to the car and left it was a miserable evening outside. It was raining, for one thing, and the canvas roof of the car was leaking. I wouldn't have minded that, only just at the loneliest and darkest part of the road I got a puncture. Well! I got out and I stood there in the rain and it seemed the last straw. But suddenly, instead of pitying myself, I felt the most violent rage sweep over me. Towards him, Richard. If only I could have confronted him at that moment, there'd be no doubt of what I'd have said. 'Why did you die, anyway?' I'd have shouted. 'Why didn't you take better care of yourself and not leave me in this mess?' And then——"

"Don't tell me. I know what happened next," Fergus said. "You had him back again, just as he always was, unchanged, amused at you."

"Yes. And I began to laugh, there in the rain."

There was silence for a few minutes. "Tell me," he said then. "What did you do about the puncture?"

"Oh, that!" She shrugged her shoulders. "I forget. What with one thing or another, in those days I was nearly always in that sort of situation. Such things were the commonplaces of my existence. I suppose another car came along, or I called at some cottage, or perhaps I walked to the nearest village. I can't remember."

"Things must have been hard for you in the beginning," he said gently. "But you managed very well."

"Oh, I don't know," she said deprecatingly. "Some things were hard in the beginning, but other things only got hard long afterwards. I'll tell you a strange thing, though, if you're interested. I don't think I fully realized until recently, but in my heart I did blame Richard all along, not for dying, but for being what he was, for leaving a void that no one less than him could fill."

They walked along a few more paces. "Is that why you didn't marry again?" he said. "It seems such a pity."

"For me?"

"Well, for you, too, of course, but I wasn't thinking of you. I was thinking of how much you have to give." But as he spoke he seemed to lose confidence in what he was saying. "I suppose giving isn't enough, though," he finished uncertainly.

Sadly, she shook her head. "And yet it was a poor kind of faithfulness really, wasn't it?"

"It's the only kind there is, I think," he said. "Do you know something?" he added impetuously. "When I was walking home last night, I was thinking about your husband, and I envied him."

"A dead man?"

"It's not as absurd as it may seem. I feel certain that I'll never have one quarter of the happiness he had."

"But you're so young!" she cried. "How can you tell what's ahead?"

He looked away. "It isn't a question of age. You know that. It's temperament perhaps or maybe it's merely chance." He looked back at her. "It's not that I haven't a normal capacity for love, either. The truth is that I have to be crazily involved or not at all. And I've never seen that kind of thing last for long. That was why, knowing what companions you were, it meant so much to me, last night, to see that you'd never lost that other quality either. Do you realise when I knew?" He faltered before the cold look she gave him, but then he rushed on. "It was when you told me about the time you stayed out all night."

"Except I didn't say that," she said crossly. "Not exactly anyway," she added, but she knew how rightly he had interpreted her vague words about that night.

"Forgive me," he said gently. "It was from your face and from the love of your voice I knew what you meant. And I was certain then of how you spent that night. You see I never really thought that kind of love could last so long. Illicit love perhaps but not married love."

Uncomfortable, she walked a little faster so that she out-distanced him by a few steps.

"I was right, wasn't I?" he called softly.

"Yes," she said at last. What was the use, now, of denying those dead hours? She sighed and waited for him. "I suppose you'd like to be married," she said, surprising herself by her words.

He answered more lightheartedly than she expected. "To the right person," he said. "You'd have been just right for me!"

It was because he said it so lightly and because she was oppressed by what had gone before that she, to, spoke lightheartedly. "Oh, don't relegate me to the past like that!" she said. "Why not say I'm a premonition of someone to come."

His face clouded. "I wouldn't say there'd be two of you in one lifetime," he said, and there was a note in his voice that was new and harsh, and, frightened by it, she was about to suggest that they turn back, when, wheeling around, he himself suggested it. "We'd better go back," he said. "Anyway, the moon has gone behind a cloud."

"Has it?" Her eyes had been upon a small field of old meadow, along the headland of which they were passing. It was so neglected that the big white daisies in it met head to head and gave it an unbroken sheen of white that in the dark was like the lustre of the moon. "Just look at those daisies!" she cried, pointing to them. "The place is getting so neglected. I'll have to plough up that piece of ground and lay it down to new grass. There is so much that is neglected."

"Nonsense, I never noticed any neglect," he said so aggressively that, in order not to be annoyed, she had to tell herself that he was speaking, after all, in her defence.

"You haven't seen the place by day," she said quietly.

"I see it every day," he said. "There isn't a bit of it I can't see from the other bank of the river. I saw you outside this morning, didn't I?"

"Did you?" It confused her to think of being seen without knowing it, by anyone. She was glad that they were nearly back. They had been walking faster on the return than when they set out, and already they had reached the wooden paling in front of the house. "You'll come inside this time, I hope, and have some coffee?"

"We'd better see what time it is first," he said. "Tim was horrified at how late I stayed last night." Raising his arm, he was trying to see his watch, as if, she thought irrelevantly, as if with that upraised arm he was trying to ward off a blow.

"Wait! There's a light in the porch," she said. "It can be switched on from outside." But the switch was almost impossible to find among the tangled and overgrown creepers. "There's neglect for you," she said as she plunged her arm deep into the leaves. "The roses are almost smothered," she said sadly. Yet when she found the switch and the light went on, the big white roses lolloped outward towards them. On long, neglected stems, blown and beautiful, they hung face down. Impulsively, he reached out and took one between the palms of his hands, tenderly, as if it were the body of a small bird. "Would you like one?" she asked, and she tried to break a stem, but it was difficult because the sappy fibres frayed before they severed.

He took it from her, pleased. And then he gave an exclamation. "Oh, look at what's on it. A cuckoo-spit."

"How disgusting. Throw it away," she said. "I'll get you another one."

But he put his hand protectively about it. "Why did you say that?" he asked. "I was only amazed that a cuckoo should come so close to the house." Then he saw his mistake from her face before he went any further. "I forgot," he said, embarrassed. "They never do come close, isn't that so?"

"Never!" She smiled. "They're never seen at all. At least I've never met anyone who saw one."

"That's right. I should have known," he said.

She saw at once that he was humiliated by his mistake, and she wanted desperately to make him feel better. "When I was a child," she said quickly, "I didn't know a cuckoo was a bird at all, but a sound, like an echo."

He didn't smile. He was looking down at the rose. On the stem, in the cleft between it and the acle of a leaf, there was a white blob, as if of spittle. "What is it, anyway?" he asked. "I've often seen it before."

"Give it to me," she said quietly, stretching out her hand. With the tip of her finger, she flicked the blob of white stuff on to the back of her other hand. "Look," she said, as the frothy secretion began to thin away, beads of moisture winking out, one by one, until, slowly and weakly on its unformed legs, a pale sickly-yellow aphis crawled out across her skin. "That's what it is," she said, but at the feel of it on her flesh she shuddered, and shook it violently from her.

"You shouldn't have touched it." Throwing down the rose, he pulled out a handkerchief and took her hand, and began carefully to wipe it all over. "It always seemed so beautiful," he said regretfully, "a sign of summer."

"Ah, well, it is a sign of summer," she said, but her mind was not really on what she was saying, because although he'd wiped away all trace of the spit, he still held her hand carelessly in his. Unused for so long to the feel of another's flesh she felt her cheeks flush. She was affected almost as strongly by his touch as by the feel of the plant louse. Shuddering again, she drew her hand away.

"You're cold?" he said.

Cold? Was it possible you could be so near to another person and so unaware of what went on within them? "You must be cold, too," she said. "Come in and we'll have a hot drink."

"We stayed out too long," he said, bending down and picking up his rose. "Next time we must manage better."

There was evidently no question of his not calling again.

"I hope you enjoyed the walk," he said easily, and then, as he was about to turn away, he looked directly at her. "Good night, Vera," He strode off down the drive.

She looked after him. Why had she enjoyed it so intensely? That was the question.

When she went inside, she attended absently to what had to be done before going upstairs for the night. Then, upstairs at last, she again went to the window and looked out. The moon, free of clouds, once more cast its lustre over everything. And, standing there, looking out, she remembered the times as a girl, before she was married, when she stood at an open window on a night like this, her heart torn by a longing to share the feelings that welled up in her. Yet later, when she had Richard there was not a single night that she had gone to the window for as much as a glance at what was outside. Always, no matter what the weather, day or the night, there was him blocking out all else. This view before her now, she had only really seen it after his death. Then, oh then its insistent beauty began to torment her. But not with the same emotion. And she thought of something Fergus had said. He was wrong. A time came when giving was enough. She stared over the moonlit fields and the high cobbled sky. And she knew what she wanted. She wanted to reach out and gather all that beauty up and shove it into his arms. To give it away and be done with it, she thought. And afterwards not ever to have to look out at it again.

Next morning, she wakened late. Downstairs there was a loud knocking on the door. It was a grey day with a mist over the river and in the fields cattle looked dark, as if they swam in the waters of a fabulous sea. The knocking came again more urgently, and she sprang out of bed and went to the window. Below, standing back from the door, she saw him just under her window, looking up. "Oh, just a minute. I'll come right down," she called down, pulling back instinctively.

"Don't come down!" he called up. "I can't wait. I haven't a minute."

"You have to go back?" This time in spite of the cold glare of day, she leaned out.

"The exam papers came," he said. "When I went back to Tim's place last night, there was a message saying they'd arrived. I have to get back. To get them finished in time, I'll have to start on them at once." He turned his head as if to listen. "Is that the bus?" he cried, dismayed. "I shouldn't have come. I'll miss it. But I wanted to tell you I was going, in case you'd be looking out for me tonight."

That he had any notion of coming that night, the third night in a row, took her by surprise. That he could have thought she might have been expecting him left her speechless.

"I'll have to go!" he cried, but he put his hand to his ear. "It's not the bus," he said, and he relaxed. "I didn't think the papers would come for a few days more. The exam was only last week. But the sooner they come, the sooner I'll get paid."

Depressed already by the day and by its cold light upon her unprepared face, and, of course, by his going, this glimpse of his unknown life was too much to endure. There was something so altogether offhand about this their last conversation that when in the distance she did hear the bus, she was not sorry. "Listen!" she said. "Here it is. The bus *is* coming this time."

"It can't be." He listened intently. It was. At once all his offhandedness left him. "What I really wanted is if you ever come up to Dublin." The sound of the bus was louder and nearer. "If you ever do come, and if you could spare the time, I needn't tell you I'd love to meet you. Perhaps you'd let me give you a cup of tea somewhere." But as he was looking nervously over his shoulder, the bus was getting nearer.

As for her, there was no time to dissimulate her pleasure. "I often go!" she cried. "And I'd be pleased to meet you." But just then she thought of a way in which she could trim the truth a little. "I was only thinking last night, after you'd gone, that I ought perhaps to give you the names of a few people in Dublin, friends of my husband's on whom you might call. People with some political influence, I mean, if you are serious about a political career."

"I am," he cried. "Write out a list and bring it up to me. That's great." Satisfied that she was coming, he hardly saw the necessity of fixing a day, and was turning away when he realised the need. "When?" he cried.

"And where?" she cried, leaning out across the sill.

"How about Tuesday next? Or is that too soon?"

There was no time to think. "Tuesday," she agreed. "But where? How about meeting in Stephen's Green? We can decide afterward where to go."

It was settled.

Or was it?

"What will happen if it isn't a fine day?" he cried.

"Oh, it will be fine," she cried recklessly. "You'll see."

It rained, after all, on Tuesday. At first, she wasn't going to go to Dublin at all, but she was too unsettled to stay at home. She'd go up for a few hours anyway, she decided. And then, shortly before four o'clock, unexpectedly the rain cleared. As she parked her car on the side of the Green, she could see through the railings that the park was almost deserted. Uncertainly, she went in through a side gate. She felt better when she saw the paths were already drying out and from the wet branches overhead small birds, plump and round, were everywhere dropping to the ground like apples. On the grass starlings and sparrows ran about like children, as if for once the earth was sweeter than the sky. Would he come? Would he think it too wet? Dispirited, she walked along the vacant paths till she came to the shallow lake in the centre. And there, by the lakeside, standing under a tree, she saw him.

It was, she thought, the suddenness of seeing him that made her heart leap; only that. The next moment, a line from an old mortuary card came involuntarily to her mind. The card had been given to her by an old nun at the time of Richard's death, and her own pallid belief in a life beyond the grave had been quenched entirely by its facile promise: *Oh, the joy to see you come.* But now the words rushed back to her, ready and apt. I shouldn't be here, she thought with terror. It was too late, though. He had seen her.

"You came?" he cried.

"Didn't you know I would?"

"It was raining."

"It stopped, though." They began to walk along the side of the shallow cemented lake. "You must have known I'd come when you yourself came," she said.

"I only hoped. Can we ever be sure of anything?"

"Of some things, surely," she said, to gain time and think what she should do. There must be no more of these meetings. That was certain. But surely she could at least enjoy this afternoon? What harm could there be in it, except for her? And then only if she gave way to barren longings that might set the past at naught. She took a sidelong look at him. He seemed so happy. What did it matter what she felt, as long as no one knew. As long as he didn't know! And he was concerned with the trivia of their conversation.

"I suppose you mean friendship?" he said. "But can there be friendship between a man and a woman?"

It was such a young question, it endeared him still more to her. She and Richard used to talk like that long ago. "I don't know," she said. "But I remember reading somewhere that there are only two valid relationships, blood and passion."

He was staring down at the cinder path under their feet as they paced along. "It's an interesting thought, isn't it?" he said. Then he looked up at her. "What about us, though?"

Disconcerted, she gave a shrug. "Oh, we don't come into any category at all," she said, "except, wait a minute, I have something for you. I'd forgotten. It justifies our association." Opening her handbag, she took out the piece of paper on which she had written a list of names. "Here are the people on whom I thought you should call."

"Oh, thanks," he said, but he took it from her absently, and without looking at it he shoved it carelessly into the outer pocket of his jacket.

"Hadn't you better put it in your wallet? I went to a lot of trouble looking up some of these addresses. And, by the way, I put a mark beside the names of a few people to whom I thought I ought to introduce you personally."

"You mean go with me?" He put his hand in his pocket and pulled out the paper again, smoothing it and looking at it this time with interest. "That's different," he said enthusiastically, but to her dismay the next minute he rolled it into a ball and tossed it into a wire basket for waste paper that was fastened to a tree. "That means you'll have to come up to town again. For the whole day next time, so we don't need the list." He smiled happily. "Let's go up this way," he said, pointing to a narrow path that ran over a humped bridge, low and covered with ivy. The bridge was little more than a decoration, for under it the water was utterly still. They stopped and were looking over the parapet.

"The water isn't flowing at all," she said. It was dusty and stippled with pollen from an overhanging lime tree.

He didn't look. "What did you mean by saying we don't come into any category?" he asked. "Is that an obscure reference to my age?"

"No, To mine," she said, and when he laughed she thought she had distracted him.

She hadn't. "I knew that was what you meant," he said. With a stony expression he looked down into the water. "Vera," he said quietly, "listen to me. Never once since the first night I met you have I ever felt you were a day older than me."

"That's nothing," she said sadly. "I never felt you were a day younger than me. But facts are facts." She straightened up and spoke flatly. "I always seem to be more attracted to people younger than me than to my own contemporaries, at least since Richard died. I was beginning to think that my heart was like a clock that had stopped at the age he was when he died, and that it was him I was looking for, over and over again, wherever I went, whenever I was in a strange place, or when I met new people."

"And wasn't it?"

"I don't think so. I think it was myself I was trying to find, the person I was before I married him. When he died, I knew I had to get back to being that other person again, just as he, when he was dying, had to get back to being the kind of person he was before he met me. Standing beside him in those last few minutes, I felt he was trying to drag himself free of me. Can you understand that? Does it make any sense to you?"

"I think so," he said gravely. "And it would explain what I said, that from the first you seemed so young to me. It was because you were making a new beginning. I felt it at once, although I knew you must be older than me, in years, I mean."

Vera shook her head. "Not years. Decades," she said.

"Oh Vera!" he cried, exasperated. "Don't exaggerate."

But she wasn't going to concede anything. "It might as well be centuries," she said bitterly.

He turned and faced her. "No," he said gravely. "Two people reaching out improbably towards each other; not impossibly." Impulsively, he took her hand. "Vera, what are we going to do?"

The first thing to do, she knew, was snatch back her hand, but someone was passing, and she could not let them be seen struggling. Instead, she looked down at her hand in his. This is the closest we'll ever be to each other, she thought. Then, when the person had passed, she pulled her hand free.

"This is crazy!" she cried. "What are we saying? I thought it was bad enough that I—" Realising what she was about to admit, she turned away abruptly. "It's just crazy, that's all. I shouldn't have come," she said childishly. "I knew the minute I saw you. I was going to turn and run back to the car, only you looked up and saw me and it was too late."

"Yes, it was too late," he said. "It was too late the first night of all."

"Oh, no!" she cried. "Not from the beginning?" It was essential she be able to blame herself, to claim complicity in letting it go on, for the course it took, for the walks, the late hours, the intimacy of their conversation. Otherwise, there would be an inevitability implied that she could not face. There would be helplessness as well as hopelessness. The tears rushed into her eyes.

"Vera, don't be upset," he said. "This may be unlooked for, but you must know it's not unprecedented?"

"I know nothing." She dried her eyes. "I've heard things, of course. I've read things. Elderly housemaids jumping out of closets at little boys."

"Vera. Shut up. Do you hear me! Shut up." He raised his hand and she thought he was going to hit her. "The question is what are we going to do?"

"We must put an end to things, that's all!"

"And end? At the beginning? You can't mean that?"

"What else can we do?"

"I don't know, not at this moment," he said, "but surely to God whatever we've found in each other, something we both know is rare, surely that's not to be thrown away, not before we've got anything out of it," he said, almost pettishly.

"What is there to be got out of it, only pain and heartache?"

"For which of us?" There was a pathetic eagerness in his voice. She shook her head. "Does that matter?"

"I suppose not," he agreed miserably, and yet instead of resignation he had a stubborn look, and he caught at her hand again. "Isn't pain the price of most things?" he cried. "You're to ready to give up, Vera. I meant what I said a while ago. There *are* precedents for this. We aren't the first people in the world to be in this particular plight. I've heard of this kind of thing, and read about it. It always seemed very beautiful."

She interrupted him. "No, it is unnatural!"

"Oh, Vera," he said wearily. "Why are you so bitter? I was only trying to say that it was something altogether outside my experience."

"And mine."

"All right," he said, "but isn't everything outside our experience until it comes into it? there was a friend of my own, a close friend, too, in my first year in college, and he was in love with a woman years older than him, fourteen years, I think. They did their best to break away from each other, but in the end they got married."

She pulled away from him roughly. "Married?" she repeated hysterically. "Anyway," she said callously, "what is fourteen years?"

He was arrested by that. "What age are you anyway, Vera?"

"What age are you?" she demanded, but she didn't really want to know. "Don't tell me," she cried, taking her hand away. She knew it was worse than she'd thought. "It doesn't matter," she said hopelessly. "Let's leave things as they are, and not show them up to be altogether farcical."

He said nothing, but she saw him wince. He reached out idly and picked an ivy leaf from the parapet and dropped it into the pond below, where it lay flat on the stagnant water.

It seemed a chance for her to say what had to be said. "We must stop seeing each other. At least by design," she added, having caught sight of his face.

"I see," he said. He stood up. "And you dismissed friendship, as far as I remember, didn't you?" he said.

She shrugged. "This isn't friendship." She glanced at the sky. "It's going to rain again," she said dully.

As she spoke, a drop of rain fell singly and heavily on to the sleeve of her blouse, and as the stroke of the hammer brings the spark to iron, the heavy drop brought her flesh to the linen. She looked down, and then she saw that he was staring, too. Without a word said, the air began to throb, and it was with love, with love and nothing less. Her eyes filled with tears. "It may be rare, love, I mean," she said, turning aside, unable to look at him any more, "but where there is love, everything is so easy. Friendship is so exacting. Perhaps that's why they can never exist together at the same time. And why they never, never, can be substituted for each other. Let me tell you something," she said quickly and urgently, although as she said them the words seemed to echo in her mind and she remembered the disastrous effect of the other incident she'd told him on the first night of all. But she went on. "One evening last summer, and I was staying with friends in Howth. After dinner, we went out on the cliff, and I asked something I'd always wanted to know. I asked why the lights across the bay were always twinkling. But I was told they weren't twinkling; they were steady. It was the level of the air in between that was uneven. Do you see?" she said sadly. "It's the same with us."

"I see," he said for the second time, and he threw down another leaf on to the water. Then he straightened up. For a moment, she thought everything was ended. "Where is your car?" he asked. But nothing was ended. "We can't settle this here," he said. "I'm coming down to the farm with you. We'll have to have a long talk." He paused. "Unless you could stay the night in town?"

"Oh, I couldn't possibly do that," she cried.

"Well then, I'll come down," he said.

"And stay with Tim?" She was distractedly looking in her pockets for the keys of the car. They were going out of the park gates into the street. But when she looked at him, she saw that he was staring strangely at her.

"Where else?" he asked.

"Oh, I know there is nowhere else," she said, but she felt the ground was slipping from under her as if she were the one who was young and inexperienced, even endangered. But it was only that she was out of practice in a game where every word, every gesture counted for ten. "I only meant that your uncle might think it odd for you to go down unexpectedly."

"I never go any other way," he said. "Are you sure that's what you meant?"

"And if it wasn't?" she asked, startled at the chancy note in her voice. "What would be the gain?"

"If we got rid of the tension that has built up between us, we might salvage something," he said, but there was a trace of despondency in his voice again. "There might be nothing to salvage," she said. "And supposing the bonds only tightened?"

"Would you care?" he asked.

"Not then. But I care now, while I'm still able to care."

"Tell me one thing. For whose sake would you care, your own or mine?"

She looked away from him, over the street into which they had entered. "Not for either of our sakes, I think," she said. She nodded at the people in the street hurrying by in all directions. "For them, perhaps."

"Don't be nonsensical," he said, and as they reached the car he caught the handle of the door. "I'll come down. And you must let me stay the night, Vera. Just to talk." He looked at his watch. "It's a bit bright to go down yet, though, isn't it? We ought to wait till it's darker, in case it would get about that I was down."

"And stayed with me?"

He nodded.

For a minute, she let herself dwell on the thought of having him in the house with her, under the same roof, however separate in all else. "I'd have to drive you up again very early before it was light, wouldn't I?"

"You could go to bed for a while," he said. "I'd call you."

She knew then that they fully understood each other. They got into the car.

"There's just one thing I have to do before I can go," he said. "I have to call at Hume Street to collect another lot of exam papers. Can we stop there? I won't keep you a minute."

She started the car.

"You didn't really think that you could walk out of my life like that?" he asked as they drove along. "I feel certain that no matter what happens you'll never altogether leave it."

She said nothing, and in a few minutes they had reached Hume Street. Before he got out of the car, he looked at her. "There's something I want to say now, before we go any further," he said. "No matter what happens, I want you to promise me that if you ever want me for anything, you'll tell me. Will you promise that?"

"Why do you want me to promise now?" she asked, she leaned across him and opened the door. "Never mind. I promise," she said quickly. Then, knowing he must have guessed what she had in mind to do, she waited till he went up the steps and she drove away.

It was nearly a year later. She had not seen him in the time between, nor did she expect to, when late one afternoon there was the sound of a car at the door. "Well?" she said weakly when she opened it and saw him standing there.

Like the first time of all, they looked at each other, and this time, too, the look was one of surprise, but not a happy surprise.

"How are you?" he asked. There was a keen edge to his voice. "I didn't need to ask," he added quickly.

"And you?" she asked. He looked well.

"I wasn't going to call at all," he said then. "But I changed my mind." He paused.

It saddened her to see him ill at ease, standing so stiffly. Why did he come, she wondered. "You were anxious about me? Is that it?" she asked laughingly, thinking that by making light of it she would dispel the shadow of what had been between them. But she saw at once she had only brought it back. In a moment, the old atmosphere of intimacy was re-created, and yet it was not the same, or anything like the same.

"It was because of the old man I called," he said dully. "He thought it odd that I hadn't come over to see you. I've been down here for two weeks."

"Ah, well," she said, "he didn't understand."

He looked at her intently. "I'm not so sure about that," he said. "I didn't tell you something he said last year, one of the nights I went back late. He gave me a queer look. "If you were better favoured," he said, "you'd be putting ideas into my silly old head."

"I'm not so sure." They were still standing in the doorway. "May I stay awhile?" he asked.

Almost imperceptibly, she hesitated, but he noticed it. "You were not going out, were you?" he asked.

"I was going out," she said reluctantly.

"Must you?"

"I'm afraid I must."

He seemed really surprised. "Will you be long? Could I come back later? As a matter of fact, I have to go to Dublin for an hour or two. I only intended calling for a minute." He looked at his watch. "I could be back in two and a half hours. Where were you going, anyway?"

"Today is Richard's anniversary," she said, still more reluctantly. I was going to the cemetery. Normally I never go near it, only I got word to say the headstone has slipped, and that it must be seen to at once, in case it falls altogether. It would break, or do damage to other graves. I have to go and see what is to be done, and make arrangements about it."

"Oh, I see," he said. "But it can't be all that urgent, surely? Isn't this a bad day to go in any case? Or do you usually go on his anniversary?"

"I told you I never go. Never, never. This is purely a coincidence."

"Well, then. You certainly shouldn't go today. Besides it's getting late. Put it off to another day."

"I think I ought to go this afternoon," she said. "I don't mind, really." Suddenly an idea struck her. "It would make it a lot easier if there was someone with me. I don't suppose——" She paused, and for a minute she thought he had not seen any connection between him and her unfinished sentence.

But he had. "Of course I'll go. There should be someone with you. You certainly should not go alone. Don't think of it. Leave it till tomorrow or the next day, and I'll go with you gladly. Better still, I'll go without you and see what's to be done. It's not a job for a woman anyway. Where is he buried, by the way?"

"Kildare."

"So far?"

"It's not so far from here, only a few minutes."

"I'd probably be going from Dublin, but no matter. Put it out of your head now, and I'll take care of it."

"You couldn't come this afternoon?"

"With you?"

"With me, of course. I know it must sound superstitious, but I hate to think of getting word about it today of all days, and not going, not wanting to go."

"Rubbish!" he said easily. "Anyway, it's my affair now."

"You couldn't possibly come now? she persisted. "Why do you have to go back to Dublin? Is it urgent?"

"Oh, it's not exactly urgent, but I'd like to go. I've arranged to give a driving lesson to someone. It need only take half an hour, but I promised to do it. A half an hour would be plenty; that's why I said I'd come back if you agreed to it, but of course the light would be gone by then, for the other job, I mean."

She was listening very attentively. "Is it a girl?" she asked quietly.

"You know it's not a girl."

"Why not? I only asked because if it was a girl I'd know you couldn't possibly break your word."

He stared. "You wouldn't mind?"

"It would be natural," she said.

"Was that your remedy? Another man?"

She didn't bother to reply to that. "Well, if it's not a girl, who is it?" she asked flatly.

"It's just a fellow who works in the Department of Education. It's through him I get the exam papers to correct."

"Couldn't you get in touch with him?"

"He's not on the phone."

She pondered this. "You could send him a telegram."

"He wouldn't get it in time."

"He'd get it afterwards, and he'd understand, surely?"

"I don't know if he would. And anyway, I couldn't leave him up there in the park, hanging around waiting for me, thinking every minute I was coming and afraid to go away."

She gave a short laugh.

"I suppose you think that if it was last summer I'd have gone with you no matter what!" he said.

"Oh, no!" she cried. "Last summer I wouldn't have let you come. I wouldn't have needed you. It would have been enough to know you'd have come if you could." Her coat was lying across the hall table. She took it up. "I must go," she said simply.

"So you were right," he said, blocking her way. "We salvaged nothing."

She put on her coat. Then she looked into his face. "Don't blame me for being right," she said. "I sometimes think love has nothing to do with people at all." Her voice was tired. "It's like the weather. But isn't it strange that a love that was so unrealised should have—"

"—given such joy?" he asked quietly.

"Yes, yes," she said. Then she closed the door behind them. "And such pain."

"Oh, Vera, Vera," he said.

"Goodbye," she said.

Goodbye.

One Summer

Above the wind and the rain she called her goodbyes to him again from the edge of the pier, as the steel hawsers splashed back into the water and the ship eased out from the dock. If there was an answering message she did not hear it in a blast from the funnel. And in the mist she could not be certain that the figure to whom she waved was him. A few minutes later and there was no distinguishing anyone. Only the portholes shone. Yet she did not leave. She sat in the car till the last speck of light was quenched in waves of darkness.

It was late when she reached home. Getting out to open the gates at the end of the avenue she could see through the trees that the light was out in her father's room. A light burned in the maid's room, but as the car swept up to the front steps this light was put out. Lily in all likelihood thought her mistress had been jilted. Vera sighed. Cramped, cold, and worn-out, she went to her room. In a few minutes she was in a dead sleep. Was it any wonder she heard nothing during the night? It was getting on for morning when Lily ran in and shook her awake. An awful moaning was coming from her father's room.

"God, Miss, I think he's dying," the girl sobbed.

"Stop it," Vera said sharply. Yet her mind fastened on Lily's hysterical words. If they were true, how badly she herself had been served by time. Alan was no further than London. It would be hours before he boarded the Orcades.

Her father moaned again. Shamed by her thoughts, she sprang up and ran across the landing. "Oh, Father, what is the matter?" she cried. But from the doorway she could tell by a strange, unnatural strength in his stare that he could not speak. His glaring eyes seemed all of him that was alive. Spread-eagled on the bed as if flung from a great height, he lay inert. Then the pain caught him up again and he was once more gathered into a living mass. Putting her arms under him she tried to drag him to a sitting position, but he gave her such a bitter look she let him fall back. Oh, why had she gone defiantly to bed without going in to him! He might have been lying miserably awake in the dark. "Don't be angry with me, Father," she pleaded, as if she were at fault, not him. Then she turned on Lily. "Stop that nonsense," she said, "and go for the doctor."

Because Lily was running around frantically filling hot water bottles, making stoups and compresses, forcing brandy between his lips. She had lights burning everywhere. Even out in the yard a light streamed unnaturally into the fields of dawn. "Oh, Miss, I hate to leave him," she said. "Wouldn't you go? You'd be no time going in the car."

Vera shook her head: It was not to have him die without her that she had given up Alan. So Lily pedalled off in the greyness and the wet.

Standing back out of range of the sick man's angry eyes, Vera stared helplessly at him. The first onslaught of pain was over, and he lay in a sheet of sweat. Yet it seemed an age until the doctor's car came up the drive, with Lily sitting up importantly beside him on the front seat, her bike strapped to the back. Vera ran down to meet them.

"Sounds like a blockage," the old doctor said, as he got out of the car. "Don't worry; we'll do all we can."

Indeed the doctor's presence had helped already, and as they went in to her father he managed a few words. "What's wrong with me, Doctor?" he whispered.

The doctor turned down the bedclothes. "Tell me, have you been dosing yourself?" he demanded.

Vera went limp with relief. So it was that? As long as she could remember he was always dosing himself. "Cleans you out," he used to say when she protested, and defiantly he'd pour himself out another spoonful of a vile concoction of cascara and treacle which he called black-jack. Turning eagerly, she was about to tell the doctor about it when a look from her father silenced her.

But Lily spoke up. "I told him he'd blast the insides out of himself with that stuff he takes, Doctor, but he wouldn't heed me."

The doctor nodded gloomily.

"It was that made him throw up too," the girl said.

"When was that?" Vera asked sharply.

"He was always at it," said the girl defiantly as if she felt herself doubted. "You could hear him all over the house." She shuddered. "And a couple of times I saw him doubled up out in the fields."

Vera put her hands to her face.

"That's enough!" the doctor said to Lily. He turned to Vera. "I'll give him something to ease him," he said in a low voice, "but I'm afraid it's a blockage all right. We'll have to get him to Dublin." He patted her on the shoulder. "I'll do my best," he said kindly, but later, when they were going downstairs, he looked more keenly at her. "You should get some sleep," he said, "You look exhausted. Let Lily sit up with him for what's left of the night."

"Oh, but she must be jaded," Vera said.

"What matter! She's young," said the doctor. Through the great high window on the landing they could see the doctor's battered car looming indistinctly in the morning mist, and as they went out on to the glittering granite steps Lily came towards them, half-wheeling, half-carrying the bicycle she had unstrapped from the car. Like the gravel under her feet, her cheeks were freshened and brightened by the damp. The stress of the night had left no mark on her. "What did I tell you?" cried the doctor, his own eye brightening. "This one doesn't need any sleep. She's fitter far than you to stay up."

The girl laughed. "A spin is what I'd like now," she said.

The doctor laughed good-humouredly, but to Vera he spoke severely. "You go and lie down," he said.

Vera shook her head. Intermittently through the hours that had passed, her mind had guiltily travelled after Alan. At one minute she thought she would wire to him. At the next she thought no. It was like the moments when she had stood on the dark pier and watched the light of the ship that carried him away from her, it came and went several times in the sea mist before she knew finally that the light was finally engulfed in it. Now in the cold air of dawn she came to a firm decision. "I can't lie down, Doctor," she said. "I have an important letter to write."

The doctor looked oddly at her. "Well, we all have our own anodyne," he said, and he got into the car. "I'll call later when I've got in touch with the hospital. Don't be blaming yourself for anything. He must already have felt some discomfort when he was taking those doses."

To satisfy him she nodded her head. But he only knew about the blackjack and the retching. What about his black moods all year, his black looks, and his fits of black, black silence? Was he not then already gravely ill? Filled with remorse, she ran upstairs.

Her father was lying as they left him. He was staring up at the ceiling. "Do I have to go to hospital?" he asked.

Had he heard what the doctor said? Or was he only trying to find out?

"Are you frightened, Father?" she asked.

"No," he said decisively. "As long as it's not what I dreaded. Anything but that."

She knew what he'd feared. But that was all she knew. The word 'blockage', so familiar, so domestic a word, had up to that moment reassured her. But was it a euphemism for what he feared? She grew rigid. If so he must not know. Then, at the thought that she might not have been there to protect him her breath caught. Others in her place would have cared for him and been kind. Lily had already shown amazing devotion. But who besides herself could protect him from a word? It was little things like this that Alan had never understood.

Her face must have given her thoughts away because the glare had appeared again in her father's eyes. "When is that fellow going?" he asked suddenly.

Was it possible he did not know? "He's gone, Father," she said. She was so eager to reassure him she made it sound as if Alan's going was something joyous. "That's where I was last night, seeing him off at the boat."

If he was relieved he was too clever to show it. Instead he shifted his position. "I knew he was no good," he said.

Sick as he was, she could not stand for that. "You know why he went!"

she said. And she had the satisfaction of seeing his eyes falter.

"I shouldn't have said that," he said humbly enough. "You've been a good daughter to me, Vera, always." Their eyes met then, and met with love. "You won't regret it," he said.

Immediately her heart filled with warmth for him until, like when she was a child, it was brimful with love. Reaching out she put her hand on his, and weakly he raised his other hand and placed it over hers again. It was like piling love on love. It reminded her of a game they used to play when she was a child. "Do you remember playing Hot hands Father?"

He nodded, and tears came into his eyes. But they were happy tears, and after a few minutes his lids closed as if he might sleep. Gently she drew her hand away.

What miracles of love he had performed when she was a child. He had made it seem that to be motherless was to be privileged. When he called for her after school his spare male figure stood out among the floppy mothers and set her, too, apart. A plain child, his love gave her sparkle. But as the years went by, his care and caution were sometimes excessive and set too high a price upon her company. Oftener and oftener her classmates left her out of their pranks and their larking. Then, if her father found out, he'd spring up, his black eyes flashing. "Never mind," he'd cry. "I'll take you." And as if by magic he'd always find where the others had gone.

There was one winter when the lake behind the school-house froze over, and a party was hastily organised. As usual she was not included, but he saw the other going skating past the house and he sprang up as if to a challenge. "We'll show them," he cried. "Wait." And he dashed upstairs to an old leather chest that stood, always locked on the landing. She'd never seen it opened. Its contents were as unknown to her as his life before she'd been born into it, yet she was hardly surprised when he drew out an ancient pair of skates. Within a minute they were at the lakeside, where they found her classmates gathered, timidly trying out the ice, venturing a little way out across it and holding up one foot, they slid along as far as their own momentum carried them. Her father pushed his way to the edge of the ice, put on the skates, and with a laugh, sped away like a bird. Out into the middle of the lake he went, and for the next few minutes he held all eyes with the capers he cut. Then, taking wing again, he came back to the shore. "Get down on your hunkers," he ordered her, and bending he tied her feet together with her own shoe-laces, and taking a piece of rope from his pocket he tied one end around her middle and the other around his own. In the blink of an eye he was flying over the ice again, only this time it was on her all eyes were centred as *she* swayed to and fro behind him, in a kind of splendid redundance, like a tassel on the end of a gorgeous cord, or the tuft on the tail of a lion.

The next day the lake had cracked like glass and everyone said they could have been drowned, both of them. Her father only laughed. "What matter, we'd have gone together," he said.

She stared in amazement. Ordinarily he was obsessed for her safety. In the evenings after he'd heard her tables and her catechism, he used to put her through a catechism of his own. "What would you do if you were chased by a bull?"

"Take off my coat and throw it over his horns."

"If your clothes caught fire?"

"Roll on the ground."

"If you were out in a thunderstorm?"

"Lie flat."

"If you got lost?"

"Stand still in one spot."

His litany, however, could not make provision for everything, Once she nearly broke her neck, when she was climbing on the roof of a shed and her foot slipped. Except that he was in the yard, and quick enough to reach out and catch her, she would have been killed. It was the first time she saw him in a rage. Marching her ahead of him into the house and up the stairs to the landing, he unlocked the leather chest. This time he took out a small revolver wrapped in a length of black calico. "Do you see this?" he asked. "Well, if anything happened to you, do you know what I'd do?" He put the barrel to his head and pulled the trigger. The sound of the empty clack was the most terrifying sound she had ever heard. But he'd gone too far. He had shown her more than her value: he had shown her where it lay—in his own eyes. From that hour her confidence diminished. Shy and distant always, she became more so. And when she was of an age to go to dances she got very few invitations. However, her father was eager to escort her himself.

"It's a good thing your old father can still pick up his heels," he'd say. Often he had the lightest foot on the floor! But one day she found him appraising her. "You'd have been better-looking if you'd taken after your mother," he said. "But never mind. You may be better off in the long run. I'd never have got anywhere if I didn't learn to stand alone." It was the first time he'd ever spoken of her mother and she was so surprised she didn't at once take in the fact that he was speaking of her own single state as if it were final. She was only twenty-three or twenty-four at the time. But over the next few years he made similar remarks and those habits of speech began to harden into an attitude. "What will you do the day I'm taken from you?" he asked once, shortly after her thirtieth birthday, but they laughed at the thought of a thing so remote. He threw back his head. "Nature takes care of everything," he cried. "Let's hope you'll have me as long as you need me."

Ironically it was that year she met Alan. They met in a public library in Dublin. She'd already seen him a few times when one day they arrived together at the library door a few minutes before it was opened. "I've seen you before," he said. "I always notice people who are alone. I find myself wondering if, like me, they dislike their fellow men." She laughed but he reproved her. "I'm serious," he said. "I hate the common herd."

After that, whenever they met, they exchanged a few words, and if they were leaving at the same time he saw her to her car. Once or twice when she hadn't the car he walked to the bus with her. He was a solicitor attached to an office in Dublin. He was interested to learn that she lived in the country. "I should have known," he said. "It accounts for a certain difference about you." From him that was a great compliment. Another day he said something still more preposterously flattering. "If I were not so set against marriage," he said, "you're the kind of girl I'd marry."

It was like a declaration. Her happiness was so great she hardly cared that when she told her father his responses were, to say the least of it, tepid.

"Wait till you meet him, Father," she said.

The meeting was a failure. To begin with her father made bones about giving her the car to fetch him from the bus at Ross Cross. He turned on her savagely, when she asked for the keys. "I'll drive you over," he said. "But why hasn't he got a car of his own?" He must be a poor kind of solicitor."

"There's no need of a car in a city practice, Father," she said, trying to bolster things up.

Her father looked up at the sky.

"Can't he walk then?" he asked. "It's a nice fine day. Is there something the matter with him?" But he threw the car-keys at her.

"Be nice to him, Father, for my sake," she pleaded before she drove away.

And when they arrived back he was civil enough. The trouble was that Alan didn't take to him. And her father saw that. "I can see why you need the car," he muttered. "He's a delicate-looking article."

"Oh, what a cruel thing to say!" she cried. "About a stranger too."

His eyes bored into her. "Is that all he is? he said. "If you take my advice you'll keep him that way. I pity the women that'll marry him. He'll die young and leave her with a houseful of brats."

"Don't worry, Father," she said. "After today I don't expect I'll see him again."

But she did, and more often than ever. Alan came down again and again, doggedly ignoring her father's rudeness. "Don't think I'm thick-skinned, Vera," he said one afternoon, "but I will not let him, or anyone, interfere in my life." It was another of those oblique remarks that she took to presage happiness.

Obliquity was in the air though, and her father too seemed to become obscure. One day he spoke of her mother again. "If she hadn't married me, she'd be alive today." he said morosely.

He'd never told her the cause of her mother's death, but she knew it had happened shortly after her own birth, and was probably connected with it. Aware therefore of a strong undertow in the conversation, she picked her own words with care, "She made her choice, didn't she?"

"Don't talk like a fool," he said.

At that she lost her temper. "Oh, what's the matter with you?" she cried. "Do you want to stop me marrying?"

He evaded her eyes. "I don't see any signs of that happening," he said. "The fellow is no more bent on marriage than I am."

"Is it Alan?" His words had stupefied her.

"Has he asked you to marry him?" he demanded.

She stared.

If never explicit of promise, all Alan's words had seemed to hold promise. They could not have been uttered by any man who did not feel himself deeply committed. Yet on them in that instant a huge doubt was cast.

"Well?" her father insisted. "Has he?"

"I don't see why I should tell you. It's my own business," she said childishly, and she trembled at the thought of the anger her words would provoke. When he said nothing at all and she was compelled at last to look at him however she saw with a shock that the rage in his eyes was a rage of pity. Suddenly she realised his dilemma. For the first time he'd come up against something he could not get for her, something that if it was to be got at all, could be got only by her. "Don't worry, Father," she said. "It'll work out all right in the end. You'll see."

From that day there was a change in her father's attitude. "Is that fellow worried about money, do you think?" he asked one day. "I never see his name in the papers. He mustn't do much court work. Of course," he said meditatively, "small court cases don't pay well. It's sales and conveyances that pay. It's on them the big solicitors make their money." It was almost comical to see the interest he began to take in the legal columns of the newspapers. "How much commission do you think he'd get on the conveyancing of a good farm, say a farm about this size?"

Unnerved by his question, she looked at him coldly. "Why?" she asked. "Are you going to sell?"

"No," he said, "but I might buy. And if I did I could give him the carriage of sale."

Her heart softened. "Oh, Father, you don't want any more responsibility at your age."

"Land is a safe investment at any time," he said soberly.

And the next time Alan came down her father was very affable. "Tell me," he said to him, "there's an out-farm at Ross Cross I was thinking of buying. Are you any judge of land?"

"But haven't you enough land, sir?" Alan said, and it seemed to Vera that he looked oddly at them both.

But her father noticed nothing. "Oh, you can never have too much of a good thing," he said recklessly. "It's not a big farm, mind you. It's only forty acres. It mightn't be worth your while having anything to do with it."

"Oh well, one must creep before one walks," Alan said quietly. "I'd be glad to act for you, sir." He'd got the point.

"Well said!" her father cried, slapping his thigh in delight. His good humour was doubled. "Come down one day next week and we'll walk the land." Behind Alan's back he winked at Vera.

When the day came for them to look at the land though, her father was moody and irritable. "This fellow can't have much to do if he can waste a whole day coming down here," he said as they drove to the bus to meet him.

"He's coming down on business, isn't he?" Vera said hotly.

"He'd want to be hard-up to call this business," her father snapped "It's not surprising he has no car."

She let the taunt pass because she had just been thinking that if Alan did have a car they could live down here and be near her father. Would that be at the back of her father's mind too? Then she saw the bus coming down the hill.

"Here it is!" she cried, scrambling out of the car, expecting him to follow. She could see Alan standing on the step of the bus, and she ran to meet him.

But Alan was not looking at her. "Where's your father?" he asked.

She looked around. Her father was still sitting in the car, black and silent, looking twice his bulk.

"There's something wrong," she cried, and she ran back. Meeting the bus was a pastime with her father. Always ahead of time, usually far too early, he'd prance up and down the road, denouncing the bus for being late. At no time else did one get such a sense of his leashed energy. "What could be the matter? Oh hurry, Alan!" she cried. But before they'd reached him he'd got stiffly out. Out on the road he looked normal enough except that there was something unpleasant about the way he dispensed with greeting Alan. And with a surly look he went ahead of them till they came to a lane, into which he turned without a word. Looking doubtfully at each other, Vera and Alan followed.

The lane was long. As they walked up it Alan chatted casually about the weather and the countryside. Her father's black mood appeared to be lifting. Then, as they were about to climb over the locked gate that led into the farm, his face darkened again and he pointed to Alan's feet. "What kind of shoes are those for going through fields?" he demanded. Alan said nothing. He just got over the gate and plunged into the long grass in his light shoes. After a short pause, her father too got over the gate. But on the other side he immediately turned up the collar of his coat, and shoved his hands into his pockets as if to imply that he had little interest in what was going on. And when they were scarcely half-way across the first field he came to a stand. "Well? What do you think of it?" he asked, turning to Alan.

"I haven't seen enough of it to form any opinion," said Alan coldly and began to walk on.

Her father didn't stir. "I've seen enough," he said. "It doesn't take me long to make up my mind."

"What are we to understand by that?" asked Alan. "That it's good, or that it's bad?"

"There's no such thing as bad land hereabouts," her father said, "but there are other things to be considered."

Miserably Vera looked at him. She could not bear the strain of waiting for Alan to speak. "There's no house on it for one thing," she said, not caring if she blundered.

Both men stared at her, her father with a glance that applauded, Alan with one she could not read. "Does that matter?" Alan asked. It was to her father he spoke, not her. "What is the need for a house on an out-farm?" His voice was so disengaged that Vera shivered. As for her father, he turned on his heel and walked back towards the gate.

An appalling feeling of humiliation came over Vera. She would have stumbled after her father if Alan had not laid his hand on her arm. "Let me handle this, Vera," he said curtly. "I must do things in my own way, not in his." Yet the expression on his face as he looked after her father was one of compassion. "I'm sorry for him," he said. "I know how he feels." He turned back to her. "But there are times when a person must put himself first. Will I be able to make you see that though?'

She was too worried to extract any sweetness from what his question implied. "We must be kind to him, Alan," she said.

He nodded. "I suppose there's no use in us all being unhappy," he said.

By then her father had reached the gate, climbed over it and got into the car. "Is he going to drive off without us?" Vera cried.

"Let him if he likes," said Alan. "We can walk. Sooner or later we'll have to have things out with him."

"Oh later then, later!" she said, and she ran after her father, but the coarse grass entangled her feet and impeded her at every step. All the same the car was still on the road when they reached it. Her father, however, was sitting in the back seat.

"Don't you want to drive, Father?" she asked, surprised. He turned his head away and did not reply.

The drive home was accomplished in heavy silence. And at the house things were no better. Her father seemed unable to stay in the same room with them. He kept going in and out. And when Lily put a meal on the table he stood up from it three or four times without explanation or apology. And his absence was as oppressive as his presence. "Is my stove lit?" he demanded at last, meaning the stove in the small room off the kitchen which he called his office. And although it was not lit, stubbornly he went down there. It was a dark little hole of a place, ell-shaped, its one window high-sashed and barred, and all afternoon Vera kept thinking of him sitting there in the cold with one leg crossed over the other, swinging his foot angrily back and forth like an angry cat swinging its tail. She could not keep her mind on anything that Alan said.

"I'd better go back on an early bus, I think," he said at last, and miserably she agreed it might be best.

"I'll drive you to the Cross," she said.

"Don't bother, Vera, I'd prefer to walk. It's a lovely evening anyway. Why don't you walk with me? Take your bike; I'll wheel it along, and you can cycle back." It was only March, and early in the month, but the daffodils were out on either side of the drive. As they walked by them the massed flower-heads shone like a lake of light. "Who planted them?" Alan asked idly.

"My mother, I think," said Vera.

Alan turned. "You think?"

"He never mentions her, you know. Someone else told me."

They walked on.

"It must be strange to know nothing about her."

Vera shrugged. But they both stopped and looked back. "I never saw so many daffodils," said Alan.

"I dare say they've spread a lot since they were put down," Vera said. Her mind was not on them, but Alan was still looking back at them meditatively. They'd even spread into the pastures indeed, where many of them were trampled and broken by the cattle, and far off in the middle of the field there were a few stragglers, that like convent girls in a convent park wandered two by two.

"I suppose you love this place?" he said.

"Wouldn't anyone?"

"I suppose so," he said reluctantly. Then, as they came to the big gates he exclaimed. "Now, there's a marvellous sight. Look." He pointed westward to where, clear of the trees, the sky burned like a sea of flame. "Do you know what I like about that? I like it because it's the same the world over. It belongs at the same time to everyone, and to no one."

But she wasn't listening. "Oh, did you see that?" she cried. Over their heads a late-returning bird had flown between them and the sun, and for an instant, pierced by the flaming rays, all but its core seemed burnt away.

Alan was amazed too. "How strange," he said. "It's like a glass bird. You could see right through it, beak, wings, feathers, all gone."

"All but its heart," Vera said softly.

For a minute he only stared at her. "Oh, Vera," he said then, and bending he kissed her. "I wanted to do that ever since we were out in the fields. And I wanted to say something, only I felt your father was listening, even when he was out of hearing. It was as if he was listening to our thoughts. He doesn't want any more land. I know what he had in mind." But when her face reddened he caught her to him. "I'm not blaming him, Vera. It's only natural he'd want to see you settled. But I can't stand him meddling. If we are to get married it must be on my terms and no one else's." He paused. "Not even yours. It's bad enough that I can't live without you."

"Oh, Alan!" The grudging way he said it did not take one whit from her joy.

But he was intent on making his meaning clear. "Some men want to marry," he said. "They're only waiting to meet the right woman. But there are others, like me, who don't want to marry at all. They are only forced into it by meeting a woman they cannot survive without."

"Do you really feel that way about me, Alan?" she asked timidly.

"Yes," he said firmly, "but I can't share you Vera. It's me or him. Oh Vera, can't you see that you've let him become so engrossed in you that his whole life has been spent on you. Not that I care about him. But I can't stand by and see you consumed, too."

"Oh Alan, you're exaggerating," she said, but she didn't know who she was defending, herself or her father. "What can I do?" she added helplessly.

"You can come away with me," he said peremptorily. "In fact that's what we've to do, we're going to go away, for a few years anyway."

"You know I can't do that," she said. "Bad enough to think of leaving him at all without going far away. And where would we go?"

His face darkened. "I knew that would be your attitude. Well, let me tell you something and you can think about it. I am going away anyway, to Australia, with or without you."

For a minute her mind blurred. "When?"

"This summer."

"Well, we can't discuss it now," she said wearily.

"Why not?"

She came to a stand. "There are so many things to be considered," she said vaguely. "For one thing there's my father's age!"

"And what is that, may I ask? Or do you know?" When she had to admit she did not know, he shook his head. "The trouble with you both is that you've lost all sense of identity. Both of you! Do you know what I think? If it weren't for you hanging around his neck all the time your father might have married again. He might do so yet, if you'd get out of the way. There's more to life than seeing one generation into the world or another out of it. I bet if you left him he'd be married within a year."

"Is it at his age?" she cried, but she saw at once she'd fallen into a trap.

"I thought you said you didn't know his age," Alan said scathingly. "Oh Vera, can't you see that without you he might begin to live again."

Such an entirely new prospect opened before her, her head reeled. "What if he got ill?"

"Is it that man? He's as fit as an ox. He could see us both down yet." Then, as they heard the sound of the bus he took her arm and shook her. "Think it over," he said.

But oh, quick upon his heels the irony of that last conversation was brought home. As strong as an ox Alan had pronounced him. The words were hardly bearable to her in the light of what followed. Alan should not be left in ignorance of it. It would not be fair to her father. It was, however, several days before she got a chance to write her letter. And when at last she began it the top of the page bore the address of a Dublin hospital.

Dear Alan [she wrote],

I'm writing to tell you that my father is ill. Oh Alan, he is very, very ill, so ill indeed that apart from any consideration of how his illness might affect us I would have written to tell you anyway, knowing you would be sad for him. It was on the very night you sailed the pain first struck him. I feel sure that, like me, you will think that very strange. And I hope that, like me, you will think that fact a sufficient reason for my writing. Anyway I cannot believe that you meant us to drop completely out of each other's existence. Do you realise that at this moment I do not know in what part of Australia you intend to settle? And that if I do not post this letter in time to reach you at Gibraltar or Aden, I may quite literally lose sight of you forever.

To return to Father, it now appears that he must have been ailing for some time, all winter perhaps. I can't help an ache at my heart when I think that if we had more patience matters might now be very different for us. Not that I am blaming you, dear, or thinking that you should not have gone, for although there can be no mistaking that Father's ailment is fatal, nevertheless his illness may be long and painfully drawn-out. Poor, poor Father. I suppose in a way my reaction to your going has been altered by these new circumstances. Perhaps now you can see that there was something to be said for my remaining behind? For my part, in spite of all the happiness I have given up, I am glad, oh so glad, that I too am not at this moment thousands of miles away from him. You will hardly believe me, Alan, but all things considered, I can almost say I am happy. Our parting no longer seems so senseless as it did the night you left.

To keep to what is relevant, I am of course doing everything I can for him, and I may add that Lily has been wonderful, but the fact is that very little can be done. He is to have a small exploratory operation, but the disease may well be too advanced for much to be done. At his age, an operation is always a risk, but the doctors see no reason for thinking he may not get through it. His heart, they say, is as strong as the heart of a young man.

I should tell you that I do not really expect a reply, although I am nearly miserable enough to crave any crumb of comfort. I will leave it to you, dear. Quite frankly at times I cannot believe you are gone.

Vera.

'PS. I did not stick down the envelope when I realised in how short a time I would have the surgeon's report. Oh Alan, things are as the local doctor feared. It is only a question of time. However, there is a further operation advised, not so much in the hope of prolonging his life as of making what is left of it more comfortable. I have given my consent. After that we will be going home, by ambulance of course, which will dishearten him I know, since I am sure he expected to walk out of here on his feet. You can imagine how I hate breaking the bad news to him. We will have to bring back a nurse too, which is another thing he will resent. I can't say that I myself look forward to having a nurse in the house, but I will try to get a pleasant and agreeable girl. I can tell you that my experience here in the past few days has taught me that they are not all angels. Far from it! But I'll do my best. Thank God I am here to see to this kind of thing for him. Ah Alan, surely now you can see my point of view? Perhaps I will expect a line from you after all, just a line, although I don't suppose your letter will alter anything in our situation, I cannot for all that hide the eagerness with which I will look for it.

Vera.'

The second operation was only successful in that the patient got over it. The pain was bought off, but at the price of new discomfort.

"I didn't realise he'd be so helpless," Vera said to the nurse as they waited for the ambulance that was to take them home. "He'll hate being carried down on a stretcher."

"He's a lucky man it's not in his coffin," said the nurse practically.

Vera stared at her. In spite of her boast to Alan, she had not in the end been able to pick and choose her nurse. She had to take the first one that came to hand. Indeed she had hardly glanced at her in the hospital, and even when they got into the ambulance she was only aware of how much room the creature took up: she was the big, hefty sort, who sat firmly planted down, with her feet apart. Her face wasn't bad, although her skin was thick, and the big brown eyes seemed lacking in expression. But there was one point in her favour, the sick man had taken to her.

"What is your first name, Nurse?" he asked. And when she said it was Rita, he started to call her that. It was extremely distasteful to Vera.

The ambulance had to go very slowly and so the journey seemed endless. "Is it far more?" the nurse kept asking. And once when they went over a hump in the road she snapped at Vera. "You shouldn't have moved him. You should have left him in the hospital."

"We're nearly there, Nurse," she said, ignoring the criticism.

The nurse shrugged. "I wouldn't answer for him if there's another jolt like that."

"Mind would he hear you," Vera whispered. "I'd rather he'd die on the way home than in hospital anyway," she added fiercely. Over the patient's head their eyes met in hostility.

When at last they got home however, and Lily came flying down the steps, all warmth and goodwill, the nurse brightened considerably.

"Upsy-daisy!" Lily cried as the stretcher listed and tilted on its way up the steps, and what might have been an ordeal was made to seem almost a lark.

"That girl would make a great wardmaid," said Rita looking at Lily after the patient was finally settled into his bed. "Had she any previous experience of nursing, I wonder?"

"None whatever," Vera disclaimed the compliment to Lily as if it had been paid to her, and, feeling that the occasion called for a gesture from her, she called after Lily, who was going to make a cup of tea. "Put two extra cups on the tray, Lily," she cried. "Nurse and I will have some too."

But the nurse called after Lily. "Put mine on a separate tray, please," she countermanded. And she turned to Vera. "Our regulations strictly forbid us to eat in a sick-room. I'd advise you not to do so either."

Vera reddened with annoyance. "Just one extra cup, so, Lily," she called out.

The sad thing was that her father didn't seem to appreciate her attentions. "Where is Rita having hers? he asked. 'Oughtn't you to keep her company?"

"I don't think she cares particularly for my company," Vera said.

But he misunderstood her. "Oh she will: she will," he said. "Give her time."

Irritated beyond words, Vera gulped down her tea and went out again to where, on the landing, the nurse was standing with her cup in her hand leaning down over the banisters. She was staring at the old prints on the wall. The house had made some impression, Vera was glad to see. "They're Malton prints," she said proudly and she let her own glance travel with pleasure around the white medallioned walls and the wide stone stairs that poured down between the iron banisters like a mountain cataract.

The nurse's voice broke in on her.

"A bit of a rookery, isn't it?" she said. "It must be bleak in bad weather. Lonely too, I'd say? Or are you used to it?"

Bleak? Lonely? Did that mean the creature might not stay? Vera stared out of the window. Stripped of leaves, the shrubs were tangled in strands of barbed brier. A stranger might think it a prison.

"Oh, it doesn't matter to me," the nurse said. "I'm only here for a while. But how do you stick it?" A faint curiosity showed for the first time in her eyes. "I don't suppose you'll stay on here, will you? Afterwards, I mean?" she said, and she nodded towards the door of the sick-room.

Vera said nothing. She felt a deep resentment. Why should this woman assume that but for her father she would be alone in the world? On a reckless impulse she said something that she knew was dishonest. "I may be going out to Australia," she said. The next minute she would have given anything to take back those words. It didn't make her feel any better that the nurse made nothing out of her lie.

"You've people out there, I suppose?" she said indifferently. "I've people out there myself. They're always writing and asking me out. I might go some time too, but I'd never settle down out there." Her expression changed. "I have other plans."

Vera stared. There was a kind of smirk in the nurse's eyes. She had a fellow, that was it. Involuntarily she glanced at the nurse's left hand.

But the nurse laughed and spread out her bare fingers. "We're not allowed to wear jewellery on duty," she said. She laughed again. "A ring above all. Bad for the morale of the patients, specially if the patient is a male. Oh, you may not think it," she said, as Vera raised her eyebrows, "but it's a fact. You'd be surprised how it depresses them, at any age." She nodded towards the sick-room.

"How ridiculous," Vera said. Yet, almost at once Alan's words came to her mind. But when those words were spoken her father was well. And sick or well, was it likely that a big lump like this would strike a spark in him? "I think you over-estimate my father's capacities," she said coldly. But hadn't she once or twice caught him looking at the young woman with a peculiar expression? And calling her Rita! She turned distastefully away from the creature. "If you'll excuse me, there are a few things I have to discuss with him."

The nurse drew herself up. "He's not able for much," she said warningly. But at that moment, Lily's voice came up from below in a snatch of song. "I tell you what!" Rita said more humanly, and she caught up the tray. "I'll take this down and give that girl instructions about your father's meals. I'm dying for a smoke." For a big girl she went down the stairs at a good lick. She was probably younger than she looked.

When Vera went in to her father he looked up. "Oh, it's you," he said, obviously disappointed.

"Yes, it's me," she said flatly. "Are you comfortable, Father? Will I fix your pillows?"

"No." Impatiently he waved her away. "Leave them. She'll do them. She has a knack."

"Well, I should hope so. It's part of her training. I don't think we should leave everything to her, all the same. Is there nothing you'd like me to do?"

He was lying back looking up at the ceiling but he glanced around the room.

"You could get her a chair," he said, "a comfortable one." He frowned at the hard bentwood chair beside his bed. "She ought to have a big armchair. Where did you put her to sleep by the way?"

"Up beside Lily," she said dully.

"Isn't it dark up there under the roof?" He didn't actually frown but she could see he was dissatisfied. And then he said something outrageous. "Why didn't you give her your room?"

"I gave her the room Lily had got ready for her," Vera said tartly, but under his stare she weakened. It would have been an awful job to move out all my things."

He said nothing for a minute and then, when he spoke he was so casual it was positively sly. "You'd have time to do it now while she's downstairs," he said.

But from below at that moment there came a sound of laughter. "I think it would be a great mistake to move her away from Lily," Vera said. "They seem to be getting on famously."

"She'd be nearer to me if she was in your room," he said.

"You seem to forget, Father, that what would be an advantage to you might not be one to her. She's not a night nurse, you know. To convenience her during the day seems quite unnecessary. We are paying her after all." But she was sorry she mentioned money. "Please let me fix your pillows, Father," she said quickly.

He waved her away again. "Leave them," he said again. Then he looked at her cunningly. "That's part of what we are paying her for, isn't it? How much is her salary anyway?"

Oh, why had she brought up the subject. "That's my worry, Father," she said firmly. Before he went into the hospital he had arranged for her to have a power of attorney. Once or twice he questioned her as to how she was managing, but only in a vague way, and gradually she had taken full responsibility. As his sole heir anyway, she felt it was virtually her own money she was spending. Unconsciously, all the same, at the back of her mind there had been times when she paused outside the sick-room, and imagined that when she opened the door she'd be confronted by him, fully restored to his old vigour, his eyes blazing, demanding an account of every penny. This, of course, she no longer imagined, but all the same she heartily wished she had not mentioned money. "Her wages are not much; really they're not," she lied. "And she's well worth every penny we pay her, isn't she?" she said, forcing out the words.

It was sad to see how readily he lent himself to her deception. "We're very lucky to get a girl like her," he said. "What's keeping her, I wonder?"

"She'll be up in a minute I'm sure, Father," Vera said, but she couldn't resist giving him a dig. "I don't think we should grudge her any time she spends below. Only for Lily's company she mightn't stay. It's very lonely here, you know, and neither you nor I have much to offer her."

"That's true," he said, but so lukewarmly she had an uneasy feeling her words had done more harm than good, because when he next spoke it was with a burst of his old energy. "What are you waiting for. Why don't you get that chair?" He closed his eyes. "I'll try and get some sleep," he said. "I want to save my strength all I can."

Save it for what? For that nurse, she supposed. Dejectedly, she left him and went out on to the landing. As she did there was another peal of laughter down below, and tears came into her eyes. Lily too had taken to the creature. What did they talk about? Probably about fellows. Vera sighed. She hoped at least they would not gossip about her. And, as she stood on the cold landing it seemed to her that in her own home she had no place. She was not wanted, upstairs or down. But just then the kitchen door opened and she heard footsteps in the hall below. Hastily she dried her eyes as Rita came running to the foot of the stairs.

"Oh, there you are!" the nurse said.

Was it imagination, or did Rita look at her with a more lively interest? But then the nurse looked more interesting to her too, less lumpy and heavy. Her big brown eyes, like berries that had ripened, were warmer, softer. And as she came up the stairs two at a time she was smiling. Halfway up she stopped. Her hands were behind her back. "Which hand will you have?" she called out gaily.

A letter?

"Lily forgot to give it to you in all the fuss," said Rita. "A little bird told me you were expecting it." So they had been talking about her. But evidently not disparagingly.

Filled with joy Vera took the letter. "Thank you," she said so earnestly Rita laughed.

"You'd think I wrote it," Rita said. "Off with you now and read it."

Vera was touched by her friendliness, and as well she felt absolved from the guilt of having said she might be going to Australia, for the letter made that seem less of a lie. But when she went into her room and sat down on her bed her heart went chill with apprehension. Suppose Alan was annoyed with her for having written. That his letter might not be a reply to hers at all simply did not occur to her, not until she was half-way down the first page.

Dear Vera,

I won't try to tell you how I felt when the boat sailed. You must have known how I'd feel. But it isn't to blame you that I write. Far from it, Vera. And I know that if you were here with me now I could imagine no greater happiness, because apart altogether from my own feelings of emptiness and desolation, the voyage itself promises to be very enjoyable. We left London—

At this point she stopped, realising he had not got her letter, and her hands began to tremble. He too was not able to endure a total severance. Her eyes flew back to the closely written page.

We left London in fog, but we weren't long at sea till the mists lifted and gave many of us, myself included, the mixed pleasure of seeing the last of the islands we were leaving perhaps forever. It was a beautiful sight, that coastline.

I have had my deck-chair put on the promenade deck which is covered, but the deck steward tells me that by tomorrow it may be finer, and probably much warmer, so if I wish I can have myself moved out on to the main deck which is open. At the moment it is pretty windy out there, and while I write this (in the ship's library which is also up on the sun deck) I can see a few hardy souls who are taking a stroll, holding on for dear life to their caps and headscarves. I could do with a bit of a blow myself before dinner, but I want to get this written, and there is not much time now before the gong goes. Dinner is served at 6.30, first sitting that is, but actually I am on second sitting, having been advised by the dining steward who is a very obliging fellow—looking already to his tip no doubt—that although the food is the same, the service at the second sitting is a bit better. Less rush, I suppose. It will give me more time to enjoy the daylight when we get further south. I expect I'll have to do a good many turns around the deck each day because the food so far seems very rich. They say that six times around the deck is equal to a mile. It's hard to believe, but everyone tells me it is so. I must say the passengers are all very friendly. Life on board is clearly going to be very sociable. There is no need for anyone to be alone unless by choice. It is surprising, mind you, how many couples have formed already. Some of course came aboard together, but in general I'd say they paired off since we sailed. There is, I suppose, a special need for friendship in those who, like me, are emigrating, and cutting so many ties.

I must tell you a funny mistake I made with regard to a couple at my table. I thought they were married because I'd seen them together in the embarkation-shed, but it seems they had just met and hooked up together. It was a bit embarrassing all round when my mistake was made known, but they took it in good part and we had a laugh over it. But oh, Vera, when I see them arm in arm, I think how lucky they are, and I can't help thinking that that is the way you and I would have been if things had gone as they should have gone for us. But I suppose it was not to be! I must try and put you out of my mind.

That reminds me, I must tell you another odd thing. Today on the promenade deck I saw a young woman seemingly like myself alone. And oh, Vera, she was so like you. It was uncanny really.

For a moment I was mad enough to think it was you, that you'd thrown your scruples to the winds and followed me. As if you would! Truly though, Vera, the likeness in profile anyway was remarkable. When she turned around I could see, of course, she was much rounder in the face than you, although there was still something about her eyes and the shape of her forehead and even the way she wore her hair, that almost broke my heart. You should have seen the look she gave me though, when she caught me staring at her. I can't say I blamed her. She must have thought I was batty staring at her so hard. I suppose I should have done the civilised thing and explained my reason to her. I'll have to do so if I meet her again at close quarters, which is likely enough I suppose, because this is not a very large ship, although the passenger list is long.

Do you know that we travelled at 17 knots yesterday and 18 knots today. These facts I learned from the bulletin board outside the purser's office. But how silly I am! These bulletins can mean little to you. Why do I tell you about them, you may ask? Ah, but tell me why am I writing this letter at all? I can hear you saying I have not the courage of my convictions. And you are right. Our decision to make a clean break was the only sane one. But do not blame me too much for trying to let myself down lightly. I promise I will try hard not to transgress again. Let us regard this as another farewell. Goodbye and God bless you. Give my respects to your father. I hope he is well. I'd like to know what he thought of our parting, but now I suppose I'll never know.

Alan.

She put down the letter. Her joy in it had been clouded. Two farewells! As if one was not bad enough. Well, by now he would have got her letter. She'd probably have another communication from him soon, a cable perhaps? And for the rest of the voyage, he need not feel so bereft. How well she knew the poignancy of the moment when that strange woman reminded him of her. She herself a dozen times, when she went to Dublin, had fancied some hurrying stranger in the street to be him, only to find that, close-up, there would be no vestige of resemblance, and what seemed a concession of memory was only an ugly trick of the eye. But oh, if that woman on the ship had in fact been her! For a long time she sat on her bed thinking of him, but although there was a chance that now she might, after all, be joining him some day, her sadness was not lessened. A forfeit had already been paid—their voyage out together.

But what was going on outside on the landing? For some time Vera had been vaguely aware of noises, pushings and shovings, and now Rita and Lily were running down the stairs giggling. She opened her door. The door of the sick-room was open too, and she could see her father lying on his side facing the wall. At her step he turned round. "Where were you?" he asked crossly. "They had to do everything themselves."

Surprised she saw that the big wardrobe in which his clothes had been kept was gone, and in its place was a moth-eaten red plush armchair that used to be in Lily's room. The pictures had been taken down too. And the ornaments were gone from the mantelshelf. "Well, what do you think of it?" he asked, thawing a bit, because he was himself so pleased.

"It's nice and airy certainly, Father," she said cautiously. Did he not see that it was the appurtenances of life that had been taken away? The bareness of the room frightened her.

"Rita is going to take up the carpet tomorrow," he said, and Lily's going to scrub the floor. It'll be cool for the summer."

Involuntarily Vera glanced out of the window. All week an east wind had driven across the land and blackened the early blossoms. "Summer is still a long way off," she said, and in her voice there must have been a latent bitterness, because he looked at her sharply. Then he reached out and caught her hand. "Do you ever hear from him?"

"Is it Alan?" she said stupidly. Alan's name had never been uttered by either of them since the day the sick man insinuated that she'd been let down. She hesitated. "I had a letter some time ago, Father."

"I knew you would," he said complacently. "He'll want you to go out to him. That will be the next thing." To her astonishment she saw that the expression on his face was one of satisfaction. "Mark my words, that's what will happen," he said. "You'll be going out to him one of these days." He must mean when he'd be gone. How nicely he'd settled things in his own regard, she thought.

She ought to be glad that he was not a prey to remorse, that his mind was at ease about her. But she could only shake her head. "Who knows," she said, and she turned away.

"That's right," he said. "There's no knowing what is in store for us."

But the bareness of the room had begun to depress her and she made an excuse to leave him.

If life had ebbed from the sick-room, the rest of the house teemed with life. Lily and Rita had only to be together in the kitchen for five minutes and the din was deafening. Rita was so different from what Vera had first taken her to be. She was so cheerful and so gay. Like a joybell she rang out happiness all day. As time went on she gave a hand with everything, peeling potatoes, scraping vegetables, drying up dishes. Prodigal of herself in all directions, she helped Vera too, mending torn linen, darning, and even doing a bit of dressmaking for Lily on the side. Her effect on Lily was extraordinary. The girl went about her work in a whirl, she too, giddily doing chores for everyone. One day she washed the doctor's car when he was upstairs with the patient.

It was with the patient though that Rita had her greatest success. Vera blushed to remember the suspicions she had had of her on the first day. It was true Rita flirted with him but this was soon understood by all to be a kind of charity. It helped the sick man to keep up appearances in the face of his steady deterioration. To Vera's amazement, Rita brought out a foppishness in him of which she herself had never imagined him capable, though she wondered if he might not be lending himself voluntarily to the blandishments; playing a part in a kind of ritual. There was about the sick-room at times the blended gaiety and gloom of carnival.

One day a strange thought crossed Vera's mind. She had often tried, without success, to imagine what it would be like to be married to Alan. Now listening to the happy babble of voices in the house, and seeing day run into day, purposeful and busy, she began to think that if she were married and had a few children, this, perhaps, was what her life would be like. To lovers, love might seem an isolated place, shutting them in, and shutting out the world, but channelled into marriage, might it not quickly become a populous place from which, in time, another generation would have to seek escape? Vera smiled at her thoughts. Her life at that moment was a good substitute for marriage.

One day there was a greater commotion than usual down in the kitchen. Curious, Vera ran down. She found Rita was standing up on a chair rummaging in the big press in the corner.

"—twenty-six, twenty-seven, twenty-eight!" Rita counted. Then, hearing Vera come in, she turned around excitedly. "Did you forget you had all this jam stored away?"

The jam! Vera had indeed forgotten.

"Why didn't you remind me, Lily?" she cried, but she knew that Lily was afraid she'd feel bad knowing the jam had been made for Alan.

"Have I put my foot in it?" Rita jumped down off the chair, but she had a pot of jam in her hand.

"Of course not," Vera said quickly. "It would have gone bad. I'm glad you found it. My father might try a little too."

"Oh good!" cried Rita, but she had no sooner poked her finger into the wax seal on the top of the jar than her face fell. "It's gone bad," she said.

Lily grabbed the pot. "I'm sure it's only the top that's gone," she said loyally. "All home-made jam is like that." Snatching up a spoon she dug into it. But the lump of pink sugar that she prised out shot into the air and clattered like a hunk of rock on the floor. Both girls giggled nervously.

"Take off a bit more, Lily," Rita urged, to cover up their embarrassment, although by the colour alone they could all see there was something wrong. A hoary whiteness glittered through the jar. "It's turned into sugar I'm afraid," the nurse said dolefully. "A pity we can't put it in our tea," she added, trying to make a joke of it.

Vera, however, was unable to laugh.

Impulsively Rita put an arm across her shoulders. "Never mind. Think what a good job you tried it out on us, and not on Someone Else."

There was tact. Vera had to smile. "I suppose we may as well throw it out," she said.

But there was a streak of thrift in Rita. "Is there no use for it, I wonder? Wait a minute, if it's turned into sugar it might be inflammable. We could use it to kindle the fire. Sugar is as good as paraffin. Let's keep it another while."

Lily was the one who had doubts. "I'd throw it out," she said flatly. "It will only draw wasps."

"Wasps?" Both Rita and Vera together pooh-pooh-ed this. "With the weather we've had for the past few summers I'd hardly know a wasp from a dodo," said Rita.

Even Lily had to admit this was true. "You'd miss them too, mind you," she said. "Summer isn't summer without them. God help them. They won't hurt you if you don't hurt them! Do you know something," she confided, "I often have to laugh at them, in their little black and yellow football jerseys."

"The Cavan colours! Oh, Lily, you're a scream," said Rita.

How Vera's heart warmed to them. They were such good sorts. In spite of the shadow of death the house was a happy one. She herself was so happy that she was hardly surprised when there was a knock at the door just then and she opened it to the postman. A second letter had come.

Like the last, this letter too was long. It was not written on ship's paper, however, but bore the letterhead of an hotel in Gibraltar. And this time Vera knew immediately that it was not a reply to hers. Without reading a line, some of the good went out of it for her.

> Dear Vera,
>   As you can see I am writing this in the Grand Hotel, Gibraltar, on the verandah as a matter of fact. I should have written last night but we had a gala dinner—the purser's party—and I confess I was late getting down to my cabin. This morning I am going on one of the shore-excursions arranged by the ship's officers and as it happens I have had an unexpected wait. But I am running on. I must explain myself. I really should have begun by telling you my reason for writing a second time. I'm sure you did not expect a letter, although this morning when I saw the mail bags on the deck it crossed my mind that there might have been one from you, oh, just a word of goodwill, Vera, nothing more, but I would have appreciated it. As it happened, we did not get our mail. Can you imagine, the launch that took us ashore was the same one that brought the passenger-mail aboard. So as we were carried away, we had the frustration of seeing the mail bags being dragged into the purser's office for sorting.

What was the meaning of this rambling rigmarole? Oh, it was too much. Vera was going to skip a bit until, near the end of the last page, a few words leapt at her.

> —and so it may be that in spite of everything, it will be to you that I will owe my life's happiness. And that, Vera, is why I write to you in such haste. I want to give you a hint of what I dare to presume may be in store for me. And I want you to know how much I hope that for you too, the same happiness may be in store, of which the happiness we had together may have been only a foreshadowing.

Bewildered, she turned back, and beside herself now, she devoured every word.

You will remember how we often spoke of destiny? It certainly does seem now that there was, after all, a strange concatenation of events in my life. Not only did I in a way initially undertake this voyage because of you, and most certainly because of you at the time I did, but it was a likeness to you that first drew my attention to Mary. That is her name. Mary Seward, the girl I told you about in my other letter. It is for her I'm waiting here in the hotel at this moment.

When I ran into her on deck the day after my last letter to you, and we got into chat, I cannot tell you how much I was struck by several other resemblances between you: small but very striking. In no time at all I was telling her about you. I found her so understanding. It was the beginning of our friendship, and now it seems that there is to be more in it for us than mere friendship. How strange to think you and I knew each other for so long, and Mary and I have just flown into each other's lives, while both of us as she put it rather beautifully, were "on the wing."

When things are settled I will write to you again. And if I am not mistaken, Mary will want to write to you too. She told me last night how very conscious she was of the part you played in our lives. She said she would like to thank you. In spite of the distance that divides you, it is my hope that you two will be friends.

But I must stop. I see her coming. As a matter of fact we have missed the main excursion. But we will hire a car and do a little tour of our own. It will probably be more enjoyable than the tour organised by the ship. But we will have to hurry, as in any event we must be back on the Orcades at 10.45 p.m. In haste, but with affectionate remembrance.

Alan.

Affectionate remembrance! It was like a line on a mortuary card. As for that sentimental rubbish from the other woman, that hurt most of all.

Oh, it was so humiliating. And what would Rita and Lily think? Even if she didn't tell them they'd probably sense there was something wrong. But as she stood miserably staring at the letter, her heart froze at a sound from her father's room. "Oh God, what is that?" she cried out loud. Headlong she ran onto the landing. But although low, those sounds had filled the house, and ahead of her Rita and Lily had raced up the stairs and were with her father. Rita was bending over the bed and Lily was on her knees mopping up the floor. "What is the matter?" whispered Vera.

Her father was almost entirely out of the bed, leaning forward in a position so grotesque that, combined with the way they were holding him, made it seem as if ludicrously he was trying to swim, or to fly. He was retching violently. And as the black bile poured out of him, it seemed that it was by its force he was splayed out over the side of the bed. "Vera!" he gasped, as their eyes met. Do you see now why I saved my strength, those eyes seemed to ask.

Then, as suddenly as it started, the retching stopped. And where before he seemed to have been flung forward, now he seemed to be flung back, his gaze transfixed.

Rita, as white as a sheet, straightened up. Her face was wet with sweat. "Another minute and he would have been gone," she said harshly. "He shouldn't have been left alone."

"Is he dying?" Hysterically, Vera tried to push past the others to get to the bed.

"Oh, not at all; he's all right now," said Rita impatiently. "We got to him in time."

Vera was shaking. "What does it mean?" she cried.

Rita swung round. "I'll tell you what it means," she said callously. "It means that you'll have to get a night nurse right away. Where would we be if this happened during the night? He could have choked."

As if she'd been struck, Vera's face reddened. "Wouldn't I have heard him?" she asked weakly.

"You didn't hear him in broad daylight, did you?" Crossly Rita wiped her hair back from her face. "A nice kettle of fish it would have been if he smothered, for me, I mean. It's high time we had a night nurse. We should have had one from the start I suppose, but I was sparing you."

"There was no need for that." The tears came into Vera's eyes. When had she been niggling?

Rita had the grace to be ashamed at least. "It's not that I'd mind getting up at night," she said. "But if I lost my sleep too often I'd be no use to you or to him. Goodwill isn't enough in nursing."

"I understand," said Vera. It took an effort to be polite.

"I hope you do." Rita looked more contrite every minute. "I want to give him an injection," she said. "I'll have to go upstairs to my room for a new needle. Will you stay with him while I get it? We can't leave him alone any more, even for a short time. You needn't be frightened. I just want to be on the safe side." As she went out of the room she looked back. "There wasn't bad news in your letter, was there?" she asked.

The letter? A thousand years could have passed since she'd read it. Alan and his bride-to-be had shrunk to specks on a very far horizon. Even the hurt they'd inflicted had been deadened, but not her instinct to hide it. "Of course not," she said quickly.

But Rita's eyes probed her through and through. "A little misunderstanding, I expect. Ah well, the course of true love never did run smooth," she said lightly. And she went out.

Vera moved over to the bed. Her father looked up at her. She bent and kissed his forehead. He *was* all she had in the world now. She had a great longing to unburthen herself to him; to tell him about her heartbreak.

But Rita was back. "A nice fright you gave us!" she said briskly to her patient as she came in the door. "Why didn't you call someone? Shame on · you!" But across the bed she winked at Vera, and bending down she smiled into the sick man's eyes and her voice was soft and cajoling. "I'm only joking," she said. "It was our fault. We shouldn't have left you alone. But it won't happen again. We can promise you that. We're going to get someone to sit up with you and keep you company at night. Won't that be nice?" When he looked startled, she gave him a playful nudge. "We'd have had one long ago only we couldn't find anyone fetching enough for you."

For a moment her father seemed to hesitate, and then, playing his part he tried to smile. "How about a blonde this time?" he whispered.

"Oh come now. I can't have talk like that," Rita said. "I'll be getting jealous."

"Oh, you'll always be my first love, Nurse," said the patient, but it made Vera sad to see that unconsciously he had given Rita back her formal title.

It wasn't easy to get a second nurse with the summer coming on. After several trips to the 'phone in the village post office Rita got very anxious.

"I wonder if we ought to try for a nurse attendant?" she said desperately. "They're sometimes very competent, and all we need really is someone to sit with him at night. And I know one who is free, a very reliable person. We were on a case together before. She's an old dear."

"Oh, she's old?" Vera was doubtful at once.

"She's fairly old. There's no denying it," Rita said, "but she's very efficient. She's had enough experience, God knows." And here it seemed she could not help laughing. "The old girl is ninety if she's a day." She was joking of course, and Lily who had come into the room and overheard her took it as a huge joke. Vera felt they could both have been less unfeeling.

Next day, however, when the old nurse stepped out of the taxi at the door Vera's own first impulse was to laugh. The new nurse looked a million years old. How would her father take this? It took them five minutes to get her up the steps. And once inside, she didn't seem to have a glimmer about direction. Several times they found her going the wrong way along a corridor, or looking for the patient's room on the wrong landing. It was nearly eleven, that first night, before they'd got her ready for her duties. She'd be almost as much trouble as the patient, Vera thought uneasily, as she said good night to her. She herself was having a cup of cocoa in the kitchen with Rita and Lily before they too went to bed. The old woman was taking a jug of water upstairs with her. Holding it out from her like a bunch of flowers, she was toddling off when suddenly there was a loud crack, as she knocked the jug against the metal tongue of the lock.

"Oh Nurse, are you wet?" Vera asked as water spilled out on the floor.

But the old nurse had heard nothing. Unconcernedly she went on up the stairs to the tune of pattering drops. Lily and Rita spluttered with laughter.

"I don't think it's amusing at all," said Vera.

But a minute later she found it hard to keep her face straight when the old thing appeared at the kitchen door. "Lily! You gave me a leaking jug," she said crossly. "There's not a drop in it."

Stuffing their fists into their mouths, Lily and Rita ran into the pantry to hide their laughing, but Vera's heart sank. How would the old woman be competent to mind a sick man at this rate? she thought. But when the old nurse was gone up again and Rita came out of the pantry she was genuinely sympathetic.

"Don't let that worry you," she said. "Your father likes her, and that's the important thing, isn't it?"

It was true that the sick man did seem to like the old woman. Was it, perhaps, that the efforts of gallantry had been a strain on him? Did he welcome the peace the old creature brought with her? There was certainly a new quiet in the sick-room. He often dozed when the two of them were together. Going into the room once it crossed Vera's mind that the old woman too, no less than her patient, was waiting for her last end. Her few words were uttered in a voice so soft they could not be heard outside the door, and when she moved around the room she made no sound in the old felt slippers she wore. Indeed as time passed it even seemed that the whole house was becoming muted.

Rita and Lily were gay as ever, but, freer now to leave the house, they worked off their excess vitality in cycle rides, and even an occasional dance in the village. And once or twice, when they had been out late, the old lady made Rita lie-in next morning. "I can rest as well in a chair as a bed," she said placidly. And indeed, the big plush armchair was as big as a bed for her small, shrunken body. "I don't need much sleep," she assured them placidly. "Anyway I'll soon have enough of it." It was impossible to tell whether she spoke humorously or otherwise.

"She sleeps on her feet," Lily said. "Like a bird on a branch."

"All the same I don't want to trade on her goodwill," Rita said.

And yet it was inevitable that they did, all of them, even Vera.

One day Vera let Rita persuade her to go for a spin with her. "You're in the house too much," she said severely. "You need to get out in the air."

"I'll cut a few sandwiches for you," Lily urged. "Make a day of it."

It was not yet the real summer, but yet it was a day such as seldom comes even in summer. The sun shone down as they rode along between the hedges, already thickening with leaf and bud, and they laughed and talked as happily as if they were one as young and carefree as the other. Rita let go the handlebars and pedalled along with her hands in her pockets, whistling like a messenger boy. They stopped for lunch on a long treeless stretch, where the banks were high but softly mounded and the ditches shallow and dry. Throwing down her bike Rita clambered up on the bank and sat down.

"Are you sure the grass isn't damp?" Vera asked, feeling it.

"Are you mad," Rita cried. "It hasn't rained for days."

But they had no sooner settled themselves, and taken out their packages of food than rain splashed on the greaseproof paper. By the time they had got to their feet it was pouring.

"Oh, where will we shelter?" Vera cried, looking up and down the treeless stretches of the road.

"Oh, come on. Let's go on," Rita cried, jumping on her bicycle. "We're already soaked to the skin."

"Look, there's a clump of trees ahead," Vera said.

But when they reached it Rita didn't stop. "Let's keep going," she said. "We can change our clothes when we get back. I love the rain." Throwing back her head, she held her face up to it. Just then the sky was split with lightning.

"Oh my God. Did you see that?" Vera's words were drowned, however, in a long peal of thunder.

"Oh, it's miles away," said Rita indifferently, although a second peal had immediately volleyed over their heads.

"We can't go on," Vera cried.

But there seemed to be a devil in Rita. "Why not?" she called back, and her voice was almost buried under the cataracts of sound.

To be heard Vera had to draw abreast of her. "It's terribly dangerous," she shouted. "Especially on a bike. Steel attracts lightning."

"Nonsense!" cried Rita. "We're safer on the bikes than anywhere. Aren't the tyres rubber?" Anyway the clump of trees was far behind.

Keeping abreast they careered along, while to either side of them the darkening countryside was lashed with light. Shrinking down over the handlebars Vera didn't dare to raise her head, but Rita, standing on the pedals, rose up and down with them, and stared out over the transfigured landscape. "Isn't it wonderful?"

"I'm scared' Vera screamed.

Rita threw her a scathing glance. "Do what you like," she said. "I'm going on. Anyway, I've got to get back to my patient. A nice thing it would be if he went off suddenly while I was sitting here under a bush."

In her fright Vera's foot slipped off the pedals and she almost fell. "Wasn't he all right when we left?" she cried appalled.

"Oh, for heaven's sake, don't take me up on every word I utter," Rita yelled back crossly. "It's just that you never can tell with any case."

As if her father was only a case. "Oh, let's get back quick," she cried, and with a new spurt she shot ahead. Obscurely she'd felt up to then that the blades of light as they scythed across the tops of the hedges would not dip to find her if she crouched low enough over the handlebars. But now she, too, stood up on the pedals and pressed them down with all her might. She too stared out over the fields, which in that eerie light were as strange as the fields of the moon. Trees and bushes, even on the farthest rim of the sky, were suddenly brought so close it seemed their branches switched her eyeballs. Near and far were one. Then, around a bend in the road, the white gable of a cottage came in sight. It seemed to rear up out of nowhere. And up its walls rode their shadows, hers and Rita's, riding like furies. "Look at us, Rita," she cried. "We're like death riders in a circus."

Then there was another flash and a second cottage rose up as if out of the earth. The walls this time were rosy pink, but to Vera it seemed they were in flames. The whole world was in flames. Even Rita was startled. "Oh God! that gave me a fright," she cried, acknowledging with a grimace that perhaps after all death could have been riding with them. When they got back at last they could see Lily's white face pressed to the window, and as they flung down their bikes she threw open the door for them and ran back, not daring to stand in the doorway.

"How is my father?" Vera cried.

Lily grinned. "He slept through it. The old girl too. I might as well have been all alone. I was scared stiff. And look. I got stung by a wasp." She held up her arm. It was red and swollen. "I knew that jam would draw them," she said. "And what do you suppose I discovered? There's a nest of them in the grass under the kitchen window. I nearly stood in it." She laughed.

Rita was the one who was cross. "You'll have to do something about that," she said sharply to Vera. "There's your father to think of. If we managed to get him out in the sun for a few hours it would be a nice thing to have him stung to death."

Bewildered, Vera looked at her. A little while before she was afraid he might be dying and now she was talking of bringing him out in the sun.

But Rita turned to Lily. "Are there any men about?" she asked jokingly, and whipping off her blouse she held it in front of the range to dry.

Vera went upstairs. Her father was still asleep. So after changing her clothes she ran down again. Rita and Lily were sitting at the kitchen table, but somehow she got the impression that they hadn't expected her to come down so soon. It was not that they changed the conversation, and Rita even drew her into it at once, but an odd look had passed between them. Then Rita addressed her directly. "I was just saying to Lily here that those summer storms—thunderstorms—are usually a sign of good weather."

"But it's only May," said Vera instinctively.

"Nearly June," Rita said.

"And those wasps," Lily said. "They're a sign of summer." But she looked guilty. "Of course this fine weather could be just a flash in the pan," she added quickly, when Rita gave her a quelling glance.

"This may well be all the good weather we'll get," Rita said. "I've made that mistake too often, spent May and June watching for the good weather, and July and August finding out it was over."

Was it possible they had been talking about their holidays? Filled with consternation, Vera's face gave her away.

"Of course I'd never take my holiday in the middle of a case," Rita said quickly. "That is, not if the end was in sight."

Relieved, Vera sat down. "I always think myself the autumn is the nicest time of the year for holidays," she said.

"Oh, the autumn is no good for anything," said Rita sharply. "The evenings are too short."

"And the nights are chilly," piped Lily.

Nervously, Vera stood up again.

Rita stood up too. "If I were to take my holidays now, while your father's condition is fairly stable, I'd be back on the job when you'd really need me."

"At the end, you mean?" Vera said quietly.

"Oh the end could be easy enough," said Rita airily. "But he could go into a coma. You might like to have me here then. All things considered, I really think I ought to go while the going is good. And the great thing is that you won't need anyone to replace me. I sounded out the old girl, and she said that if you put a stretcher-bed into your father's room she could easily manage single-handed. It isn't everyone would do it, mind you. Wasn't it a godsend it was her we got. She's as good as two saints rolled into one."

So it was all settled. Only her assent had been needed. "Wouldn't we have to consult the doctor?" Vera asked desperately.

"Oh, doctors are usually considerate enough where private nurses are concerned," said Rita lightly.

"You could get round him anyway, Rita," cried Lily. "You could tell him one of your family was sick."

Vera's heart sank.

How false had been her feeling of solidarity with them. These girls had their private lives which at all costs they would safeguard from interference.

Yet, when the day came for Rita to leave, her concern for Vera was genuine. "Do you think you'll be all right without me?" she asked anxiously for about the twentieth time, as Vera and Lily stood on the steps, waiting to see her off. There was a car calling for her.

"Her fellow," Lily whispered to Vera.

But Rita wasn't happy. She was restless and uneasy. Suddenly she frowned. "The wasps' nest!" she cried. "We did nothing about it. Oh, perhaps I oughtn't to go at all. Not that I really think your father will ever stir out of doors again," she said quickly, "but there's the old girl to consider. What if she got stung." It wouldn't take much to finish her off I'd say." She wrung her hands.

"Don't worry," Vera said placatingly. "I'll attend to it at once. Tomorrow."

"But how? That's the whole point. It may not be as easy as you think."

"What about tar?" Lily cried. "We could pour it into the nest at night when they're all inside?"

Rita shook her head. "Too hard to handle. You have to heat it and that's very dangerous." She shuddered. "But you could set fire to it perhaps, with petrol."

"Not so near the house!" Vera cried. "The whole place could go up."

Rita bit her lip. "Wait!" she cried. "Have you a gun? You could fire a shot into it, at close range. But can you handle a gun?"

"I'm sure I could manage," Vera said.

"Well then, there's no more to worry about." Leaning forward, Rita strained to see the road through the trees. "Here's my friend," she said as she saw a car. "I told him I'd meet him at the gate," and catching up her bag she gave them both a quick kiss and ran down the steps. "Goodbye," she called back. "Goodbye."

Looking after her, Vera felt curiously bereft. She looked at Lily.

"Well, that's that," Lily said, as they turned and went back into the house.

Had the sun gone? Had the birds stopped singing? It was hardly possible that one person's absence could have made itself felt so immediately. Yet, before the day ended the house was like a tomb. Certainly the kitchen became one. The leaves of the trees had thickened and the shrubs grown dense, and although the upper rooms were above the level of their shade, the lower part of the house was as dark by day as if evening had prematurely fallen. Once about four o'clock when Vera went down to make a pot of tea, it gave her a shock to see two birds that chased each other dash in one window and out the other, as if indeed it were a deserted place.

But one afternoon while Vera was upstairs mending a sheet, the silence of the house was shattered. Voices? Like a twitter of birds they rang out, only louder and more inconsequential. She thought she recognised Rita's voice, and then, unmistakably she heard Rita's laugh. Throwing the sheet aside, Vera ran down the stairs.

"Oh, there you are!" cried Rita gaily. She ran forward and kissed Vera. "I was just telling Lily here that I got bored in Dublin and I came down to stay with cousins of mine who live near here, and today I hopped on the bike and came over to see how you were getting on. Talk of a busman's holiday! How are you? And how," she asked quickly as an afterthought, "is your father? I must go up and see him before I leave. Not that I can stay long," she said, glancing at her watch. Then she laughed. "What I'm dying to know is how you're getting on with Her Nibs?"

"Oh, she's been very good and kind," Vera said sincerely.

"Not a bad sort at all," said Lily, but she giggled. "She's a howl really," she said. "I never stopped laughing since you left."

Vera looked at her with astonishment. When had all this hilarity taken place?

"Oh, I didn't let on to you," said Lily, turning to her. "She was going to leave several times only I got around her to stay. There was one time and she'd her bags all packed and ready for off! She thought she was in a madhouse. There was the jam for one thing." She turned to Vera. "You remember just after Rita left there was a cold spell and one evening we thought we'd light a fire, but the kindling wood was wet and I was down on my knees puffing and blowing at it when—"

Suddenly Rita gave a screech. "Oh, Lily. Don't tell me. I know what happened."

But Lily put her hand over Rita's mouth.

"Let me tell it," she begged. "I've been dying to tell someone."

She turned back to Vera. You came in. "Did you try putting jam in it, Lily," says you. You should have seen the poor old thing's face. But that wasn't the worst. That afternoon she was having a cup of tea when you walked in with the master's gun in your hand and—"

"Oh, Lily!" Rita knew what was coming this time too.

"Wait! please, please," pleaded Lily. "Let me tell it." She turned back to Vera. "The poor old thing looked up. 'I thought it was the closed season,' she said. 'Oh,' said you, 'I'm only going out in the garden to shoot a few wasps.'"

"Oh no." It was too much for Rita.

Screaming with laughter, the two girls sank down on the kitchen chairs, their feet sprawled out in front of them.

"To think I never noticed a thing!" said Vera so sadly Rita was sobered.

"Ah, you were too anxious about your father," she said kindly. "You didn't tell me how he is? Ought I go up and see him, or do you think it might only disturb him?"

A week earlier there would have been no question of her not seeing him, but now Vera had misgivings. "Would you like me to tell him you're here," she said after a minute, "and see what he says?" And without waiting for an answer she slipped upstairs.

In the sick-room the windows were thrown up, and the whole room was filled with a myriad of small sweet sounds, the hum of insects, and the songs of birds. And when Vera went softly in there was a whir of wings as the swallows under the eaves swooped back and forth from their nests. The old nurse and her patient were both awake, but although they were not speaking Vera felt as if she was intruding. It was as if they were communicating in some way beyond her understanding. These unspoken messages were deep and meaningful. How could she ever have been so mistaken as to think that life had ebbed from this room. Dying too was a part of life. For a minute she stood unobserved in the doorway. Then she heard Rita's footsteps on the stairs and she stepped back quickly, closing the door.

But Rita had seen into the room. "Oh, what a change there is in him," she whispered. "And in such a few short days." Gently she put her hand on Vera's arm. "It looks to me as if he's near the end," she said. But, seeing

Vera's start, she spoke sternly. "You're lucky, you know. The end is going to be very easy." Then drawing Vera towards the stairs she went down a few steps. "It's funny the way things work out, isn't it? We only thought of that old woman as a stop-gap and now it looks as if it was God who sent her to you. I don't think you'll need me back at all,"she said firmly.

"Oh, Rita," Vera cried. "We couldn't do without you."

Rita shook her head. "It's not my business, I know," she said, "but think of the saving. I don't know how you're fixed with regard to money, but there's no sense in throwing it away."

"The money doesn't matter," said Vera in a flat voice.

Rita shook her head. "You'd be surprised what a financial drain it can be, a death in the family, I mean, specially coming after a long illness." She threw up her hands. "When all is over there's an avalanche of bills. I've seen people crushed by them. Yes, crushed!"

"Oh, Rita," Vera cried, putting out her hands, "I can't bear to think of the house without you. And what will Lily do?"

"Oh, a pity about Lily!" Rita said. "She'll be getting married one of these days. She can live on the thought of that. As for you, won't you be going to Australia?"

It was a long time since Alan's name had been mentioned. Vera had begun to think Rita and Lily both suspected that there was something wrong.

But Rita's face was guileless. "It's a pity you can't be there for the Australian summer," she said. "Not, God forgive me, that I grudge your father his last days, but it's a shame to lose the chance. Ah well, it's only one summer."

Vera looked at her. She was so strong and young. One summer more or less would indeed matter little to her. Unable to bear her secret any longer, she blurted it out. "I may not be going out at all."

But Rita missed her meaning. "Oh, is he coming back?" she asked "I can well believe it. I know lots of people who didn't like it out there. Still, it's a pity you didn't have the trip. Ah well! maybe you didn't miss much. You might have ended up with two winters in the one year." Uncontrollably she yawned. "Oh, I'm jaded," she said. "I was at a dance last night. Late hours flatten me." She looked at her watch. "I'd better be off."

In the days that followed it became clear to Vera that her father was dying at last. His world was shrinking smaller and smaller. In the beginning of his illness, when there was a noise downstairs, or in the yard, he'd sometimes ask them not to slam doors, or let things fall, but after a time when there was a noise he'd only look startled, and his eyes would dilate as if with fear. Soon sudden sounds in the sick-room gave him a violent start. His world had narrowed down to the bed on which he lay and his face seemed to wear an habitual look of surprise. At first Vera thought it was that he could not believe the pass to which he had been brought, but slowly she came to realise that it was the old life of health and normality in which he could not believe. When a light went on he was surprised. When Lily brought his tray he was surprised, and he was surprised again when she came to take it away. And once when Vera herself went into his room he seemed to find her presence so startling she had to protest.

"Where did you think I was, Father?" she cried. Was it possible that deep down in his heart he did not trust in the finality of her break with Alan? Did he think she had deserted him after all? In that moment she made up her mind to tell him the truth. And so one day while the old nurse was taking a nap she sat down on the side of his bed. "There is something I never told you, Father," she said quietly. "Alan has gone out of my life for good."

Weak as he was, he was able to hide his reaction. "What matter," he said dully.

Stung by the apparently indifferent words, she was about to move away when she was struck by the depths of pity in his eyes. It was not a rage of pity, like long ago, it was a pity that embraced them both. And he did not need to explain it. She knew he was asking himself what anything mattered when all came to this in the end.

Then he took her hand. "What does your mother's loss matter now to me?" he said sadly. "Some day it will be the same with you." It seemed a strange and unreal analogy, this analogy between her and her dead mother. And yet it was valid she supposed. A silence fell as they pondered their separate aspects of the same thought. Then he spoke again. "Vera, do you think there's a meeting in the next life?" he asked suddenly.

"I don't know, Father," she said, confused. Not for years had she given the matter thought.

"Because I don't," he said vehemently. "When they dig the black hole and put you down in it that's the end of you."

"Oh no!" Vera's heart cried out against the thought of facing into that nothingness, that nowhere. "Of course there is a hereafter," she cried. "Otherwise what would be the meaning of love?"

Weak tears came into his eyes. "Do you really believe that, Vera?" he said.

Partly lying and, like himself, partly wanting to believe it, she nodded.

He closed his eyes. "It would make up for everything," he added, almost under his breath. Then he opened his eyes wide. "Just to see her. Just to see her again is all I'd ask."

Vera's own eyes widened. "Who are you talking about?"

"Your mother," he said, and he looked surprised. "Who else?"

The Mock Auction

The bloom of summer was on Miss Lomas. She was as plump as a goose. She had put on weight in her years at Brook Farm and took a large fitting now in skirts and blouses. Gone, long was the time she could struggle into the costume she had worn on the day she accepted the invitation of the Garret brothers to preside over the fine old house which would otherwise have been a liability to them. They had bought the property solely for the sake of the land. To have allowed the large beautifully proportioned house to go to rack and ruin just because the farm was to be an outfarm, would have been outrageous.

It was a matter of luck for all concerned that Miss Lomas had been on hand to run it in a befitting manner.

The costume Miss Lomas had worn the day she first went up the graceful flight of steps to the hall-door of Brook Lodge was still as good as new, stowed away in the hinterland of her clothes closet along with other costumes and coats of that bygone time. She kept plenty of moth balls in the pockets of those once modish garments but the garments themselves only saw the light of day once a year when she took them out, gave them a shake and hung them by an open window for an airing. Occasionally the garments at the back like a crowd at a football match, had pushed forward those in front, and it was difficult to shut the closet door. Miss Lomas had to bump it shut with her ample bottom.

Ought she to have given those old clothes away to someone needy, someone less fortunate than herself? This question sometimes crossed her mind. But to whom would she give them? In order to preserve the sort of privacy proper to a place like Brook Farm she had from the start kept the neighbours resolutely at arms-length. And in the succession of young servant girls the brothers were always hiring to give her a hand, there had not been one who would have appreciated the quality of such clothes, neither the superior fabric nor the elegant cut. Anyway the bulging closet was in tune with all else at Brook Farm, where plenty was the order of the day. Indeed what might appear plenty to some men would have been frugality to the Garret brothers. Jokingly Miss Lomas used to say there was as much left on their plates after they had eaten their fill than would have satisfied other men to have set before them when they took up their knives and forks to attack a meal. As for herself, she wasn't slow in acquiring the same breadth and scope as her patrons. She regarded herself as one of the family and daily thanked her lucky stars that she had not let herself be persuaded by so-called wellwishers that her financial arrangement with the brothers was too free and easy. She knew what she was doing. She was more than content with her position. No salary however generous would have allowed for her spending so lavishly on herself as she was at liberty to do if she wished every Saturday night, when, in the Garretstown trap, she went to town to pay the week's bills and order supplies for the week ahead. In town after she had settled the Brook Farm bills, taking out the fat wad of notes that Joss Garret, the older brother, had stuffed into her hand before she set out, she paid each bill, painstakingly and slowly peeling off note after note as if it was hard to get it to come away from the wad as the rind from a thin skinned lemon. There would have been lashings over to pay for a box of face powder or a bar of perfumed soap or some such little fal-de-la. She did not feel such purchases could be strictly regarded as household expenditure, although the cost would have been a drop in the ocean of the considerably large amount of change she attempted to hand back to Joss the following Monday morning at the beginning of her first full week in her new employment. But Joss, who was the most generous of men, awkwardly pushed the proffered money back into her hand. He was downright embarrassed. "Keep it, Miss Lomas! Keep it!" He muttered. "You might need it during the week. One never knows what expenses may crop up unexpectedly and I sincerely hope you did not deny yourself anything you needed." Although a bachelor, (due no doubt to the frailty of his sister, Joss had an ornate understanding of women) so with a delicacy equal to his own, Miss Lomas did not press the point, or upset him by ever raising it again.

Of course when she got to know the brothers better, she saw the common sense behind the words of Joss. For, what with replacements of crockery, cooking utensils and household linen, to say nothing of replenishments of food and cleaning materials for the huge store cupboards there was always good use to which the money could be put. Every single bit of that money was ploughed back into Brook Farm, even taking full account of the trifling odds and ends she began to buy herself when the brothers had made it abundantly clear that this was part and parcel of her deal with them. She soon saw for herself that it would not have been in the best interests of the property that she herself look less than her best. Was it not because of how she graced the top of the dining room table as well as being answerable for the provender upon it that she had been invited to reside in the dear old house in the first place? The truth of this was brought home to her when remarkably soon after she had become established there an unexpected development took place. She was exceedingly gratified by it and she saw at once it would be both gainful and pleasurable to all concerned. She was quite struck by how quickly the brothers saw that Brook Farm would be an eminently suitable place to fulfil their occasional obligations to entertain the big cattle men and jobbers, with whom they did business, without putting undue strain, as hitherto, upon the household at Garretstown House, which although it was presided over efficiently and elegantly by Miss Garret put a costly price on that poor lady's health and nerves since she was virtually a semi-invalid. The new plan was put into action at once. In no time at all Miss Lomas had made Brook Farm a homelier and happier place than Garretstown House had ever been, a smaller, but, in her opinion a nicer house. The modest garden that lay between it and the road was full of trouble-free secluded bowers, and far prettier, she thought, than the large formal grounds that surrounded the larger property. Taking all with all Brook Farm was an ideal place to bring warm-hearted cattlemen back for a meal at the end of a long tiring fair day.

The only pity was that Joss and George themselves could not more often eat there, or indeed live permanently there because in spite of their money they were men of simple ways who went about the countryside buying and selling their own stock like plain farmers. Needless to say they were infinitely larger minded than ordinary farmers and certainly did not make a display of their wealth, but one had only to look at their sister to see the stock from which they had been bred. Just to consider the paper-thin soles of Miss Garret's shoes was to know that never in her life had *she* stepped into a pad of cow dung.

Not that Miss Lomas herself was one for traipsing through fields. She got a good grasp of all that she was required to know about farming from the account books and the farm correspondence which she in the main handled. And of course she learned a lot by listening to the talk at table whenever she put up a lunch for a vet or a land inspector, or on the even happier days when the brothers themselves arranged to eat with her if they were shearing sheep or dosing cattle, it being obviously more sensible for them to remain at Brook Farm for their mid-day meal rather than lose precious time going back and forth between it and the big place.

There was nothing Miss Lomas liked better than getting up a decent meal for men capable of appreciating it. Hearty food for hearty eaters was her motto. After warning the men that the plates were mad hot, although never as in lesser establishments disfigured by oven marks, she would ladle out huge helpings of prime beef cooked to a nicety and plentifully doused with gravy from rich pan-liquor. She would eagerly grasp her own knife and fork and eat up with as much gusto and relish as any man.

When the meal was over and the room still reeked traditionally of whiskey and tobacco, Miss Lomas made a point of taking leave of the company to go down to the kitchen and personally supervise the making of the coffee. Unfailingly Joss would spring up to pull out her chair, and invariably he would pay her a nicely phrased compliment. "Where would we be without you, Miss Lomas. You are the heart of Brook Farm."

"Ah, but where would I be without Brook Farm?" She would invariably reply.

Then as George chimed in with generous words of his own, echoed by the guest if any, Miss Lomas would let the beam of her smile sweep over the table, stopping short only at Christy.

Who was Christy?

Christy was the fly in the ointment at Brook Farm. He was a partial orphan, the son of an older sister of the Garrets who had died in childbirth soon after having married unsuitably, unhappily, and also unhealthily to judge by Christy's looks.

Poor Christy had a yellow face, weedy yellow hair and even the whites of his eyes were yellow. Miss Lomas could not stand the sight of him. It was a thorn in her flesh that he was sometimes taken to be a relative of hers. "Don't class me with that fellow," she would say quite crisply for one of her soft nature. Nor did she hesitate to freely voice her opinion to Joss that it had been a mistake for the Garrets to take Christy to live with them at all. He would have been far better left with his father's people whom he took after in more ways than one. Christy had profited nothing by being reared from birth at Garretstown, and when Brook Farm was bought and it was arranged that he would sleep there to keep her company, Miss Lomas would frankly have preferred a dog.

There was no blood bond between Miss Lomas and any of the Garrets, none whatever. Some vague connection may have existed going back to a distant marriage, but it fell far short of a bond of blood. And from the shadow of charity that hung over Christy Miss Lomas was careful to stand well clear.

The Garrets were obligated to her, not she to them. Furthermore, since at times several days might lapse without the brothers setting foot in Brook Farm at all, Miss Lomas, in their absence was regarded by the local people in the light of its Regent. Time was, when it was thought she might one day be its Queen, but if such a notion had ever entered her own head, she had promptly put it to rout. It would not have been proper for her to be residing there at all if there had been any element of that sort in her relationship with the brothers. As things were, they always made sure to be out of her house by nightfall, unless a jobber from Scotland or Northern Ireland had to be given a bed, on which occasions, such was their sense of decorum, the brothers would request her to make up a bed for one or other of themselves as well, to make sure the proprieties were safeguarded. Not that anyone would have found the smallest cause for scandal in her being alone in the house with any of the cattle dealers who came there. They were Nature's gentlemen to the core. Most of them were married men, with whose wives Miss Lomas had been made acquainted by proxy, and to whom from time to time she despatched little gifts of hand-made crochet, soda bread or country butter. It could almost have been said of the Garrets, herself and the cattlemen that they were one large happy family. It would have been hard to untangle the debts and counter-debts, that over the years had grafted them together. Miss Lomas was truly part and parcel of Brook Farm.

"And when my day is done I will not be taken far away from here," she frequently said, looking out of the window towards where, beyond a thin belt of fir trees that separated it from Brook Farm, an old over-grown cemetery could be glimpsed.

Once or twice it had occurred to Miss Lomas that she ought to ask the brothers to buy a plot for her in that cemetery, knowing they would never refuse her anything. But sensitivity held her back. Being Protestants, the Garrets themselves could not be buried in that little cemetery. Unfortunately however Christy was fully entitled to this privilege, for, among the many other mistakes his mother had made, she had married a Catholic. To fortify herself against the unpleasant thought of being buried within the same acre as him, Miss Lomas nourished the hope that the miserable fellow might yet take himself off out of their lives before he had need of a grave, sickly and all he looked. In spite of his spinelessness he would hardly put up forever with the humiliations that were heaped on him by his uncles in their disappointment at how he had turned out. Failing his departure however Miss Lomas consoled herself by thinking that sickly or not, he would, most likely on account of his youth, outlive her, and her bones would have returned to dust by the time he'd join her. For surely she'd be the first of all of them to go, even before poor Miss Garret because as everyone knows invalids hang on like burrs to life. It was therefore a great shock to Miss Lomas, one fine day when Christy ran in from the yard where they were skulling cattle to say that Joss Garret had dropped down dead on the cobblestones. "He died without making a will too," Christy panted. But Miss Lomas was naturally only concerned with getting down to the yard.

In the yard however arrangements were already underway for the body to be brought back to Garretstown. Somehow or other in her grief and confusion Miss Lomas had assumed that Joss would be carried in to Brook Farm. She couldn't help thinking how much better she'd lay him out than would be done up at the other place, for all its grandeur. But she stifled this unworthy thought and hurried to ready herself for going over to Garretstown, where she knew she'd be needed. She had already given orders for the Garretstown trap to be sent to fetch her.

Arriving at Garretstown, Miss Lomas found, as she expected that she had no time to think of anything other than planning the enormous quantities of food and drink that the sad occasion would demand. It was not until late in the day that she got an opportunity of a private word with George. To her surprise, like Christy George's first words too were about wills and testaments. Unlike Christy of course George only intended to reassure her about her position, a reassurance she herself had never for a moment deemed necessary.

"You see, Miss Lomas," George explained, "Up to the time we bought Brook Farm, our entire estate was held in a family trust and because my brother and I were always so close to each other, our personal monies were in a joint account. It is therefore only with regard to Brook Farm that there could be any difficulty because for some reason of convenience at the time of the sale, the precise nature of which I forget, it was not important, Brook Farm was bought by Joss in his own name and we never got around to remedying the matter. It was very careless, but these things happen. Unfortunately, since Joss died intestate, the place will have to be sold." When, at this, Miss Lomas started violently, George held up his hand and begged to be allowed to continue. "I will, of course, be the buyer. I will buy into the family estate by private treaty. There is no cause for concern. Things will go on as before, except for the sorrow of our loss." He stood up. "There will be no change, Miss Lomas."

Joss was laid out in one of the upstairs rooms at Garretstown House and people thronged the stairs all the next day and late into the night on the eve of the funeral. Miss Lomas was up to her eyes catering for them. On the day of the funeral however she could not suppress a feeling of anxiety, which arose in her when she saw the large mob of Christy's relatives on his father's side, who felt free to call to Garretstown and who had the effrontery to push into the dining room and eat and drink their fill of what she had thought she was providing for a select company. Although she herself was rushing frantically backwards and forwards seeing that empty meat platters were replaced by full ones, and glasses kept topped up, it did not escape her notice that the undesirables stuck very close together, their heads in a bunch. They were hatching trouble. She felt sure of it. And she wondered how George kept his equanimity.

As for Christy himself, he was a new man, all energy, all life. Once as she passed him he spared her a word. "They say George can't buy back the farm, except by public auction," he said. A nerve in his left cheek was jumping as if for joy.

Although her own head was throbbing, Miss Lomas gave him a piece of her mind. "What kind of a gom are you?" She said. "You're like a man in one end of a sinking ship laughing at those in the other end."

Yet, before she left for Brook Farm in the early hours of the morning, she sought out George. She found him graver than before but still calm and collected.

"Be so kind as to step into my study for a moment, Miss Lomas," he said, escorting her to a chair and sitting down patiently beside her. "I have to tell you that since I last spoke to you, I have learned that nothing can save Brook Farm from going under the auctioneer's hammer." Seeing her begin to tremble, he took her hand and pressed it. "Not because of local pressure, mind you, that is only ignorant gossip. It will have to be auctioned because of the covetous curs you saw here tonight, those relatives of Christy's. Those curs did not come to pay their respects to my poor brother, they were here to see what gain might come to them from his sudden death. They weren't slow to find out my intention of buying the place by private treaty, and knowing that Christy would be entitled to a cut of the purchase money, they put him up to demanding his cut in cash instead of adhering to my advice that, as one of the family, he be a party to a plan I had outlined to him. By this plan he would have to allow his share, like mine and that of my sister, be reabsorbed into the estate, a plan, which as you can imagine, would be vastly to his ultimate advantage. It would of course be a long-term policy, but for a half-wit like him that's the only kind of policy I could advise. However if a fistful of money was what he wanted, I would have been prepared to give it to him. But do you think those curs were satisfied? Not them! If you please they did not trust me to put a fair price on the place. It's *them* who are insisting on an auction. I wouldn't put it past them to rig the bidding."

"But how will they gain by an auction?" Miss Lomas couldn't help interrupting.

George gave a mirthless smile. "Because in an open market the whole thing would have to be a cash transaction, and it was the cash they had their eye on. They knew their Christy. Did you never hear that a fool and his fortune are soon parted? If Christy got his share in coin, they knew they could count on getting their hands on most of it. That's the principle behind their conniving. I hear they are already trying to persuade the poor fellow to go back and live with them." At thought of the like happening, George threw his eyes up to heaven, although Miss Lomas, if left to herself, would have seen nothing wrong with any proposal that would take Christy out of her hair. Her hopes in this respect however were quickly quenched. "Ah, but I'm able for curs like that," George's voice rose so high that Miss Lomas glanced anxiously at the door to make sure it was shut. "They won't get away with that. Christy will not leave Brook Farm. As for his relatives, they'll soon be scuttling back to their kennels. You see, I've just had a word with Parr."

"Mr. Parr?" At mention of the solicitor's name, Miss Lomas let out a long pent-up breath. She knew Mr. Parr well. Brook Farm would be safe in his hands. Many a meal the solicitor had eaten there. He was a fox if ever there was one but very civil, and fox or no fox, he never left the house without remarking on how well she kept things. On his last visit, indeed, he had been extraordinarily warm and natural for a man of his profession. He stayed talking to her in the front hall, not heeding that Joss and George, had had his trap brought round, were waiting to see him out the gate. He persisted in telling her all about a sister of his whose husband had just died leaving no money and a large family. He even took out his wallet and showed her a photograph of the children. "They are fortunate children, Mr. Parr," she'd said that day with genuine fervour. "They will be safe in your hands."

And so, too, would Brook Farm.

That conversation was some time ago of course and Miss Lomas called her wandering thoughts to order because George was still trying to explain the present situation to her. "Tell me, Miss Lomas, did you ever hear of a mock auction? You didn't? Well, that's what's going to be held at

Brook Farm. Let me briefly explain Parr's plan. The house and lands will be put up for public sale alright, and the sale announced on bill boards pasted to every telephone pole in the country, as well as publicised by notices in the columns of the national as well as the provincial newspapers. Then on the day of the sale, the place will be knocked down to the highest bidder."

Miss Lomas had been perplexed from the start, but now her perplexity would have reached alarming proportions if she had not detected a playful glint in George's eye. "And do you know, Miss Lomas, who the highest bidder will be?" he asked. "You don't. Well I'll tell you. It will be Christy, no less!" Now George was laughing openly at her confusion, but his kindliness prevailed over his amusement. "No need to be alarmed. Parr has everything in hand. He has arranged that I will go guarantee for Christy so he can borrow the purchase money from the bank, but only on condition that immediately after the sale he signs a mortgage for as near as no matter to the same amount as the Loan. Do you follow? In this way, he won't lay hands on a penny piece. *He* will be the nominal, but I will be the virtual owner of the place. Then, when his false friends slink away, after letting a little time pass, I will persuade him to sell back to me, this time by private treaty and at a fair price." In spite of his undoubted grief for the death of his brother, Miss Lomas saw George's eyes light up with triumph at the manner in which he would beat his enemies. Not that Christy was an enemy. On the contrary, George proceeded there and then to explain that Christy would fare far and away better under Parr's plan.

"He will of course get paid a certain amount of cash, but Parr has thought up an arrangement by which he cannot squander it. To tell you the truth I have sometimes wondered if I tried hard enough to guide the poor young devil in the right path. I felt I would be wasting my time. But after we've handled this tricky situation, I'm going to make it my business, henceforth to try to steer him in the right direction. I'll see to it that he cuts off all connection with the other side of his family at least until he sells the place back to me. If I can persuade him to keep the transaction quiet, and clear out of the country altogether, take himself off to Canada or Australia and make a new start, I might raise the price I'd give him. It wouldn't be a bad thing to feel I might be making a man of him after all. If he does well wherever he goes, it would be an interest for me to follow his progress. I might even think of making a voyage out to see him sometime. Those foreign places get a lot of the sun. And then, of course, in the natural order of things, when the last of us dies he will be entitled to the whole property. It's not a bad proposition for a lout like him." But here, to the distress of Miss Lomas, George seemed to lose his pleasure in the plan. "Not that in my opinion, there will be a lot left when that day dawns. My sister, in spite of her weak constitution, may live as long as Methuselah. There's no one like an invalid for dragging out life to the bitter end, and draining away family resources however abundant." He stood up to go.

Miss Lomas, as always had to acknowledge the wisdom of his words, but she had one question she had to put to him. "Will Christy agree to all this? That's the problem as I see it," she said.

"I don't know," said George simply and sincerely. "Parr seems confident that if we butter the fellow up enough the notion of being a big landowner will ensure that he will agree to anything. Parr is also going to give him a few words of advice about keeping clear of his father's people once he's a man of property." Here George went to the door. He looked very tired but Miss Lomas was touched to see he still had thought for her. "Rest assured everything will continue as before. I will continue to graze the land as hitherto, and of course, be responsible for the expenses of running the house."

Miss Lomas made a valiant effort to appear happy but she still had a niggling worry. "If Christy agrees to this plan, how long will it be before you buy the place back from him?" She had dire misgivings at the thought of being dependent on Christy for even the shortest of time.

George laughed. "About a few weeks," he said offhandedly, and then, although he had opened the door, he shut it again. "I forgot to tell you the most important part of the plan," he said. "You must forgive me but the fatigue of the last few hours is taking a toll of me. The main reason I brought you in here, in the first place, apart from its always being a pleasure to see you, was to tell you that a bit of penmanship will be demanded of you too, dear lady, in connection with this tiresome business. On the evening of the sale and after the signing of the mortgage, I will be presenting Christy with an account on behalf of the Garretstown estate, for a number of items for which the estate has been out of pocket going back to the day poor Joss bought Brook Farm, or at least for as far back as is allowable under the law of statutory declaration. The total of our outlay will be chargeable to the new buyer, and he will have to accept legal liability for that sum in the eyes of the law." All at once George sat down again. "Poor Christy. I could almost pity him," he said. Miss Lomas too, felt a sudden softness towards the fellow, but George had once more risen and gone to the door. "You understand the part you have to play in this, I hope?" He said quietly. "You must see to it that all the indoor expenses of Brook Farm over the past years, will be drawn up in ledger form. And I expect the total to come to a nice tot. Do you get me?" Seeing that she had only dimly got the drift of things he came back up the room. "Don't worry. I will get Parr to explain to you. Parr will make everything as clear as daylight."

Yet a few days later when Mr. Parr called to Brook Farm and had a long talk with her, Miss Lomas was still muddled in her mind. She kept asking question after question. In the end, Mr. Parr threw up his hands in near despair.

"Miss Lomas, you are far too conscientious. There is no need to be so exact. All that really matters is that you come up with a final figure which, while not necessarily larger than the amount expended over the years, will at least not be smaller. Keep in mind the possible value I have put on this place, which I will tell you in confidence later, and aim at producing a figure which will approximate to the difference between that value and the amount of the mortgage we'll be getting Christy to sign with which I will also see you are acquainted. You'll have to make a guess at some of your figures but make a good guess. Then he, who was always so formal, winked at her. "Don't forget it's a Mock Auction," he said, and he winked a second time.

It was not however until after she had consulted her cookery books and pondered what she felt to be analogous instances of mock-cream and mock-turtle that Miss Lomas got any real grasp of what might be meant by mock auction. And Christy? Did he know what was afoot, she wondered. He certainly gave no sign of knowing. But then George might not have intended telling him anything until the last minute. The fellow was so used to being ordered around, told to do this and told to do that, to run here and run there, to open gates and shut gates, to chase sheep and count cattle, he'd probably sign on the dotted line without raising a single query. He was however notably more silent than usual. On the other hand, the servant girl of the moment, was full of gab. She could talk of nothing else but the auction. And on the eve of the Big Day when unfortunately Miss Lomas was forced to keep her until late in the night to help pluck and stuff a few extra fowl that she had decided at the last minute might be necessary, she found her downright impertinent.

"It's only a mug's game, being too particular," said the slut when Miss Lomas insisted on the pin feathers being singed. "There may be the crowd of all times here tomorrow but it won't be for what they'll get to eat they'll be coming."

Miss Lomas was outraged. "Better to be safe than sorry," she said, "Although I agree that there may be a large crowd of viewers, but there are not many people hereabouts with money enough to bid for Brook Farm."

"Isn't that what I was trying to tell you," the girl said. It won't be only bidders will be here. There'll be gawkers galore as well."

Miss Lomas looked in some dismay at the load of food on the kitchen table, but she quickly recovered her calm. "If that is so those people won't be brash enough to come up to the house," she said. "The auction will be held down in the yard, you know." All the same her heart sank. Privately, she too, was coming to the conclusion that there could be a lot of people who'd come out of sheer curiosity. People might guess that George would have a trick card to play, something up his sleeve. She realised suddenly that very few people had come to view the place. That was odd. They had all been strangers to her too, but of course they could have been stooges dredged up in the town by Parr. Certainly few of them had walked the land, or not in earnest, and none of them had asked to inspect the house.

Perhaps she had prepared too much food? She belatedly remembered that George had stipulated that only the principals were to receive hospitality. All of a sudden she felt uncertain and out of her depth. So late that night when she was alone in the parlour and George called out to Brook Farm she was exceedingly glad to see him.

"You're worrying unduly I tell you," he said. "What does one duck or one goose too many matter at a time like this? If you are thinking of Christy's relatives. Those interlopers won't darken the door, when they discover they've been outwitted? Our food would stick in their gullets this time. They'll be a sorry breed that ever questioned my honesty. That reminds me. Have you anything to add to that list of expenses you gave me? I hope nothing was omitted. If so it can be added in pen and ink. Think hard! Meals for drovers? Did you, for instance, think of that item?"

"The drovers never got more than a bite in the kitchen with the servant girl, a few odds and ends that would otherwise be thrown out," Miss Lomas said wearily.

"No matter!" said George. "Put down a figure for those meals. We have to have entries for everything we can rake up. It is essential that Christy's immediate profit on the place will be as hollow as a blown egg. I don't think you've caught on to our plan at all." It was as near as George had ever gone to being cross with her and Miss Lomas got flustered.

"Maybe I ought to make out a new list," she said although she couldn't help glancing at the clock.

"Do so by all means if you think you can improve on the total," George said. "There's one point I ought to have stressed, which is that Parr will see to it that you will get away with anything you put down." But again, as always, his innate goodness came to the fore. "Look here, it's getting late and I can see you're tired. Don't bother with a new list. The first one will serve well enough. But there is one thing I must ask you. Have you given any consideration to the final item, the one you left blank?

Miss Lomas had not forgotten that she'd left a blank. She had done so deliberately. She simply could not believe that George would press her on that sore point. Reaching out to him with her two hands, her eyes appealed to him for understanding of her feelings.

"No salary I could possibly invent would come anywhere near to equalling what I got out of Brook Farm over all those years," she cried. "Put down whatever figure you yourself think proper."

"Ah," said George. "Are you sure about that?" Miss Lomas nodded vigorously. "So you did get the idea?" George said with a quizzical smile. He was touched. "Tell me, Miss Lomas, when you were a child, did you ever play a game, a game that began by asking the other player to think of a number and then. ..."

"Then double it?" Miss Lomas asked timidly.

"Yes, Yes and add 5," George prompted.

"And then double that again?" Miss Lomas had got the hang of it.

George was so pleased he slapped his thigh the way he did when he'd tell her he'd bought a herd of cattle for next to nothing.

"You've got the idea, alright," he said. Then producing her original list from his pocket, now neatly typed, he scribbled a figure in the blank space. "Sign this," he said handing the list to her. "And just in case the solicitors on the other side should be foolish enough to contest it, you might as well put your initials at the end of each page."

Partly in embarrassment and partly in jollity, Miss Lomas half-averted her eyes as she complied. She was about to hand it back to him when George put his finger on one particular line. "Just initial that item he added casually."

With a flourish Miss Lomas put her initial everywhere George told her, but again took care not to look at the figure entered as her supposed salary. She didn't expect George to notice her squeamishness but she was pleased to see he was aware of it.

"You are worth your weight in gold, Miss Lomas," he said solemnly. "You have taken good care of Brook Farm all through the years. God grant it will take care of you too, to the end."

Miss Lomas felt like kissing his hand.

*   *   *

Next day, on the spur of the moment, Miss Lomas decided not to show herself in the yard at all.

"It was a great mistake to hold the auction here at all," she said to the servant girl. "It should have been held at Garretstown House, or better still in the auctioneer's office." It upset her to see people streaming in the gate and slouching around the yard. It was also extremely difficult to keep the servant girl from running in and out between the house and the yard.

By eleven o'clock a tidy knot of people had gathered around the farm cart on which the auctioneer would stand when he proceeded to dispose of the farm. This casual group was disposed to be talkative, until shortly before noon a silence fell when there was a stir in the crowd and Miss Lomas saw that Christy had arrived back, accompanied by a mob of relatives. But when the auctioneer, who arrived almost at the same time, took up his stand on the cart, to her relief she saw that at a sign from George, Christy broke away from his companions and took up his stand in front of the cart. She breathed a great sigh of relief. She concluded that all would be well. Then a new annoyance presented itself. The servant girl had escaped her again and, most unsuitably, wormed her way through the crowd to Christy's side. There was no calling her back.

On the stroke of noon the auctioneer gave the dash-board of the cart a crack of his stick, and a few people who had been skulking in the sheds and hay barn came sheepishly out. Others, who stayed in the shelter of the outhouses, only craned their necks forward like ganders. Then just as the auctioneer was about to open his mouth, an old clucking hen that was roosting in the haggard flew down into the crowd.

Miss Lomas gasped. Mercifully, the servant girl dived on it, and clapt it up in her apron. How was it Christy hadn't the wits to do anything about it? She turned back to attend to a few last minute preparations. If the meal was to be ready on time she herself had better start frying the liver and kidneys that were to embellish the fowl.

It seemed only a minute later that the girl came running back into the kitchen.

"It's not over, is it?" cried Miss Lomas.

"All but the cheering," said the girl with a laugh. Miss Lomas didn't know what she meant, but she handed over the frying pan.

"Don't forget the rule I gave you. Kidney well done, liver less so!" But her mind was not on the meal. "What did you do with that old hen when you were coming in? You didn't let it go again?"

"Oh no, miss," said the girl. "I gave her to Christy to hold."

To Christy? And of course he took it. A fine figure he'd cut with the old clucking hen under his arm when the auctioneer would call him up to sign the papers. Ah well. Perhaps it would further Parr's plan to have the fellow shown up for a gom. It would let people see that George Garret was able for all mean-minded connivers. Hearing voices approaching the house, she ran to open the door to them.

There were only three people; George, Mr. Parr and Christy. Apparently, the auctioneer and his clerk had been let take themselves off.

"Well, I'm glad that's over," George said, and he reached for the decanter. "We must give this man a drink, Miss Lomas," he said, nodding at Parr. "He's not used to being out in the open air." He filled out a good stiff drink for himself too. He looked as if he needed it.

"Well! How did it go?" Miss Lomas asked anxiously looking from one to the other of them, her glance resting last, but longest on Christy, who had slunk in last. Prompted perhaps by something in Miss Lomas's face, George too turned around and looked at him.

"Liven up there Christy," he said, and he gave him a clap on the back that nearly jolted the teeth out of his head. "You're a man of property now, the owner of a big farm with nothing to do for the rest of your life only scratch around for the money to pay for it." Turning to Parr, he laughed. "Well, Parr? We foxed them nicely, didn't we? Did you see their faces? They never knew Christy here was such a man of substance." After he let himself down into the big mahogany carver at the head of the table, he made as if to rise again. "Excuse me Christy, it's you ought to be at the head of the table now," he said.

"Ah, leave him alone!" said Miss Lomas unexpectedly. "There's no use making any more game of him than is needed." She looked at the poor fellow and not for the first time she wondered if there was a ton of him in it at all. It was impossible to know what he thought or felt.

"By the way, we mustn't forget to have him sign the mortgage,

George," said Parr, as if Christy wasn't present at all.

George paused with a forkful of kidney half-way to his mouth. "It wouldn't do to forget that, would it?" He said but he laughed. "Do you know something. If I was to drop down dead this minute, like my poor brother, Joss, I'd rather see Christy here," he pointed at him with his fork, "I'd rather see Christy here walking off with the place than have those mangy relatives of his rob him of a penny." Abandoning his jocose manner then, he turned solemnly to the solicitor. "Weren't they the fools to stand out against me?" He said, but before Mr. Parr had time to answer, George threw a glance at the clock and snapped his fingers. "I nearly forgot. There are cattle coming from Dublin this morning. They were to be at the station before noon. Christy! Quick! Eat up and off with you over the fields. I've arranged for a drover to come from Dublin with them, but he'll need help." It was the sort of job Christy always got, but Miss Lomas was surprised at his being given such a menial job today of all days. Christy too seemed stunned at the order. He got to his feet more sluggishly than usual. "Don't forget it's your own property you're looking after now!" George called after him, winking openly at the others.

It was Miss Lomas who remembered the mortgage. "He didn't sign it," she cried, and she got to her feet with such haste that her chair over-turned as she ran and banged on the window-pane. Mr. Parr too sprang to his feet.

"Well, well," said George, "you must both of you have a very poor expectation of my longevity." He wasn't in the least worried.

"Tut-Tut," said Mr. Parr. "These things are a matter of routine."

Miss Lomas however had got too much of a fright to be politic.

"Think of poor Joss," she admonished. "Think of how quick he went!"

Sobered, George himself stood up. "I suppose we'd better get him to sign it." Picking up a big cut glass ink stand and a pen, he followed Mr. Parr, who was in the hall getting into his overcoat unaided.

"Are you sure you won't wait for coffee?" Miss Lomas asked.

George however was tapping the face of the clock. "Is that clock fast?" he asked, as if she had detained him long enough already. A few minutes later the cob was trotting down between the clipped laurels of the drive and out through the gates on to the road where it was soon hidden by low branches of chestnut and sycamore in young, sweet leaf.

Miss Lomas listened till the last clip-clop of hooves died on the air. She had the oddest notion that there would not be many more big spreads to prepare at Brook Farm. Then she walked down the drive and closed the gates. But as she slammed them shut, and pushed the iron bolt down into the spud-stone, she felt a certain sense of security and as she walked back she looked appraisingly at the old house with its many-paned windows, one to the right being the front window of her own little bedroom, a room that was in fact the largest in the house, but when speaking of it, she used the diminutive from a feeling of homeliness. It was the same feeling of homeliness and love that often made her refer to the whole house as a little treasure.

What a pity the men had to rush away, she thought. This was the time they would pull their chairs over to the fire to let the food settle on their stomachs. Today, since there was no sense in wasting a good fire, she sat herself down in one of the big plush armchairs and in a second she had fallen asleep. She did not wake until tea time when the maid came in, and poked the fire, splashing the fire-light momentarily around the room. "Is Christy not back yet?" she asked, but immediately she regretted having spoken. It was not customary for her to comment on either his goings or his comings. Changes there might be in the days to follow but she was convinced there would be no change in her attitude to him. She affected a light laugh. "He must be worn out," she said, "signing himself into a big farm one minute and signing himself out of it the next!"

"The one is easier done nor the other," the girl said, looking at her slyly. Miss Lomas would have been upset if she had not had manifold experience of the meaningless remarks made by ignorant girls for the sake of hearing their own voices. The one was still particularly talkative. "If the Garrets wanted to sell this place tomorrow, they couldn't do it without asking leave of Christy!" she said.

"Nonsense," said Miss Lomas. "I hope you, and others of your kind, won't put foolish notions of that kind into the fellow's head. When he comes back send him in here to me and I'll put things in their proper light for him."

*   *   *

In the days that followed there was little or no change in Brook Farm. At the end of the week, although he had not once set foot in the house, much less partaken of a meal, George took out his wallet and handed Miss Lomas the same sum of money as always.

As time went on George did of course come to the house quite frequently, but he came only to talk about some small problem that had arisen. He also brought cattle dealers and jobbers to the place, as regularly as before, but now it was never for more than a drink. They were never asked to stay for a meal and never never to stay the night. All in all, life thinned out at Brook Farm. Miss Lomas tried to tell herself that she was getting on in years, and that in a way it was just as well there was less excitement about the place. She persuaded herself that a bit of peace and quiet would almost have been welcome if it were not for Christy, but there was a big difference between silence and surliness. It never ceased to amaze her that he could be so different from his uncles, who had closely resembled each other.

Miss Lomas felt a catch in her heart whenever she saw George; he was *so* like Joss, the same heavy build, the same hearty red face and the same bloodshot eyes. It never crossed her mind that he might also have the same constitution, until one day, less than two months after the death of Joss, the Garretstown trap came in the gate to the front door, the harness splattered with foam from the mouth of the cob and the yardman that drove it incoherent. He was trying to tell her something about George.

"Is he dead?" cried the servant girl who had run out after her.

"Hold your tongue," said Miss Lomas, but she knew from the palpitations she got, that something serious had happened. "It could be just a dizzy spell," she said to the man and told him to wait while she got her coat. "Even if it *was* a heart attack," she pronounced a few minutes later as she was scrambling into the trap, "it must have been a mild attack or else he would have been gone at once. Mark my words, he will be all right when he gets a bit of rest. Well? What are we waiting for?" she asked impatiently, as the man made no move to go.

"I thought Christy might be coming with us."

"Is it him?" said Miss Lomas scathingly. "He'd be the last one I'd want to see if I was ill, and I'm sure his uncle would feel the same."

"I only thought . . .," the man began when reaching across him, Miss Lomas whisked the whip out of its socket and gave the mare a flick on her glossy rump. "Why do people always look on the gloomy side? Things will be all right, you'll see," she said. Then as the cob broke into a trot, she settled herself more comfortably on the horse-hair cushions. "Wonders can be worked nowadays even with the heart," she said and it occurred to her, that had she been in the yard when Joss had had the stroke, she might have been able to save him, although they said he was stone dead when he fell. All you had to do was just rub the chest clockwise above the heart. Or was it counter-clockwise? No matter anyway. Joss was dead and gone. And by all accounts, George was not only still alive but the doctor was with him. He would be all right.

Minute by minute as the trap spanked along the road Miss Lomas felt less alarmed. It was odd the way things worked out. Instead of being threatened, it seemed that her authority had increased, because for the time being at least, she would most likely be taking charge at Garretstown House as well as at Brook Farm. Not that she'd fancy sleeping there. She might have to spend a night or two there perhaps—she had brought her night things—but on no account would she stay there indefinitely. For twenty years she had not slept one night away from Brook Farm, and she did not believe she would close an eye any place else in the world. Turning around she looked back fondly at it. "Isn't it a little gem?" She said to the yardman.

In spite of the sad nature of her ride, Miss Lomas could not help but respond to the beauty of the countryside. She rejoiced to see that already the dog-roses had budded, and when she saw a large, pale blossom that had flattened wide open, she beamed upon it. After that however she closed her eyes because the trap had rolled past the boundary of Brook

Farm where the hedges were always as neat and trim as if they were pared with a nail scissors and they were passing between the ragged hedges of neighbouring farms.

The neighbouring farms were an eyesore to Miss Lomas, the gaps in their mearings stopped with dead branches, and between the fields instead of gates discarded bedheads. Oh, how she despised the mean and petty economies by which the local farmers, not having the broadness of the Garrets eked out their scanty profits. When Garretstown was reached at last, Miss Lomas sat up straighter. "Pull up," she called out unnecessarily when they reached the hall-door.

All was bedlam at Garretstown. Miss Garret, most unsuitably, sat weeping in the kitchen, weeping noisily. The two maids appeared to be at a loss. They did nothing but run up the stairs and then run down again. It was high time someone took charge. Taking off her hat, Miss Lomas dealt first with Miss Garret. She led her back to the drawing-room, and, as an undertaker might compose a corpse, she composed her. This she did so well, that although Miss Garret still wept, she thereafter did so silently and decorously. Then, Miss Lomas, with maids scampering before and after her went upstairs.

But at sight of George Garret she gasped. How could such a big man like him have shrunk to nothing in the few short hours since she'd seen him last? Blenched and enfeebled he lay on his bed.

"George," she called urgently. "George? It's me. It's Miss Lomas." But bending closer she could see that for the moment at least he could make no response. "How long has he been like this?" she asked sharply of those at his bedside. Startled she saw that one of them was Parr. He was seated at a table drawn up at the other side of the bed. On the table he had placed a large lamp with the shade off and in front of him he had a sheet of foolscap and a large silver inkpot from the library, and into the inkpot every other minute he dipped his pen, after which, each time he gave the pen a little shake that scattered ink on the floor.

"Mind there! You'll destroy the carpet," Miss Lomas warned before she took in the purpose of the lawyer's presence. "What are you thinking of?" she cried then. "This man is in no condition to attend to business." Mr. Parr, however, must have seen a flicker in the eyes of his client, for disregarding her, he called to a gawk of a clerk he had with him, and together they tried to drag George Garret upright, as they might have tried to pull a beast out of a gripe.

"Stop that!" Miss Lomas shouted. "Can't you see he must store what small strength he has left in him? Where is the doctor? Does the doctor know about this carry-on?"

Mr. Parr gave her a scathing glance.

"The doctor is gone. There's a limit to the skill of all men," he said. "But doesn't all the world know that any man, sick or well, is the better for knowing his affairs are in order?"

"But this man's will is made. It is in my possession, locked in the closet in my room, as you must surely know."

"That may be," said Mr. Parr, "but there is one small matter outstanding, Miss Lomas, and if possible it ought to be regularised."

Miss Lomas hardly waited for him to end his sentence. "This is no time for small matters," she cried. "I suppose you mean money? Money, money, money! You'd think it was the only thing on this earth. Well, let me tell you something! All the money in the world would not be worth one hour of this man's life! And anyhow, believe me, your purpose may best be served by letting him sleep."

Mr. Parr was not to be patronised.

"If it is sleep!" he said. All the same he stabbed the pen into the inkwell, like a labourer sticking his spade into the ground, and he wiped his hands. "God knows where you get your optimism," he said. "In my opinion, he's as good as gone."

But if Parr was not to be patronised, Miss Lomas was not to be flustered.

"All the more reason to leave him in peace," she said, "Thank God I've always been above money."

"Your generosity does you credit, Miss Lomas," said Mr. Parr drily.

"Don't forget where I learned it!" Miss Lomas admonished him as she turned back and looked sadly at her old friend. As she did there was a rattle in his throat that made her whole body go cold. But she kept her head even in her fright. "Have Miss Garret brought up at once," she said to the maids.

"Better get Christy too," said Mr. Parr, "and get him fast."

But Christy was already at hand, standing in the passage outside the sick-room, where a small group of the servants and workmen had gathered.

*   *   *

When George Garret breathed his last, a deep silence fell not only within the house but outside too. It seemed as if the fields, and indeed the whole world, had gone silent. The lawyer was the first to make a move. He was deadly tired. His one thought was to get away before commotion set in. Indeed as he went stiffly down the stairs one of the maids ran past him going full tilt, and in the kitchen there was a clatter as someone let fall a pile of plates. He would have to have a talk with Miss Lomas later, but he knew that tonight she'd have her hands full. He had not reached the foot of the stairs however before he heard her call down that she wanted to speak to him.

"Do you know the first thought that came to my mind when all was over?" she cried, "Only for me Christy would at this moment be the master of Brook Farm."

Shocked as he was that she could be so down to earth at such a time, Mr.

Parr was too tired to be cautious.

"By God, Miss Lomas," he cried, "I don't know that you've any great reason to congratulate yourself. Christy's signature on that mortgage only complicates matters. For me, at any rate. Better he were left in full ownership. The Garrets owed the poor devil something. In an estate, the size of the Garret estate, one out-farm is a drop in the ocean and I thought that if Christy were to get Brook Farm outright, without being indebted to the bank, he might be amenable to accept it as his full share of the family trust. Now there's no knowing what will happen." He shook his head. He looked dead beat. "It's my guess Christy could be gom enough to try and raise the money to pay back the mortgage. There would be no shortage of people at hand to encourage him in such foolishness. I'm afraid we'll have to contend again with those ravening relatives of his, only now they'll be ten times as vicious having been tricked at the Mock Auction." Seeing that Miss Lomas had bristled, he opened the door. "Well, we can't worry about it at this moment. Things may sort themselves out," he said hoping to fob her off for the time being with a few easy words.

Miss Lomas was not to be fobbed off, though.

"What were those papers you were trying to get George to sign?" she asked.

"What do you think? I was trying to get him to write off the mortgage."

"I thought it was money that was in question," she said faintly.

Was she a fool? Mr. Parr wondered what in the name of God did she think a mortgage was all about if not money? He was in no mood for such imbecility. For her part Miss Lomas was trying to figure out how the mortgage which had been intended to put everything right, would appear now to have landed them in a worse plight. She dimly discerned there could be trouble ahead.

"But if there was no mortgage on the place, couldn't he sell it?" she asked.

"He could," said Mr. Parr without blinking, "but don't forget George was too far gone to hear me much less understand what I was trying to get him to do. Poor George!" Mr. Parr shook his head sadly. "The truth is, Miss Lomas, I thought George should be given a chance to die without having his shabby treatment of Christy on his conscience."

"George was going to buy the place back from Christy when he judged the time to be right," Miss Lomas protested.

"Ah yes," said Mr. Parr, "but unfortunately we are not judges of what time we are allotted for future actions, whether good or bad. That reminds me, Miss Lomas, I have a suggestion to make to you. I think that while you and I can still keep our own slate clean, I suggest we destroy that list of expenses that was drawn up for the running of Brook Farm for the past decade. The document is still in my safe. George did not get round to presenting it to Christy. Perhaps in this matter he was waiting till he judged the time to be fit. But if Christy has to meet that bill too he will be left stripped as bare as a bone. Things might have turned out alright if George had lived, but now there is no one to stock the land and keep the buildings in repair."

Miss Lomas felt suddenly slightly better than she had for some hours. She had not realised Christy's position was so bad. "Maybe he'll take himself out of here altogether," she suggested hopefully.

"And where would he go?" Parr asked sourly. "No. It's my opinion he will hang on here if only by the skin of his teeth." Then the old man looked up at the ceiling of the room where the corpse lay and with a disregard for the dead which was very shocking to Miss Lomas, he shook his fist, "George Garret would have done well to ascertain the state of his health before he laid plans for beggaring his nephew," he said.

Miss Lomas could not let a slur like this be put on her old friend, no longer able to defend himself.

"The idea was to make a man of Christy," she said coldly, "to force him to emigrate and start a new life, perhaps in the colonies."

"Is that so?" said Parr sarcastically. "Well, I can tell you, Miss Lomas, George did his work altogether too well in every regard. For one thing he puffed poor Christy up with a bogus sense of his own importance and encouraged him to see himself in the light of a big farmer for all that he hadn't a penny to his name."

"Do you really think he'll hang on at Brook Farm?" Miss Lomas cried in open disbelief of such a thing being possible.

"I don't think it. I know it," said Parr. "I've already had a few words with him. In his own interests I suggested that he ought to start looking around at once for someone to graze the land but he scoffed at the idea." Miss Lomas stared at him she was amazed that Christy had the guts to make a stand against Mr. Parr. It crossed her mind that he might have a side to him that she had never seen. She'd want to be careful not to antagonise him too much. Unexpectedly she found herself flying to his defence. "Christy was quite right about one thing anyway. Tenants at Brook Farm! The idea was unthinkable.

"They would only have grazing rights," Mr. Parr said, making a visible effort to be patient. "How else will he get a pennypiece on which to live?" he asked.

Miss Lomas did not answer for a moment. She was rethinking the whole matter. Could there not be a compromise. After all there were tenants and tenants. Certain tenants could in fact be most acceptable.

"You, Mr. Parr, will, I take it still be continuing to administer the Garret estate, and I suppose you will have to hire a farm manager? Surely you could get him to rent the land here. That ought to be acceptable to Christy. After all the Garrets are his own flesh and blood."

"You don't know Christy, Miss Lomas. He is as stubborn as a mule. And I may tell you that you don't know me either. I expect of course that I will be looking after the interests of Miss Garret but no way will I tangle with Christy. As a matter of fact that was another disservice George did his nephew. He should not have alienated him from his father's relatives. Bad and all as they are, they were the only friends the poor devil had in this world, but such as they were they were better than no friends at all. Although there would be no immediate gain to them in the way things turned out, they might have seen it to their advantage in the future to have Christy struggle out of his difficulties. They might have succeeded where I failed and persuade him to sell the land. But they have washed their hands of him since he signed the Mortgage. They feel it was him not George that tricked them."

Miss Lomas sank down on the step of the stairs.

"Oh what will happen?" she whispered.

"Nothing good. You may be sure of that," said Mr. Parr. "Christy will be in a pretty pickle. I had thought for a moment when I saw him up in that room standing beside the corpse that I might make an effort to get the bank to allow him a second mortgage, a small one, just enough to buy a few beasts and give him a chance—a slim one I admit—but still a chance to get on his feet. After all if he can hang on long enough he'll be heir to what's left of Garretstown although that won't be much if the old lady lives much longer. So in the end I decided against doing anything, mainly I may say, in his own best interests. If there was one good thing to be said in favour of George Garret's behaviour it was that idea he had in the back of his mind about helping Christy to emigrate, but I reluctantly came to the conclusion that there might be only one way to do that now and that is to starve him out. It might be the kindest thing to do under the circumstances."

To the surprise of the old solicitor Miss Lomas laughed, although it was a mirthless laugh. It was just that this was hardly a plausible plan to put into execution at Brook Farm, where more food went into the pig's bucket than went into the mouths of many of their neighbours.

"I'm afraid it would be hard for anyone to starve at Brook Farm," she said, but she noticed Mr Parr looked oddly at her.

"Look here, Miss Lomas, it must be getting on for morning. You're worn out like myself and no wonder. I'd take forty winks if I were you before you do another thing. I suppose you'll be staying the night here?"

"Here? Why should you suppose that?" Miss Lomas asked.

"Well, for one thing, there are the funeral arrangements to be made," said Mr Parr censoriously. "Miss Garret is in no condition to attend to such matters." Then when Miss Lomas made no answer, he realised that she was going to let bedlam take care of bedlam.

"Perhaps I had better put a notice in the newspapers saying that the house and funeral will be private," he said. Considering the magnificent way she had coped with the refreshments at Joss Garret's funeral, he didn't expect for a moment that she would really let people go away from George's grave without as much as asking if they had a mouth on them.

But Miss Lomas was turning away.

"Do what you like in the matter. I'm going home," she said wearily.

Dawn was coming up over the trees when Miss Lomas climbed stiffly into the trap. The night which had brought the chill of death to George Garret had brought the full softness of summer over the fields he had left behind. And as she drove along the road in the early light, instead of a single dog-rose, there would have been dozens to delight her, but she saw nothing. Worn out, she jolted up and down on the seat of the trap, as blind to their beauty as if she too was boxed up in her coffin. And when the gable end of Brook Farm came in view, a sight which in the past had always given her pleasure, it seemed that the great stone house had suffered a metamorphosis, turned into an abstraction, a cause of dispute.

"What time will I come back for you, ma'am?" asked the yard man. His simple words made Miss Lomas uneasy. Having reached Brook Farm she never wanted to stir out of it again, ever. Who knew what might not happen in her absence?

"They can do without me today," she said. "I have affairs of my own to concern me," she said. The man was surprised but not unduly.

"I suppose you'll have a lot to do before leaving," he said off-handedly.

Miss Lomas started. "What made you think I'd be leaving?" she asked sharply, but Mr Parr's words about starving-out Christy came back to her. How could that be done while she was there? Surely Mr Parr didn't envisage her leaving? The idea was preposterous. Everyone knew her position at Brook Farm. She went into the house. Her mouth was parched for a cup of tea, but it was too early for the servant girl to be in and she didn't feel fit to wrestle with the kitchen range. Christy would probably be back soon and he'd attend to the range. She had not seen him since those last confused minutes by his uncle's death-bed. Going upstairs, she lay down on her bed, meaning only to stay there a short time but it was evening when she woke. Christy apparently had not shown up all day.

"Where can he be?" she enquired anxiously of the girl.

"It's late in the day to start worrying about him," said the girl.

Such impudence was staggering. It was all Miss Lomas could do not to give her notice on the spot, but she thought better than to introduce more disorder than that which seemed already to be threatened. She refrained from further enquiries about the fellow. Maybe he had made up to his aunt and got round her to let him stay the night at Garretstown?

Christy however had not stayed the night at Garretstown. This was clear the minute his step was heard on the stairs late that night. He had drink taken. "Where were you?" Miss Lomas demanded. "I hope you weren't foolish enough to be discussing your business with strangers."

Christy gave her a cold look.

"My father's people were as much my own blood as those on the other side. But they've been put against me now. I have to look elsewhere for support." She looked after him. There was no knowing what hands he'd fall into now.

Miss Lomas didn't see Christy again until he came into the cemetery the next day and he was accompanied by a couple of scruffy fellows of about his own age. Miss Lomas herself had been brought to the cemetery in the Garretstown trap, but she took care to stand apart from the other mourners. In the absence of Miss Garret, who had been in no condition to attend, Christy had to be considered the chief mourner. Mr. Parr was there of course. And there was a small knot of maids and workmen from Garretstown. Miss Lomas deliberately stood at a distance from all, she wanted it clearly understood that she was representing Brook Farm. She felt numb. Even the sight of the glossy coffin did not awaken any emotion in her, other than to compare it unfavourably with the one in which Joss had been laid, for the ordering of which she herself had been responsible. It was not until that other coffin was lifted up as custom demanded, to let the more recent one be put on top, that her heart was stirred, and her own troubles were for a moment forgotten. Both coffins were new and strong. What matter anyway whether a coffin caved in or not? What did anything matter to the dead? The living were more to be pitied than them. All the same, tears came into her eyes. How upset the brothers would be if they could know the annoyance she was being caused. It was with this thought in her head that, after the last sod was thrown down on the two coffins, she made her way over to Mr. Parr.

"I must have a word with you," she said urgently.

Mr. Parr inclined his head. "Can't it wait a day or two?" Parr was curt. "Normally, I would be reading the Will to Miss Garret after the funeral, but since she's still in no condition to take it in, I was going to postpone doing so until later in the week. It will give us all more time," he added enigmatically.

"For what?" said Miss Lomas so loudly Mr. Parr looked around uneasily. Then he looked back at her and tried to assume an expression of sympathy.

"I know it will be a wrench for you to leave Brook Farm, Miss Lomas," he said guiltily. It seemed the most tactful way to refer to the inevitable changes that would have to be made.

"What do you mean? You know that Brook Farm is my home. I've invested the best years of my life in it," said Miss Lomas, and her voice rose shrilly. "I have no other place to go."

So she was going to be troublesome too? A caustic look came on Parr's face. "If you feel so strongly about it, why don't you buy the place yourself." he said.

"With what?" Miss Lomas asked, looking at him as if he was mad.

Parr's eyes narrowed. He was not sure if she was clever or merely stupid. "It was just a manner of speaking," he said. "I only meant to convey that I knew how highly my clients valued your services. And indeed so well they might. There are not many people who would have given so much over and above what was demanded of them."

"Demanded?"

Mr Parr coughed.

"I know," he said slowly, carefully choosing his words. "I know too how greatly your services exceeded your renumeration, but you always struck me as a thrifty woman."

Miss Lomas stared. It was a matter of pride with her that no one knew her business, but never for a moment did she expect that the family solicitor would have been excluded from confidence with regard to her relations with the Garret brothers.

"You don't mean to say you thought I was paid?" she cried, as if he had cast a slur on her. "Surely you knew my position in Brook Farm?" Suddenly panic seized her. Did she know it herself? And more important still, what was her position *now*? She did not at all like the waspish look on Parr's face.

"I may be wrong," the solicitor said, although the tone of his voice made such a supposition ridiculous, "but I seem to recollect that at the time of the auction there was an item in the list of expenses, an item supplied by you, Miss Lomas, in your handwriting authenticated by your signature, and further to that, initialled on every page, an item which represented a salary, a salary going back over many years, and which, I must add, struck me, even at that time, and in spite of my client's well-known generosity, to say the least of it, as adequate. He coughed. Not to mince matters, it was a remarkably generous salary, Miss Lomas. To tell you the truth, I didn't think we'd get away with that item. You must have a nice little nest egg stashed away." That ought to fix her, he thought.

"Oh, but you forget," said Miss Lomas, and Mr. Parr was startled by the simple and artless look on her face. "You forget that list was made up for the mock auction. They were mock figures. George worked out what he thought was a suitable figure."

"May God forgive him," said Mr Parr, and when at that moment Christy passed them going out the gate of the cemetery, heavily escorted by a dubious looking lot of young fellows his own age, the solicitor threw up his hands.

"Two leeches! Not one!" he cried. "George Garret was not as smart as he thought he was." Then controlling himself with difficulty, he put his hand on Miss Lomas's arm. "I can't believe that you will make trouble, Miss Lomas," he said, but when she shook off his hand, he raised his voice. "I must warn you, that if you do it will be the duty of the law to take action."

Miss Lomas looked around nervously to see if they were overheard.

"I'll say nothing now, Mr. Parr, except that your attitude is very strange. As to the law!" She drew herself up. "Let me tell you it is not the law has the last word in this country. I have my rights and everyone knows that. I tell you plainly here and now that I intend to stand upon those rights."

The mourners were beginning to leave the cemetery, but many of them were waiting to offer her their sympathy. "You see!" she cried, triumphantly turning her back on him and proceeded gracefully to shake hands with all and sundry.

After a few moments however as she stood in the wet grass receiving the sympathy of the farmers' wives, whom she knew only slightly, it began to dawn on her that their condolences seemed to be offered less on the death of George, than on her own predicament. Breaking away from them abruptly, she went out of the gate to where the trap was waiting. But on another impulse she ignored the trap and started to walk down the road. It was an aggressive action, and she saw Mr. Parr looking after her with his lips drawn together as tight as if they had been sewn up with string, like she herself had always made the servant girl sew up the vent of a chicken to keep the stuffing from falling out.

It was a good thing she had not let the girl come with her to the cemetery she thought as she walked along the road because the fresh air made her quite hungry. The girl would have something prepared for her when she'd get home. But the thought of the servant girl was not altogether a happy thought. If there was to be unpleasantness between herself and Parr, who would pay the girl's wages? Ah well, the girl had a good home at Brook Farm, and that was not something to be ignored. The work ought to be lighter now too. She decided not to worry.

It was some time before Miss Lomas reached Brook Farm and when she got no reply to her knock on the hall door, and had to trudge round the back, it was with surprise she saw that it was Christy who was in the kitchen standing beside the range.

"How did you get back before me?" she exclaimed. He had not passed her on the road.

"There are fields attached to this place as well as a house," he snapped back. Miss Lomas agreed to ignore Christy's bad humour. "What are you doing with that filthy teapot?" she asked. In his hand he had a battered blue enamel teapot used only for handing out tea to casuals in the yard.

But Christy had a true economy with words, making question answer question. "Do you want a cup?" he asked, noisily clapping the lid on the pot. "If you do you'd better take it while it's going. There's no use waiting for the skivvy to get it for you. She left. She was no fool that one. She saw the writing on the wall."

"Nonsense!" said Miss Lomas. "She couldn't leave without giving notice."

Christy gave an ugly laugh. "There's no class but has some privileges. Are you going to have a cup of tea or are you not?"

"Well, if the girl is really gone, we had better eat a proper meal," Miss Lomas was about to take the teapot from him but he was already emptying the kettle into it. "I'll have enough to do without washing up odd cups and saucers all day," she cried.

"It's hardly worth your while making a compliment out of yourself," Christy said bitterly. "I won't be here much longer. No one is going to buy a place with a murderous mortgage on it."

"Can't you let the land?" she asked. But she saw that Mr. Parr was right. His relatives had had enough of him. They'd seen there was nothing now to be gained by them. Was he going to quit, walk out of the place and not give it a thought? All along she had wanted to get rid of him, but in the light of Parr's attitude to herself, his going might be far from the best that could happen. She drew herself up with all the dignity she could command upon a stomach so empty. She'd put guts into him if no one else did. "Since when have other people dictated what was to be done at Brook Farm?" she demanded.

"Tell that to Parr!" said Christy crustily.

"I have already done so," said Miss Lomas and she felt she had made some impression on the fellow until he stepped over close to her.

"It's a laugh to hear you talking about rights," he said. "Weren't you the one that laughed at my rights, in spite of them being down on paper and registered in the Office of Deeds." He came closer still. "By all I hear, too, there might be no mortgage at all only for you!" There was an ugly look in his eyes.

The sight of him had always been distasteful to Miss Lomas. She had always thought him a weakling. Perhaps she was wrong about him? Perhaps for all his weediness he could be a bully? And if he was going to leave, he might in his malevolence do her harm before he went. Overcome by fear she had an impulse to run. Only where would she run? Anyway, deep down in her, another fear was growing. If Christy went, she'd be utterly alone, and although the house was only a few yards from the road she had preserved its privacy so well up to now, it might as well have been a vault. Desperately she summoned up a cunning not native to her.

"Why are you so sure it would have made all that difference whether the mortgage was signed or not?" she said. "This is not a case in law you know, it's a matter of human decency. You don't think they can turn you out, do you? Do you imagine for one moment anyone from hereabouts is not going to take your side in a case of clear injustice. What kind of neighbours do you think we have?"

Christy listened, but he shook his head. "There are more people in Ireland than the people hereabouts. What about strangers," he said. "My position will soon be known all over the country and there'll be some scoundrel ready to take advantage of me."

Miss Lomas scoffed. "How big do you think Ireland is? Don't you know that where land is in question, Mizzen Head is only a stone's throw from Fair Head! Word will be passed along, you'll see, and there won't be a man in the length and breadth of the country will as much as cheat you out of a blade of grass. The Irish are still Christians." She saw that her words were sinking into him. "Where's your big talk now about ownership?" she demanded. "Who have you been mixing with these last few days? It's to me you ought to listen! You'll be no man if you let Parr drive you out of here. He won't put me out, I can tell you! And now," she cried, trying to affect a lighter tone, "we'd better eat something. We'll need to conserve our strength for what may be ahead." Stepping brightly over to the bread-bin she lifted the lid with a flourish. At once her smile faded. "There's no bread," she said.

Even Christy was taken aback. He held out the tea-caddy from which he'd made the tea. "That was the last of the tea too," he said.

Not possible! There had never been any shortage in Brook Farm. Miss Lomas hurried over to the big store press. Except for a few jars of mint-sauce, chutney and cayenne pepper, the shelves were empty. When the girl was going she must have cleared out everything in the press and taken it with her. "What will we do?" she asked, stunned. It was a strange quarter from which to look for help, but surprisingly Christy was resourceful.

"Well, we can't live on air," he said rooting around in his pockets. Taking out a fistful of small coins he made a careful selection from them. "I'll go to the shop for a loaf of bread and a bit of tea and sugar."

Miss Lomas looked at him. Survival for both of them depended on solidarity. She'd have to take her chance with him and she was prepared to do so with as much good will as she could summon to her aid, until, at the door, he looked back and fixed her with a cold eye. "Can I get anything for you?" he asked.

"I'll get my purse," she said hastily. Standing at the window, watching him go out to the yard and take down an old push-bike that hung by its front wheel from a meat-hook in the haggard, she wondered what would she have done without him. There was a trace of manliness in him after all, especially in the way he threw his leg over the bar of the bike, and lowering his head over the handlebars charged down the drive. In spite of the vigour of his pedalling however, the bike soon began to wobble from side to side, and going out the gate, he nearly brought the gate-piers with him. She saw with disgust that he had not taken the trouble to pump the tyres. It was not to be wondered he was a long time away, and that he came back on foot.

"It's in the ditch," he said, when she asked about the bike.

Counting out her change, Christy took a number of brown paper bags out of his pocket. Miss Lomas hustled over as he put them on the table. Sugar? Butter? Small quantities, but that was what they'd tacitly agreed. And bread? Yes, but why two loaves? They would get stale. But what was this, though? More tea? More butter? Slowly she understood. Going over to the press she got down two canisters, instead of one, two butter dishes and two earthenware jars for the sugar, and started to divide out their rations. She was about to empty a ration of sugar into one of the jars when she saw there was still a bit of sugar in the bottom of the jar. Startled, she looked at Christy for direction. Silently Christy gave it. Diving in his dirty hand he transferred a fistful of it to the other jar. Then with a down-turned thumb he indicated she could go on pouring. Thus was shared out the dregs of the Garret bounty.

Making sure to use a spoon of tea from each caddy, Miss Lomas made a fresh pot of tea, and put the teapot on a tray along with two cups and saucers, ready to be carried into the dining-room, when Christy reached out roughly and took off one cup. Again with a down-turned thumb he indicated that she was to fill it. Miss Lomas looked uncertainly at her own cup. To eat in the kitchen would save steps, and if she didn't get a cup of tea quick she'd drop. Also, with the servant girl gone there would be no loss of face. She left down the tray and sat herself opposite Christy.

The meal was eaten in a brutal silence. Miss Lomas was so hungry she gulped down the tea and dragged at the thick bread as voraciously as Christy, who always had the manners of a pig. All the same, she was grateful when after he'd finished, he went over to the sink and held his cup under the tap. At least he didn't expect her to wait on him.

What would he do next, she wondered? Would he be going over to Garretstown? She guessed that if she asked he would not answer, so she made what she could of the fact that when he went out he wore no coat. Through the window, she saw him walking around the yard. From the way he poked his head into one shed after another she thought he was looking for something until he went over to one of the field-gates and leant across it staring down at the grass, she felt that he was probably seeing Brook Farm for the first time.

Looking around her, she felt she herself was certainly seeing the kitchen for the first time. She had never spent much time in it. And this, she now saw had been a mistake. It was nowhere as clean as she'd always insisted the rest of the house be kept. She rolled up her sleeves.

Miss Lomas spent the best part of the morning looking for things. Where were the scouring brushes kept? Where on earth were the floor-cloths? And in searching for these things such dirt came to light behind presses and on the top shelves of cupboards. She could hardly credit her eyes. When Christy got back late in the day, she had heaped up in the middle of the floor, a clutter of rags, old newspapers, empty cartons, and half-empty saucebottles, he stood in the doorway and let out an oath.

"Have you turned the place into a dung-heap already?" he said, and wheeling around on his heel he went out again.

Tears of humiliation came into Miss Lomas's eyes. Her head ached. And she was hungry again. Had Christy gone off for the evening? Could he be so spiteful? Perhaps he was gone to buy food for their supper? On the other hand he hadn't asked her for any money. As the evening wore on and there was no sign of his return, she lost heart. If the hens had not stopped laying, she could have had an egg. Or if there was anyone to wring the neck of one of the old hens she could have put it in a pot. But perhaps it was as well not to do that, since somehow or other in their new partnership she felt that everything out of doors was Christy's province. She could boil up a pot of potatoes, of course, but she'd have to go out and dig them, and, although her footwear was not as foolish as that of Miss Garret, her shoes weren't up to the soft trackless loam of the potato patch, and in the end she made do with another cup of tea and a few more cuts of bread.

At twelve o'clock that night when there was still no trace of Christy, Miss Lomas climbed the stairs utterly exhausted. It was near morning when she heard him come in. It would hardly have seemed worth his while going to bed at all except that judging by the way he was stumbling around he'd be safer off his feet than on them. More to contend with. Miss Lomas sighed. Up to this she had not known him to drink hard. Indeed he had not been one to consort with anyone much less with hard drinkers. She listened for a while to him cursing and muttering. Where had he been? Worn out, at last she fell asleep and did not wake until late. The first thing that struck her next day was the deadly silence of the house. By contrast, outside in the open-air the sound of birds singing and cattle lowing was so loud she might as well have been out in the fields. Small wonder, she thought, when going down the stairs, she saw the hall door was wide open. It had blown open in the draught from the kitchen door which was also wide open. The whole house was as cold as a windowless ruin. Shivering, Miss Lomas closed the doors, and unconsciously took comfort from the solid blocks of furniture and the fat padded armchairs. It would take some wind to blow them away.

But although she had closed the doors the sound of lowing cattle was as loud as ever, louder in fact. Running to the window she was just in time to see a young lad from Garretstown going off down the road driving the entire stock of Brook Farm, cattle and sheep, ahead of him, and belting them onward with George's ash plant. Every field on the farm was empty. Every gate was open, including the road-gate.

"Christy! Christy!" she shouted, and she ran to the foot of the stairs. But even when she went up and banged on his door, the only sound she heard in the room was the creak of bed-springs as its occupant turned over heavily. She went downstairs again. For years she had been handed a cup of tea in bed before she put a foot on the floor. Now she'd have to wrestle with the range.

The range went against her. It was noon by the time she got the kettle boiled. There was no stir from Christy. It gave her a queer feeling to think of a grown man lying all day in his bed like a hog. She tried not to think about him as she went about gathering up the heaps of sweepings she'd been too tired to collect the night before. Then, unable to stand the hunger any longer, she foraged out an old pair of Christy's boots that he had long ago discarded and went out to the field to dig up a bucket of potatoes.

There wasn't much butter left to put on the potatoes, but she ate them greedily all the same, and after she'd eaten she felt a lot better. Putting a plateful of the potatoes into the oven for Christy, she went into the dining-room and looked around to see what was to be done there. Before Joss died, it had been her intention to renew the loose covers on the chairs, and indeed, she'd meant to have the room re-painted and re-papered. Now she could not help but feel she'd been caught on the wrong foot. Telling herself however that soap, water and good honest sweat could work miracles she boiled up a tub of water and whipping off the covers she plunged them into the suds. Vigorously she doused them up and down, but very little dirt came out. Instead the water began to turn pink. The dye had run. Ought she to have put something into the water to keep the colour fast? Salt? Soda? What? Well, at least they would be fresh and clean smelling, she thought, as wringing them dry, she went to put them out on the line, but it had begun to rain and she had to bring them back and leave them piled up in the sink. Taking up a scrubbing brush she decided to attack the paintwork. It was while she was on her knees scrubbing the wainscot that Christy appeared in his stocking-feet.

"You're taking off more paint than dirt," he said contemptuously. Looking down at her handiwork, Miss Lomas saw his words were true. She got to her feet. Her back was breaking. She ought as a start to have tackled an easier job. So when her eye fell on a small grease stain on the wallpaper above the sideboard, she felt to remove it would be a task so simple as to be almost pleasurable. Getting a hunk of bread she pulled out a lump of dough and vigourously rubbed at the red flock wallpaper.

Perhaps the bread should have been stale? The stain seemed only to spread. Or perhaps she hadn't rubbed hard enough? Leaning forward she was scrubbing with all her strength when to her stupefaction a long triangular strip of the paper gave way under her finger. First it crumpled like a concertina, and then opened out again to stream out from the wall like a pennant. Utterly disheartened now, Miss Lomas threw the bread on the floor which was already scattered with large crumbs. She crept back to the kitchen as to her lair.

Christy's dinner was still in the oven.

He stayed away all that day too, and when night came and Miss Lomas crawled up the stairs and threw herself on her bed, too tired to undress, she slept so heavily she would not have heard him come back if he had pulled down the staircase.

Next day she woke at cockcrow. Knowing now how hard the range would be to light, she got out of bed at once. The previous night she had shoved a few sticks of kindling into the oven to dry, but when she pulled them out, out too came Christy's stale plate of dinner, which fell on the floor with a clatter and broke in two. Looking down at the pieces, she consoled herself that the plate would in any case have been impossible to clean, the blackened potatoes were stuck as fast to it as a pattern. Then as she stopped to pick up the pieces, she saw something else to upset her. Under the range there was an empty whiskey bottle.

No wonder he didn't eat if he spent the day drinking. Where did he get the money for it? Like herself, he had never been asked to give up change when he ran on an errand, but if he had hoarded anything it couldn't be much. There might, of course, as Parr said, be people willing enough to advance him a few pounds on the strength of the fine farm that was in his name, mortgage or no mortgage.

Just then outside in the yard Miss Lomas heard the same lowing of cattle that she had heard the morning before, but this time looking out, she saw eight or nine lean and scraggy heifers and a small flock of sheep running in the gate, with Christy running after them, as lively as a bee.

So his consorting had been to some purpose? He must have codded his new cronies into giving him a loan on the strength of his expectations from Garretstown. Dear God—the next thing they knew he'd be sent to prison. But for the moment all that mattered was that he'd got hold of a bit of money. Momentarily, her heavy heart was lightened. She went to the door to call him for a cup of tea. After he had penned up the sheep and closed the heifers into a near field he came into the kitchen, and as he came in, he put his hand in his pocket and pulled out a small parcel of meat and threw it on the table. Then, as an afterthought, from the same pocket, he took two letters, bloodied by meat stains. He held one out to her. She saw at once it was from Parr. The other she assumed to be addressed to himself, probably from the same pen. Impulsively, she went over to the range and lifting the lid, she threw the letter, unopened, into the fire. Christy appeared to take no notice of her action. "Where's the tea?" he asked, taking down a cup from the dresser and reaching for the teapot.

What was in his letter, she wondered? But there was no sound from him but the gulping down of the hot tea. Then, suddenly leaving down his cup, he went over to the range, and lifting the lid he dropped his own letter into the fire. Fast though the flames fastened on it, Miss Lomas saw that it too was unopened. "Are you mad?" she screamed. "You don't know what may be in the letter. It was from Parr, wasn't it?"

Christy leered at her. "If you didn't care what he had to say, why should I?" for the first time since George died, he looked her in the eyes, and Miss Lomas realised that her feelings towards him would never change. All that had happened was that where they had previously been divided by hatred, they were now bound by it.

After Christy had swallowed the last of the tea, he went upstairs to his room. Miss Lomas thought he'd gone to bed because he had quite evidently been up all night, but in a minute he came down again with an old shot-gun that he kept for potting at rabbits.

"If anyone wants to know who is the owner here," he said truculently, "he can look for his answer down the barrel of this gun," and going out into the haggard, he sat down on a heap of hay, facing towards the road, the gun across his knees.

Christy sat on the heap of hay till noon.

When he showed no sign of coming in for his dinner, Miss Lomas brought him out a plate of potatoes. "How long do you think you can keep up this game?" she asked. He made no effort to answer her but she was beginning to realise that those who live together in hate learn to make a language of silence. And in that language nothing need go unsaid.

Christy didn't leave the yard till dusk, after which he made no attempt to do jobs that badly needed to be done. During the morning one or two neighbouring people passing on the road had looked in through the gate curiously but no one ventured to come in.

The next day was wet, but the only difference this made to Christy was that he sat a bit further back in the haggard. That day too he sat there till dusk. That night he fumbled around the yard in the dark and in some sort of way got a few jobs done that could not be left any longer undone.

Was he going to spend the rest of his life sitting on a heap of hay? Miss Lomas wondered.

On the third day however Miss Lomas caught the sound of a trap on the road. Could she ever mistake the trot of that cob? Running to the back door, she called out to Christy. "It's Parr," she warned.

Christy too must have heard the cob but he did not get to his feet and to her astonishment the trap did not stop. Indeed, when it reached their gate, it flashed past faster and Mr Parr was looking straight in front of him between the ears of the cob as if Brook Farm was less than nothing to him.

With a broad grin, Christy got to his feet and threw down the rifle. It had not been loaded.

Reluctantly Miss Lomas had to express approval. "He knows what he's up against now," she said timidly.

Christy who had started to whistle, stopped short. "If I could get rid of you as early I'd be right," he said.

It was just like him to take the good out of a thing. All day, his words rankled, and that afternoon for the first time in years, she went up to his room and distastefully eyeing its condition, she attempted to make his bed. The room was in a bad state. She ought not to have left it to the servant girls all those years. She filled two dustpans with cigarette butts alone, and there was such a smell she would have opened the window, only the sashes were stuck. All in all, she was nearly sick to her stomach before she got out of the room. It was no better than a pig-sty. But pig and all that he was, she felt he'd be grateful to her for her concern on his behalf. Not so. That night, when he went upstairs she heard him cursing and swearing. And next day his door was locked.

*   *   *

Casual callers had never been encouraged at Brook Farm. Now hardly a soul ever appeared. If someone did venture in the gate, even if it was only a neighbour, Miss Lomas always summoned Christy who in his turn always picked up the gun before he went to the door to find out what was wanted.

In time, Miss Lomas found herself handing him the gun when she called him. And whenever he went out to the fields or even to the yard, he carried it under his arm like a cattle stick, although as often as not he carried it barrel backwards. But Miss Lomas had to admit the gun spoke loud, and what it said carried far. Soon no one at all came near the place, unless an unwary rate collector or warble-fly inspector, who'd scurry off down the drive a lot faster than he'd ambled up it. Christy got the name of being an ugly customer.

One day however a stranger appeared while Christy was in town. Miss Lomas ran into the hall and dragged at the hall-door, but the door was swollen with damp and by the time she got it open, the stranger had already gone around the gable to try the back door. Miss Lomas was thrown into such a flurry by her own temerity, and also by a fear that Christy might return, she flew after the man like a hen flying out from under a farm cart. Without waiting to find out why the man had called, Miss Lomas began to talk to him herself.

"If it's Christy you're looking for," she cried without preamble, "you're lucky it isn't him that's here. He'd run you off the place. He's trying to best the Garrets, you see." Here she gave a loud scoffing laugh. "Him! that has no claim at all on the place. It's *me* that has the claim," she cried hysterically. Then controlling herself, she leaned forward confidingly. Don't let that worry you though. You did right to come. A wrong impression was put abroad about me. Do you think I relish the way the place is going to rack and ruin? Me, who always put the interests of Brook Farm above all else. Wait a minute, sir, and I'll get my coat and show you over the house." As she spoke she was looking anxiously around in case Christy might be coming back. "Wait another minute, sir," she said. "I have a better idea. If you'll be so kind as to take a quick look around the yard, I'll ready up the rooms a bit for your inspection."

Hurrying back into the house, she dragged a brush over the floor of the kitchen and rubbed ineffectively with her apron at the tea-stains on the table. Then she ran out again but there was no sign of the stranger. Instead Christy was standing in the middle of the yard, a sneer on his face.

"Begod," he said, and he gave an ugly laugh, "you did my work better for me than I ever could do it. That poor devil thought it was into the hands of a lunatic he got. There'll be no more intruders here at Brook Farm from now till the day one or other of us is boxed up for the clay."

Miss Lomas felt the truth of his words fasten upon her mind like a clamp, fixing her to her fate. Across the neighbouring fields, flattened by winter, the cemetery was plainer to be seen than usual. But even if she hung on till her end came, could she be sure where she'd be buried? Then a queer and terrifying thought came to her. If she died here alone in the house with him, would Christy bother to have her buried at all? She looked at him. He was staring at her malevolently. From romances she'd read as a girl, she'd known that eyes could speak love. She had never known they could more eloquently speak with malice. She shivered and went back in the house.

From that day the silence between the two of them grew until it was as thick as the grass in the understocked fields, the ragged scutch that invaded the driveway and pushed up between the cobbles in the yard. Looking out sometimes at this neglect and decay, Miss Lomas muttered to herself. But if Christy heard her, he shut her up quick. "Put a sock in it, will you, for God's sake," he'd say.

Yet, sometimes he too muttered to himself as he shuffled about.

Miss Lomas never rightly knew what he did all day long, although she had to admit he kept himself occupied. Sometimes she'd see him with a hammer in his hand bending over a piece of farm machinery. At another time, she'd hear him driving in a paling post into the ground in a far field, the blows of the mallet echoing back, heavy but irregular, and with long intervals between blows. Or else he might come into the kitchen and rummage about for a bit of string to patch up the harness of an ass he'd got somewhere or other. She grudgingly admitted he was making as good a fist of things as could be made, all in all.

In the old days farm horses and carts, the pony and trap and all the farm machinery, had been kept at Garretstown, and it had been workmen from Garretstown who cut the hedges at Brook Farm, weeded the garden and scuffled the paths. As for odd jobs like taking a jackdaw's nest out of a chimney, cleaning the gutters, opening a blocked drain or cutting timber and splitting it into logs for the fire, who else would have done these things?

Now such jobs had to be left undone. At first, Miss Lomas was only concerned about the neglect inside the house, but gradually she realised that the neglect outdoors had a more direct bearing on her domain than she'd taken into account. When the drainpipe over the back door got blocked, she had to step through a puddle as big as a lake every time she went in or out. And when a slate blew off the roof just over her own bedroom, the rain came down in a waterfall on to her bed and she had to move the bed in the middle of the room. Inside and out, the place was becoming a shambles. It was no worse, of course, than the small farmhouses round about, but if Christy was satisfied with this comparison, she was not.

Once, as she stood in the doorway looking out at the dandelions and nettles that had sprung up in every crack and crevice of the yard, she couldn't control her tongue. "That's a nice sight," she spat out at Christy.

"At least it's more natural to see things growing outdoors than indoors," said Christy, and following his glance Miss Lomas saw a dirty big toadstool sprouting in the corner of the kitchen ceiling. Speechless, she stared up at the ugly sight. Then, getting a broom handle she hit at it as if it was a living creature. When it splattered all over the floor, she felt like a murderer.

Strange to say, the house had deteriorated faster inside than outside. The yard didn't really look much worse after six months, for whereas weeds wither and die, and each Spring they had to make a fresh start, the dirt and grime indoors was cumulative, and in places that she could not reach, like the top of presses and cupboards, dust lay as thick as plush.

As well as that, Miss Lomas would have thought that it would have taken centuries before her large stock of linen and crockery would be exhausted, but as the kitchen cups got cracked and plates got chipped, it wasn't long until she had to draw on the good china that was hitherto kept in the dining-room cupboard. Upstairs too, when a sheet tore, or wore thin in the middle, there was no one to mend it and she had to encroach on the bed linen kept for the spare rooms. Then came the terrible day when she found that damp had mildewed even the unused sheets, and they too had rotted. Damp was eating up everything, even the plaster from the walls. She felt it could eat the flesh from one's bones.

The first winter of their unhappy partnership, Christy cut down any trees that were not too big for him to fell alone. These logs had to be used for fuelling the range and so the kitchen was the only part of the house that was reasonably warm. At night the only way Miss Lomas could get warm was to sleep between the blankets, which meant that these too in time got discoloured and threadbare. As for Christy's room, now that he kept it locked there was no knowing its condition. As she hurried past it a smell came out under the door, but soon this smell was indistinguishable from the smell all over the house. She had almost given up scrubbing and washing, for her labours seemed only to hasten disintegration. Curtains and loosecovers at first faded, then frayed, and finally they flittered into ribbons that fluttered about in the constant draughts that went criss cross through every room.

One day as Christy and herself were eating the pot-full of potatoes which had become their staple food, there was a clatter in the dining-room, and when, wordlessly, they ran in there they saw that a piece of the plaster cornice had fallen from the ceiling. Christy looking morosely upward, "The roof will fall in on us next. We'll be driven out by the rain and the weather."

"Not me!" cried Miss Lomas stubbornly. "I'll stand on my rights to the end."

"Begod, that won't be long now by the look of you!" he said cruelly.

Miss Lomas had not heard him however. Picking up a piece of the fallen plaster she'd gone back into the kitchen with the tears pouring down her face. "Poor Brook Farm," she said to herself. "Poor, poor Brook Farm."

It was a long time since Miss Lomas had cried and even now she did so silently and hopelessly. Not till a ray of sun came through the grimy windows, did she take heart from the fact that the fine weather had come. She went out into the yard. Alas the bright sunlight only showed up the utter desolation of the land. The fields were as bare and trodden as a strip of commons. The hedges were woody and gapped at the bottom and their tops reared up into the sky as if to fence out the birds. A few scrawny cattle came and went where they liked. The wire mesh that had once enclosed the flower garden in front of the house was long rusted away. Now the little garden was palisaded only by nettles. At that moment there was a beast standing under the dining-room window.

"One of those bullocks will put his horns through the window yet!" she said out loud, not knowing or caring if Christy had heard her or not. He had heard her alright and when he went out, although there was a leer on his face, she thought he was maybe going to mend the fence. But it was to scull whatever few cattle he had left.

The sculling of cattle was always done at Brook Farm, but in deference to the susceptibility of the women in the house, even the servant girl, the beasts were done in a shed and put out in a far field till their poor heads healed, although George and Joss always did it as humanely as possible. Now Christy did it himself, and he did it in the yard, clumsily and cruelly, and afterwards, smeared with gore, the beasts blundered around the place where Miss Lomas could not but see them and share in their agony.

That afternoon when she had occasion to go into the parlour, looking out the window, she saw the same poor beast of the morning, his head glittering with dried blood, his eyes blinded with clipped hair. Unnerved she ran back into the kitchen where Christy was washing his hands in a basin at the table. "Oh, take him away! Take him away!" she screamed with her hands to her own head.

"He'll be taken away soon enough," Christy replied.

Miss Lomas took her hands down from her head. Lately the fields had seemed more silent and empty than ever. Was that poor beast the last on the land?

"Won't you be buying more cattle?" she asked. The next minute she could have bitten off her tongue. Her own small store of money was long gone. It was Christy now who provided them both with tea and bread, and the odd bit of meat or bacon that kept them alive. It was he who had paid the rates and the interest on the mortgage. Moreover he was smoking now as well as drinking, and he was never without a copy of the Racing Gazette sticking up out of his pocket. Where could he find the money for all this save by selling beast after beast?

With no cattle on the land, the real despoiling of Brook Farm would begin. Now he would start to sell anything he could lay hands on.

At first Christy only sold the grain-bins and feed-troughs, turnip slicers and tree guards, articles that he could take away in a wheel-barrow. Then he pulled the corrugated iron off the sheds and sold it for scrap. Then except for one at the road, he sold the gates. What next, Miss Lomas wondered, as she watched these items being wheeled down the drive. Searching the house, she found a key that would lock the dining-room door. But a month or so later she heard a splintering sound one day and found Christy had put his shoulder to the door and got in. He came out with two chairs.

"Well?" he said, confronting her. "Which do you want, an empty house or an empty belly?" After that, every piece of furniture in the house went the way of the chairs. And as the days got cold and winter advanced, he pulled up paling posts and sold them for firewood.

Another day standing at the window pinched with cold, Miss Lomas saw him trundle off to town with a barrow of rotten stumps he'd dug out of the ground. She wished she herself had the strength to drag up a few roots because the only fire they ever had now was a blaze of twigs she pulled out of the hedges, or a branch brought down by the wind from high trees on the mearing which he hadn't dared to cut. She let the blaze die down when she'd boiled the kettle or got the spuds cooked. Staring into the cold and empty grate one evening although it was only five or six o'clock she went to bed to try and keep the life in her body. The thought of the winter was unbearable to her. It was not so bad for Christy who was still young and had no aches and pains in his bones.

But one morning on waking, she was startled to hear a roar in the flue of the dining-room chimney which ran up behind the mantlepiece in her own room. She jumped out of bed in a cold sweat thinking the house was on fire. There was a smell of smoke and she could hear a crackle of sparks. She ran down the stairs, but halfway down she heard Christy moving about below, and her panic was allayed. At the same time she saw that the door of his bedroom was open and she couldn't resist looking into the room as she passed. She hadn't seen into it for years.

Compared with the general neglect of the house the neglect in Christy's room was classic. The floor was carpeted with butts, and there were so many old yellowed copies of the Racing Calendar piled in the corners they acted as tables and chairs, of which there were none. But it was the bed that struck Miss Lomas. She knew that no more than herself, Christy could not have much left in the way of blankets to put over him at night. His coverings, like hers, would be mostly made up of old jackets and coats. But this morning his mattress was bare. She hurried on downstairs, although she couldn't bear her own footsteps for the roar of the fires, because through the banister rail she could see that the kitchen range, too, was blazing like a furnace, although its roar stopped for a moment as Christy who stood in front of it stuffed another armload of paper on top of what was already fiercely burning.

"What are you doing? You'll set the chimney alight," she cried but she got her answer from an old straw suitcase open on the floor. She hadn't seen it since the day Christy first came to Brook Farm. But she remembered it well. Only an orphan would have had luggage like it. Now, with its webbing ravelled, its strap as hard as iron, and the catches red with rust, it was a stranger sight than ever. But into it Christy had stuffed all his worldly goods, among which she saw with concern the stub of a shaving stick. "You're not leaving, Christy?" she cried, but to Christy, intent on trying to get the catches to fasten, this question seemed so superfluous he laughed.

"Maybe you didn't hear the news," he said, knowing well she had no way of hearing anything except through him. "The old one up at Garretstown was taken to hospital to a public ward in a public hospital," he added with an emphasis on some of the words the significance of which escaped Miss Lomas.

It was so long since Miss Lomas had thought about Miss Garret she didn't at once know to whom he so vulgarly referred. "Oh, is she dying?" she cried.

"No such luck," said Christy, "It's not a real hospital, it's an old people's home where she'll be preserved like a mummy for another half a century. There can't be much left of the Garret estate, at this rate there'll be nothing at all for me. The game is up at last. I listened to you long enough, I'm getting out of here. I'll be gone to Dublin on the next train and I'll be there in time to catch the night boat for England. I know Parr!" He looked at her viciously. "He could have the law on us for the damage that's been done here."

Miss Lomas quailed before the spiteful look he gave her but his words themselves she regarded as rubbish. "Any damage that has been done is only the result of neglect," she said with dignity. "And whose fault is that?"

"Ah, you're a bad case," Christy said and he gave a laugh. Having got the catches on his case closed, he hoisted the case under his arm, like he must have caught up the clucking hen on the day of the Mock Auction, then, leaving it down again for a minute he took out a cigarette and going over to the range he lit it from the dying embers. Miss Lomas felt he would as lightheartedly lit it from the flames of the house. For a minute they stood looking at each other. Then, on an impulse, Christy put his hand in his pocket and threw down on the table a ten shilling note so dirty and crumpled it was almost objectionable. "That might hold your bones together till they come and take you away," he said, as, with another laugh he went off.

It was all so sudden. Miss Lomas stood in an empty house, outside which were the empty fields, and a terrible panic seized her. Christy had become almost as much a part of Brook Farm as herself, and at night when she used to lie in bed in the house that had lost most of its window catches and locks, she had nevertheless felt lapped around with a strange protectiveness that emanated from him, even if, as often as not, he was half a mile away stuck in a furze-bush, dead-drunk.

He mustn't go, she thought, and she ran to stop him. But Christy had already got as far as the road where a dilapidated motor car was waiting for him. When it started up it made such a racket her cry to him was lost. She went back to the house in a daze.

All Miss Lomas could think to do at first was make a cup of tea, but like the day after George's funeral when she looked into the tea canister there was only tea-dust in it. Dully she stared at the ten shilling note that lay among the crumbs on the table, but it was so long since she had handled money it seemed of no more use than a toffee-wrapper. Disdaining it, she looked away. Had she not always been above money? Indeed it seemed to her at that moment that the world had really no need for it. She felt sure that if only people would behave properly money could be done without. Had she herself not proved this? But to whom? Only to herself, she thought sadly. Suddenly the scales fell from her eyes. They had all of them, Parr and Miss Garret and Christy, they had all thought it was money she wanted. Oh, what a dreadful mistake! What a terrible misapprehension! She must remedy it at once, she thought. Immediately! She must go to town and have it out with Parr.

Climbing the stairs, Miss Lomas for the first time in a long while, felt purposeful and confident, and when she opened her closet door it gave a great lift to her spirit to smell the camphor that had successfully battled for so long against destructive moths. That smell was like a promise that all would in the end be well.

How wise she had been to spare her best garments and not put them over her in bed at night as she had often been tempted to do. Fumbling among the clothes, she pulled out the last costume she had bought. It was the smartest, the most high-class, the most costly costume she had ever bought. Stepping into the skirt she pulled it up proudly. She felt she was being proved right in one thing anyway; good quality garments never lost their shape. That was true, but alas, she herself had lost shape. She might as well have stepped into a rain-water barrel. For a moment she almost gave way to despair. But diving into the closet again she brought to light the old costume she had worn the day she first walked in the door of Brook Farm. Hadn't she always said that if you kept a thing for long enough you'd find a use for it in the end? Everything seemed to be working to a pattern. When last she wore this suit she was as slim as a stem, and now, again, she was as thin as a stalk. Except for the padded shoulders and the fact that the skirt was hobbled, the costume looked very well on her, she thought. The skirt was a bit long, but considering that she was wearing Christy's shoes, this was an advantage. Her feet were so swollen there was no question of trying to squeeze them into any of the neat little shoes that had stood patiently for so long on the floor of the closet. Hats were a different matter though. And gloves. And handbags. Taking down a hatbox covered with wallpaper patterned with violets faded but recognisable, the dear little flowers, she selected accessories to match the costume. It was a pity that every looking-glass in the house had been broken or sold and the one in her own room so spotty there was no seeing oneself in it. So although she couldn't appraise her appearance, she drew herself up and confidently went downstairs. To give an auspicious start to her mission, she tugged at the front door till she got it open.

It was many years since Miss Lomas had been on the public road. Motor cars now, and not traps, flashed past. She was a bit put out when people she met did not appear to recognise her but she gave no sign of caring. And when three or four small children, open-mouthed fell into step behind her, she would not have sent them back if she had not feared their mothers might miss them and worry on their account.

It was a long walk to the town. It was tiring too, but like an engine excitement drove her onward, and at last she got to the outskirts of the town. But so many new houses had been built in the town since she'd last been there she doubted whether she'd find her way to the main street so when, passing a row of dismal cottages, recollecting that in one of them the widowed sister of Mr. Parr used to reside, she had an impulse to stop and enquire if the lawyer's office was still in the same place. But she decided against stopping, thinking that having prospered he would no doubt have arranged for his nieces and nephews to reside in a better quarter. Anyway she had seen a very common looking girl standing in the doorway with curling pins in her hair. Certainly Mr. Parr's dependants no longer lived there. She hurried on.

Mr. Parr's office was where it had always been. It had not changed much since the days when she used to sit outside in the trap and hold the reins while George Garret went inside. But mistaking a new bronze plate for tarnished brass, it seemed to her that perhaps he had not prospered as much as she would have thought. From this observation indeed she took such heart that upon pushing open the outer door, and finding herself confronted by two other doors, one marked Enquiries and the other Private, she had no hesitation whatever in making towards the latter, until she was stopped short by a loud voice. "Where do you think you are going?" the voice called out.

Startled, she stopped dead but next minute, seeing she had only to deal with a raw young man, weedier even than Christy had been at his age, his face covered with pimples, Miss Lomas brushed him aside. Grasping the door-knob she went through the private door with such force that even without recognising her Mr. Parr gave an exclamation.

"Good God!" Parr said, then, seeing who it was, he repeated his exclamation. "Good God!" What in the world had brought her to town? Was she ill? She had shrunk to half her size. He was appalled at her condition. And what of Christy? Queer gossip about the pair had reached him from time to time. But the fears roused by such stories were instantly dispelled by a look of loneliness in her eyes that vouched for her virginity. An unexpected feeling of pity for her came over him. "My dear Miss Lomas!" he cried out.

Miss Lomas, too, was stirred at sight of Mr. Parr in the flesh, if such words could be used to describe the leathery little bat she saw before her sunk in a swivel chair he was barely able to swivel. Stretching out her hands, she ran forward to him as if laden with bounties. "He's gone!" she cried. "Gone at last! Poor Brook Farm can yet be saved."

Mr. Parr sank lower into his chair. She could only mean Christy. The fellow must have heard about Miss Garret. "Ah!" he said. "No doubt word reached him that Miss Garret was taken from Garretstown?" The old calculating look she knew so well had come back into his eyes.

Miss Lomas nodded and taking out an elegant but discoloured handkerchief, she wiped a dry eye. "How is the poor thing?" she asked. "I never knew her intimately, you know." Leaning forward she spoke more familiarly. "I may as well tell you, Mr. Parr, I never cared much for the poor thing. Just the same I think it is not at all suitable that the poor thing should be put into a public hospital, a kind of a home not much better than a poorhouse, Christy said."

So Christy had not been a complete fool. He had come to his senses at last and seen the writing on the wall. But Miss Lomas was still concerned about Miss Garret.

"Is it known to whom the poor thing will leave the estate when she does die?" she asked. "Surely that person can advance the money to see she has proper care to the end."

Mr. Parr gasped.

"You can't have forgotten that there is a family trust. Christy is the sole heir but he was a wise fellow to skedaddle. He could have found himself in a worse plight than when he inherited Brook Farm. Debts are all he would inherit."

"But surely Miss Garret must have some personal effects that she would be free to dispose of in her own right?"

"It is true I believe that she has a few, a few baubles which," Mr Parr coughed discreetly, "which she insisted on leaving to me, and so I had to advise her that as a beneficiary under the testament I could not act for her in that matter and that she would be obliged to make her will with another solicitor. However I understand from him that they are merely small objects of sentimental value, to her I mean, but otherwise worthless."

Miss Lomas seemed momentarily at a loss.

"Well that is too bad but I will come to the point of my visit here," she said. "It is my opinion that Miss Garret must be taken out of the place where she has been put and brought to Brook Farm where I can take care of her and where she can be given some comfort and companionship in the end of her days. You and I both owe it to George and Joss to see this is done."

Mr. Parr gasped. Noting that she hurried on, "I am aware that some repairs will have to be carried out before it is possible to receive her, and some essential replacements of crockery, linen and the like will have to be made. But thank God the house is there and available to us in order that we can perform a great charity."

Was she mad? Not for the first time Mr. Parr wondered about this.

"But Brook Farm is *not* available to us," he shouted, "Why can't you get that into your head? You never had any right there, much less me. And whether Christy is gone or not, and even if we never hear from him again, he is still the lawful owner. Your intentions are of the best. They do you credit, Miss Lomas, but I'm afraid they cannot be implemented."

At these words the dejection which descended on Miss Lomas was such as Mr Parr had never before seen come over any human being. And yet he himself felt relieved. Now at last, she, too, would have to take herself off, although God knows where she would go. She'd be off his hands anyway and at the moment that was all that seemed to matter. But suddenly Miss Lomas rallied.

"Christy?" she cried. "If he is our only hope now we must get him back. A motor car came and took him to the station, but the next train to Dublin is not due to leave for at least two hours." She sprang to her feet. "You must go to the station at once and get hold of him."

"For what in the name of God?" Mr. Parr was suffering such palpitations he thought he was going to have a heart attack.

"Because you just said young Christy has come to his senses at last. He knows he has reached the end of the road. He is desperate Mr. Parr. He will almost certainly be prepared to do business with anyone. He will sell Brook Farm this minute even if he only gets half the price of the mortgage. Indeed I believe he is so desperate he'll probably sell it for a song."

"You might be right," Mr. Parr said dryly, "but can't you see it's too late in the day now to find a buyer. Are you blind to that as well as to everything else?"

Miss Lomas drew herself up and something of her old authority returned to her voice.

"It's you that's blind," she said, "can't you see it's you yourself who must buy Brook Farm, and you must act fast if you're not to lose a golden opportunity, an opportunity that only comes once in a lifetime. Quick! Where is your coat! there is no time to be lost. If he's not in the station he'll be in the nearest bar. And if he's half-seas over when you find him, that will work to your advantage. If he has a consort of scroungers with him, that too will be in your favour. They won't be too drunk to see that they may still bleed him a bit." Here she threw a look at the clock. "The banks are still open. They'll see to it he can cash your cheque. Don't forget your cheque book. And here's another thing, be sure and take your clerk with you to be a witness to the transaction. He'll hardly be needed here while you're away. Anyway, I can stay here and give what assistance is needed maybe to answer the bell or admit a client if one calls. I can provide him with a chair and say that you were regrettably called away on urgent business but would be back shortly." In a matter of seconds she had him on his feet and in his coat. "Isn't destiny extraordinary," she said, "George always said there is a right time and a wrong time for everything we do. I used to wonder long ago why you never did buy a farm of your own."

"I never got much encouragement to do so," said Mr. Parr, "Never from the Garrets," he added acidly, "If you remember they regarded me highly as a lawyer but never lost an opportunity of saying they did not think much of me as a farmer, although I managed all their affairs for a considerable number of years." He leaned forward. "Don't you remember, Miss Lomas, that not long before he died George said in your hearing that one day in the open would be the end of me. They didn't think a man was a man at all if he wasn't big and red-faced like themselves."

Miss Lomas was surprised at a semi-quaver of bitterness in his voice. In the past she had sometimes wondered how he had taken the Garrets' jibes at his white face and skinny legs. Then she had been on the side of the mockers. Surprisingly now she felt more like siding with him. "Ah well! We can't all be big and beefy!" she said. "And isn't it odd it's them and not you that's now six foot under the sod" When a squint of gratitude came into his eyes, she didn't miss it. "It's my belief that you will make as good a fist of farming it as anyone. After all, what is there to it, only watching the grass grow and telling a fat beast from a thin one?"

Mr. Parr seemed somewhat taken by surprise but he bowed in gratitude to her tribute. "Thank you, Miss Lomas," he said.

"It's true!" said Miss Lomas. "If only that terrible Christy had not let the place go so far downhill. It's only fair to warn you that there will have to be a lot of money spent on the land and the outhouses. Ah well," she said practically, "we can't have our loaf and eat it at the same time. Think of the bargain you'll be getting." Seeing that Mr. Parr did not look as happy as he ought, she patted him on the shoulder. "Little by little, that's the way we'll tackle the job. We must keep a proper balance, you know." And when as he still looked glum she gave him a little shake. "Cheer up!" she said. "It won't be too hard to put the place to rights if we go about it with the proper spirit." Indeed she herself was overcome by such a rush of energy and enthusiasm it seemed to her that when she'd get back there that evening she would turn out every room at Brook Farm and overtake in a few hours all she had failed to accomplish in a decade. But this rush of vitality brought a rush of blood to her head and she flopped back again into her chair. And when she tried to rise a second time, her legs wobbled and a sweat broke out all over her body. "I think I'm going to faint," she gasped.

Mr. Parr scrambled to his feet. "Help, help!" he shouted, although, almost before the words were out of his mouth, as if he was listening at the door, Miss Lomas, thought, his pimply apprentice ran in. "Quick! Get this woman a cup of tea," cried Mr Parr, "and some sandwiches, anything at all, as long as it's quick."

But weak as she was Miss Lomas heard what the young fellow said. She always had good ears.

"Who is the Old Bags anyway?" the young man asked.

Pained, Miss Lomas closed her eyes. "Is it wise to let such an ill-mannered pup come into contact with your clients?" she asked weakly, but feeling she had been unkind, she modified her criticism. "Perhaps the young man is delicate that sallow skin, those pimples."

"Delicate?" cried Mr. Parr. "Is it that fellow? Well, let me tell you if he's delicate, it's not for want of food. That fellow has been plied with the best, the same as his sisters and brothers, since the first hour he came into my care."

"Oh dear me!" Miss Lomas's hand flew to her heart. "He isn't your nephew, is he?" she cried in embarrassment but it was an embarrassment that was put to rout by one of those impulses of generosity that had characterised her in the old days. "The poor boy," she said. "I'm sorry for him." Suddenly she sat up, full of life once more. "Why didn't you send him out to me at Brook Farm?" she cried. "There's nothing like the country for putting red cheeks on young people. Indeed if it comes to that, there is nothing like it for putting manners on them too. Oh dear, what a pity to think of all the summers that young fellow could have spent out there with me and his brothers and sisters too for that matter." Distressed she sighed. "Well, it can't be helped now," she said, but she looked peculiarly at the old man "So you never married?" she said with a look as belittling as the gaze of an undertaker sizing him up for a coffin.

"I may not have married, Miss Lomas," Mr. Parr said sourly, but I have had a full share of life's responsibilities. And I am by no means rid of those responsibilities either. You may not know it, living as you have done in such unnatural seclusion, but when I took over the care of my poor sister's children they were already a neglected lot. It was not easy to rear them from such a poor start."

"You don't tell me? Bad enough to be saddled with them, without them being ailing and difficult." Genuinely sympathetic, she reached out and manacled his hands in a warm moist clasp. But she had seen that the word saddled was too strong a word to have used; it had put him in a poor light. No doubt when his nieces and nephews were growing up, he had found some sort of fulfilment in the rearing of them. It must even have given him pleasure to pay for their books and satchels, their little boots and mufflers. And when he called to the cottage where they lived and for which of course he would have been paying the rent, it must have made him feel good to have them throw their arms around his neck and hug him in thanks for the bag of sweets he would most likely have pulled from his pocket. Ah! but it must have been a different matter altogether when he wakened up to the realisation that for all he had spent on them they were far from being what they would have been had they been his own. Then the boots and books he had so magnanimously supplied would have been taken for granted, and he would have had to put his money into giving them the airs and graces they now clearly lacked. Nevertheless, no matter what, she thought he should not have let them grow up in the town. "There's no use crying over spilled milk, I suppose," she said briskly.

"Weren't you the foolish man to let the Garrets ridicule you out of trying your hand at farming. Isn't it the only way of life that is natural to any man." She paused. "You could have added to your income too, and for all your money, I daresay you could have done with a few extra pounds, having had extra burdens to carry. To say nothing of the young people themselves who would have reaped a harvest richer than gold!" But here, as if her words had set up an echo in her mind, she leant forward excitedly. "Do you remember George Garret always said the land was so good at Brook Farm that if you sowed farthings you'd reap sovereigns?"

"That's right, I remember well. Many a time he said it," said Mr. Parr. "Tell me, would you say it was very run down, the land, I mean?"

Miss Lomas pondered the question. "It's the house I'm worried about," she said. "I think the sooner you come out and inspect the place, the better."

It was at this point a tray arrived, with tea, bread and butter and slices of cold ham, and although Miss Lomas fastened a famished gaze on it, she took time for a quick look at the young man who carried it before he went out again. "He certainly isn't as robust as I'd like to see him," she said, "it might be a good idea to send him out right away. Can he drive a car? If so, how about having him drive me back? Then he could give you a report on the place and whatever one may say about one's own, they can be trusted better than strangers. She had poured out a cup of tea and taken a sip, when she had another idea. "Why not have him stay out there tonight?" she said. "He could have Christy's room! If he gave me a hand, I wouldn't be long getting it to rights. It would need a good cleaning out of course. You know what Christy was like, but it might be advisable for him to bring a few blankets with him too," she said. Here, however Miss Lomas could no longer refrain from falling on the food, but before taking her knife and fork to the ham, felt obliged to add another recommendation. "And some supplies perhaps," she said, as casually as was compatible with her famished state. Mr. Parr got to his feet.

"When I come back from the station, I think that I will leave you home myself, Miss Lomas," he said. "We can discuss a lot of matters on the way out. And now I'll leave you for a brief time to finish your meal in peace." Calling his nephew to accompany him he hurried out. Miss Lomas nodded her thanks to him as she stuffed a forkful of ham into her mouth.

*   *   *

It was late in the afternoon when Mr. Parr and Miss Lomas drove out of the town. Mr. Parr had thought it wise to leave his nephew behind for the moment. He had made a very good deal with Christy but it was as well to keep things quiet until he had possession of the deeds and cleared his entitlement.

"How did Christy react to it all," Miss Lomas asked.

"Well as you said he was slightly befuddled. He actually wanted to take less than I offered."

They had made one stop, because they were passing the family grocers where she used to deal, Miss Lomas gave an exclamation. "The supplies!" she said, and remarkably nimbly she hopped out of the car. "I'll tell them to put them down to you, I suppose," she said before she dodged into the shop. It was half an hour before they were on their way again. This time, more accustomed to the newfangled vehicle, Miss Lomas sat happily looking out at the countryside. It was a stuffy way to travel compared with an open trap in which one got the air, and an unobstructed veiw, but of course it was faster, because in no time at all they were near to Brook Farm. They ought surely to coming in sight of it? They had turned around a fence from which, in the old days, the gleaming white gates could be seen. She stole a look at Mr. Parr's face and it was by the dismay on it, she realised that they were already at the gateway.

The gate was open, but not thrown wide in the hospitable way of old, when Christy would have been sent running down at the sound of the trap. It was only half-open, its broken hinges having caused it to list and drop, leaving one end stuck like an anchor into the thick mud that totally replaced the washed river pebbles with which it used be annually surfaced. There was no sign of the spud-stone, or else it too was sunk into the mud.

The old solicitor stopped the car.

"How are the cattle kept from straying out on the road?" he asked.

"The land is empty," Miss Lomas whispered.

Mr. Parr shook his head. "How do we get in?" He tugged at the gate but it did not budge. Yet in the mud of the drive he saw the tracks of a cart. After a closer scrutiny he saw that the cart had come out through a gap in the hedge where a number of rotten planks and a sheet of warped roofing-iron had been thrown across the ditch. The old man eyed this pass-way distrustfully. Getting back into the car he parked it carefully on the far side of the road and proceeded to help Miss Lomas down. "We'll walk up if you don't mind," he said, and he began to make his way up the drive through the puddles and potholes. "Ah dear!" he murmured again and again when, sidestepping a puddle, he nearly had his eye pulled out by a briar trailing out from a hedge. Through a gap in the hedge he saw with alarm the barren state of the land. Field ran into field, and the headlands could only be distinguished by an abandoned ploughshare or a rusty harrow through the iron ribs of which the grass had grown, riveting them like skeletons to the earth. "Ah dear! Ah dear!" the old man kept muttering, and even Miss Lomas plodding along beside him, was hardly prepared for seeing from without the neglect with which she was more familiar from within. Even she had not realised what a shambles had been made of the actual farmland. She gave her attention to the house.

Poor Brook Farm. The windows were broken, the paint peeled away, and from the gutters there spilled out a filthy green fungus. As for the roof, not only were there the holes where tiles had blown off, but the whole roof sagged in the middle like an old mattress.

At last the pair reached the place where formerly the driveway had swept inward towards the hall-door, but humbly Miss Lomas plodded past this point and went around the gable to the back door. Mr Parr followed wordlessly and when she stood back to let him pass into the kitchen, he was so appalled by the dirt and decay that he gladly sank down on a backless chair she proffered him. Following his astonished gaze Miss Lomas too stared around. Rot, woodworm, rat holes and holes where fixtures had been torn out of the walls, the place, even on that summer evening, was like a sieve. Except for the chair on which he sat and the grime-coated kitchen table, the kitchen was bare, while through the hall-way it could be seen that the parlour too, that once was stuffed with armchairs and carpets, was now as empty as a shed. Miss Lomas felt the moment called for some comfort.

"We were lucky to get the place before he did irremediable harm. Christy, I mean," she said. She pointed up at a hole in the lath-and-plaster of the ceiling overhead. He'd have torn out the laths for firing, only he couldn't reach up to get at them," she said. "If you stand here, and look up, you'll see where he tried to bring them down by battering at them with the handle of the sweeping brush." But as she pulled at his sleeve her own foot suddenly went down through one of the floor boards, because this spot on the floor was under the spot in the ceiling that was under the spot on the roof where the tiles had blown away and let in the rain. To pass off the awkwardness she laughed, although her foot hurt. But Mr Parr didn't join in the laughter. "It will cost a King's ransom to put this place to rights, if it can be done at all," he said sharply.

For a minute Miss Lomas said nothing. Then she too spoke with some asperity.

"All that need be done at the start is put an appearance on the place."

The phrase was so quaint Mr Parr was taken aback. Mistaking his sudden scrutiny of her face for interest in her proposition Miss Lomas's own face lit up with eagerness. "What would it involve but some slates on the roof, a few tins of paint, a length or two of new timber and a couple of pounds of nails." As she saw his eye rest on the broken window in the kitchen she frowned impatiently, not at it but at him. "That's nothing," she said. "There's a few panes gone elsewhere in the house too, but glass is cheap. If only there had been a bit of putty put in these window frames from time to time, the glass would never have fallen out. Indeed if there had been money made available to me for polishes and cleaning powders, there mightn't have been any repairs needed at all." Suddenly she ran out into the hall and called the solicitor to come after her. "The rest of the house is very well preserved," she said, "only for a few damp spots. Would you like to look around?" But although they had not noticed it steal into the house, the gloom of dusk had come down on Brook Farm. Nothing daunted, Miss Lomas looked around for matches. "There are no lights in the front of the house, I'm afraid," she said. "The bulbs have all blown, and some of the switches are defective. With years of damp and disuse wires perish, you know. In any case it would not have been safe to have light bulbs in empty rooms where they'd only be left burning day and night by irresponsible people. As a matter of fact, even in the old days, I was worried about the wiring here. It was not in a very good state when the Garrets bought the place. They were always intending to renew it. I myself was always pressing Joss to have it done," she paused, "before the little upset occurred." But seeing Mr. Parr look startled she lowered her voice—"his death, I mean!" She thought he was even more startled at this, but it was hard to see anything dearly now in the dark. "The re-wiring of the house ought to be attended to at once. There's nothing as dangerous as faulty electricity. And now is our opportunity to get it done at a low cost," she added, as if she were speaking to a child, and she pointed to a rat hole, "now while there are holes and cracks everywhere the wires can be run through the house without taking up floorboards and splintering the wainscot. You know what electricians are!" Then suddenly she had an inspiration. "I suppose one of your nephews wouldn't happen to be handy about the house? Would there be one of them that could attend to the wiring for instance? Think what a saving that would be! And at the same time he would be getting the benefit of the fresh air and the wonderful peace and quiet of the country. How about the young man I saw in your office? How about him?" She paused and then she leaned forward and spoke in a loud confident tone. "I don't want to frighten you, but by the look of him I'd say the sooner you get him out here to Brook Farm the better. In fact I'd say there is no time to be lost. I still think he ought to come out right away. Tonight."

Mr. Parr said nothing for a minute. The various expressions that had crossed over his face since she first burst into his office had mingled into one overall look of panic. Inside his waistcoat his heart was hopping about like a frog. "Tell me, Miss Lomas," he said, and he took a little backward skip as if to get away from the sound of his own voice. "Tell me! How do you think the local people will take to the notion of my having bought the place?" He looked very perturbed.

Miss Lomas was quite unperturbed. She gave a sidelong look at him. "How are they to know you didn't buy it long ago!" she said. Mr. Parr gave her an uneasy look. Miss Lomas hurried on. "Anyway why should anyone know your business until we are good and ready to let them know." She drew herself up proudly. "It was not for nothing that I always preserved the privacy of Brook Farm. What more natural than that now, with Miss Garret in a home and Christy gone off that you would have to be here a lot—and your nephews likewise. It will take a bit of time to counteract the impression you gave by your former indifference but no one will question what you do, if you go about it gradually. You must however start to show some interest straight away, to walk around the fields, be seen attending to mearings and gates at first, before later going a bit further. If one of your nephews, the young fellow I met, was to show an interest too and be seen cutting a few hedges, or painting the gates, in no time at all it would be thought natural that he'd sleep here as well in order to get an early start in the mornings with so much to be done." She stopped short to ponder some problems she couldn't take time to explain. "On second thought, I think he had better not come out tonight, but wait till he's been remarked paying an odd visit, or eating an odd meal here. Do you get me?" She gave him a wink. "And from that," she cried, her excitement rising, "it would be a small step for the girls to spend a few days of the summer here—making it seem like a little holiday. Oh, how wonderful it would be, for all concerned to have them here," she cried, clasping her hands over her chest, so that in the dark, it seemed for a moment that once again she was the big goose-bosomed woman of long ago. "Summer is not far off, you know," she warned, "and you know what the summers are like out here. You could eventually all come and go as you wished. I'm sure your sister would benefit from a change. As for you!" She looked at him so penetratingly that the whole cast of her thought was for a moment darkened. "Oh dear, isn't it a pity you couldn't have bought the place long ago," she said. "Think of how different everything would have been!"

There was such a note of regret in her voice that they both sighed.

"My dear Miss Lomas," said Mr. Parr, "Brook Farm in the old days would have been far too grand for the like of me!"

"Nonsense!" said Miss Lomas. "And even if that was the case, you can't say it's too grand for you now."

Unfortunately at that moment, her eye caught the glint of goldleaf on a fragment of a Crown Derby saucer that was stopping a mousehole near the door, and she recalled all the good times which had gone. "Oh, poor Brook Farm!" she said again and this time tears gushed into her eyes.

"You really love the place, don't you Miss Lomas?" Mr. Parr said, profoundly struck by her grief.

Miss Lomas made no attempt to wipe away her tears. She just looked into his. "Don't you?" she asked.

Mr. Parr peered around. His reply was non-committal but Miss Lomas could read him like a book. "I suppose it would do no harm to start repairing the ravages at once," he said, "or at least put a stop to the inroads of decay."

Halfway down Miss Lomas's cheek a tear dried up and did not fall. "That's the right spirit," she said.

It was now so dark inside the house that instinctively Mr Parr moved towards the door. Miss Lomas followed. Outdoors there was still a little light, at least in the sky, and against it Brook Farm reared up in all the strength of its hand-cut granite stone. It was, indeed, a gem, and for all the decay within, it was as if some concept of beauty had outlived its execution in perishable form. As for the land, was not the earth at all times indestructible? Across the dark fields it was no longer possible to see the copse of conifers that marked out the cemetery. But Miss Lomas no longer felt her interest in the cemetery so obsessive, or her appointment with it so imminent. She turned eagerly to Mr. Parr. "I did not ask about the girls at all," she cried apologetically. "How are they? They must be young ladies by now. Dear me. We must make great haste if we are to have the place suitable for them. It is so important for young ladies that their background be as gracious as possible. Oh, it will be really wonderful to have them here. It will be just like the old days—only gayer." As she saw Mr. Parr seemed to falter, she caught his arm. "It is not money that makes a house into a home," she said, "it is the presence of people. I wish I had a glass of wine to offer you, so that we might celebrate this happy solution to our difficulties."

As if he felt giddy, Mr. Parr seemed to reel slightly. "Is it wise to go so fast?" he asked nervously. Miss Lomas swept aside such timidity.

"If we are to be ready for the summer, we must start at once," she said. "I'll see you tomorrow, I suppose. I'll be up at dawn, astir with the birds."

One Evening

While they were talking Larry leaned his bike against the sooty sycamore tree in the street outside her door. Daylight was leaving the sky. Soon he'd have to go home. He had reached out to grasp the handlebars when the street lamps went on. Startled, he looked up as around them pale light fell like rain. But they, under the dome of leaves, were sheltered from its downpour. A new magic came into their encounter. It was harder than ever to part from her. Overhead, the dusty, toughened leaves of summer appeared thin and silky, as in springtime. If only it was spring and he need not be afraid that they'd be separated when the long school holiday came to an end.

To be nearer to her, he bent forward and rested his elbow on the saddle of the bike, but the springs shifted and, if he had not shot out a hand and steadied himself against the tree, he'd have been sent spinning.

Eileen tittered.

Furious, Larry straightened up and adjusted the saddle before placing his elbow on it once more.

"You nearly fell on your face!" Eileen said.

"And you'd find that funny, I take it? I could have been hurt."

"That's what I meant," said Eileen. "It's a wonder to me you weren't killed years ago on that old bike."

Mollified by this admission of having known him for years, if only by sight, he gave the frame a rattle. "It's only fit for scrap," he said, but he felt disloyal. Except for it, he'd never have struck up acquaintance with her. A fellow couldn't walk up and down a street he didn't live on, several times a day, at that, but on a bike it was different. On a bike he could be going anywhere. "I won't need it after this summer, anyway," he said. "Have you decided what you're going to do next year, Eileen?" He ignored the fact that he'd already asked the same question twenty times.

Eileen tossed her head. "I won't go to the 'Uni', anyway," she said.

At the abbreviation he squirmed. His father said only outsiders used it. "But don't you want to?" he asked, amazed.

"My sister didn't go, and Pa says she's earning more than any girl with a degree after her name."

"There are more important things in life than money," Larry said hotly.

"Oh, I know," Eileen agreed. "But she has a fellow, as well. She goes out with him every evening. He's crazy about her. When he leaves her at home at night, they stand under this tree for ages, kissing and kissing. I can see them from my window."

"It's well for them," he said impulsively.

"What a disgusting thing to say!" Eileen cried. Seemingly, though, she was not too repelled, because, putting out her hand, she stroked the handlebars. "You'd never sell this old bike, would you?" she asked softly. "It wouldn't fetch much, it's so battered and rusty." She laughed. "I used to hear it rattling down the street and I knew it was you, even before I'd met you. Properly, I mean. I remember how you used to stand up on the pedals when the saddle was too high for you. You've no idea how funny you looked."

"I only did that when I was getting up speed. You used to look pretty funny yourself on your brother's bike with your leg under the crossbar."

"Oh, do you remember that?"

She seemed delighted, but he'd meant to annoy her the way she had annoyed him. First, all that stuff about her sister, and now this harking back to when they were kids. Gulping down a mouthful of the warm summer air, he thought of a compliment so daring that he felt it must by its utterance turn all their yesterdays into one long tomorrow.

"A nice sight you'd look now on a man's bike," he said. And to him the words were so full of innuendo that a smirk came on his face.

But Eileen drew back as if she were stung, and there was fury in her eyes. He thought she was going to slap him. "How dare you speak to me like that!" she cried. "Only I know what's wrong with you I'd never speak another word to you ever again in all my life. But you're just peeved because you have to stay home with your mother this evening, and it Sunday at that."

It was a mean, mean thing to say, but she had reminded him of the lateness of the hour. "What time is it?" he asked urgently.

Eileen looked oddly at him. "It must be queer having your father away all week."

"What's queer about it? Lots of men are only home at the weekends."

"It's hard on your mother, though, isn't it—if they get on well together, and all that?"

"What do you mean, 'if they get on well together'? You'd think they were a cat and dog."

Eileen laughed. "I know some people and they might as well be cats and dogs." Then she frowned. "It's hard on you, too, isn't it? being all that close to her, I mean."

He wondered what she was getting at; but he could not delay to find out. He sat up on the saddle of the bike, yet kept one leg still on the ground and one hand against the tree.

"I'll have to push off," he said dejectedly. Eileen had rested the toe of her small patent-leather shoe on the pedal of the bike, and when he did push forward her foot slipped. "Now who nearly fell on her face?" His spirits were restored: the conversation had come neatly round full circle.

"Well, I like that!" cried the girl. "There's all the difference in the world between falling and being pushed."

His good humour trebled. Now he had the advantage. "Well, so long," he said, and he wheeled out into the centre of the road and faced for home.

There was nothing like a bike. Standing on the pedals, he pressed down hard on one and then the other, making the old crock rock like a boat. By the time he'd reached the street that went down to the canal alongside which he lived, he'd got up such speed that, as a bird on the hover dips a wing, he had only to drop his shoulder and the bike turned into the sloping street. Then, near the end, dipping the other wing, he swept into Wilton Place.

Between the houses on the Place and the canal bank was a private park, triangular in shape and rarely entered. Such residents as held keys had long ceased to go there. In the middle, the trees had been cut and their stumps were overgrown with moss and ground-ivy so that it was like a forgotten cemetery of a minority sect, Moravian or Huguenot, closed to burials; abandoned. Yet, inside the railings, suckers had sprung up and shrubs and bushes had grown from seed, and here too the trees had not been cut or even pollarded, so that their great, spreading branches filtered the light of the street lamps.

Larry saw at once that there was no light in his own house, or at least not in the front. Moreover, there was something about the dark façade that somehow suggested total darkness.

It was odd. Instead of flinging the bike against the railings and running in, he took a wide sweep out into the roadway to see if there was any light reflected from the tin roof of the coal shed at the back. Craning his neck as he circled outwards, he nearly bashed head first into a car that was parked with its lights out on the other side of the street. He saved himself just in time, and was startled to discover that it was his father's car. But, if his father was not gone, why was the house in darkness? And why was the car on the other side of the road when there was plenty of space for it outside their own door?

Then he saw there was a figure at the wheel, sitting silent. It was his father.

Larry's first thought was that his father was dead, but as he jumped off the bike and let it clatter to the ground the headlights were abruptly switched on, almost blinding him.

"Oh, Father, what's the matter?" he cried. "Why haven't you gone?"

Overcome by fear, he caught at the door handle, and tried to drag the car door open. Immediately, his father's hand shot out and pulled it shut again with a slam. "Don't mind about me. Go in to your mother," his father said.

"But the house is all dark, Father. Where is she?"

His father said nothing for a minute. Then he slumped down on the seat. "I think I killed her," he said in a quiet, soft tone. "You'd better go in."

"Father!" He could not tell whether to believe or disbelieve, but he started to whimper. "Oh, Father, Father." Once more he tried to get into the car, dragging at the handle which his father still held tightly pulled against him. "Oh, Father, what will you do?"

Abruptly, then, his father let go the door, which flew open, causing Larry to fall backwards. And as if he had shaken off something irritating, his father started the engine.

"Where are you going?" Larry cried, agonised.

"Get into the house," his father ordered.

"Will you come with me?" Larry asked; but even to himself this seemed unreasonable. "Just as far as the door," he pleaded. "Or let me come with you."

Through the window his father stared at him. "Why?" he said dully, and then, as if his foot had slipped off the clutch, the car leaped forward.

For a short time, the evening was filled with the sound of the departing car, and then there was nothing but the hum of the spokes spinning round on the fallen bicycle.

When the spokes stopped spinning at last, Larry picked up the bicycle and walked it across the street. Inside the front gate, he propped it against the base of a stone balustrade that led up to the hall door. Here, at one time, a plaster cherub had played a flute, but flute and cherub had long been entombed in ivy.

Normally, Larry would have gone in by a door under the steps, because at that hour it was in the basement he would be most likely to find his mother. But noticing that the drawing-room window was open, he went up the steps. By leaning over the balustrade, he might be able to look a little way into the room.

When he reached the top step, however, he was able to see well into the room, for particles of light from the street lamps fell leaf-like through the trees. When the real leaves swayed, the golden foliage swayed, too, this way and that. It was when one of those golden ovals fell evenly over her face that he saw his mother. Still and silent, she was sitting in an armchair under the open window. He was so used to seeing her on her feet, she hardly ever sat down except at meals, that he was shocked by the sight of her. And why did she not call out? She must have seen him. Then the leaves swayed again, and although he could still make out a white blob in the dark he could no longer distinguish her features.

What could he do? There were no people in the street. If there were, how could he approach them? What would he say? Supposing he were to shout, just for anyone to hear, anyone, the people next door or a passerby? But his mother too might hear him, and no matter what was wrong, she would want him to behave in a seemly manner. At last, because he could think of no other way out of the situation, he pushed open the hall door and went in. Taking a deep breath outside the door of the drawing room, he edged around it.

A large splash of light had fallen once again on his mother's face, and he saw that her eyes were open.

"Son!"

"Oh, Mother, Mother!" he cried, his voice torrential with love. "Oh, Mother, Mother!" Rushing into the room, he threw himself on her, sobbing with relief.

But, bracing herself against the weight of him, she sat bolt upright. "What is the matter with you?" she asked angrily.

"Nothing, nothing." He didn't care that she was cross as long as she was all right. He caught up her hands and began to kiss them. She pulled her hands away.

"What is the meaning of this?" she demanded. "What is wrong with you? I knew there was something the matter the minute I saw you on the steps. Why were you creeping up like that? And why didn't you speak?"

"Oh, Mother, you don't understand. Father told me——" But he stopped, frightened again.

"Oh?" she said queerly. "Oh?" And she lay back on the couch. "So you met him?"

But, surely, sitting there at the open window in the dark, she must have seen him talking to his father. He moved back from her. "I'll put on the light," he said, trying to be matter of fact.

She reached out and caught his hand. "Not yet," she said, and there was a pleading note in her voice. "It's beautiful here with the light coming through the trees. I've been sitting here"—she paused—"some time," she finished lamely.

In the dark, he raised his eyebrows. It was not exactly that he thought she was lying, but that he suddenly felt the truth might be more complex than he knew. Then she gave his hand a playful slap.

"Why did you come in the hall door?" she said. "I hope your shoes are not muddy?"

Annoyed, he pulled back.

"I expect you're hungry," she said when he made no answer. She sighed. "I suppose I'd better start getting the meal," but she did not stir.

"I'll lay the table," he said quickly.

She still made no effort to rise. Instead, she beckoned him back, although he would not have seen that she did were it not for a splash of lamp light that fell on her arm at that moment when the wind stirred the leaves of the trees outside in the little park. "I've never talked much to you about your father, have I?" she said, and guessed that she was trying to be casual. "You've never been interested," she added more coldly, having seen perhaps that he'd stiffened. "A girl would have been," she flashed, "but not a boy. Ah, well. That's another story. Nevertheless, there are certain things you ought to know, things that in later years you will want to know: would in fact resent not knowing." Feeling perhaps that this onslaught had subdued him, she settled back into the cushions. "It was in a room like this," she said, "with the street lights coming through the trees like this, that your father first told me he loved me." Some prudery made her interrupt her story. "We weren't alone, of course. My mother and my sisters were in the next room." She paused. "The door was ajar, always." Having eased some scruple, she rushed on. "I was playing the piano, and your father came and leaned over me." But the emotion of that dead moment was dead, too. She faltered. "I remember the tune exactly," she said, as if hoping to regain some of the rapture of her memories. "Every note of it," she said. "Although, as you know, I haven't laid a finger on the piano for years." Her voice changed again. "I see you didn't notice that? You never thought that odd? And yet I used to play with great taste, if not indeed with distinction, even after you were born." To his astonishment, there was now a note of admonition in her voice. "Surely you must remember my playing to you when you were little?" she demanded. "We had a game. I was a cat and you were a mouse. And as you ran your little fingers up the keyboard I ran mine after you, only you were on the treble and I was on the bass, and you didn't know the difference. You thought the cat's paws made more noise because he was bigger and stronger. You used to beg me to let you be the cat. Do you mean to say you don't remember?" She stood up. "Let me show you. It will all come back, I feel sure."

In utter consternation he stared at her. Not for years had the piano been opened. Not since he used to pound on it with clenched fists when she was out of earshot, pretending it was the sound of cannon. He could hardly believe his eyes when she started taking down the silver frames, the vases of dried honesty, and the Venetian glass bluebirds that had stood for a decade undisturbed on the piano top. It was a shock to see how roughly she handled them. And, when she began to pull off the heavy, handmade runner that covered the instrument all over like an altar cloth, he shrank into himself at the thought of the queer, light-coloured wood of the casing being exposed with its birdy-eyed graining and its curlicues. Pianos weren't made of that kind of wood any more.

And so, before a note was struck, he braced himself for the unpleasant sounds that would come from the damp, stuck-together keys. The bass would be no louder than the treble: the cat no better than the mouse. But things were worse than he'd feared; when his mother ran her hand up and down the notes neither bass nor treble was distinguishable under the knocking sound of the wooden hammers from which the moth-eaten felting had worn away. Not noticing that anything was wrong however, his mother began playing with both hands, without music, throwing her head back, her body swaying in time to the notes.

"Well, son?"

Hoarsely, he spoke over the din. "I thought we were going to have our supper?"

Throwing her head back still further, so that she could look at him where he stood behind her, she said archly. "Time enough. You can't be all that hungry. I want to play something special for you. It's a tune your father used to beg for whenever I lifted the piano lid." She stopped playing. "I hope I'll be able to get the opening bar," she said, dropping her hands into her lap. He felt she did this only for effect.

"I forgot to tell you," he began desperately, "that I have to go out tonight."

She had lifted her hands again and they were poised over the keys, but at his words she let them fall with a thump on to the keys. "But it's Sunday night."

"I know," he said weakly. "I'm sorry." Then he had a cunning thought. "There's no special reason for me staying, is there?" he asked. If, like his father, she too was trying in some crooked way to tell him something, well, then, let her tell it straight out. Or else let her keep it. One thing they had both told him without knowing, that they had failed each other. "You don't really want me for anything special, do you?" he repeated, risking the question in pity for her as he stood in the doorway looking back.

She made no answer except to strike a chord and start to play the tune again loudly. That was the way his father let out the clutch and drove into the night.

"I won't stay out late," he said, but either she didn't hear him or she scorned this sop. Turning, he ran down the hall in dread that she would follow him. But it seemed that it was only with the tune she tried to follow him, thumping harder on the keys. And even in this purpose she was defeated because the thick walls, the lath-and-plaster ceiling, and the heavy wooden floorboards absorbed what little music there was left in the old instrument. And after he left the house, the only sound that came out into the evening air was the knocking of the clappers and the thump of her foot on the pedals.

Grabbing up the bike, Larry threw his leg across the bar. A last qualm came over him at the thought that his father would blame him for leaving her alone, but his father's stature had been diminished. A man had to be a man. Love could not be kept for ever in the third person, past tense.

A Pure Accident

"Put it out of your mind so, for good and all, will you!" said the Canon. "You know my mind in the matter. It's not a cinema or a public-house we're dealing with, it's the house of God." The old priest prised himself out of his armchair. "I'll have no hailstorms of light raining down on the heads of my people. We have lights enough."

It was dismissal. The three men sitting around the fire seemed to have no choice but get to their feet and move towards the door after their pastor, but at the door one of them hung back.

"We were only thinking this time of one light in the porch, Canon," Murty Kane said, "Or in the chapel yard?"

"No matter," said the Canon. "It would still mean rewiring the whole place, and after that there'd be no stopping you. You'd soon have the place lit up like the Aurora Borealis." He himself laughed good-humouredly at this sally, but then the others did not, he looked more closely at them. "Hold on a minute. Did I ever tell you what I saw when I was in Rome?" he said jovially. "It was when I was over for the Papal Jubilee, you won't believe it but I saw a sanctuary lamp wired up for electric light. Can you beat that. It's dead against the rubrics." He leant forward confidentially. "We had a joke among ourselves, the Irish contingent. We used to laugh our heads off. You know the old proverb 'the nearer the church the farther from God'? Well, we used to say. 'The nearer to Rome the farther from God'."

Here Andy Devine did laugh faint-heartedly, but neither of the others did.

"There was one other point, Canon," Murty Kane said stoutly. "If you'd consider the rewiring, we could keep down the number of lights, but we'd be able to have other amenities like heat."

"Only a few radiators, Canon," Andy interjected nervously. "One in the sacristy, maybe, where the clergy have to robe, another up near the altar, maybe, to keep the altar-linen from getting mildewed, and another somewhere in the body of the church."

But at a look from the Canon his voice tailed off.

"Oh, so you have something new to bleat about," the Canon said. "Well, come back so; come back, by all means." He closed the door which he had been holding open. He made a feint of squeezing himself down into the tight tub of the chair again, but before doing so he cocked an eye at them. "I suppose, of course, that you're acquainted with what happened up in Dublin when fellows like you started putting heaters and radiators into the fine old Georgian buildings, those priceless treasures of the nation? Well, in case you didn't, let me tell you. They fell down: that's what. Dry rot, that's what. Incubators they made out of them, and millions of eggs, larvae they're called, hatched out overnight. The damage in Mountjoy Square alone ran into millions, to say nothing of the danger to life. A nice set of eejits you'd look if that happened here. You'd never know but the roof might be brought down on top of the congregation and kill them all." He let go the chair and stalked over to the door and held it open again. "Will you never get any sense?" he asked querulously. In the doorway, however, he seemed unwilling to let them go without a more genial note.

"I don't suppose you men are in the habit of making a visit to the Blessed Sacrament on your way home, but if you should happen to take the notion tonight, just say a few prayers as you stroll past. Don't attempt to go into that chapel." Surprised, the men who had been looking down at their feet, looked up. "I've planted Father Patton down there," said the Canon proudly, and he lowered his voice. "This time I'm determined to catch that thief."

It was a hard name for a petty pilferer. The men stirred uneasily and looked down at their feet again. Despite the small number of coins ever put into it, the poor box was periodically rifled.

"It's a matter of principle," said the Canon. "I've sent Father Patton down there to hide in the porch to see if he can catch the thief red-handed."

"Some child, I suppose?" said Andy, feeling that some sort of apology was called for from the laity.

"A nice kind of child," the Canon snapped. "My only fear is that Father Patton will jump out on the wrong woman."

But here, all three men looked up in surprise.

"How do you know it's a woman, Canon?" said Alphonsus Carr.

The Canon gave him a scathing look. "Is there ever anyone else in the chapel at night only old women? Bundled up in corners, mumbling and jumbling, and thumping their craw. Mea culpa, mea culpa! Titillating themselves with piousity, that's all, with not a jot of real religion in the lot of them. They ought to be at home looking after their families. But oh no. They must have their nightly jaunt. I often say they couldn't be kept away if it was Satan himself was sitting inside in the Tabernacle, instead of the Son of God."

But the men weren't listening. Who was it? It could only be someone known to them, well known, a neighbour, a customer, perhaps a relative? They were suddenly all so tense that Alphonsus laughed nervously and nudged Andy.

"It must be your sister Annie, Andy," he said. You could set your clock by Annie's step going down to the chapel every night at exactly the same time.

"That's who it is!" said Andy, glad of a chance to laugh, because the whole notion of the trap scared him.

"I'd ask you to take this matter seriously, men," said the Canon coldly. In particular he turned to Andy. "I certainly hope your sister won't go down there tonight. She could upset the apple-cart altogether." Then, as an afterthought, he laid his hand on Andy's arm. "I'd like you to know it wasn't of her I was thinking when I criticised the other women of the parish. Your sister Annie has no claims on her. A widow woman can do what she likes. How is she, by the way?"

"She's well, thank you, Canon," said Andy, but his face flushed. He wished his sister's name had not come up. He did not look directly at the Canon, nor at his friends, feeling that his own position was never properly understood with regard to Annie. It was true that she had reared him and his younger brothers and sisters when their mother died, and that as soon as they were old enough to look after themselves she took herself off to America, out of their way. When she came back to Ireland it was by choice she lived alone. He, and his family, had been willing enough to have her live with them, but she was dead set on being independent. She'd made a bit of money in America.

"Ah, she's all right as long as she has the little bit of cash," said the Canon. "I hope she doesn't squander it on votive lamps and the like. That money doesn't go into my pocket, you know. Tell her that!"

"Oh, she's sensible enough, Canon: no need to worry about her," said Andy, telling himself his words were true.

The Canon nodded. "All the same, I hope she won't put a spoke in Father Patton's wheel tonight. Poor Patton, I'm afraid he's no man for this job. He'll botch it. If he finds any candles lighting I hope he'll have the sense to quench them, or else all he'll catch will be a cold in the head."

When the men did laugh at that, the Canon was better satisfied to let them go. His voice became more amiable. "Poor Patton," he repeated. "You'd feel sorry for him if you'd seen him going out tonight. He was in a blue funk." All of them for a moment thought about Father Patton: a large man of middle years, whose bulk made him look aggressive, but who in fact was timid enough, and whose demeanour in the presence of the Canon was abject. "It's hard to see what sends the likes of him into the Church at all," sighed the Canon. "They do their best, I grant you, but they don't have the right motive at the start. Pushed from behind, that's what they are. Oh, the mothers of Ireland have a lot to answer for. When I was in Maynooth I used to see them on visiting day walking around the grounds with their poor weedy, pimply-faced sons, wrapping their own mufflers around the poor fellows' necks, and giving them their own gloves to put on their hands, instead of letting them stiffen into men of their own making. Ah, the right kind of mother is a rare creature. My own mother, God be good to her, would sooner have seen me a bank manager, but when I made my choice she put all her weight behind me. No wonder I have contempt for poor slobs like Father Patton." Then his face grew stern again. "I hope he won't scruple putting out the candles. That chapel is a regular Crystal Palace at times, with candles and colza lamps. What do you think? Will he have the wit to quench them?"

Was he joking? A Crystal Palace? The men stared at each other.

But the Canon had opened the door of his study and was showing them into the hallway. "We can only hope for the best," he said affably. "Goodnight, men."

It was not customary for the Canon to accompany his parishioners to the hall-door, but when he slammed it after them, a light over the steps was usually switched on from within. However, as soon as they got to the bottom step, this light went out abruptly. And, accustomed as they were to being thus plunged into darkness, there was always a slight shock. On this particular night Andy stumbled over the iron footscraper. "The sky seems to have clouded over since we went in," he said, to cover his confusion.

Alphonsus looked up. "I thought the forecast was for frost," he said. "It may come later, of course."

The Canon's driveway was short but dark and the men had to pick their way carefully on the thick gravel that rolled under their feet like shingle. Away to the left, there was a glow in the sky, like the afterglow of sunset, but it was in fact a reflection of the lights of the town.

"You'd think it was the city of Dublin," said Murty sourly.

It was a sore point with all three men that the Market Square was so well lighted. In the evenings it became the centre of all activity; all conviviality. On fine evenings people stood about in the Square reading the paper by the light of the shop windows as if by daylight. The big shops had to have spikes set into the window-sills to prevent them being used as public benches. But shops like their own in the back streets might as well put up their shutters once darkness fell, for all the business they'd do.

"Does it pay them, I wonder, to burn all those lights?" said Andy, coughing gently as he looked again at the glow in the sky.

"They may have no option," said Alphonsus. "It's probably a condition laid down by their insurance company." His friends understood, of course, that he was speaking especially of the public-houses.

"I suppose you're right, Alphonsus," said Andy. "God knows they need light with the footless crowd that's in there at night. They spend most of the time stumbling in and out to the lavatory in the yard."

By now the trio had reached the end of the Canon's drive, and, feeling their way, they found the latch of the wicket-gate, and went out one by one on to the road.

"You'd think the Town Council could have put a few more lamps on this road, seeing it's the chapel-road," said Andy.

"Why should they?" Alphonsus dissented. "The chapel is the concern of the Canon. It's up to him to see that the area around it is lighted. I don't think it would be too much to expect him to put one light over his own gate."

At that Murty gave a short laugh. "Are you joking?" he said. "He could hardly do that when he won't put one in the porch of the chapel. After tonight we may as well throw in our hand. We'll never best him now. It's my opinion that man wouldn't part with a penny if it was to save his soul, in a manner of speaking," he added awkwardly, when the others sniggered.

But whether or not the joke was intentional, his companions, not being responsible for the irreverence, felt free to go on laughing, until Murty himself sobered up. "Has he much money, would you say?" he asked. "The Canon, I mean."

Alphonsus shrugged his shoulders. "Who knows. And there's another thing I often wondered. Where *does* a priest's money go anyway when he dies?" Murty asked after a minute or two. "Can he leave it to anyone he wants, or does he have to leave it to the Church? Come to think of it, I never saw a priest's will in the paper. But I suppose it's seldom a priest has anything to leave behind him."

"Oh, I wouldn't be too sure of that," Alphonsus said. "A will doesn't have to be published in the papers unless there is a specific bequest to charity."

But here Andy interrupted him. "Ah, sure, God help them," he murmured, "who'd expect them to give anything to charity when their whole lives have been devoted to the sick and the suffering. To say nothing of the dying and the bereaved. It would only be fair play that they'd be free after their death to leave any few pounds they might have to a niece or a nephew. After all, their families were deprived of them as wage-earners, and I'm told that in some cases their families have to go on contributing to their support even after they're ordained, for holidays and such like."

"Well you can't say the Canon takes many holidays," said Andy, striking a nice balance between censuring and condoning. "But most of them make out all right. They don't have too bad a time, all things considered."

This was the part of the evening he enjoyed best when, after a scrap with the Canon, they strolled home, their humour restored by their own affability.

They had now passed the last lamp-post between the parochial house and the chapel, and when they had gone beyond its hooded circle of light, ahead of them, blacker than night, loomed the chapel and its sepulchral yard. Instinctively the men came to a stand at the gateway and looked inward. Ordinarily, through the narrow windows, there would be a soft glow of candlelight, but tonight it seemed as black as pitch. It was not even certain whether the door of the big front porch was open or shut.

"Father Patton must be still in there," said Andy, and he shuddered. "I wouldn't like his job." He peered in the gate. "He couldn't have put out the sanctuary lamp, could he?" he said then, in a shocked voice.

"What harm if he did; it's not a matter of dogma," said Alphonsus impatiently. "It's only a pious custom." He too, was straining his eyes into the dark. "It is lighting anyway," he said, as in the deep recess of the sanctuary he could just make out the imprisoned flame burning in its pool of oil, but dispensing no rays.

Murty turned and looked across the road.

"Look: There's his car," he said. Pulled in under the trees on the opposite side of the road was the curate's old car.

"He didn't catch anyone yet so," said Andy, vaguely relieved. "Maybe his car was seen."

"Just as well," said Murty. "What loss is a few coins compared to someone's character?"

Openly relieved, the three men were starting to walk forward again when they heard bright ringing steps coming towards them in the dark.

There was no mistaking those footsteps.

"It's Annie," Andy said, and he couldn't keep dismay out of his voice.

"Do you think we ought to warn her?" Murty said, and his voice, too, was oddly urgent.

"No, no. Why would we?" said Andy, pulling himself together. He was oddly nettled by Murty's concern. Anyway, his sister was stepping out so briskly she was almost abreast of them.

"Goodnight all," she said, in her clear voice that always surprised people by its youthful note. The next minute she had passed them and turned in the chapel gateway. They heard her heels tap-tapping on the hard impacted gravel.

"Isn't she an active woman for her years?" said Alphonsus.

"She was always the same," said Andy. He was pleased at the compliment to her. "That's what I remember most about her when she was young. I'd lie in bed at night listening to her feet on the flagstones down in the kitchen, until the sound would put me to sleep, like music. And I missed it when she went away to America." He laughed softly. "When she came back, though, the time she was staying with us before she got her own little house, it used to drive us all mad then to hear her tapping about below until all hours. One night I asked her to take off her shoes, but the next day I had to tell her to keep them on, because in her stocking-feet she hammered around even harder."

"Oh, she's a strong woman: there's no doubt of that," said Murty. "And let me tell—" But here he stopped, as the night was rent with a scream. "What was that?"

Shocked, they all came to a stand. It was the scream of a young woman. And yet it must have been Annie.

"It couldn't be Annie," said Alphonsus, speaking for them all, but they started to run back to the chapel gate, when suddenly Father Patton's voice was heard. They stopped.

"Ah, she got a fright, that's all," said Andy, reassured.

They listened.

"In the name of God, what's the matter with you, woman?" the curate cried. "Get up out of that!"

"Oh, Father, I'm sorry." It was Annie's voice. It was a relief to hear it so normal. "I didn't see you standing there in the dark, Father, and then when I brushed against you and you moved, I didn't know who it was." But here her voice wavered and the listeners lost something. The next minute there was another small scream but again Annie's voice came to them clear and strong. "Don't! Don't, Father," she cried. "I'll get up by myself, if I'm able."

"Oh, Father, I think I'm hurt," Annie said, and she gave a moan.

Murty started. "Did you hear that?"

"Wait Murty," said Andy, and he put up his hand. "We don't want to embarrass Father Patton."

They listened.

"Of course you're hurt," said the priest. "Wouldn't it hurt an ox to come down on his backside the way you did, but it isn't going to do you any good to lie there on the ground. Get up out of that. I've got the car outside and I'll run you home." He must have tried to lift her again because Annie gave another scream, or a sort of scream. The three men waited no longer.

"We're here, Annie," Murty called. "You'll be all right."

Andy addressed himself to the curate. "She'll be all right, Father. She only got a fright. You'll see?"

The clouds had thinned out and the faint light in the sky made it possible for them all to see each other. Annie lay on the ground, the curate bending over her.

"Such a night as I've had," said the curate, straightening up. "This is the last straw." He stepped back and looked in the direction of the parochial house. "That scream must have been heard all over the town," he said. Then he turned back. "What kind of a woman is she to scream like that? And what's the matter with her that she won't get up?" He pushed Andy forward. "Make her get up!"

But Annie caught Andy's hand. "I'm sorry, Andy," she said. "I couldn't help it. I think I injured myself. My side is very sore."

Only the last word caught the priest's ear.

"Sore? he shouted. "What else did she expect coming down on her arse like that? We've got to get her out of here. If this caper gets to the ears of the Canon there's no telling the harm it could do me. I'll tell you what. I'll bring the car in here. Let you three get her on her feet."

"Wait a minute, Father," Murty called after him. "Maybe we ought to get a doctor to have a look at her before we try to move her."

"Is it out to make a show of me altogether you are, Murty Kane?" the priest cried. "It's bad enough that some other old woman may come along any minute and start poking her nose into our business. Here, I won't wait to get the car. Give me a hand with her and we'll carry her out if she won't co-operate."

The path was narrow, and to lift Annie, Andy and Murty had to step on to the grass verge. Under their feet was crisp and brittle. Looking up, Andy saw that a high wind had cleared the sky and now it was dizzy with stars. The forecast was right. There was frost after all. "Be patient, Annie, be patient. We're doing our best," he said, embarrassed by the way she kept moaning.

At the gate, Father Patton let go his hold to run across the road and bring over the car. As it swept around in a circle, the headlights for a moment seemed to ripen the frosty grass to a golden stubble. Then Father Patton shut off the lights again and got out.

"All together, men," he said, and they bundled the woman into the back seat.

When they arrived at Annie's little house, they had more difficulty getting her out than they had getting her in, but they managed it. Where was the key of the house, though?

"It's in her bag I suppose," said Andy, seeing with surprise that through thick and thin Annie had held tight to her bag. But now the shabby black bag gaped open. Father Patton shook it. "The key must have fallen out; we'll have to bring her to your place, Andy," he said.

Gathering every dreg of strength left in her, however, Annie cried out in anguish. "No, no, no! You can't put me into that car again. Is it trying to kill me you are?"

"Don't heed her," cried Father Patton. "Catch her up there."

This time, though, when Annie was in the car and Andy had squeezed in with her, Murty stepped back.

"You can leave me out of this from now on," he said.

Father Patton turned and gave him a look, then he dived into the car. "Come on," he said to the others. "We're in trouble enough as things are."

A big, heavily moving man, Father Patton usually drove slowly, but tonight as the car careered along, although Alphonsus caught first at the the door-handle, and then at the back of the driver's seat, he was rocked violently from side to side, and when, without slowing up, they shot into the lighted Square, he saw that the priest's face was livid and fixed in a stare. Fearfully Alphonsus looked back at the others. On the back seat Andy had put his arm around Annie, hugging her to him like a lover. Brother and sister stared in front of them unseeing; the eyes of one prised open by fear, the other by pain. The next instant the car hurtled down another side-street and all was dark again. At Andy's gate it stopped, and Father Patton turned around and he too looked into the back. "What kind of a heart has she, Andy?" he asked.

"Oh, her heart is all right," Andy answered. "As strong as a lion."

But suddenly, with a convulsive jerk, Annie pulled away from her brother and caught at his arm. "Andy!" she cried, "there's something sticking into my arm!"

Before Andy could say anything the curate's voice rose in fury. "What's wrong with her now?" he yelled. "First her arse, and now her arm!"

Alphonsus drew a sharp breath. "Look here, Father," he said hotly, "this is the second time tonight you've used that word."

"Oh please, Alphonsus, please!" Andy pleaded. "Father Patton is upset too. We must make allowances."

But Annie had leaned forward and caught Alphonsus by the hand.

"Could there be something broken inside me, Alphonsus?" she cried, and she pulled his hand down. "Feel!"

Taken by surprise at the strength of her hands, Alphonsus felt his own hand pressed against her thigh, from which, although muffled by clothing, something hard stuck up.

"Christ!" he exclaimed, and dragged his hand free. "It's a bone."

"Oh no, no, no!" Annie started to cry.

Everyone else was struck dumb, and the curate, putting his hands up to his head, began to sway back and forth. It was at that moment that the lights of another car behind flashed over them like the beam of a lighthouse.

"A car? Stop it!" cried Annie. "For God's sake don't let it pass."

Andy and Alphonsus got out to flag it down, but the car was already pulling up beside them, and out of it jumped Murty Kane, shaking his fist in the air.

"Did you think I was going to stand by and let you add murder to everything else," he cried, but the doctor who accompanied him and was getting out on the other side cut him short.

"That's enough, Murty," he said. Taking a torch out of his pocket, the doctor flashed it into the priest's car, and ran his hand over Annie's body. Straightening up he hurriedly started to prepare an injection. "What kind of fools are you?" he said in an angry voice. "God alone knows what damage you've done. But after this at least she won't feel any more pain till you get her to hospital." He put the syringe back into his bag. "You'd better get her there as fast as you can." As no one moved, he looked sharply at the priest. "Pull yourself together, Father. You're not out of the wood yet."

Like a sleep-walker, Father Patton turned on the ignition. Then, as Andy was about to squeeze into the back again the doctor took him by the arm.

"Get into the front, you," he said. Without a word, Murty and Alphonsus stepped aside and, as when a hearse is about to drive away, they took off their hats. "There's just one thing," the doctor called out, dragging open the door again. "I'll be 'phoning the hospital—where do you want her put, in a public or a private ward?"

The curate's foot was on the clutch. He turned to Andy. "You said she has some means, didn't you?"

"She has a little," said Andy. "She was a thrifty woman." He looked into the back seat as if for confirmation, but Annie was already unconscious. "I suppose she deserves the best after all she's been through," he said.

"She'll get that in either place," said the doctor curtly, and then ignoring Andy, he spoke to the priest. "We don't want to cripple her in every way. What do you think will be the outcome of this? Will she get compensation?" As the priest gave no answer the doctor slammed the car-door. "Settle it among yourselves," he said impatiently. "Money may not be the worst of your worries."

It was three days before Andy saw his sister. Her bed was in the centre of a large room, and when he edged around the door two nurses were cranking up a kind of jack which slanted the bed upwards. Although flat on her back Annie was looking straight at him.

Brother and sister stared at each other.

"How are you, Annie?" said Andy.

It was one of the nurses who answered.

"Oh, we're splendid," she said brightly, and she looked at Annie. "Aren't we?"

Annie's eyes were very bright. "They operated on me, Andy, I have a silver pin in my hip," she said. She paused. "I'm told I stood it well. What did they tell you?"

"Oh, they work wonders nowadays," said Andy quickly. One of the nurses, the younger one, had gone out of the room, and he wished the other one would go too. "You've a nice room, Annie," he said.

Annie looked around the room. "Yes, it's nice," she said politely.

"Did you see her flowers?" the nurse asked.

Looking, Andy saw that in a vase beside the bed there were several sprays of leafless white lilac, on long woody stems.

"Alphonsus and Murty sent them," said Annie. "Fancy lilac at this time of year, Andy."

There didn't seem to be any perfume from the fronds of forced blooms. "They have no smell," said Andy.

Both Annie and the nurse seemed surprised.

"What else could you expect at this time of year?" said the nurse, but bending she looked more critically at the lilac. Then she snatched at a spray and lifted it out of the vase. Shaking off the water, she examined it closely. "This one can go," she said. she snatched out another. "And this one too."

"Oh, Nurse, they're still fresh," Annie protested.

But the nurse was scrutinising every stem, her practised eye finding the first frail freckle of decay on the lovely lilac petals. "I hate the smell of rotting flowers," she said. "They don't last any time in these overheated rooms." Breaking the discarded branches in two she threw them into a waste-can. As she did, a faint scent was shaken from them, and for an instant it streamed in the air. She turned to Andy. "You may stay as long as you like!" she said affably, and she went out.

Left alone, the sister and brother looked at each other again. "How are you feeling?" Andy asked.

Annie, however, was looking past him towards the door which the nurse had left ajar. "Why didn't she close it?" she asked. "There isn't anyone outside, is there?"

"No, who would there be?" said Andy. "Didn't Alphonsus and Murty send flowers?" He spoke as if answering a charge against them.

"Oh, I didn't expect them to come," said Annie. "Not so soon anyway. They'll probably come in some time in the car with Father Patton."

Andy's face brightened. "Oh, is he coming?" he asked. "When? Did he send word?"

"No, but don't you know he will," said Annie. "I thought he might have come with you today."

Andy looked down at his feet. "He had to go to a funeral today. Anyway, he was very upset, Annie."

"About me?"

"Upset generally."

There was a short silence. Again Annie glanced at the open door. "You're sure there's no one outside?"

"Ah, who would there be?" said Andy irritably for one of his disposition.

"Well, shut it, will you?" said Annie, and her voice too was short. When the door was shut they both felt better. "I'd like him to know how sorry I was that I gave him all that trouble, but the pain put everything out of my head. Oh, Andy, wasn't it an unfortunate thing to happen? And in the chapel of all places."

"Now, now, Annie," said her brother. "What difference where it happened? But as this bit of philosophy didn't seem to help Annie, he plunged in the opposite direction. "All the more reason to take it well," he said. "There must have been a purpose in it. My advice is not to think about it. Make the most of things while you're here. Make a holiday out of it!" he cried, his voice rising.

Annie tried to smile, but as she did so the remaining sprays of lilac caught her eye and she frowned. "That lilac wasn't in the least withered. She wouldn't have been so quick to throw it out if it was her own, or if she'd paid for it with her own money." Then, surprisingly, she giggled. "Of course, it wasn't my money either." Her face clouded once more. "Who is paying for everything, Andy?" she asked anxiously.

"Now, now," said Andy soothingly. "Your job is to get well and not to be worrying about things like that."

"But who will pay it?" she persisted.

Andy stood up. "When you talk like this, it's time for me to go," he said. "Worry isn't good for you. All you have to do is lie back and let them put you right. Be glad you're well cared for and comfortable."

"Oh, there's no doubt I'm well minded," said Annie. "I'd be having the time of my life if I wasn't worrying about who's going to pay." It seemed however as if the visit had taxed her strength because she closed her eyes.

"Well then, don't dwell on it," said Andy, and as he thought she seemed sleepy, he got to his feet. He might as well go.

At the end of a month Annie was let try out her legs. She was very nervous but the rest in bed had done her good and she looked well. Along with worrying about the bill, though, it bothered her that Father Patton had not called to see her, although Murty and Alphonsus confirmed what Andy had told her earlier: the curate was in a bad state. They kept telling her that her accident had shaken him. Yet, at the end of another month Annie was still expecting him. Andy had come to dread the mention of his name. "You don't understand, Annie," he said. "We're all worried about him. There's a great change in the man. He looks dreadful. Only last night we were saying that this thing is getting on his nerves."

"Does he ask for me?" Annie asked.

"Well, the fact is," said Andy, "we don't see much of him. He went away somewhere the day after the accident, didn't I tell you that? You know he never goes anywhere, but now he's always taking off on short trips without telling anyone, or saying where he's going. Murty thinks there must be something on foot. He thinks it could be down to his brother's place he goes. He has a brother, a chemist somewhere in the Midlands. We used to think there was no love lost between him and the brother, but maybe the brother is going to put up something towards your expenses."

Annie sat up straighter. "And who'd put up the rest?" she asked eagerly. "The Canon?"

"Are you raving, Annie?" said Andy. "Isn't that the whole trouble? The Canon knows nothing about your accident. He knows you're in here, of course, but he doesn't know why." Annie's brightness faded, and Andy saw she really didn't look as well as he'd thought at first. "One good thing has come out of it all," he said nervously. "We're determined to try once more to get a light put in the porch of the chapel. You'll have the satisfaction of knowing that what happened to you won't happen again, anyway."

Dully Annie looked at him. "It's not much satisfaction, is it?" she said.

"Oh, come now," said Andy. "You're getting depressed. Do you think you might rest if I wasn't here?"

"No," said Annie. She looked at the clock. "Anyway I have my therapy at four o'clock. They've been taking me down in the lift, but today they're going to see if I can manage the stairs." She looked around. "I've got a new stick. Did you see it? The other one belonged to the hospital. This one will be my own." Suddenly her face clouded again. "Who's going to pay for that?" she cried. "It isn't an ordinary stick. It may look ordinary but I'm sure it will cost a lot. And the therapy? What will that cost? It will be extra, on top of everything else."

Andy said nothing for a minute. Then he had an idea. "Maybe all this therapy, as you call it, isn't necessary. When they get people into these places they take advantage of them; you know that."

"Do you think so?" Annie's face puckered. "I'm having massage too, did I tell you that? They say my muscles will seize up if I don't, and then I'd be a real invalid. Oh Andy, will I ever be able to manage when I do go home?"

"Oh, we'll face that when we come to it," Andy said hastily. "The bill is enough to worry about now." The last words dropped out accidentally, but it scared him to see how they affected Annie.

"I thought you weren't worried about that at all?" she said.

"I'm not really," said Andy hastily. "Maybe no one will be called upon to pay," he added recklessly. "The Church is very influential, you know."

When Annie brightened again, he was tempted to leave while her spirits were up, but she leant forward eagerly.

"That's what one of the wardsmaids said. She was telling me about a woman who got a fortune in compensation."

Andy interrupted her. "I'm surprised at you, Annie," he said. "What does a wardsmaid know about such things? This is not America, you know." It was her years in America that blinded her to the difference between people, he thought. Annie lay back on the pillows.

"I've been thinking a lot about America since I came in here," she said, and she looked around her. "This room is a bit like my room in the apartment-house in New York. I was thinking it was a pity I came home when I did. I'd have made a lot more money by now."

"You did well enough," said Andy curtly, "and there's no use crying over spilt milk."

The next week when he came in to visit her, Andy saw at once that Annie was very upset. She was up hobbling round the room, and didn't hear him come through the door until he spoke.

"Oh Andy!" She sort of ran towards him, which was very distressing because of how she lurched and rose, lurched and rose. Like a boat, he thought. He took the stick from her and made her sit down. "Oh Andy!" she cried, "they mentioned the bill. They asked me if it was to you they'd send it."

"To me?" Andy was speechless. His eyes fastened on the stick. She was right, it wasn't an ordinary one. It had a rubber hand-grip, and at the base it widened out into a flat metal disc that was set in a sort of rubber coaster. He had no idea what a stick like that would cost, but it wouldn't be cheap; that was certain. All the pent-up worry of the past months broke suddenly. "Annie, you wouldn't consider, would you—" He stopped. "I mean the simplest thing might be to pay the bill yourself? But at the look of panic that came over her face he patted her on the knee. "When you come home you could talk it over with Father Patton. You'd only be advancing the money, as it were."

Annie shook off his hand. "Where would I get the money?" she asked. "I'd have to sell my American shares, and then what would I have to live on?"

Andy couldn't answer this directly, but he shook his head. "I never felt happy about those paper investments," he said.

"Oh Andy!" No wonder the family business had gone downhill. A thought, the very opposite of what she had lately been thinking, about staying in America, came into her mind. She ought never to have gone. She sighed. One or the other. Certainly as a business man Andy was a poor specimen. Then she straightened up as well as she could. "I'll have to see a solicitor, that's all," she said.

Andy started. "And what solicitor do you think you'd get?" he cried. No decent firm would take the case, once the clergy was concerned. "I'm telling you, the best thing would be to pay it if you could at all. You wouldn't lose by it, Annie. I feel sure of that. You'd get it all back a hundred-fold."

Annie looked up. It was as if all along there had been a stupid misunderstanding that had suddenly been cleared up.

"From whom?"

Her brother seemed surprised that she should ask. "From the Giver of all things, Annie. Who else?"

"Oh Andy, You gave me such a disappointment." To her brother's dismay her eyes filled with tears. And he realised that he had never before seen her cry, never in all his life, not even when he was a child and she was only a young girl, shouldering alone the burthen of their orphaned home.

"Oh, you might get some shady solicitor to take it on," he said quickly, in order to let her down a bit more lightly. "You wouldn't stoop to that I know," he added. But how did he know she wouldn't? He himself was overcome by such misery he put his head in his hands. "Oh Annie, Annie, is there no way we could get the money and at the same time spare Father Patton?" His mind was so muddled he hardly knew what he was saying.

But like long ago. Annie's mind was crystal clear, and her voice a crystal bell. "Spare him from what?" she asked. Pushing aside the medicine bottles on the bedside table, she took up a pen. "I'm going to write and tell him to call. You can give him the letter on your way home, or put it in his letterbox if you like."

"Oh Father!" Annie cried out in genuine surprise and pleasure when the next morning, before she was out of bed, the door opened and Father Patton lunged into her room. In the small room he looked bigger and bulkier than ever. Annie felt that if she were on her feet there wouldn't be a place for the two of them in the one room. She waited nervously for him to speak. As he said nothing, she glanced at the window where a spate of rain rattled on panes. "What a terrible day to have brought you out, Father."

But she felt frightened when the curate moved over towards the bed. "It's not the weather that's bothering me," Father Patton said. As he came nearer, Annie saw that his hands were trembling. "How are you?" he asked, but seeing that she was looking at his hands, he stared down at them himself. "That's nothing," he said, and he raised his arm to expose the armpit. "Look at that sweat. It keeps pouring out of me. My suit is destroyed. And my other suit is worse, the one I was wearing that night. I sent it to be cleaned, but they couldn't do anything with it, the armpits were rotted. I'll have to throw it away."

"You got a shock, Father," said Annie gently. "I know that, and I'm sorry."

The curate looked strangely at her. Disarmed by her gentleness, he relaxed. "What in the name of God were you doing that night creeping about in the dark?" he said. "If you'd any sense it's at home in your bed you'd have been, an old woman like you." But here he drew himself up. "That's not what I came to say though, I came to make it clear that I have no money to pay your bills."

"Nobody expects you to pay anything, Father," said Annie, less gently. "Nobody expects a priest to have money of his own." She was totally unprepared for the effect of her words on him.

"Ah, you're wrong there," he yelled. "You'd be surprised how many of them have money. Some I know seem to make out all right—holidays in Kilkee, and a decanter always at their elbow—but let me tell you it's not the parish that pay for it, it's their own families. That's where I lose out, with only one brother and him with a grudge against me. "Unable to stay still, he began to pace around waving his hands. Then abruptly he came to stand again at the foot of the bed. "The day after it happened I went and had a talk with him. Do you think I got any sympathy? None. But I might have known. He was always sour about the money that was spent on me. Only for that he'd have been a doctor instead of only a chemist, and in a small town at that. So you see," he said, leaning down heavily on the iron bed-rail, "you're flogging a dead horse."

Dazed by the spate of words Annie's head began to reel, but she forced herself to concentrate.

"What about the Canon?" she asked.

Father Patton let go the rail. "Is it him?" he cried. "Your fall must have made you soft in the head. Isn't it his meanness has me the way I am."

Annie didn't flinch. She put her hands under her and hoisted herself up in the bed. "Then what about the Bishop? Couldn't you approach him?"

As if unable to believe he had heard right, the curate glared at her. "It's easy to see how little the laity know about the clergy," he cried. "Don't you know that would be playing right into their hands, giving them the chance they've always been looking for?"

Annie put up her hand to her throat. He was suffocating her with words.

"The chance for what?"

The priest glared again. "As if you didn't know. I could be clapped back there again," he said wildly.

"Back where?"

"Oh, you know very well. Nobody ever mentions it, but I'm not taken in. It's known to all, John of God's, that's where! Don't pretend you've never heard."

For the second time Annie felt frightened.

"You're letting this get on your nerves, Father," she said.

Her words were ill-chosen. "There, you see!" he cried. "The same thing on your tongue as on everyone else's. 'It's your nerves, Father. Steady down, Father. Pull yourself together, Father.'" He had caught the bed-rail again, but now his hands were shaking so much the bed rocked like a cradle.

"Oh Father, Father, please!" Annie's face twisted with pain, but it wasn't certain whether it was caused by the shaking of the bed or by the priest's words.

Ignoring her cry and with a wild look on his face the curate went on. "My only chance is to keep in the Bishop's good books." Then suddenly another aspect of the situation seemed to strike him. "It's your only chance too," he cried. "Don't tell me you're blind to the advantages for you in me getting a parish, or even getting out of this one and getting away to some parish where I'd have some sort of life of my own. But one word of this in the ear of the Bishop and all hope of that is gone forever. And let me tell you that it would be the end of your expectations too. Don't think my ruination would do you any good." But the thought of his own ruin overwhelmed him. "How would you like to have it on your conscience that you destroyed me?" he cried. He let go the rail, but he could not stop talking. "If you've once been in John of God's they have it marked up against you for life. It wouldn't make any difference my being as right as rain, like the last time."

To make sure she was heeding him he gave the bed-rail another rattle. "There was nothing wrong with me the last time either, only that I was a gom: I didn't realise all the other fellows were going through the same thing as me, only they were always rushing about on the hurley field, and running up and down in the mud till they stupefied themselves, but I kept trying to work everything out in my head, walking the floorboards at night, all alone, destroying my strength, and getting unfitter and unfitter to make up my mind about anything. A few fellows left that year, but I kept going round in circles till it came to the point where I was told I'd be put out. That was when the real trouble began. My mother wouldn't hear of them putting me out. She said it was only nerves. She held that I'd be all right if I got a bit of peace and quiet." Here the priest's voice sank so low Annie could hardly hear it, and leaning his two elbows on the rail he hid his face in his big hands. When he looked up again there was no expression at all on his face. "My mother was right about one thing, God be good to her," he said. "There was nothing wrong with me. After a few weeks of sleeping late and walking in the garden of the Home I was well enough to go back to the seminary, and they let me go forward for ordination. Not with my own class-men, though. I was put back a year. And that was where I lost my foothold. I fell behind, and when you do that you never catch up again. I ought to have had a parish long ago. Doesn't everyone know that?" When he first started talking Father Patton was very wild and distraught, but it seemed that unravelling his thoughts and going back to those early days gave him some peace. "I wouldn't have minded being delayed in getting a parish if I had been sent to a place where the parish priest would be on my side, and put in a good word for me. They can do that, you know. They often get the ear of the Bishop at Confirmation, or at the Priests' Retreat, or better still, in places like Kilkee or Tramore, where they all flock for their holidays. But the man I'm up against wouldn't put in a good word for a saint. And he gave up going on holidays years ago. He wouldn't give it to say he'd spend money on himself in case his curate would expect to have some spent on him. And it's not as if I could hope he'd be called to his reward, because he's the kind will live for ever. I'll never get a parish. Never! I'll always be like a cockroach, crushed under somebody's foot."

To Annie's consternation tears suddenly brimmed into his eyes and spilled out and ran down his face, even into his mouth. "A cockroach," he sobbed.

Utterly shocked, Annie stretched out her hands to him. "Please don't, Father."

But once started, the crying couldn't be stemmed.

"Oh stop, Father, stop, stop, please!" Annie cried to no effect. Catching at her stick that rested against the bed-table, she tried clumsily to get out of bed and go to him, but the stick fell and the medicine bottles on the table wobbled as her arm knocked against them. "You'll be heard outside, Father!" she cried. "The nurses will hear you, they'll come in to see what's the matter." Indeed, just then she heard the rattle of crockery outside the door. "Oh quick!" she cried. "They're bringing around the dinners. They'll walk in on us." Pulling out a handkerchief she tried to throw it to him, but it fluttered on to the counterpane halfway down the bed. "You don't want to be seen like this, do you?" she pleaded.

It was too late. The wardsmaid had come in the door. She was a big country girl and she was holding the tray so high she didn't at first see the visitor. But Father Patton turned on her.

"Put down that tray and get out of here quick!" he shouted.

The girl's mouth opened and she came to a stand in the doorway. The tray tilted.

"Watch out! You're going to spill that slop." Father Patton's swollen eyes travelled over the girl. "Put it down and get out, like I said!" he cried. "Stir your stumps!" But as the girl, blushing furiously, stood rooted to the floor, he snatched the tray out of her hands, and planted it down himself on Annie's lap.

"Oh mind, Father, it's scalding hot!" the girl cried, coming to her senses.

"It's smells good I must admit," said the priest.

Its homely smell seemed to settle him down. He bent and smelled at the soup. Impulsively Annie lifted the spoon.

"Would you like to taste it, Father?" she asked, and then she caught the bowl and held it out to him. "Why don't you have it all, Father? I don't really want it. Do, do!" she urged.

Unexpectedly the wardsmaid spoke. "I could get more."

"No, no," Father Patton said. "I was only curious to see what it was like." He turned to Annie. "You know the kind of muck I get thrown up to me in the parochial house." Taking the spoon however he stirred about among the coarse-cut leeks and potatoes that floated in the soup. "What's it called?" he asked.

"Cocky-leaky, Father," she said.

Instantly the priest let go the spoon, which fell back into the soup-plate, splashing the soup over the sheets.

"That's enough out of you!" he cried. And catching the girl by the arm he pushed her out of the room. "Did you hear that?" he demanded of Annie. "You'd think butter wouldn't melt in her mouth, and then she comes out with the smut. Oh, I know her kind. And I know how I drew the smut down on me. It was mentioning her ugly stumps of legs that did it. They're all the same. They think that's all you're interested in. But she was wrong for once. Whatever else I may be, I'm not that kind. I didn't fail in that respect." Then, out of nowhere, an erratic gust of confidence seemed to blow over him. "Maybe I'll get a parish yet," he said, "and maybe sooner than we think too." To her astonishment. Annie thought he winked, but then she realised it had been only an involuntary twitch of his eyelid. "Do you know what?" he said, "I'm glad I came." Visibly now, minute by minute, he was pulling himself together. "You're not in as bad shape as I thought you'd be. You could be a lot worse. You'll see, things will work out somehow. Wait till you get home. One thing nobody seems to realise is that when you get home again you won't need as much money as before. You won't have the same chance to spend it, for one thing, and you won't be able to run about looking for ways of doing so either. The mistake all old people make is thinking that their needs will always be the same. You'll manage; you'll make out." He came nearer. "Let me give you a piece of advice. Don't let that brother of yours off too lightly. I've been making enquiries. Wasn't it you reared him? Has he no gratitude? I was told you used to be seen around the town, and you only a child, with him in your arms, when you ought to have been out enjoying yourself, courting and the like. He must have a short memory. You may not be able to make him pay the bill, but he ought at least to help out after you go home. Independence is all very well, but it can have its bad side too. Does it occur to you that you may be doing him great harm by letting him sneak out of his obligations? Oh, you didn't think of that? Well, it's time you did. I heard a friend of mine, another priest, talking along those lines some time ago, and he claimed that if you let people turn their back on the aged and the infirm, the next thing they'll want is to get rid of them altogether. Euthanasia! the same thing as is being done every other day up in the cats' and dogs' home in Dublin; putting the poor unwanted things to sleep, by scientific means, of course, only it's no different from the old way we all did it, tying them up in a sack with a big stone at the bottom, and dropping it in the water butt."

But Annie put her hands over her ears.

"Oh please, Father, please!" she cried, and then she took down her hands and her eyes flashed at him. "I think you'd better leave," she said.

"What's that?" As suddenly as the ranting began, it stopped. What did she mean? Hadn't she sent for him? What had changed her mind? For the first time since he came into the room, he really looked at her. Was it because she was a woman? That seemed the only possible explanation. Old as she was, and past it all, her flesh sagging, she was a woman all the same. He didn't know much about women. Were their minds as private as their bodies? In the seminary as a student he was supposed to know as much about them as doctors did, but only from text books, charts, and diagrams. And after he was ordained he didn't trouble any more about them. He had written them off: it was easier that way. But suddenly, where once he used to think sex was the only difference between a man and a woman, it seemed, now, that maybe it was the only thing they had in common. He found himself thinking back to one day when he was nine or ten. Someone told him how his mother had carried him inside her before he was born, and at the thought of something moving in the stomach, something soft and slimy like frog-spawn, he supposed, he'd felt so queer he'd gone out to the coal-shed and been sick.

"Are you feeling all right, Father?" Annie was stretching out to him with her hands, trying to reach him. He drew back. With an effort he recalled that she had just said she was sorry she'd asked him to come to see her.

"What are you going to do?" he asked.

"I don't know," Annie said. "I'll have to think. I'll stay here till the end of the week anyway." As if she was worn-out, she leant back against the head-board, and her doing so had a touch of finality to it. "A week is a long time," she said in a low voice. "Anything could happen."

Father Patton raised his heavy eyelids. Could she be ailing from something other than the fall? She'd failed a lot: he saw that now. Inside him, a horrible hope leaped to life. He couldn't smother it, but he knew he had to hide it. "You might win the Sweep, is that it?" he said, and the jaunty words made him feel so much better that a real solution occurred to him: an immediate one. "Couldn't they give you a job here in the hospital? Wheeling around the meal-trolleys, maybe, or something like that?" But he'd forgotten her injury, and the stick. "Well, they might find something for you," he added lamely.

Annie shook her head. "Don't worry about me, Father," she said. "You've other things to worry about."

What did she mean by that? Was she going to take advantage of his having let her see he'd been upset? Just in case, he'd better cut her down. "You're over-reaching yourself I think," he said.

But she looked back at him with a steady eye. "Am I?" she said.

Outside the door there was again a sound of crockery rattling.

"They're coming with more of their muck," the priest said.

"Yes," said Annie. "You'd better be going, Father."

When he got outside the door of Annie's room, Father Patton mopped at the sweat that had again broken out on his forehead. Then a faint chill of ether penetrated his nostrils. He kept the handkerchief to his face as he went down the corridor towards the stairs. Through the large windows on the landing he saw that the rain had ceased and a high wind was shaking the trees in the park across the street. Anxious to get out in the fresh air, he almost ran down the stairs, and when, on a lower landing, he met another wardsmaid coming up the stairs against him with a tray, he would have crashed into her if she hadn't flattened herself to the wall. Lazy sluts, still only bringing around the soup, he thought. Then he stopped short. "What is the name of that soup?" he demanded roughly, not caring that he'd nearly frightened the girl out of her wits.

"Cocky-leaky, Father," she whispered.

Taken aback, he caught her arm, spilling the soup. He looked around to see if the other wardsmaid was anywhere in sight. The corridor was empty. There could have been no collusion.

"What sort of a name is that for a soup?" he asked less crossly.

"I don't know, Father," she said. "We have it once a week."

Father Patton stared at her. For some reason he felt better. But why? Leaving the girl to stare after him, he went down the last flight of the stairs, and strode along the bottom corridor until in front of him he saw the glass doors through which he had entered the building. He pushed open the door and went out on to the steps. The air was fresh against his face. A cold sun was trying to struggle through the clouds, but in the wind its pale light was blown about like candleflame. He stood on the steps for a moment, looking across the street into the park. Over there everything was stirring, the leaves, the thin branches near the tops of the trees, and now and then a heavy branch swayed. And when a sudden flock of sparrows rose into the air he laughed to see how the high wind blew them about like leaves. Yet all this movement made him feel light-headed.

Carefully he went down the steps. Reaching the last step he stopped again. Every movement in the sky was reflected in the wet pavement so that it seemed as if the world was upside down, and that it was the heavens, and not the earth, was underfoot.

Slowly he went over to the edge of the kerb where he had parked his car. He came to a stop again. At sight of the car he shuddered. It was so old, so dented, so pockmarked with rust; it was like a car you'd see abandoned in a back street, the upholstery ripped open, the springs and padding protruding like guts. He could almost get the smell of it from where he stood: a smell of stale cigarette butts and sweaty feet. He couldn't bring himself to get into it. Rotten poky box of a car! He shook his fist at it. "Box!" he shouted out loud. "Box! Box!" but when some children playing in the street laughed, he moved hurriedly away, and having no particular place to go, he crossed the street and went into the park.

His life had been all boxes, he thought. First there was that box of a cubicle in the seminary. In it he was more awkward than most, being bigger boned than most. After that it was box after box; nothing but boxes: confessional boxes, poor boxes, collection boxes, and pamphlet boxes. Even God was kept in a box, closed up and locked into it. For what else was the Tabernacle only a box?

With the shock of this last thought, Father Patton came to a halt, and looking up he saw that he was standing under a tree covered along its sooty branches with young green leaves. He put up his hand impulsively and broke off a branch. He only wanted to look more closely at the tender young leaves; but there was something shocking about the white inner skin of the wood that was bared. Yet at the same time, the splintering sound of the breaking branch made him feel good. He broke a second little branch, and after a moment another, and suddenly he knew why the sound had made him feel good. He looked around the park with its pattern of paths leading, one to a little glade, one to a fountain, one to a bandstand, and one to an ornamental lake on which he could see swans gliding freely and serenely. He would watch those swans for a start. After that, perhaps he'd go back to see Annie again?

But for the moment it was enough to be there in the park. Around him, like the sparrows, people were appearing from all sides to enjoy the unexpected sunlight.

The Lost Child

Leaving Mike to park the car, Renee got out and ran up the steps of the church. Iris could give a hand with the children. As long as she had come with them she might as well be put to use. She herself was entitled to a little solitude after that nerve-racking drive up to town with them all gabbling away unconcernedly about matters totally unrelated to the ceremony. Iris of course had been sceptical from the start, and Mike most probably thought it a pity she hadn't taken the step years ago and saved everyone a lot of misery. Well, it was her soul, not theirs.

But she had reached the porch, and without waiting to take holy water, she pushed open the baize-lined doors and went into the dark interior. Oh, the peace of that vast empty place of God. She closed her eyes. Enough to have reached it, she thought, when, behind her, she heard Iris and the children: Iris clumsily trying to push open the baize doors without letting go the hands of her niece and nephew.

"Where do we go, Renee?" Iris whispered. "Do we sit with you?"

Renee trembled with annoyance. "I haven't the least idea," she said. It wasn't as if this was the first time her sister had set foot in a Catholic church.

But Iris was not to be put off. "I suppose we may as well go down to the front," she said, and she gave Renee a nudge to go forward.

Renee drew into herself. "Why don't you wait for Mike?" she said, and this time there was such an edge on her voice it cut her free again, and Iris let her go. Detached again, Renee started down the aisle alone, as if she were a bride. And then halfway down, inside the altar rail she saw a single prie-dieu that could only be for her. At the same time the sacristan stuck his head out of the sacristy door and gave a signal, not to a choir of course, but just as punctual as a peal from the organ Father Hugh stepped out on to the altar, ready and robed to receive her, his Ritual in his hand. After genuflecting smartly before the Tabernacle, he turned and smiled at her. Opening the brass gate in the altar rail, he beckoned her to pass inside, and motioned to her to kneel on the prie-dieu. Nothing could have been more simple or yet more solemn, but apparently now Mike had parked the car and joined Iris and the children, because behind her once more Renee heard them all coming down the aisle, the adults on tiptoe, their shoes creaking, and the children's feet clattering. She deliberately closed her eyes and waited till her family got themselves into a pew. But why had they felt obliged to plank themselves down in the very front row? For there they were—she couldn't resist a glance back—strung out in a row like birds on a clothes line, although when Mike saw her looking back, he got down on his knees at once, and made the children follow suit. Iris didn't budge, though. She evidently intended to stick to her guns and remain seated throughout. On all their faces, even on Iris's, there was such a look of expectancy that Renee suddenly felt foolish. What did they expect? Yet she herself was surprised at how quickly the ceremony was over. She had been received into the Church. She was a Catholic at last.

Replacing the silk marker in his Ritual, Father Hugh shook hands with her in the most ordinary manner. Then he opened the brass gate again and preceded her down into the body of the church. There he shook hands warmly with her family, beginning of course with Mike, then the children, and then, with a slightly exaggerated politeness, with Iris.

Ought he to be asked to lunch? Renee wondered, but said nothing. Apparently Mike did not think it necessary; he just gave Father Hugh a nod and stood up to let his wife into the pew. He and Father Hugh were old friends. "Move up there, children, and let your mother kneel down," he said out loud as if they were not in a church at all. "Goodbye Hugh," he said, also out loud. "We'll see you during the week, I suppose?"

"That's right," said Father Hugh, and with a smile that embraced them all, he went back through the brass gate, shutting it carefully after him. Then, genuflecting in front of the altar he went into the sacristy with the quick impatient steps of one on familiar territory.

For a few minutes they all remained on their knees except Iris. Iris was examining the mortuary plaques on the wall. She seemed bored. Renee turned and looked at the children. The expectancy was gone from their faces too. For them the ceremony had probably been a bit of a frost.

To recollect her thoughts, Renee would have liked to cup her face in her hands, but since this was a gesture reserved by born Catholics for the moments after Communion, she was afraid it would seem over-enthusiastic. It might annoy Mike. In spite of his wish that she should become a Catholic before they married, he had afterwards settled down to the idea of her never turning, and indeed, secretly he distrusted converts. It was incredible really to think how stubbornly she had resisted this step which in the end she had so willingly, so eagerly taken. For although at no time had she been prepared to lose Mike rather than give way, she'd gone very near to it once or twice. That was because of the hullaballoo his mother had made. Not that her own mother had been much better because when she finally consented to a Catholic wedding her mother behaved very badly.

"What on earth do you mean, Renee? You can't mean it will be held in the sacristy, the actual ceremony?" Her mother was outraged. "How can you tolerate that? How can you allow your marriage to be a hole and corner business? It's an insult to your parents and your friends as well as to yourself. As for the slight cast on Iris, that is the worst of all."

"Oh, I don't mind, Mother," Iris said. "It's just that I don't understand, that's all. What does my religion matter? I'd only be a witness."

Their mother had been somewhat placated.

"Anyway Iris you don't want to be a bridesmaid again, do you?" she said. "You know the old saying, three times a bridesmaid never a bride."

It was then Iris had said a very odd thing.

"Everyone doesn't set the same value on being a bride," she said. "I'm content never to marry if I don't meet a man of my own kind." She might as well have struck Renee between the eyes. And she knew it. "Forgive me, Renee," she'd said. "I'm jealous, that's all." And she ran over and gave her a kiss.

But her explanation simply didn't wash because Iris was the beauty of the family: she could have had any man she wanted; she always had had any number of admirers. No one could understand why she didn't marry. If she was disturbed about Renee's marriage it could only be supposed she was bigoted, because she was fond enough of Mike as a person. Indeed it was she who, in the end, spoke to their mother and told her the mistake she'd be making if she took any more risks with Mike. Their mother took the advice. And on the day of the wedding it was their mother who impressed everyone by being briefed-up on procedure, not only genuflecting but making the sign of the cross as well.

"There!" she seemed to say, flashing her eyes at the in-laws. "That is the behaviour *I* expect from people." Iris of course had needed no briefing, having been at school in a convent in Belgium. She was a past master at dabbling her fingers in holy water, and passing it on, continental style, to her neighbours. She also had met Father Hugh, and had got on so well with him she felt better about everything. Really the wedding had gone off remarkably well, and it hadn't been in the sacristy after all but in a side chapel.

When they came back from their honeymoon though, and her mother came to visit, she barely concealed her contempt when Renee served fish on Friday. And later she nearly hit the ceiling when she heard her grandchild, Babette, was to be baptised a Catholic.

"But I promised, Mother; You know that."

"I only know that such a promise should never have been extracted," said her mother. "It was given under duress, emotional duress."

"Oh, give over, Mother, will you?" Renee had said. "Do you want us to be happy or do you not? Can't you see I'm only doing it to make things easier for Mike?"

"Why can't he make things easier for you?"

"Well, for one thing!" she cried, "his mother would have made life worse for him than you're trying to make it for me. In any case, Mike is bound under pain of mortal sin in this matter."

Her mother gave her a scathing look. "And you are willing to let your children grow up in the same stupid bonds?"

"Oh Mother, please, please," she said wearily. "You don't understand, that's all. I care more about Mike than I do about any church, his or mine."

To give her mother her due, that had silenced her. As for Iris, by then she had met so many priests through Mike, most of them having been at school or college with him, and she'd got on so famously with them, it began to look as if she too would turn.

All the same the sisters had had one bitter argument years later when Renee had started to receive instructions for her entry into the church. They had gone to Achill on one of their week-end trips, and Iris had gone with them. They were staying in a small hotel close to the shore and after putting the children to bed they had gone for a stroll along Dugort Strand. As they walked along the shore they had to pick their steps, because the tufty shore-grass was dotted with half-concealed stones and they could easily trip and twist an ankle. Suddenly Iris stopped.

"I thought the rocks along here were all a natural formation," she said, "but look, surely there is some attempt at pattern in this?"

Mike and Renee stopped too and looked where she pointed. It did seem there was a regularity in the disposition of the small rocks at their feet, some forty or fifty at least. There was no cutting or marking on them and yet they seemed to have been set down deliberately by the hand of man.

"Let's see if the guide book has anything to say about them," said Mike, taking it out of his pocket. "You're right, Iris," he said, commending her. He looked around him to take his bearing from the over-hanging cliffs and then turned to calculate the distance from a small pier to the left of where they stood. "This must be it," he said, "it's indicated on the map too. And it has a name, Cillin na Leanbh, that means Cemetery of the Children." He looked proudly at Iris. "I bet there aren't many people who spot this. He was too pleased with himself to see there was anything wrong with Iris. On the contrary he patted her on the arm. "Weren't you smart, Iris. Only for you we would not have seen it."

Renee however had sensed trouble. Iris was staring around her at the bleak and lonely shore, with not a soul in sight. "Why did they bury them here? Why not in the ordinary cemetery down in the village?" The harsh air had reddened her face but that was not enough to account for her excited look. Renee did not know what could be wrong, but she felt uneasy. "It's much more beautiful up here anyway," she said, hoping to dismiss the matter. And she began to walk on. In any case, she herself had had enough of the place. There was something oddly disturbing about it. But Iris stood stubbornly where she was and looked not at Mike but at her sister. "It's certainly beautiful, but that's hardly the reason for the choice," she said.

What was she driving at? Did she suspect some kind of superstition which she attributed not to the ignorance of a peasant community but to their barbarous religion?

"Is it because they were illegitimate?" Iris asked then bluntly, and there was such a note of fierceness in her voice that at last Mike realised there was something wrong.

"Certainly not," he replied. "The Church does not discriminate in such cases as long as the child is baptised." His voice was vibrant with self-righteousness. "I've never seen one of these places before," he said, "but I believe they were common at one time, and there are some in other parts of the country." Confident that he had stamped out his sister-in-law's spark of rebellion, he turned to take his wife's arm with the intention of complacently walking on, when Renee pulled away.

"But that's inhuman," she said. "How must the poor mother have felt?"

"Don't mind the mothers," Iris cried. "How would anyone feel, any proper mother?" Unconsciously the sisters drew together.

Against them Mike stood at bay. Then, although they knew he detested crudity of any kind, the two women were startled at what he said next. "It's no worse than what is done every other day in hospitals and nursing homes."

"And what is that?" It was Renee who had asked, and in a whisper. Mike shrugged his shoulders. "How do I know?" he said harshly, "but I'm pretty sure they don't hold a full funeral for a foetus."

"Oh Mike! That word!" It made Renee feel sick. And he knew she loathed it. He must be very upset. She looked out over the sea where a last cold glitter of light came from under the clouds. It might easily rain. "Oh, come on, let's not talk about it any more," she said. "The custom is obsolete anyway." Warning Iris with a look, she began to walk back to the hotel.

But one morning in the following week, when they were back home, Iris drove up in her car; the tyres screeching on the gravel. She marched into the house, holding up the handbook of the Antiquarian Society.

"Listen to this," she commanded.

'Immediately on the cliff edge at the east end of Dugort Strand a number of small rough and uninscribed slabs are to be seen. This spot is locally called Cillin na Leanbh. In this spot are buried the bodies of unbaptised children, and a rough slab is erected over each. There is no enclosing wall and the grave stones are only just visible through the heather. The custom of burying unbaptised infants on useless pieces of ground like the present site was formerly common throughout the whole country and—'"

Here she paused dramatically, and, leaving down the handbook on the table, she quoted the rest from memory,

'but to a large extent the custom had now ceased.'

To a large extent. Do you hear that? In other words, it has not ceased: it is not obsolete. Oh Renee, are you prepared to accept things like that?"

Renee was in fact shocked but she found Iris interfering. "I'll take it up with Father Hugh," she said, and, having said that, she felt no obligation to listen to any more ranting from Iris.

Father Hugh, however, needed no new issue to arise in order to urge Renee to go slow about a final decision. That was one of the things that surprised her; the thoroughness of her instruction: it amounted almost to unwillingness on the part of the priest to receive her into the Church at all.

"What is the hurry?" he asked smiling. "Your faith will be all the stronger if it comes as a result of living with a good Catholic like Mike."

"What if it's the other way round?" she asked, unable to resist the quip.

"Fair enough!" said the priest, and he laughed outright. And although at the time her Protestant probity resented what she felt to be an attempt to ingratiate himself with her, yet she knew he was incapable of duplicity. It was just that, like his Church, he believed too staunchly in the superiority of the male intellect, he couldn't imagine Mike being influenced by her in such a matter.

And yet, in the end, it was the maleness of the Church that had, as Mike put it, hooked her. She could lean on it. "Or was that a silly way to put it, Father Hugh?" she asked one day.

"My dear," he said, "have you never seen how, in pictures of the Good Shepherd, the lost lamb leans against Jesus, trusts himself to Those Arms? I think Mike expressed himself very beautifully. We Catholics do lean on our Church."

That somehow settled it. And here she was today, a member of the Church, having entrusted the full weight of her soul upon it. But suddenly, with a start, she realised she had not said one prayer, had not offered one word of gratitude to God for the grace that had been bestowed on her. Yet she must have been on her knees for ages. The others were getting restless, the children were beginning to bicker wordlessly. Babette was pulling her brother's handkerchief from him, using her strength meanly, letting him think he was getting it one minute, and then tugging it away. She could easily pull him off the edge of the pew on to the floor. What a howl he'd give then! Renee realised she'd have to be content with one quick prayer. First however she glanced at Mike. She couldn't help noticing that he looked bored. The children too in spite of their bickering had a subdued look. Poor little things, for them the ceremony was probably a disappointment compared with the solemnity of their own First Communion Day still fresh in their minds; the feasting afterwards, the sugar kisses and silver-papered presents from friends and relatives. Even Iris looked disappointed, having memories, no doubt, of her schooldays in the convent in Courtrai where even the Protestant boarders shared in the First Communion goodies, amassing heaps of iced almonds, virgin white and tasting as sweet as scent, to make caches against the lesser, leaner days of the calendar.

Oh, those years in Courtrai. Renee was ashamed to think she had lived under the same roof with the Blessed Sacrament and had been so indifferent to it. Nostalgia for those bygone days made her want to throw her arms around Babette. She stood up and joined them in their pew.

Taking this to be an end to praying, the child whispered to her. "What are we going to do next?"

"Have lunch," said Mike, overhearing her. He sat up and began to dust his knees. "We may as well get out of here, hadn't we?" he said, in what would have seemed an irreverent tone if it weren't for the devout way he was making the sign of the cross at the same time. "Are you ready, Renee?" he said quite roughly for him, but she understood. Distrusting the convert, he had been afraid she'd expect to stay there half the day. So, after one piercing look at the Tabernacle, suffused with joy, she too got to her feet. In the aisle she took care to genuflect quickly, and as if carelessly, like a born Catholic.

When they reached the door, a bit dazed she was about to step out into the sunlight, forgetting to take holy water, till Iris stretched out her hand. Then, hastily dipping into the font she passed a damp touch to Iris in the continental manner. Poor Iris. Little things like that made the whole thing more palatable to her. Renee wondered why, in fact, her sister had come with them to the church. It must have been out of regard for the children: to help make it an occasion for them. Renee's heart smote her again. They must all feel very let down. In addition they were probably hungry. It was past noon. She herself was not hungry but she did feel very tired. She wished they were going home to spend the rest of the day normally. She turned to Mike, but it was hard to see what was in his mind. He wouldn't be human if he wasn't thinking it a pity his mother had not lived to see this day. Yet Renee herself could not truthfully regret her mother-in-law's absence: the old woman's satisfaction would have been so tactlessly evident, the ceremony would have been really objectionable for Iris.

"It was nice of you to come, Iris," she whispered impulsively, giving her sister's arm a squeeze as they went down the steps.

"Oh, not at all," said Iris. "I thought it would be expected of me."

"Do you mind awfully?"

"Why should I?" her sister said. "It's entirely your concern." But something in her voice struck Renee as odd, and she looked enquiringly at her. What reservations did she still have?

"What is the matter, Iris?" she asked, putting all the warmth she could into her voice, because now she was very, very tired.

But Mike was all for moving off. "Where are we going to eat?" he asked, and unconsciously with his hand he felt inside his jacket to make sure he had his wallet. That always meant he had planned an extra-good meal.

"Where would you like to go, Iris?" Renee asked, anxious to give her sister the choice.

"Oh, anywhere suits me," said Iris. "Oughtn't you to have the choice? Sort of like long ago when one was the Birthday Girl!"

They all laughed at that, the children loud and boisterously.

"Well, the Birthday Girl has no preferences," Renee said truthfully.

Then she hesitated and turned to Mike. "Perhaps not an oriental restaurant though, on account of the garlic."

"But I thought you loved garlic?" Iris was astonished.

"Oh?" Renee stopped dead. She blushed and dropped her voice. "Didn't you know? Didn't I tell you? We're going to have another child. I meant to tell you but I kept forgetting: it seems so far off, it won't be till October, nearly November."

When Iris said absolutely nothing even Mike got nervous and broke in. "We're not even sure yet."

Renee smiled gratefully at him. "That's right. We could easily be mistaken, although I don't think so." Then she laughed. "We could put it to the test, of course, by going to an Indian restaurant. One smell of garlic turns me inside out, in the early stages anyway."

Iris missed the joke. Her face had become deadly serious.

"We most certainly won't go anywhere that would upset you, Renee," she said.

"Oh, I was exaggerating," Renee said. Renee disliked the solicitous note in her sister's voice. There was nothing she would hate more than this and that would be an obstetrical chat. Hoping to deflect her sister's interest in her condition, she reached back into the conversation and tried to salvage the topic she had a few minutes before allowed to founder. "Was it an ordeal for you, Iris? The ceremony I mean?"

"Oh no," said Iris. "I always knew from the moment you married Mike that you'd turn one day. But I must say that in view of what you've just told me, I am worried. I wouldn't have thought now the most appropriate time for making decisions of any kind."

"Well, really!" Renee was so taken aback she gasped. "You don't mean because of my pregnancy? You can't mean that? That it has clouded my judgment? After all, I've been in this condition on two other occasions and I didn't change my religion. Oh Iris, you fall so short of understanding."

But Iris looked her straight in the eyes.

"That's right, I do," she said, and catching Babette's hand she bent down and gave the child her full attention. "Where would you like best to go?" she asked.

Never having expected to be given the choice, both children nevertheless were ready with an answer. "To the Zoo!" they cried. "The Zoo!"

Renee could have shaken her sister. The Zoo was out of the question. Better an oriental restaurant, garlic and all, than the Zoo. Out of her depth, she appealed for help to Mike. "Think of the smell in the Lion House," she said. "I couldn't stand it."

The damage was done though. Babette was pouting. She had been angelic, up to now, and who would dash the hopes of an angel?

"Why can't we go to the Zoo?" the child demanded.

They all came to a stand.

"Because this is your mother's day," said Mike. "It's her, not you, who is to be considered."

"Why did Iris ask us, so?" Babette took her hand away from Iris and caught the hand of her small brother.

Behind the children, Iris was making signs, and silently forming words with her lips. Renee was unreasonably irritated. "What are you trying to say?" she asked out loud.

Betrayed, Iris flushed. "I only wondered if they knew."

"No, they don't," Renee snapped. "Perhaps it's time they did." She was almost frightened by how tired she felt now. .

Mike raised his eyebrows. "Isn't it a bit early to tell them? They'd get an awful disappointment if it was a false alarm."

But the children had got wind that there was something concealed from them.

"Oh, what is it? Tell us!" they cried. Feeling certain they would be told, their sulks gave way to excited anticipation and they began to hop like hailstones on the pavement.

"Tell them, Mike," said Renee.

"I suppose we may as well," said Mike, and then as the children clutched him and rocked him from side to side, their excitement became contagious and his face broke out in the first real smile of the morning. "Your mother has been planning a surprise for you," he said.

"It's not something specially for them," Renee intervened. "Don't raise their hopes too much. It won't be arriving till—"

"Oh, Mummy!" They'd guessed, and stunned by joy, the children stopped hopping up and down. After that one exclamation they fell so silent Renee laughed. Then she realised she must seize her advantage now.

"So you see, about going to the Zoo—" she began, but Babette needed no explanations.

"Oh, *of course*, Mummy, you must do what you want." And then, more prescient than anyone could have supposed, she ran over and whispered in her ear: "Why don't you go home, Mummy, and lie down. We'd be good. And you'd get a rest from us."

"Would you like to do that, Renee?" Mike asked, partly surprised, partly relieved. "You would?" he said, answering for her when he saw the look on her face. "I think it's a very good idea. Look! Let's do it in style," he said. "Let's send you home in a taxi. It's not very extravagant. It won't cost more than your share in the meal. And you do look deadly tired." He turned back to the children. "Let's put her into a taxi right now." And from a hackney rank just opposite them, he hailed a cab.

A wonderful feeling of being minded, taken care of, came over Renee as Mike put her into the taxi cab. As she sank back on the seat she saw that Mike too was delighted with the way he had handled things. Only as the taxi moved off did she think of this. She wound down the window. "What about you Iris? Will you be all right?"

Iris probably didn't hear her, but by the look on her face she was taking things good-humouredly. Anyway, Renee didn't really care. She leaned back and closed her eyes, prepared to give way to utter exhaustion, but as the taxi gathered speed she found it irksome to keep her eyes closed. Was it possible she wasn't tired at all, only anxious to be alone? To be truthful she felt lively and full of energy. She really ought to have gone by bus. The exercise would have been good for her. She smiled to think how Mike had treated her as if she was made of glass when she was expecting Babette, or at least had tried to do so until she showed him what it said in her precious manual on childbirth, how important exercise was in pregnancy.

Oh how she had sworn by that manual when she was expecting Babette, and even during her second pregnancy. This time she'd felt so confident she hadn't consulted it once.

"You've got the knack, old girl. You don't need it any more," Mike said, although he had, at the time, been very impressed by the way she'd read up, briefed up, on childbirth. As a business man he'd felt this was because she was a University graduate. He was always telling people how she'd learned to drive from a handbook, and how when they'd inherited the farm where they now lived, she had read up on pasture management, the making of compost and animal genetics, until she knew more about farming than him, although he'd been brought up on a farm. To top off his praise of her, he'd beam as he added that she'd had her babies by her book too. And he felt sure that was why they were so strong and healthy, and yet fine boned. He was so proud of Babette's clear skin and her beautiful auburn hair, although she knew he had misgivings about the boy's hair. It was so very strong and abundant. "It was all those carrots you ate, Renee," he said one day.

She had found it very easy to defend herself because the boy had such a happy disposition. "Les carottes sont pour faire rire," she said. Then thinking of carrots reminded her that she had intended to buy some lettuce when she was in Dublin. In spite of owning a farm, they often had to buy some of the ordinary vegetables. It just didn't pay to grow them out of season.

The taxi was now turning into Thomas Street. Perhaps she could get some greens at one of the street barrows. No. The vendors were packing up and what was left was strewn around the street, wilted and yellowing, disgusting, simply disgusting. The discarded outer leaves were trodden into the ground, rotting and beginning to give off a stench. Heads of lettuce were already a liquid mess.

Seeing the lettuce Renee smiled. Lettuce always reminded her of a time when Mike's younger brother called to tell them his wife was expecting her first baby and poor Mike started to recommend that she drink lots of water and eat plenty of greens, when his brother cut him short and said his wife was a healthy woman and didn't go in for food fads. How Mike and herself had laughed at the time and later, more unkindly had remembered the conversation whenever they saw his pasty faced progeny. Yet they too had grown up into fine strong children.

At this point Renee looked out of the taxi window. They had come to the end of Thomas Street and were turning down by St. Patrick's Hospital. Her last chance of getting vegetables was gone, but it was just as well because she'd forgotten she'd have to lug them across the fields. That was something they had neglected, the making of a proper driveway into their house which they'd built down near the river. They had never regretted siting the house far in from the road but as their money ran out they had had to postpone the making of the avenue for a while since nothing would satisfy Mike except tarmacadam. In summer of course they had got away with it driving through the fields and even when winter came had been lucky in that the ground was hard and frosty, but now, with a touch of spring in the air the ground would soon begin to get soft. Even today Renee wondered if it was fair to ask a taxi driver, a city man, to risk it. Anyway the walk through the fields would be pleasant. It would give her an appetite, for although she was eating well enough she did not have the same eagerness for food she had had when she was carrying the other two children.

For a moment Renee let her thoughts dwell on her unborn child. What sex would it be, she wondered. She had read somewhere that it would soon be possible to determine the sex of a child before birth, but somehow the idea of such a thing did not appeal to her. It would surely in some way interfere with the mystery of carrying an unknown, but living creature within one's body, feeding it from one's own bloodstream and sustaining its life-breath with one's own heart's pulse. But suddenly Renee felt a slight shadow fall over her happiness, because of course it was not only the flesh of our flesh we passed on to our children but something of our intellect and personality as well. A faint shadow fell over her happiness as she thought dismally of a number of unpleasant relatives that she and Mike had on both sides, people whose traits it would positively pain her to think of passing on to a child. And yet the secret seeds of ancestry were already at work in her womb. Against such an unwelcome thought she closed her eyes and leaning back on the leather seat of the taxi deliberately summoned up memories of those she loved who were so lovable. Perhaps the new baby might even be like herself or Mike? Vaguely an image began to form in her mind of a broad stream flowing strongly, but, going upwards against the current like a salmon going upstream to spawn, she saw a tiny infant.

Oh dear! She sat up with a start. She must have been asleep. The taximan, following Mike's instructions, had crossed the bridge over the Boyne, but finding no driveway or gate piers on his right as he had expected, but only a gap in the hedge with a pole across it, leading into what looked like a rutted cow-path, had cruised past it and gone on till he came to the cross-roads a couple of hundred yards from the farm. There he stopped, confused, and it was probably when he stopped that she woke.

"Oh, we've passed the entrance," she cried. "It's just a gap in the hedge," she said, but seeing the dismay on his face she laughed and assured him she didn't expect him to go down to the house. "I'll get out here in fact," she said, "and *then* you can continue without turning. Just go right here and you'll come out again on the main road. It will be slightly shorter too," she added.

For her it would mean a slightly longer walk, that is to say if she took a short cut through a small beechwood that divided their property from a neighbour's, but on a day like this it ought to be heaven in the woods. She got out and paid the fare, but the man did not immediately drive away. Perhaps noticing her high heels, and remembering Mike's decidedly citified appearance, he was thinking it odd they lived so far from Dublin.

"Have you much land?" he asked with the innocent curiosity of a Dubliner.

"Only a few acres," she said and she smiled at him. "It's not a real farm. We just graze a few cattle, just let them fatten on the grass," she explained patiently as to a child. "No cows, no pigs."

He nodded, obviously not fully understanding and then after a last look over the fields he let in the clutch and began to move away. Standing on the roadside, Renee waved impatiently at him, glad he was gone, because it would have been awkward getting over the rickety fence into the wood. The old fence was so shaky she could not let her weight rest long on it, but had to jump down on the other side. Fortunately the ground was not as soft as she thought. There was a hard core still in it after all.

It was beautiful in the wood. Walking over the dried leaves between the trees, she felt an increasing sense of well-being. Everywhere there was evidence that spring was on the way, although everywhere too there was evidence of the damage done by winter. There were two big trees blown down and several trees had branches broken. Then when she came to the end of the trees and out into the fields she noticed as never before how winter had flattened the grass. In places it looked more like a lawn than a pasture. And what was this? She stopped. In the middle of the field through which she was walking there was a huge stone that she and Mike had let fall from the tractor one day last summer. They had been drawing stones from the ruin of an old stone cottage for a dry-wall they were building at the end of the garden. They had got the loan of the tractor and they had had a young local boy to help them load the stones, but this big one rolled off after the boy had gone home to milk his father's cows, and it was far too heavy for them to lift alone. They left the tractor back, but every week they meant to borrow it again and get the boy and fetch the stone, but when the wall was finished without it, they forgot all about it. Soon the grass grew over it and hid it from sight of the track by which they went in and out. She went over to it. It was huge, and she now saw that it was roughly chiselled, perhaps by one of the old monks to whom the land once belonged. It would have been a pity to have cemented it in a wall. It would make a marvellous feature on the lawn, a focal point, with bulbs planted around it. It would of course be an awful job to move it now because it had sunk into the ground and was tightly stitched down by scutchgrass. Still it ought to be possible for a strong labouring man to lever it up with a crowbar and roll it up a plank into a wheelbarrow. With the toe of her shoe she prodded it, but it didn't budge. It was firmly rooted to the ground as a tree. Still the thought of salvaging excited her and walking on she found herself stepping out faster as she planned where to place it and what to plant around it.

At last she reached the gable end of the house, and there, in the warm bulb border under the wall she saw that several crocuses had thrust up their wiry green tips. But when she went closer she laughed out loud because two or three of them, no, four or five, oh lots and lots of them had thrust themselves upwards in such a frenzy of growth that they had shot out of the ground altogether and lay on top of the clay. She'd have to put them back. Perhaps she could push them back into the ground with her fingers she thought, or make a hole with the heel of her shoes. No, she decided, better do things properly.

Eager to get into the house and change into more comfortable clothes to go out again and use up all this energy that was surging through her, she turned around to the front door. It was extraordinary how everywhere, simply everywhere she looked, there were things that needed to be done which, she and Mike, blinkered by winter, had not noticed. And when she got to the door and put her key in the lock she saw something that would have to be done at once, today. How had she not seen it before. Her precious, precious old rose Gloire de Dijon, whose young shoots had prematurely put out spurts of tender pink leaves in the shelter of the house, was blasted by frost at the tips of its branches. If those blackened tips were not snipped off immediately the whole shoot would die, possibly the whole bush. Without going into the house, Renee hurried around to the potting shed and got the pruning shears. It would only take a few minutes to attend to the rose at least.

Half an hour later, Renee was still hacking away at the rose bush. There had been more damage done than she'd thought. And from the Gloire de Dijon she'd gone on to inspect the Madame Alfred Carrière on the terrace. It, too, had dead shoots. Less rare than the Dijon but more beautiful, it was a larger bush. She had transplanted it from their former garden, and once she'd tackled it she'd let herself in for a really tiresome job. When she'd finished at last, she sat down on the steps up to the door to rest before going inside and getting something to eat. She certainly had an appetite now. She was famished. A few minutes after she felt like getting up she'd gone into the house and made a pot of tea. She was just about to put it on a tray and take it up to her room, when she happened to look out of the kitchen window. Good Lord! What did she see at the end of the garden but their long awaited load of manure. It had been promised for so long she'd given up hope of its ever arriving, but it had evidently come while they were away. Almost knocking over the tea in her excitement, she ran to the window to make sure she wasn't mistaken. Not having stall-fed cattle they had to depend on local farmers for an occasional load of manure for the garden. This always involved an endless humiliation of begging and endless broken promises, because although to her, manure was something money could not buy, the farmers felt they were only humouring her by giving and never considered it of much consequence to deliver it until it suited them, such as some day when they were clearing out a shed perhaps. It was always when she'd given up hope of getting it that a tractor would roll up with a big load of it. Or else like today, she'd come back from town to find a load dumped down in the most awkward place possible.

But oh, what an unsightly place it had been dumped this afternoon. If only she'd been at home. And why on the lawn? It was down at the end of the garden, not near the house of course, but it would ruin the grass, burn it to the roots if it wasn't moved within a few days. It was very near the herbaceous border too. She opened the window and leant out. How maddening, simply maddening, a lot of the wretched stuff had toppled into the border. That at least would have to be removed very quickly. But by whom? She didn't have the car to go looking for a man to do it, and it was unlikely that she would be able to persuade anyone to spare a man on such a fine day for what would be considered a frivolous occupation, a woman's caprice. She stood for a moment wondering if there was anything she could do. Then putting down her cup of tea she went out to assess the situation. Perhaps there would not be as much damage done as she'd feared.

In the garden, she was sorry she went out at all. It was pretty bad. The big heap of dung was fresh and still steaming, and had been thrown down so carelessly that the whole of one side had collapsed and flowed like lava into the border. It had entirely engulfed the smaller plants, and several of the larger plants further back were up to their necks in it.

She could have cried. It had almost buried her beautiful Chinese peonies that were due to flower for the first time this summer, their leaf buds had already unfurled. She'd have to save them if nothing else. Trembling with annoyance she ran back to the tool house and got a fork, just an ordinary garden fork. She had never been able to handle the big five pronged manure fork which a man would have used, and with which short work would have been made of the job. Oh, if only Mike was home! but he'd hardly be back till dark. "Damn Iris!" she said out loud, as if all this was her sister's fault. She knew she was unreasonable but she repeated it. "Damn Iris." Catching up the fork she set to work with a will.

To clear the manure from the peonies was not such a big job after all.

She used her hands most of the time and there was enough space around them to just clear it away to either side of them so it didn't touch the plant itself. There were spaces of bare clay between these larger shrubs and they would benefit by being enriched. And it wasn't long till she had freed a few bushes of sandalwood and several clumps of lavender, just by shaking them! The smaller plants were a different matter. On them the manure lay in such thick wet slabs it would have to be forked off and flung back on the heap.

It was no joke, this job, but she got through it quickly enough and had just heaved a sigh and decided to stop when she noticed the main heap still looked very top-heavy. Unless a few forkfuls were taken off the top it could topple over again and her labour would be in vain. Taking a deep breath she set to work once more.

This time it was really tough going: The dung, heavy with urine was a dead weight and every time she dug the fork in, it let out an evil smell. Compared with compost it was very unpleasant. Her compost heap was a pride and joy to her. She'd made it by the book too, putting everything into it, grass clippings, withered leaves, the tops of plants when they'd finished flowering and were cut down; everything, everything. She often went out with the tea strainer and threw the tea leaves into it. The same with coffee grounds and eggshells, although the egg shells had to be pounded into small bits or they'd take too long to decay. Mike used to laugh at her in the beginning, but in time he was impressed by the results. He'd plunge in his arm and bring out a fistful to show a vistor, opening his hand slowly to let the friable soil run out like sand between his fingers. It was amazing to think that a mass of refuse and offal could turn back into sweet-smelling loam. Compost was so different from this heap of filthy stuff that took so long to decompose. Yet, dug into the ground, this too would be transformed. She took another deep breath and stuck the fork into the heap again, and with an effort raised another layer of it. The next instant she let the fork fall and put her hand over her mouth in disgust. Ugh! under the hot coverlet a mess of worms snuggled. Stabbed by the bright light, they blindly and clumsily began to uncoil. The sight was nauseating, but she kept her head, realising that if they crawled back into the darkness of their nest she would be liable to uncover them with every other forkful, whereas now, if she gritted her teeth and acted fast, she might lift the whole disgusting posse and fling it out of sight. Taking up the fork again she lunged it under the sprawling creatures. But oh God! she'd bungled it. The vile things had already squirmed away in every direction, twisting and turning and crawling over each other, and one or two of them that she got on to the fork tumbled off it and fell on to her shoes.

Sickened, she threw down the fork. But oh God, oh God, oh God, a worm was impaled on one of the prongs. Utterly demoralised, her impulse was to run into the house, but how could one, above all someone in her condition, deny even a disgusting thing like that, any creature, its right to life? She'd have to free it. Putting her hand on her stomach, feeling she was about to retch, she took up the fork a third time and with her foot she tried to dislodge the writhing thing skewered on the prong. No use. Only with her finger could it be done.

But after she'd freed it, the mangled worm, still writhing, dropped to the ground in two halves. As if her hands had been in contaminated water, Renee frantically wiped them on her skirt, on her sleeves, on her jumper, but all the time she was watching the little mutilated body, unable to tear her eyes away. It was cut in two. But *both* parts of it were writhing. Its entity doubled and therefore its agony too was doubled. Oh God, could no part of it die?

With a scream she ran towards the house.

"Renee? What's wrong with you, Renee?"

It was Mike. They had come home earlier than she expected but Mike was the first to reach her. He took her in his arms. "What were you doing? What is the matter? You look so green!" Then he took in the situation. "I thought it was to rest you came home early?" he said angrily, although at the same time his arms closed tighter and more lovingly around her. "What on earth made you take on a job like that?" he asked. "Particularly at this time?"

She pulled away from him. "You know we always agreed there was no need for a woman to coddle herself just because she was expecting a baby. You always went along with me that work never did any harm, that it was only nervous exhaustion that could do damage." She was sobbing and gulping words that broke from her involuntarily. "You always said you were glad I didn't trade on pregnancy in order to get out of obligations. And this job was *most* urgent." His face was so impassive she pounded his chest with her fists. "You can't turn on me now. You've got to take the bad with the good. Oh, I never knew you were so mean. Before Babette was born, don't you remember, the nurse said that if I didn't go into labour next day she was going to get me to move the furniture. She said that in the maternity hospital where she was trained they always got the patients to lift the beds when they were going past their due time, and rearrange them about the ward." She looked at him. She'd told him this once before and he had been amused and even interested. She thought he'd laugh but it was Iris who answered her, having let the children into the house.

"The maternity nurse may have told you that, but she was probably joking. In any case, what she meant was that they did it to induce labour. If you had come full term it would be a different matter, but in your present state there's absolutely no excuse for having taken such a risk." Iris was furious. She actually took Renee by the shoulders and shook her.

Renee turned on her. "Are you trying to teach me my business?" she cried, but even in her distracted state she was appalled at the viciousness that underlay her words and she wasn't really surprised when Iris burst into tears. "Oh please don't cry, Iris!" she begged, because she guessed suddenly that her words had struck home harder than she intended Iris was lonely. And suddenly she remembered something her sister had said on the eve of her own wedding, which she had not understood at the time and thought very odd. Iris had said that she would never marry unless it was to someone of her own kind, and it had seemed then that she meant someone of her own persuasion. Now with a blinding illumination she realised Iris had not meant that at all. Renee had been hurt and had harboured the hurt over those years, thinking Iris meant that she'd settled for marriage with the Catholic Mike for fear of not finding anyone in their own church. After all it was a minority religion. "I'm sorry Iris," she said, not clear why or for what she was apologising.

Then, as if the whole world was made of crockery and she had let it fall, her ears were filled with sounds of clatter and breakage. Only the voice of Iris came through to her, talking to Mike, not to her.

"Let's get her up to bed," Iris was saying, and one on each side of her they got her into the house and up to her room where the children stood huddled together, and stared at her uncomprehendingly.

It was good to be in bed. There was a great luxury in lying down while outside it was still daylight, and only the sleepy note in the throat of a bird gave any indication that evening was approaching. And now here came Iris, smiling and kind again, with a tray of supper for her and Mike, with the early edition of the evening paper he'd bought in town and forgotten about in the fuss.

"I don't deserve all this attention," she said. "I'm as fit as a fiddle. I just got worked up over those nasty worms. I feel marvellous."

"That's good," Mike said, but he was looking anxiously at her all the same and Iris was looking at her very keenly too after she'd left down the tray.

Uneasily Renee's glance went from one to the other of them. "You don't really think I did myself any harm, do you?" she asked. Then she clapped her hand over her mouth as if her question had been irrelevant because she knew where to find her answer. "Where is my book?" she cried. "The baby manual, that I relied on so much when I was expecting the other two. I forgot all about it this time but I remember it said something about taking things easy in the early stages, specially on certain days of the month. Oh Mike, Mike! How could I have forgotten that? It was so expressly stipulated."

Mike pushed her back more firmly against the pillows. "There is only one thing expressly stipulated now and that is that you stop worrying and after your supper you try to go to sleep."

Renee glanced out the windows. "But it's still daylight."

"Is it?" Mike said wearily and he too glanced out of the windows. "No matter," he said. "When Iris has given the kids something to eat I'm coming to bed myself. "Although," he said "that may not be an easy job" as there were ominous sounds of disorder below. Those children have had a long day." Then he hastily corrected himself. "They've had a great day, a day in a lifetime, but like all of us they are over-excited. If you're not going to eat any more Renee I'll take your tray. Try and sleep. I'll be up as soon as I can."

Mike did come up early, but Renee had not slept. She had not put on the light even when dark fell. Filled with a curious peace, she'd lain back on the pillows and gradually the dreadful fatigue she had experienced, lessened. She had only to be quiet, she thought and she would be free of all the tension that had had her in its grip. "Don't put on the light Mike," she called out to him, "unless you want to read or something. I'll just run out to the bathroom and now that you're with me I'm sure I'll go right to sleep," she said happily.

"How do you feel?" Mike asked, more soberly.

"I feel fine, just fine," she said and she ran into the bathroom. A moment later, standing on the cold tiles in the bathroom she heard Mike's name called out again and again. By whom? A hot sweat had broken out all over her body and it preoccupied her so much she could not concentrate on who it was who was calling him.

"Mike! Mike! Mike!"

"For heaven's sake, what's the matter Renee?" Mike ran into the bathroom and turned on the light.

All Renee could do was point to the floor where splashed on the white tiles, serrated like a star, there was a large splash of bright red blood. "I'm bleeding," she said, and she began to cry.

Mike was both relieved and cross at the same time. "You gave me a terrible fright," he cried.

"But don't you realise it means there's something wrong."

Mike was now rested and relaxed. "Hold on to yourself old girl," he said. "Don't get hysterical again."

She supposed he was justified in his remark but this was something serious. "You'll have to call the doctor," she said.

"At this hour?" He looked critically at his watch. "Have sense Renee." Reaching for a towel he bent and wiped up the splash of blood. Then he put his arm around her. "Get back into bed," he said. "All the doctor would do would be to tell you the same, to lie down and wait and see how you are in the morning. It's such a small amount of blood I'm sure there is nothing abnormal about it. One swallow doesn't make a summer as they say and I'm sure one drop of blood doesn't mean you are haemorrhaging." He was trying to drag a smile from her but he could see she found his humour forced, and that the word haemorrhage had scared her.

"Do you mean a miscarriage?" she cried.

"Oh, look here, Renee. Which of us is the woman, you or me? You may not be pregnant at all."

The surprise of this suggestion gave Renee a brief respite from panic. She even laughed, and allowed herself to be brought back to bed.

"What a fool you'd look," Mike said, "if you brought the doctor out here at this hour for nothing. In the morning, if you like you can ring him and have a test. You'd be having one anyway eventually, although I must admit you usually waited till it was pretty obvious." Renee laughed at that, but Mike did not. "I may as well say Renee I was surprised you took it on yourself to be so sure of your condition, telling Iris and the kids. I suppose you were going by that blasted manual."

"Oh, but that's the whole point. I forgot about the manual. Oh Mike get it now, will you, please. Run down for it. You'll find it in one of the drawers of my desk somewhere at the back. You may have to hunt for it, but I'd love to glance through it."

"Oh, cut it out, will you?" Mike was as near to ratty as she'd ever known him, but he kissed her. "You look marvellous. There couldn't be anything wrong. You did look awful in the garden when we got home, and simply ghastly a moment ago in the bathroom, but you look your old self again now. How do you feel? That's the real test I'm sure. Tell me honestly."

Renee had to admit to feeling all right. "Except I'm a bit scared. I can't help it. For the baby, I mean."

"Oh nonsense. It will be a tough little beggar like his sister and brother." Getting into bed he switched off the light and in a second he was asleep. Lying beside him, a small seed of resentment in Renee's heart had no time to germinate because a second later she too was asleep.

It was towards daybreak, although it was still dark outside, before Renee woke again. She got up and sat on the side of their bed, her legs dangling.

"Mike, will you ring the doctor now. I don't like to get out of bed just in case there's anything wrong," she said.

She herself had wakened in full possession of her fears of the previous night, and it was hard to realise that Mike did not know what she was talking about.

"Oh that?" he mumbled then, remembering the blood. He sat up. "Did you sleep well? How are you now?"

"Everything seems alright," Renee had to admit, "but I'm still very worried. And it's not good to be upset, you know that."

"All I know is that it's damned early to ring any man, even a doctor, unless it's a case of extreme emergency."

"Anxiety is a matter of urgency in some cases," Renee said hotly. "He's probably up already anyway. And he might be going away for the day, or starting his house calls early. That's the worst of living in the country and having to depend on one doctor. We've got to catch him before he's made his plans for the day."

Mike however was clearly reluctant to make the 'phone call. "Maybe Iris would ring him," he said.

Renee started violently. "Did Iris stay the night? You didn't tell me."

"I thought it might frighten you," Mike said cautiously.

"Then you *were* worried," she countered.

"Not about your physical condition," he said, "but about the state you'd got into. You don't realise what a dance you led us!"

"Oh Mike, I'm sorry," she said. "We'll wait a little longer if that's what you think is right. After all, as you said, I may not be pregnant at all." She calmed down. "I honestly am beginning to think that perhaps it is a false alarm."

Two hours later, however, when they had decided it was no harm to ring the doctor and he had in fact come and gone, Mike ran up the stairs two steps at a time.

"Well whatever it was, it was not a false alarm," he said, and although Renee knew he was trying to make light of the whole business, his face was white and strained. "He says there's no need to worry unduly about last night. But you are to stay in bed all day. And he will call again this evening. He left a prescription for some tablets for you to take as well. Iris has gone to town to get them made up. She'll be back as quick as she can."

Renee didn't feel quite such a fool as she'd done earlier. She was lying with her two hands down by her sides. Then she thought of the long day ahead and there was so much to be done.

"I don't suppose he means me to lie flat on my back," she said. "Not all day? I'm sure I can sit up," she said, starting to do so. "I could get some mending done or some letters written." It was unthinkable to lie idle doing absolutely nothing.

Mike, when he spoke, was very terse. Their roles seemed to have been reverted. "I'd do as the doctor says if I were you. He was adamant about your lying down. You've chanced enough already." Only that she knew him so well she would have been terribly hurt by the tone of his voice, but she knew it was due to a sort of inverted concern.

Then Renee glancing at the clock, looked sharply at her husband. "Aren't you going to the office this morning? There isn't any reason to stay home is there? You're late already, but there's still a lot of the day left."

"Oh well, Iris is here anyway," Mike said, not noticing he was hedging. "Anyway I rang to say I might not be going in today." He went over to the window and from the window to the mantlepiece where he fiddled with the clock. From that he went over to the small bookcase where they kept special books and began to read the titles like a visitor. There was a restlessness about him that was uncharacteristic.

Renee watched him nervously. "Do stop buzzing around like a bluebottle," she said.

Immediately he came over and sat at the foot of the bed. "Renee, how did the doctor establish that you were pregnant?"

"He examined me of course, how else?" she said impatiently.

Mike either did not notice or else ignored her impatience.

"A manual examination?"

Renee sat up.

"Mike are you crazy? What does that matter?" She found this intimate interrogation almost unnatural, until suddenly Mike's face went to pieces as if he was going to cry.

"I just wish we had sent for a doctor from Dublin," he said.

"From Dublin? Why on earth?"

"Oh, I suppose it doesn't matter," Mike said and he stood up.

Renee felt like laughing outright into his face. "Now who is making a mountain out of a molehill? Everyone has the highest opinion of this old doctor."

"That's true," Mike said, but unconvincingly. "Oh, I know I'm being stupid," he added hastily. "It's just that I remembered something I heard when I was in college and I suppose it unnerved me."

"What was it?" Renee's voice was like a knife.

"Oh, it was something I overheard one day years ago, when we were students. I was talking to a few medicals, standing about in the Main Hall. I just happened to be with them. I wasn't even interested in what they were saying. I may even have got it wrong. I'm sorry I mentioned it. There's no sense in telling you about it."

Renee's cheeks flushed. "Don't be a fool, Mike. You've got to tell me now that you've mentioned it. Can't you see that? Go on. Tell me."

Renee did not usually relish hearing his old college reminiscences. They were usually too boring for words, but this was something different. Once he started he'd have to finish it, it was obviously preying on his mind. "Go on. Get it off your chest," she said flippantly, because for all his protestations she couldn't help being amused at how confidently he launched out into what he wanted to say once he'd got a hearing. It was just the way the children acted.

"Well," he burst forth. "As I said, I was talking to this group of medicals. They had just come from their oral examinations and they were in top form because they seemed to think they'd done pretty well. They were just waiting for two pals of theirs who were still in the Examination Hall. Apparently they take them in pairs. But when one of the two came out he told them he was worried about the poor devil who was still inside. He himself, like the others, felt he'd got on alright, but he said the examiner was grilling the other poor fellow because he'd made a colossal mess of one question. He was asked what he would do if he was called in to establish pregnancy at an early stage."

"Go on," Renee said quietly, but her heart had begun to beat violently.

"Well the fellow who was telling the others knew the right answer, but he could do nothing to help his pal and he nearly passed out when he heard him say he'd give the woman a manual examination."

"What was wrong with that?" Renee was getting more and more alarmed.

"I didn't know naturally, but the others were very upset. They said he must be a fool not to know what he'd have on his hands in five or six hours—a bloody great haemorrhage."

Renee was stunned. She was almost as much stunned by Mike's telling her than she was by what he had said. And Mike too was suddenly stunned by the realisation of his idiocy in telling her.

"I shouldn't have told you," he said miserably. "But they were only medical students, *all* of them, and maybe their pal was right and they were wrong." He was trying desperately to undo the harm he couldn't but see he had done. "I never heard the results," he added frantically. "In fact I think that fellow turned out to be a first class obstetrician in the end."

But Renee was not even listening. She felt a strange sense of being exonerated from her own mistake. If she were to lose the baby it would not be her fault, but the fault of the doctor. Seeing Mike's agonised face she put her hand on his knee and patted it.

"We'll just have to wait and see Mike. Perhaps it's no harm to be aware that there could be trouble. And don't forget the tablets. Iris will soon be back with them. And medical science has made immense strides in recent years. Drugs can work wonders. Let's not lose our heads. I feel fine. And I think you should go to the office. There's no sense in you hanging around here all day."

Renee continued to feel fine all day and when Mike, who did go to the office, came home he was delighted with how she looked and in what good spirits she seemed. Iris and the children had already eaten, so he had his own meal put on a tray to take it upstairs and eat it in Renee's room. She was in exceedingly high spirits. He'd rarely seen her so full of gusto. Telling funny stories and positively giddy, when without warning she stopped talking in the middle of a sentence.

Renee had felt her thigh flush uncomfortably. For a second she had got frightened but telling herself it was just sweat and that she had too many blankets over her, she was leaning forward to throw them back, when she realised that under her the sheet was wet.

"Mike! Mike!" she screamed. "Get the doctor quick."

It was upon them.

After 'phoning the doctor Mike ran up the stairs and caught her hands and held them so tightly she thought he'd break her fingers.

"Did he say what I should do?" she asked.

"No, just that he'd be here in a few minutes." She noticed he himself was perspiring visibly. Poor Mike, he'd gone through a lot.

"Don't be frightened Mike. I'm not! she said, but she thought it odd how eagerly he grasped at her reassurance.

"Not even if you have to go to hospital?" he asked, and then he gulped out the rest of what the doctor had said, that he had arranged for an ambulance to be here also as soon as possible. Having got out what he had dreaded telling her, he stood up and tried to adopt a practical every day attitude. "What do you think you ought to take with you? I'll get your overnight case."

"Oh Mike!" It was true that she wasn't frightened, not now, not anymore. She just felt humiliated. "You'll come with me in the ambulance won't you? They'll let you I hope." But what was wrong *now* she wondered because Mike's face had gone white, even his lips were white.

"I've just thought of something. How will the ambulance get in here?" he cried. "The fields will be all muck. It's been raining for the past few hours. I had a hard job getting in myself without getting stuck, but I know the ropes. Oh Renee, I think I'd better go down to the road and see what can be done. We may have to get a tractor to tow it in here."

"Did you say it was raining?" Renee asked, ignoring the rest of what he'd said. "I would have thought there was a frost. I feel so cold." Then she remembered that a moment before she'd felt too hot. She'd started to shiver uncontrollably. The flow from her body had not stopped, it seemed to have thinned but not ceased. And no sooner was Mike gone down the stairs than it came on again, heavy and thick. Exerting all her might Renee pressed her thighs together. It was impossible to accept that she could not control this onpouring.

The minutes flew past. Mike hadn't packed the case. And where was Iris? She had probably taken the children into the kitchen where their voices would not reach upstairs. The whole house was so silent. What time was it? She took up her watch from the bedside table, but she had forgotten to wind it. Not knowing the time, brought a new panic. All sense of time collapsed. Why had Mike not come back? Who'd get her down the stairs? The thought of being moved an inch terrified her. She felt as if all the blood in her body was seeping away, an image of ice-floes jostling each other down an Arctic river in flood, and at that moment a clot of warm soft matter left her body.

"Mike! Mike!" she called out again despairingly this time, but it was Iris who ran up the stairs. "What's the matter?" she said. "Everything is under control. They are having a bit of trouble getting the ambulance across the fields but Mike is handling it. It got stuck a few times but they've shovelled gravel under the wheels. Don't worry. I think Mike is going to drive it."

Then he won't be with me, Renee thought, but she didn't care any more. A strand of her hair had fallen over her face and when she had tried to brush it aside, her hand failed and fell back. She tried again. This time she could not raise her hand at all and the strand of hair on her face felt like something crawling across her flesh. Am I going to die; she thought. Strangely the thought was translated into words, in a voice thin, faint and far, far away.

"Hush, hush," Iris said and her voice had such a loud rushing sound of a torrent, a waterfall. It was deafening, yet she could do nothing to block out the noise. And why didn't her sister answer her question. If she was, they ought to tell her so she could put up a fight. She'd pull herself inward with all her strength and make a cage of her ribs to stop the leaking away of her life.

Then a strange woman came into the room, followed by a man in uniform, and next minute Renee felt herself being lifted out of the bed. How often in the city she'd seen a stretcher being taken from an ambulance and carried up the steps of a hospital and she always had a feeling of pity for the patient being tilted helplessly on the canvas, but now all that concerned her was the delay.

"Oh, where is the ambulance?" she asked, but no one heeded her and vaguely she understood that she was already in the ambulance and that it was moving away from the house. "I want to talk to my husband," she said imperatively. No answer. The woman in white who was sitting right beside her didn't seem to hear.

Then there was another convulsive movement in her body and another mass of pulp passed out of her, and then another and another. Just then though, a dazzling idea came into her mind, although where it came from she could not say. Had she read it? Had someone told her? No. It was she herself who had made a great discovery, the discovery that, quite simply, a human being could go on living even after the body had been emptied of all the things that were supposed to be vital for survival, lungs, liver, kidney, even the heart. For of course those blobs and clots, those ice-floes, could not just have been blood. They were all the organs requisite for living.

Her insides had been cleaned out as she herself had often cleaned out fowl. Yet here she was still alive. If only she could get up she felt sure she could walk about, could run. She might perhaps be light like a bird. If that was so maybe she could fly? She was amazed to think that she had come by this knowledge by intuition alone. But that was the way Newton had discovered gravity. Oh, she'd have to tell someone, but not this stupid nurse. And anyway she was deadly tired. First she must sleep. Just before closing her eyes however, the ambulance stopped and Mike got in and the nurse changed places with him.

"I only had to get them out to the main road," he said.

What gibberish was this Renee wondered. Why couldn't he let her sleep?

I'm still alive, Renee thought, when, without opening her eyes she heard voices talking, yes and calling her name, but it was as if they were on a far-off shore, while she was being washed about in a cold mist-filled sea. Struggling to wade ashore, she suddenly felt Mike's warm hand clasping hers and, opening her eyes she knew immediately that she was in a hospital room, bright and sunny, and filled with flowers. Mike was bending over her and kissing her hands. Kissing and kissing them, and looking at her as if he could never get the full of his eyes of her.

"Oh Renee! Thank God. I thought you'd never come out of the anaesthetic. I was terrified."

"But why?" Renee did not understand. She was so warm and comfortable, so happy.

"What time is it?" she asked.

He didn't bother to tell her. "They said you were never in any real danger but I was beside myself with worry. You were so weak and you kept asking if you were dying."

"Dying?" She laughed. It seemed a very ridiculous question. Then she remembered the baby. "Oh Mike, did I lose it?" she whispered.

Mike hesitated a moment. "Bother the baby!" he said then. "It was you that mattered."

Sobered, Renee closed her eyes again and her joy in the sun and the flowers faded. "Why wasn't I more careful?" she said, and from under her closed lids tears streamed down her face.

"It wasn't your carelessness that did the harm. It was the ignorance of that fool of a doctor."

Renee opened her eyes and now they were tearless. "There would have been no heed of him at that time if I had not been such a fool myself." Then, in a loud voice, not caring that the nurse had come into the room, "I killed our baby," she said, and she began to cry loudly and without restraint.

"Nonsense," the nurse said and she rushed over to the bed, but she addressed herself to Mike. "This is only to be expected," she said. "I must get her to stop talking now and get some rest. She'll feel better later." Renee registered the words with scepticism.

Did she feel better when she woke again? At least she felt like sitting up and putting her arms into the sleeves of the flowery bedjacket the nurse held out for her.

"A present from your sister," said the nurse, and although Renee was glad to see she was not the same one that had come with her in the ambulance, but young and pretty, she still could not put on a pretence.

"It's not an occasion for celebration," she said, although just then Mike came in the door armed with more flowers.

"Well, we feel like celebrating," he said as he kissed her tenderly. "I know how you feel about the baby. I was only being facetious because I was so happy." He must have been very happy because his next remark was certainly facetious. "There are plenty more where that one came from," he said.

Renee pushed him back from her because of the nurse. "You're crumpling the bedspread," she said.

But the young nurse who had heard, was delighted with Mike's remark. "We'll have you back here with us within a year," she said. "How many will that be, you'll have? I mean how many children?"

Renee was given a jolt. "Isn't that odd, Mike," she said, turning to him. "I'd forgotten the children. I never once thought of them at the end. I only thought of myself. I thought I was dying. I didn't even think of you, Mike." In case he was hurt she put her hand on his arm. "What did you *feel?*" she asked. "When you thought I was in danger, what was *your* first thought?"

Mike's face so strained, even now when the danger was over, became normal for the first time in twenty four hours. "Do you really want to know what I thought?" he asked with boyish gleefulness that was very endearing. "Well, the first thing I thought was that the farm was in your name. That's honest Renee. I know it sounds awful but it's *honest*. Of course a minute after I was horrified. But now that you're so well I *do* think it's rather funny."

"Don't explain." Renee took his hand. "I know exactly how it was. And I'm so glad you felt you could tell me. That is the reality in our marriage, isn't it? We are truthful with each other always, no matter what. And it was the proper thing to feel too, dear, because, if I had died, it would have been you who'd have to be responsible for them, you who'd have to do everything alone, rear them, educate them—simply everything. I suppose that is why I didn't think of you and the children. I knew where you were and that you were all alright, but I must have felt I could be going into the unknown. And our poor, poor baby. Where was it going?" The tears came into Renee's eyes again but she blinked them back. "Can I get up?" she asked. "I want to tell you something. It's just come back to me. I had the most awful dream about the baby, a queer dream. I dreamt I was at home and I was going out to the garden when I looked out and saw three men digging a hole under the big elm tree on the lawn, the one with crocuses under it, and when I went nearer to see what they were doing I saw a naked baby lying on the grass. I didn't know they were digging the hole to put the baby in it because I thought the infant was alive, but when they'd dug deep enough they went to lift it up and then I knew that was what they intended and I began to call out to stop them but no sound came. You know how that happens in a dream. But, Mike, they weren't able to lift the baby. They kept trying and trying but they couldn't and then I realised the baby wasn't made of flesh and blood, because I could see through it like you'd see through a soap bubble. I could see the grass through it and the crocuses. And yet it was alive. It was moving its limbs in a way a normal baby would do. Oh Mike, I was so happy because I knew then that they could never lift it and they couldn't put it in the hole. I thought it might perhaps float away from them up into the sky. Then I woke up. And I saw you and I forgot about it." Suddenly she began to cry again. "Oh Mike, why didn't we take more care of our baby?"

"Hush, my darling," Mike said, and he kissed her again.

Renee submitted for a moment to the happiness of being loved. Then uneasily her mind strayed back to their baby. "Had it begun to live I wonder? And where is it now? What do you think Mike?"

Mike had lost his bearings, and felt that he might also lose his head. He looked to the nurse for help. She came over to the bedside.

"We must not overdo things during the first few days," she said to Renee. "Easy does it. You may feel well but I bet you wouldn't like to be asked to run ten miles." She gently led Mike towards the door. "She'll be as gay as a lark by the time she's ready to go home."

Only this wasn't so: it wasn't so at all. As the days passed Renee got more uneasy, not less. At times she was deeply depressed. And when he came to see her, Mike was no longer happy and loving. He didn't bring the children to see her again after their first visit, which had not been a success.

"What is the matter, Renee?" Mike asked miserably on the day before she was due to go home.

"I don't know. I just keep thinking of the baby."

"I see," he said shortly, and he left shortly afterwards. Then, that evening when she wasn't expecting any visitors, he walked into her room. "Guess who is coming to see you in a few minutes," he said. "Father Hugh. It was Iris who suggested it. She is bringing him in her car. He's going to talk to you about that graveyard we saw in Achill. That's what has been on your mind, isn't it?"

Renee stared at him, first in amazement and then in dismay.

"I had forgotten all about that," she said. She was sobbing when Iris and Father Hugh arrived. Mike confronted them at the door. "She says she'd forgotten all about Achill," he said accusingly to Iris.

Iris walked past him and went straight to the foot of the bed.

"Here's Father Hugh, Renee. Aren't you glad to see him no matter what?"

Father Hugh approached the bedside. "I hear you are worried about your little baby's soul, Renee," he said levelly. "But you know God's love is infinite, don't you?" When Renee stared at him coldly and said nothing, his tone changed. "Would it make you happier if I told you there was a growing body of opinion in the Church that the Vatican may be prepared to admit to error in teaching about Limbo. It was never a dogma you know." Then, when Renee turned her head away Father looked over at Mike. "Who was her doctor?" he asked. "Was he a Catholic? Some doctors are very scrupulous and they have been known to give lay baptism to unborn babies."

Suddenly Iris gasped.

"Please!" she said. "I've heard of those amateur baptists and what I heard turned my stomach."

Shocked by the tone of her voice, Father Hugh looked at her.

"Iris. I thought you brought me here because she was worried about her baby's soul?"

Unflinchingly, her face cold and proud, Iris answered him. "Well, I'm glad to say I thought wrong! After all, what does the Church know any more than the medical world which is not prepared to be definitive about the issue."

Renee stared lovingly at her and stretched out her hand, which Iris immediately took and held fiercely. "Iris is right," she said. "Whether the idea of Limbo is a dogma or not, why were no women given a say about it? Mike," she commanded. "Tell him about my dream." To her surprise Mike's face was dark with annoyance.

"Look here, Renee," he said. "You're not going to give up your religion, are you? Not when you've only just adopted it! It would have been far better if you'd never turned. What will people say? What will I tell the children?"

Father Hugh put his hand on Mike's shoulder. "Stop shouting at her," he said. "Conversion is like vaccination. If it didn't take it didn't take. There should be no more said about it."

Iris couldn't help laughing. She relaxed visibly. "Anyway it's not her faith in God that is in question." She turned to her sister. "Isn't that right Renee?" she asked. "But now I hope you can see why I didn't want you to rush into a religion that makes everything so complicated and involved, so hard, so *impossibly* hard."

Renee nodded. "I know you meant well Iris," she said. Her own concern at that moment was for poor Mike. He looked so down in the mouth and distressed. "Don't worry Mike. I don't intend to give up my religion but there is a lot in what Iris said, and I do think women ought to be allowed to have more voice in the Church. I suppose I probably was unconsciously worried about the baby's soul. And Father Hugh was very kind to come to see me. I accept what he says about trusting in God's love for us. Thank you, Father," she said. But she saw that the priest was staring very strangely at Iris.

"I didn't think you were interested in theology," he said, half serious and half jokingly. "I'll tell you what we'll do," he said. "When our patient comes home and has built up her strength, we'll have it all out, the three of us. And you too Mike of course," he added quickly, although it was clearly an afterthought. "It will be a regular Round Table. We'll thrash out anything and everything that worries you. Calmly."

"And truthfully?" Iris stabbed. "With no false loyalties."

Father Hugh laughed. "No holds barred," he said.

At that Iris laughed again and Renee thought how well she looked, how pretty. Not since they were both young girls had she seen her so well, really beautiful.

Father Hugh noticed it too. He couldn't seem to take his eyes away from her, as if he had just seen her for the first time. "You are a man after my own heart Iris," he said, and, again, Iris found this so funny she laughed once more. They were both laughing. As for this Round Table, it seemed a good idea, since they both were so engrossed in the present discussion. They had gone on to some other doctrine now. They had forgotten all about her. And as long as Mike was happy she was glad to be forgotten. After all her main responsibility now was to get strong again. Mike seemed quite happy now too. She took his hand but she held it very lightly. She was getting so sleepy and after a minute she closed her eyes, but the next minute they flew open again as she remembered once more what Iris had said about never having met anyone with whom she felt a kindred spirit or something like that. But what about celibacy she thought. Oh, everyone was very much more involved than she had realised when she was receiving instruction. So this Round Table was a very good idea. They could all iron out their differences to their heart's content. Then she closed her eyes again, and deliberately shut out the lovely room that was transfixed with light, and everything in it, the masses of flowers and Mike smiling at her so happily and Father Hugh and Iris looking into each other's eyes.